JUSTICE BY THE POUND

JUSTICE BY THE POUND

A NOAH SHANE THRILLER

IVAN WEINBERG

CURTIS BROWN UNLIMITED • NEW YORK

To the memory of my sweetheart, Marilyn, and to my children, Darin, Bo, Jason, Aaron and Amanda, whose love and support has held me up and made the seemingly impossible seem possible. Family is everything.

PROLOGUE

A midnight onshore breeze eases the late-summer heat, rustling palm fronds a hundred yards from the sea. Farther inland, cloaked in bougainvillea, stands a whitewashed Spanish-tiled mansion. Except for the moon, the lights of the isolated compound offer the only illumination over several miles of coastline. A warm, welcoming glow emanates from ground-floor windows.

Nearby, a secluded pool shimmers a deep blue, around which shadows dance as tiki torches flicker. The sounds of syncopated mariachi trumpets, guitars, violins, and close harmonies rise above the crashing surf. Revelers in G-strings and brightly colored shirts are gathered on the patio, their laughter mingling with the music, heightened by coke and Michoacán. Several couples move to the salsa rhythms while others wander off into the moonlight. Despite the late hour, servers in white coats still pass among the all-male cadre of guests.

A quarter mile down the beach, one couple wades in solitude. Three inches shorter, the younger man is the more muscular, youthfully handsome, with dark, wavy hair. His companion, comfortably proportioned, is graying, his gentle eyes lined by years of laughter. He speaks quietly, insistently.

They stop, and the conversation intensifies, soon punctuated by shouts. A compassionate hand reaches out, but is slapped away. Face contorted, the younger man whirls and bolts, splashing through shallow foam and up onto the sand. Hesitating, he falls to his knees, sobs racking his shoulders as the soothing voice moves toward him. He suddenly turns and hurtles upward, overpowering his approaching counterpart and driving him onto his back, rigid fingers constricting his airway. Legs thrash, and torso writhes, as the struggle becomes desperate, but no one hears the frenzied gasps and gurgled pleas.

In time the bucking slows, then ceases.

As he stares down into lifeless blue eyes, the assailant feels his disbelief morph into anguish, and his weeping begins again as he slowly shakes his head, the terrible reality washing over him. Cheeks streaked with tears, he leans down and kisses the unresponsive face repeatedly, as though it might magically undo his atrocity. Then, utterly spent, he lays his head on the motionless chest and closes his eyes.

PART ONE

NEOPHYTE

"A wise man gets more use from his enemies than a fool from his friends."

—Baltasar Gracián

CHAPTER ONE

The sun cut a hole in the clouds and in seconds blasted heat and light onto the white sand.

Leech Jaqua exhaled a lungful of cheap, harsh tobacco as he slogged up the beach. "El Ropo," he scoffed, grimacing down at the loosely packed Mexican cigarette pinched between his yellowed fingers. He flicked it, half-smoked, into a pile of stranded seaweed as he passed, his white loafers sinking deeply with each step.

Every inch of Jaqua's bony body was covered: black shirt, black slacks, white belt, white Panama hat, cheap mirrored shades, nothing exposed to the 103° midday sun but a pockmarked jaw and neck slathered with 70 SPF sunblock. Mixing with sweat, the viscous white lotion formed rivulets that stuck his shirt to all the wrong places.

A high-pitched, distant voice, barely audible over the relentless sea breeze, caught his attention, and he looked up. Carl Mumford was gesturing wildly from a breach in the rocks a hundred yards away. Jaqua cast him a dismissive wave. "Okay, okay, keep y'pants on, I'm comin'."

Squinting into the glare as he drew nearer, he could see that Mumford was leaning over a nearly naked body, clad only in a two-tone G-string.

"Why do I always draw this shit for duty?" Jaqua grumbled. The inflection was authentic New Jersey, as was the chronic pessimism. "Fuckin' faggots. Can't watch 'em every goddamn second." He squeezed into the rocky cleft and winced reflexively. "Jeezus," he rasped.

Lying face up at the end of a furrow in the sand that stretched nearly down to the surf, the corpse had begun to bloat with the heat, the hermit crabs having already found the open eyes. Clumps of green bottle flies roiled around the nose and mouth. Even in the gusting wind the stench was formidable.

Jaqua shuddered, snatched a filthy handkerchief from his pocket, and pressed it over his nose and mouth. "This the place those kids said he was? I thought it was further up."

Two teenagers had found the body on their way out shrimping that morning, and had brought the news back to the compound.

The short, round black man looked up. "Nah. Must be a different body those kids saw. Prob'ly got dead fuckers all up and down this beach."

"Awright, awright. Get him in the bag. I'll call the house and tell 'em to send the boat." Jaqua fished in his jacket for his cell. "Everybody's a fuckin' comic."

Perspiration glistened on Mumford's slick, brown scalp as he pulled a body bag and gloves from his duffel. "Say this guy was some kinda stockbroker?"

"Yeah, Van Zandt. Warren Van Zandt. He's been down here a buncha times."

Mumford eyed the pink-and-yellow flowered thong and dragged a sleeve across his forehead. "Guess I just don't get it," he muttered.

Jaqua dialed, then shouted to make himself heard over the windblown static. "Okay. We got him. Quarter mile up the beach. Right, north." He clicked off, and his gaze drifted up the shimmering cliff. "Fuckin' heat," he said, mopping his face with the handkerchief.

"What? Y'ain't a sun worshiper?" Mumford chided, wrestling the semi-stiff meat. "Thought we were gonna lay by the pool after this."

"Only pool in my neighborhood was Manny's Billiards."

Jaqua's attitude grew more tentative as he dialed the cell again, this time to Oakland for instructions. There'd be hell to pay when they got back; this was exactly what they'd been sent down there to prevent. "Lovers' fuckin' hassles, man," he said, tapping in the number. "I knew this'd happen someday."

Ten minutes later the heavy-plastic, green body bag lay at the edge of the surf as the Boston Whaler nosed up onto the beach. Jaqua and Mumford hoisted the corpse over the rail, shoved off, and jumped aboard as the Mexican pilot revved the 210-horsepower Mercury engine, swung the boat around, and bounced it through the spray of several incoming waves toward open water.

"So, we gonna feed this mothafuckah t'the sharks?" Mumford asked, once they'd cleared the breakers.

"Too easy." Jaqua shook another "El Ropo" from the pack. "Orders are to schlep him back to Oakland and dump him in the Emeryville sewage plant."

Mumford's head slowly rotated, brow creased in a disbelieving frown. "Say, what?"

"Yeah. They don't want any snoopin' around down here when he doesn't show for work Monday."

Cupping his hands against the oncoming gusts, Jaqua lit the brutal smoke as the sleek, white, open boat powered forward. "I gotta get outta this line of work," he said, exhaling into the wind. "Shoulda opened that fuckin' grocery store with my uncle in Hackensack."

"What's the difference?" Mumford scoffed. "You'd'a been sellin' fruit, 'steada just baggin' it."

CHAPTER TWO

Showing age and little maintenance, the '92 Nissan four-door sedan was mostly a faded maroon, though its left front fender was adorned with gray primer over a semi-sanded Bondo patch. Proceeding north on Market Street in West Oakland, it coasted up to the blinking red signal light at East 14th, then moved slowly through the intersection. As it accelerated down the dark, deserted block, a black-and-white OPD cruiser lurched out of a service alley and fell in behind it, bar lights swimming. The Nissan veered sharply to the curb and stopped, the driver's window rolling down.

Pablo Ruiz's first instinct may have been to run, but having lived in the Oakland barrio all of his twenty-three years, at that moment he knew one thing for sure: best to make it absolutely clear that he knew who was in charge.

The police vehicle eased to a stop close behind, its headlights and both spotlights bathing the run-down sedan in an intense glare. Patrolman Vince Mathers had eleven years in, but he was still cautious as he approached the driver's side of the Nissan, flashlight raised high in his left hand, right hand resting on his service semi-automatic, its holster unsnapped. Shining the light inside—first the back seat, then into Pablo's face—Mathers illuminated the dark, boyish features, and ultimately played the beam down over the Raiders jacket and jeans. His partner, Terry Stills, remained in the squad car, running the tag on the computer.

"Driver's license and registration, please." The voice was low and firm, attention focused on Pablo's hands as the nervous young man leaned forward and slowly opened the glove compartment. He extracted a wrinkled registration certificate and handed it over, trying hard to control his trembling. Equally slowly, he leaned forward, reached into his back pocket, and drew out his wallet, sorted through the bits and pieces, and finally produced a license card. The officer slipped it under the clip on his citation pad along with the registration, and studied both under his flashlight beam.

"Pablo Ruiz?"

Pablo didn't look up. "Yes, sir."

"11601 Forty-Sixth Street?"

"Yes, sir."

"You ran the stop back at Fourteenth, Pablo. We put those there so citizens don't kill each other. You a citizen, Pablo? Or just another La Raza punk who got up here in somebody's trunk?"

This was already heading in a bad direction. Pablo struggled for an answer. His face felt stiff, frozen.

"You always drive like that, Pablo?"

"No, sir. I do not. I am sorry." The words were clipped, distinct.

"Out kinda late, aren't ya?"

"I was on my way home."

"Don't fuck with me, Pablo. Forty-Sixth is on the other side'a town. You been drinking?"

"No, sir."

The officer looked down at him. "Blowin' some weed?"

"No, sir."

"So where you been?"

"With friends."

Mathers bent down, inhaling deeply through his nose, trying to detect any suspicious odors. "Whaddya got in the trunk?" Again the light shined into the back seat.

"Nothing."

"We gonna find any guns or drugs if we check it out?"

"No, sir."

Mathers abruptly opened the driver's door. "You wanna step out of your vehicle?"

Pablo slowly slid out and stood tentatively.

"Around to the rear," Mathers ordered. He leaned in and snatched the keys from the ignition.

Having developed no information concerning the Nissan, Stills exited the cruiser, approached from behind, and stopped, silhouetted against the black-and-white's brightness, as the bar lights continued to strobe red and blue. A female R.T.O.'s voice squawked intermittently over the service radio's external speaker. Mathers tossed the keys to Stills. After several tries, one key turned in the trunk latch, and the rusted hinges creaked open.

Stills scanned the interior, pulling at several cardboard cartons. "What's all this?" he asked.

No answer.

Mathers turned. "Pablo! He asked you a question."

"It-it is butter."

Mathers smirked, shaking his head. "You a dairy farmer, Pablo?"

Pablo's mind was racing, dark eyes widened, chest pounding.

Stills extracted a one-pound package of partially frozen butter from one of the cartons and held it up, then tossed it back in the trunk.

"Lotta butter here. Where'd you get all this?"

No response.

"Where'd you get it!"

"I-I was taking it home."

"Home for what? A chili bake-off?" Stills cast a glance toward Mathers.

"Run it," Mathers instructed. "See if there's a 459 with butter anywhere near this twenty." He turned back to Pablo. "Must be a couple hundred pounds of butter, *pen-day-ho*. What were you gonna do with it?"

A beat, then: "I was going to sell it."

"I'll bet you were." Mathers grabbed his jacket sleeve and yanked him toward the front of the patrol car. "Up against the hood and spread 'em, amigo. You know the drill."

Pablo turned back, pleading, reflexively trying to pull his sleeve loose from the officer's grip. "But, I must get home. I did not-"

He saw only a dark blur a nanosecond before the flashlight hit him full on his right cheek, and he went down hard. His world was now high-pitched and ringing, rimmed with dancing lights. Flat on his back, he cowered from the indistinct mosaic of flared nostrils and clenched teeth looming a foot above him, as blood streamed from his split cheek and oozed from the back of his head. Gasping for breath with Mathers' knee crushing his chest, he was vaguely aware of a distant, mechanical, singsong female voice somewhere in the surrounding miasma.

"Unit twenty-six... 459 at the Safeway market... Code R... Eighth and Market... Foremost dairy truck... frozen butter..."

Mathers turned to Stills, shaking his head and grinning. "Six blocks over," he said. "Am I good, or what."

• • •

"Ohhhh, Jeezus," Noah Shane groaned, gut churning, eyes squeezed shut. Alameda County's newest Assistant Public Defender had already missed his first two days on the job. There was no way he could make it three and stay employed.

The sudden, intense wave of nausea took him back to fourth grade, when Neil Suggins had doubled him over with a sucker punch. It was about who would bat first in the game of playground work-up. He'd looked Neil straight in the face for a full five seconds as he unbent, feeling the whole time like he would throw up, and then he'd flashed a forearm up under Suggins' jaw and put him on his backside. Noah checked his watch. *God. Eight-thirty already.*

Pulling himself up on an elbow with effort, he swung his legs over the side of the bed, rose unsteadily, and hobbled to the bathroom. He leaned forward on the ancient freestanding basin and winced at the hideous image in the mirror. His mind was thick; his thoughts came slowly. Twisting on the cold water, he doused his face as the phone rang. Instinctively he moved toward it, then waved it off.

Voicemail answered over the speaker; then, "Noah? Sandy. If you're there, pick up." A beat. "If you're not, we're in deep shit, man. Better make it in today. I don't think this's gonna keep 'til tomorrow. I mean the man is talkin' about the next guy on the waiting list. Says they need someone like now. So call my cell if you totally can't make it happen. I'll try to cover. Or call the front desk, 510-387-9822. Extension 5714." Pause. "Don't blow this goddamn job, Noah. We need this." Click, and a dial tone.

What? Waiting list? It was only Wednesday and he'd called in twice already to say he was sick.

Ducking his head under the faucet, he ran the icy tap water through his black kinky mop, then straightened, again staring into the mirror. He examined his coated tongue as the water streamed down his face. *Better. Upgraded to shitty.* He peeled off his T-shirt to reveal a naturally chiseled chest covered with black, fuzzy fur.

After brushing his teeth and swirling a cupful of mouthwash, he grabbed the thermometer from the medicine cabinet, stuck it in his mouth, and wandered out of the bathroom. Across the room, the kitchenette counter was piled high with dirty dishes. On autopilot, he pulled a packet of prefab coffee from a jar next to the coffee maker, scrutinized it doubtfully, and tossed it back into the jar. As he opened the sparsely stocked cupboard, his eyes fell on a can of chicken noodle soup. *Not much better.* He winced but opened it anyway, poured the contents into a small bowl, added water, slid it into the diminutive microwave, and tapped *Start* as he withdrew the thermometer and scrutinized the tiny numbers.

One-oh-three. Jeezus. Couple more lousy degrees and he'd be a clinical fatality. How the hell was he gonna pull this off? Probably dying!

As the microwave did its thing, Noah pulled out clean skivvies, a pair of khakis, and a white shirt from the bureau next to the bed. He withdrew his one sport coat—gray herringbone—from the armoire, chose the dark purple tie, one of two, and draped the whole ensemble over the back of the overstuffed chair in front of the TV. Pouring the warm, weak chicken broth into a cup, he took it with him back to the bathroom, cranked the shower on cold, then gingerly took a sip and set the cup on the sink. Instantly his enraged gut raked another wave of nausea through him, and he retched into the commode.

Noah was moving at maximum flu-speed, and it was 8:55 by the time he was shaved and dressed. He grabbed his jacket and headed to the door, then stopped, turned, and surveyed the wreckage.

The Larkin Hotel was a dingy flophouse inhabited by an assortment of drunks, disabled, crack whores, and degenerates a step above homeless, in the heart of the Tenderloin in downtown San Francisco, the City's red-light district since Gold Rush days. The quarter was flourishing in 1898 when Tessie Wall, one of the neighborhood's flamboyant madames, opened her first brothel. Only a few short years later, the area took a major hit in the 1906 earthquake and fire, and was almost completely destroyed. But the need for love and adventure being what it is, the Tenderloin was immediately rebuilt with some hotels and restaurants opening as early as 1907. By the 20s, the streets were rife with speakeasies, and in the 50s and 60s, jazz establishments dotted the landscape, hosting such luminaries as Miles Davis, Dave Brubeck, and Thelonious Monk. This was the same era that Dashiell Hammett's Sam Spade haunted the sector in search of the *Maltese Falcon*.

But now those days were alive only in the history books. Urban exodus had resulted in an inability to fill the mostly single-occupancy hotel rooms and studios. By the mid-70s, the Tenderloin had suffered a devastating vacancy because of its lack of family apartment housing. In the wake of the Vietnam conflict, an influx of poor Southeast Asian refugees took advantage of the situation, entering into dense multiple occupancies of the small spaces, and leading the colorful district into free fall.

By the time Noah found his way to his third-floor walk-up, shortly after entering Hastings College of the Law four blocks away, the neighborhood was mostly cheap dives, sex shops, and shooting galleries. His garret was admittedly grim, but he answered to no one. The once off-white, now light brown, paint was chipping off the walls here and there, but the studio was cheap, convenient, and he had definitely made it his, embellishing it with a wealth of old sports memorabilia.

There were the hard-to-find Johnny Unitas and Bob Waterfield posters. An ancient photograph of Ruth at Yankee Stadium, doffing his cap after a monster shot to center, hung alongside Ripken taking the victory lap when he retired after 2,632 consecutive games. Noah's eyes paused on Ripken. Sixteen years without missing a major league appearance. Astounding. *Must've played with a one-oh-three temperature at least a few times.* Jackie Robinson and Branch Rickey stood grinning at home plate at Ebbets Field, a centerpiece of baseball history. And then there was the bat Duke Snider used to take Whitey Ford deep to left at Yankee Stadium in the '55 series, or so they said at the flea market. Who knew? It was the right vintage, but certification of its authenticity wasn't really the point. It was the aura of endurance that stirred Noah. There were definitely great athletes playing today, but the guys on these walls had forged their souls in the crucible of time. In the end, it wasn't the beauty of the dance so much as the determination to persevere, no matter what. Those rugged faces in the old photographs, etched with their bring-it-on mentality, were epic. The force was with them, no doubt.

His furniture, a selection from St. Vincent de Paul, was just now heaped with the detritus of five days of the plague: clothes, towels, magazines, to match the dirty dishes in the sink. Against the wall, under the quarterback posters, stood his one luxury, the 43-inch Samsung flat-screen LED TV from Best Buy. A definite necessity, this was his window into the world of his only addictions, the NFL, the NBA, and the MLB. He took a deep breath, shrugged, stepped out, and closed the door behind him.

Wiping the beads of sweat from his forehead with the grainy woolen sleeve of his blazer, he gazed tentatively down the three flights ahead of him, and clutched the rail in preparation for the descent, like planning the first step in the trek down Annapurna.

Three stairs down, he heard the muffled sobs. Approaching the second floor landing, he saw her, sitting on the bottom step, long blond hair disheveled, head in hands. Beneath a soft pink sweater, her delicate shoulders jerked spasmodically as she wept almost inaudibly, unaware of his presence.

"Hi, Lisa," he murmured, squeezing by in his semi-fog. *Okay, something was really wrong, but with Lisa something was pretty much always really wrong. He just couldn't get into this right now. He was going to catch hell as it was, maybe even lose the job.*

She looked up, her light blue eyes devoid of makeup and dulled by anguish. After regarding him intensely, pleadingly, for an instant, she looked away, tried to speak, couldn't, shook her head, bunched up her right sleeve above the elbow and touched it to her eyes, and then the soft sobbing resumed.

Stomach still seething, Noah pasted a sympathetic look as he rounded the wooden railing and started toward the first floor. Two steps down, he hesitated, stopped, still considering. *Shit. No way.* Then he turned, climbed back to the landing, and sat next to her.

"What's up, Lees?" he asked, stretching an arm around her. She collapsed on him, burying her head in his herringbone shoulder.

"Okay, okay," he whispered, "tell me about it." He snuck a look at his watch. "But can you maybe give it to me in kind of a nutshell? I'm totally pressed for time."

"It—it's Maggie," she snuffed.

He was immediately alarmed. "What happened to Maggie? Where is she?"

Lisa Sanders and Noah had become friends soon after he moved into the Larkin. Her apartment was on the floor below, so he passed through her world several times a day. They enjoyed a good-natured repartee, but the core of the relationship was his immediate and lasting bond with Maggie, her seven-year-old.

Although he was tempted by Lisa's soft smile and smoldering innocence—assets that were her stock in trade—he had resisted so far on the several times she'd invited him to her bed. She was entirely too needy. He definitely wasn't against the one-night stand on principle, but he knew this one would become hopelessly complicated, stood a good chance of disrupting his connection with Maggie, and then, of course, there was the bottom-line concern about *treyfe*, and the risks of sex with a hooker.

"A cop and some woman from Child Protective Services came this morning when I was getting her ready for school," she managed, trembling convulsively and rubbing her red nose with the back of her hand. "They gave me a paper saying they were taking custody, said I could request a hearing, but they were going to hold her in the meantime." She searched his eyes, one and then the other, seeking reassurance, fighting the tears.

"Why?" he asked.

"I couldn't do anything, Noah. They just took her."

"But why…" He glanced down at the two raised red tracks in the exposed crook of her left elbow. He knew why.

"It was that same woman from CPS who came to talk to me a couple of weeks ago." She started to weep again. "Oh, God…"

He also knew there was no way they were going to let her keep her daughter unless she got into a program and cleaned up her act. Even then, it wasn't a sure thing. He had hoped her devotion to her child would supply the necessary motivation. She had told him more than once that she saw Maggie as a fresh new version of herself, maybe her chance to really do something right. But so far, status quo.

"Where's the paper they gave you? Lemme see it," Noah said. *What was he thinking?* Sanity suddenly caught up with instinct. "Wait, wait, Lees," he added. "I got this new job. I gotta get over to the East Bay. Why don't you just slip it under my door. I'll have a look as soon as I can. I'm sure there's something we can do."

She looked up at him, imploring. "You think? I mean I've only told them I'm unemployed. I don't think they know that I'm—"

"I get it," he interrupted. "So we'll put together a game plan." He stood and pulled her up. "I really gotta go. You get over and see Maggie as soon as you can. She'll be up at Juvenile Hall on Twin Peaks. You know where that is?"

Lisa nodded.

"Tell her everything's gonna be fine, that I'm workin' on this. She's gonna be scared stiff. I'll check out the papers and get with you tomorrow after I've had a chance to see what they say."

He squeezed her hand, continuing to nod as he backed away. "I want you to hang in there, Lisa. We'll work this out," he promised, having no idea what he was going to do. "But you gotta be there for her."

"What would happen if you weren't around, Noah? I mean, how can I thank you?"

"We'll thinka something." He tried for the sly smirk, but it came out more of a grimace.

Actually seeing him for the first time in that moment, she couldn't hide the concern that crept across her face. "You okay?" she asked. "You don't look so good."

"I'm fine. Just a monumental aversion to work. See ya."

He descended the remaining steps and emerged from the front door of the hotel into the sun on the building's eastern exposure. After standing on the stoop for a few seconds to get his bearings, he started down the front stairs, again steadying himself with the railing as he struggled to remember where he'd left his car. One of the serious drawbacks of the neighborhood was parking. Spaces were always at a premium at night when he rolled in, necessitating a morning search that often took him a number of blocks afield. Reaching the sidewalk, he peeled off his sport coat, threw it over his shoulder, inhaled deeply, and paused before starting up McAllister.

"Morning, Margaret," he said, squinting against the glare.

Nothing. He stood, waiting the obligatory twenty seconds as his eyes followed the line of cars creeping down toward Ellis. Then a deep, gin-soaked rasp emanated from under the stairs.

"Mmmmorning... Nnnoah."

After a thankfully more-limited-than-usual search, he discovered the elephantine, gray '78 Dodge four-door sedan five blocks away, over on Turk. Littered with empty beer bottles, old magazines, half-eaten fruit, and God knows what else, the aged vehicle emanated a ripe, organic aroma that was overwhelming to many, particularly on hot summer days, but Noah found the scent nostalgic, reassuring. Besides, the radio worked, and he'd been told when he bought it that the engine had been rebuilt at some point. He and this old relic had come a long way together, through three water pumps, a starter motor, and two transmission overhauls since junior year at Stanford, and it was still pretty much going strong.

He snatched up the sweatshirt from the driver's seat, lightly dusted it over the plastic brass-colored *Captain America* nameplate affixed to the dash, pitched it into the back, and slid in under the wheel. When he turned the key, the engine moaned. *The Captain sounded almost as sick as he was.* After several attempts, the ancient rusting metal came to life. Noah rolled down his window, let the clutch out slowly, and the old war horse lurched out noisily toward the Bay Bridge.

CHAPTER THREE

White foam gushed over the concrete wall of the hundred-foot-wide cistern, reminiscent of the spillway at Hoover Dam, sweeping tons of muddy-brown sewage through a twelve-foot-square steel lattice and down the cavernous drain. Vincent Spunelli's aging, practiced eyes scrutinized the process through his metal-rimmed sunglasses, as he strained for a better view.

Standing on the steel catwalk above the rim of the cauldron, Spunelli straightened and ran callused fingers through his graying hair, then leaned forward with interest as the fluid level in the tank dropped to four feet, three feet, two, and there it was. Though it was still slathered with solid waste, as the powerful surge of water tossed it about, he could see that the yellow-and-blue-blotched form was unmistakably a naked human body, wedged fast in the mixing blades of Number Three Effluent Tank at the Emeryville Sewage Treatment Plant.

"Okay, Toby!" Spunelli shouted over his shoulder toward the glass-enclosed control cabin on the tower that extended fifteen feet above the vat's rim. "Cut it to forty GPS!"

The bearded operator adjusted a sliding lever on the left side of a control panel that rivaled a 747's telemetry console, and the force of the falling water diminished. Spunelli walked around the catwalk to a position directly above the body and looked down. The upper torso was hidden behind the blade, legs flopping like an inflatable plastic doll under the swirling pressure.

"Shut it down!" Spunelli yelled. "We don't wanna saw this guy in half!"

The roar of rushing water diminished further, then ceased, as the remnants of liquid and solid waste twisted into a vortex, disappearing down the drain. Spunelli swung a rubber-booted leg over the railing, stepped onto the top rung of the steel ladder, pulled the green mask that hung around his neck over his nose and mouth, and slowly descended. At the bottom, he waded into noxious fluid that was still a few inches deep. Standing over the corpse, he studied the huge, waxy lacerations on the head, neck, and shoulders, but he saw no blood. Despite the vigorous washing, the body was still covered with patches of feces. Stuck head first in the apparatus, the face was hidden behind the immense mixing blade. The grotesquely bloated remains revealed little of their characteristics in life, though a shriveled member identified the form as that of a male.

"Christ…" Spunelli winced, shaking his head and exhaling forcefully inside his mask. The manager of the largest sewage plant in Alameda County, he'd seen, and smelled, a whole lot of God-awfulness in his thirty-six years on the job, but never the likes of this.

Several of the other workers had gathered at the railing above and were peering down.

"What is it, Vinnie?" one of them posed.

Spunelli gazed up, a look of wonder on his sixty-two-year-old countenance as he pondered the fortuity that this was the first body he'd fished out of a vat. It was truly astounding that one of these morons hadn't fallen in at some point over the years. Seemed like County always sent him the cretins. The near-normal IQs went to Public Works, maybe Building Maintenance. Always would. But this guy clearly wasn't one of his. God only knew who he was, or how in hell he got in there.

"Just call the cops, willya?" he instructed to none of them in particular, exercising the usual Herculean restraint it took to conceal his disgust. All three remained rooted. He rolled his eyes and heaved a sigh. Four more years and he was home free. He could stand anything that long. Hell, he'd hung in all these years already, hadn't he?

"For chrissakes, call the goddamn cops!" he barked. They looked at each other, then one finally broke away and wandered down the ramp toward the guard shack, craning to gape back at the grisly scene.

Fifteen minutes later, an unmarked tan Oakland PD Crown Victoria coasted through the facility's front gate and stopped next to Number Three Tank. A heavyset, 6'0" detective emerged and strode up the ramp toward the rim where the gawkers were standing. As he neared the top, Spunelli came down to meet him.

"Ned Swarth, Oakland PD," the detective said, not extending a hand. Although he was unclear on treatment plant etiquette, he figured that one of the rules would probably discourage shaking.

"Spunelli," was the response.

"So whatta we got?" Swarth asked. He'd done sixteen years in police work, the last twelve in Oakland assigned to homicide. Though he'd seen most of it, this was his first DB in a sewage vat.

"Well, I guess you know we got a corpse," Spunelli responded. "But, now, who he is, or where he came from, that's beyond me."

"How'd you find him?" Swarth grunted, looking down into the empty cistern.

"Blade jammed. When we couldn't free it with the usual maneuvers, we had to drain the tank, and there he was."

"You sure it's a male?"

"Body's not in the greatest shape, but that much you can tell."

They arrived at the rim directly above the cadaver, shooed the rubberneckers, and looked down.

"Guess it's like you said," Swarth observed. "I'm goin' down for a closer look."

Spunelli peeled off his rubber gloves. "Better wear these," he said, handing them to Swarth. "We try to keep things clean, but it is actually sewage we're dealing with here. And watch your step. Might be pretty slippery."

With the wash down complete, the waste was virtually gone. Swarth struggled to balance his 240 pounds as he descended, gripping the wet handrails and lurching down the narrow ladder. He stepped off the last rung and squatted next to the body. After a few moments, he backed up and snapped several photos with his cell phone. The lab techs would get more detail in the evidentiary photographs, but he routinely took a few preliminary snapshots for the early pages of his murder book. This one was a bit more of a struggle than usual, operating the camera app through rubber gloves. He returned the phone to his pocket and hauled himself back up to the catwalk.

"I'm gonna call the coroner," he puffed, stepping over the rail and pulling off the gloves. "Can they get the body outta there, or d'ya have to dismantle the mechanism?"

"Nah," Spunelli said. "We've disengaged. It'll freewheel now."

Swarth handed back the gloves as they walked back down the ramp together.

"Hell of a way to go," Spunelli said as they neared the police vehicle.

"Guess he was lucky, in a way," Swarth countered.

Spunelli cast him a quizzical glance. "How's that?"

"He's got at least two bullet holes in his head."

• • •

As the bridge girders swept past rhythmically, Noah's muddled thoughts drifted to the day ahead. He was good at first days, at being the new guy, and even with the current gut rot, he'd manage this one.

When he was firing on at least four of eight cylinders, he was actually bright, likable, and made friends easily. His soft, Semitic brown eyes seemed to survey the world at half-mast, projecting an air of indifference that others found compelling. Dark, rounded, Mediterranean features, and curly, low-maintenance, dark hair completed the "careless disinterest" image.

His ease in unfamiliar situations probably stemmed from entering no less than nine new schools as a kid, before graduating high school. His parents split before they were thirty, leaving him to be raised as an only child by a narcissistic mother who was more focused on landing a second husband than on dealing with the needs of her precocious youngster. They had moved frequently to accommodate her jobs and whims. Father was an Ivy League-educated engineer from Beverly Hills, who was AWOL during Noah's childhood. After the divorce, Shane the elder had quickly re-married and started a new family; within a few years, business prompted a move to the Middle East, with him remaining in the picture only to the extent of the occasional card on birthdays and holidays. At first, Noah saved the exotic stamps; later, he just pitched the whole thing.

Eventually Noah's mother found another spousal victim, and he was dispatched to boarding school in the Tehachapi Mountains, east of Santa Barbara, where, as an angry adolescent, he excelled in football and wise-mouthing. Most of his teachers respected his academic ability despite an aversion to the attitude. At 6'1" and 190, he was a gifted high-school quarterback with the tools to succeed at the next level, but after a promising freshman season as a walk-on at Stanford, he struggled through a spotty sophomore year as a sometimes starter, and quit at the end of the season because, he said, he wasn't getting enough playing time.

On nearing the criminal justice complex on the fringe of the West Oakland ghetto, navigation became tricky. The employment letter had come with directions to the Public Defender's office, but they were abysmal, the streets being all one-way in the wrong direction. Finally, Captain America swung into the parking structure down the block from the courthouse. Swept by another urge to heave as he got out of the car, Noah sucked in a few deep breaths, and the nausea subsided. Grabbing his jacket, he plodded up 6th to Washington.

It was 9:45 by the time he passed through the glass doors in the black alabaster façade of the Allen E. Broussard Justice Center. This had been the old Oakland Municipal Courthouse at 600 Washington Street before the Municipal and Superior Courts were unified in 1996. Back in the day, Municipal Court judges sat as magistrates. Theirs was the business end of the criminal justice system where the whole process began, and where the countless misdemeanor cases were administered and tried. Now they were all the equivalent of Superior Court judges, but the Broussard Center—named for an African-American Oakland son who had risen from humble beginnings to the state Supreme Court—still served as step one for the unfortunates entering the criminal justice system for the first time, and the court structure remained upside-down. Because the newcomers entered through the magistrates' departments, these settings could have offered a unique opportunity to send first time offenders in a better direction if only time and funds were invested in creative solutions. Sadly, populated with entry-level DAs and PDs, and many judges who were just biding their time to high-pensioned retirement, they were the low end of the criminal justice totem pole. Result, a cattle-call mentality that specialized in deals, delays, logistics, statistics, and calendar clearing, rather than bringing justice to the community, and pointing young souls in jeopardy toward a rising trajectory. The up-and-coming and experienced lawyers and judges fought their way to the felony departments, where the stakes were higher and the visibility greater, but the chances of redirecting the paths of the defendants in any meaningful way hovered pretty close to nil.

A deputy sheriff stood next to the metal detector just inside the door, inspecting bags, as Noah waited in line in his stocking feet, devoid of belt, jacket, or cell phone. A pretty leveling experience.

"PD's office?" he asked the officer as his belongings passed through the x-ray machine on the conveyer belt.

Without looking up, the deputy jerked a thumb over his shoulder toward a bank of elevators. "Sixth floor."

Noah steadied his sensitive stomach as the elevator ascended. At six, he stepped out into a large, brightly lit linoleum foyer and walked across to a glass wall on which bronze-painted letters declared ALAMEDA COUNTY PUBLIC DEFENDER, OAKLAND DIVISION. Beyond, a sparsely furnished, government-issue reception room accommodated several potential clients who sat on blandly colored, somewhat soiled, couches and chairs. Next to the coffee urn against the far wall, two well-scrubbed, dark-skinned preschoolers sat at a toddler-sized table and chairs, one absorbed in a coloring book, the other piecing together a jigsaw puzzle. Pausing momentarily, Noah wet his parched lips, shook his head a tad to clear the haze, straightened his tie, and pushed the door open. *Show time.*

CHAPTER FOUR

"Siddown," was Noah's gravelly, two-syllable welcome to the professional world, as a briefly visible woman slid the frosted-glass window open, then closed it with a decisive clunk. *Okay. Step one was always trial by secretary, no?* He picked up a dog-eared six-month-old *People* magazine, settled onto the couch, and paged mindlessly for what seemed like forever, his frontal lobes pounding.

Oakland Division occupied the whole of the fifth and sixth floors of the Broussard Center. The Alameda County PD was ensconced in seven different locations, including the Main Office on Lakeside Drive, which housed the administrative functions. There were four branch offices, divisions, in local communities, and they, together with Oakland Division, were nestled beside the various former municipal courthouses, the pits where the criminal-litigation rubber met the road. Investigation Division was quartered at the old Courthouse, over on Fallon next to Lake Merritt, the meandering, aquatic crown jewel of Downtown Oakland.

"Mr. Shane?"

He looked up to see a slender, attractive African-American woman in her early thirties, dressed in a navy business suit with a red silk scarf at her neck, standing at the door next to the reception window and carrying an armload of nondescript materials.

"That would be me," he said, rising to greet her.

"I'm Bobbi Matthews, assistant to Mr. Stark, our managing PD here at Oakland Division. Why don't you come with me, and I'll show you the office." She had a glittering smile, great teeth.

Bobbi ushered him through the front door, pausing at a desk just inside the frosted reception window, where an obese woman sat, wearing a light brown dress and black horn-rimmed glasses, engrossed in a tatty magazine.

"This is Raylene Baldwin," Bobbi said.

"I've had the pleasure," Noah responded. "Nice to see you again."

Raylene slowly raised her attention from the magazine, fixing him with a tired, just-what-I-need—another-smart-ass-kid-PD look. Then she returned to paging through the glossy pictures without speaking.

Noah followed Bobbi through a government-gray carpeted, open work area, reminiscent of a newsroom at a metropolitan newspaper. Crowded with some thirty-five cubicles where the attorneys sat, the room was rimmed by glass-enclosed offices, conference area, and utility space. At mid-morning, with court in session, the place was nearly empty.

"You know," she said, her smile never fading, her pace never slackening, "I've got to tell you that your absence was noted. Raised a little concern around here. The brass were close to moving down the list to the next candidate." She glanced at him out of the corner of her eye as they zigzagged through the maze of cubicles.

"Yeah, my friend Sandy—ah, Garren Sutherland?—mentioned that. Been flat on my back with a hundred-and-three fever since the weekend, with the kind of rock-and-roll gut I wouldn't wish on an enemy."

"Wonderful," Bobbi said, wrinkling her nose.

"I actually called a couple of times to let people know."

"Okay. Just a word to the wise. I think you made it in under the wire, but we had a full indoctrination Monday for the new arrivals. So you'll have to pick up what you can on the fly. People are pretty busy."

"I'm a quick study."

"You'll need to be."

Bobbi led him into a spacious, unoccupied conference room, in the middle of which stood a long gray metal conference table, surrounded by sixteen metal chairs. Windows covered with aluminum Venetian blinds looked out toward Broadway, a block over. The morning sun bathed the room in banded sunlight. She put a stack of forms on the table and pulled out a chair for him. He sat and looked up at her.

"So after I fill these out, I'm official?"

"Not quite," she said, opening the door. "You still gotta meet the boss."

Twenty minutes later, after completing the forms, but still feeling somewhat washed out, Noah got up to survey his surroundings. He pulled a crim-law text from a metal bookshelf and paged through. He examined the photos on the wall, admiring the magic-marker mustache and goatee on a portrait of the governor, when the door opened and Bobbi returned.

"Mr. Stark will see you now," she announced.

James Stark was taller than Noah had expected, perhaps 6'2". Though balding, he was slim and looked younger than his 47 years. The shirt was a subtle pink stripe, monogrammed at the pocket. A charcoal pinstriped suit-jacket hung from a hanger on a clothes tree in the corner. The blue-silk tie and matching suspenders rounded out an image that struck

Noah as a bit opulent for a PD, especially one who inhabited a cramped office with a metal desk. Stark extended his hand with a forced smile.

"Jim Stark," he said, as though it should be immediately recognizable. Noah's aversion was instantaneous.

"Welcome aboard," Stark continued. "Did Bobbi get you set up?"

"She did. Loaded me with forms."

Noah took a seat in one of the client chairs as Stark settled behind his desk, his smile morphing into a slightly skeptical look, one eyebrow raised. "So we were a little concerned with whether you were going to show up. I would've thought you'd have been more anxious to get started."

Noah fixed him with a serious stare. "Y'know, I've been laid up with the most god-awful flu since last weekend. Definitely would've been here, but I thought it best not to expose the office. I did call in a few times with updates."

Stark measured him a beat, countenance unchanged, and then the smile returned. "Well, you're here now. You up for it?"

"Been talking to Sandy and Kate. They make it sound great."

Noah, Sandy, and Kate Waverly, members of a law-school study group and close friends, had come to the Public Defender together from Hastings.

"Sandy?"

"Garren Sutherland."

"Oh, right. I was going to ask you about Kate. Charming girl. How long have you known her?"

"We've been together since the beginning of third year. Guess it's over a year now." He hoped the "been together" part cloaked the relationship with some degree of ambiguity.

Stark started to add something, thought better of it, then said, "So listen, Noah, I've got to get over to Main Office, but I just wanted to open the lines of communication, and tell you that if there's anything you need, any questions, well, just know that my door is always open."

"Thanks."

"Okay then. I guess that's it." He stood and grabbed his jacket. "Bobbi'll get you a desk, a phone, and an assignment. I don't know exactly what's going on this morning, but she'll find you something." As he made for the door, the smarm continued. "Well, good luck. See you around campus."

Noah's main reaction was relief that there was no more talk of going back to the waiting list. He wandered out, found Bobbi's office, and poked his head in. She was on the phone, but beckoned him to a chair, then made the inch sign to indicate she'd only be a minute. He amused himself with Snapchat on his cell while she droned on about calendars and courtroom assignments. After a few minutes, she hung up.

"So?" she said, with a cheerful smile.

"Stark said you'd have something for me," he said, pocketing the cell.

"He would. Didn't say what that might be, did he?" She picked up a stack of files and began thumbing.

"Did not."

"Okay, let's see…"

Finding one that needed work, she opened it. "All right, here's one. It's an interview you can cover in the City Jail. That lovely building over there?" A thumb over her shoulder indicated a gray, windowless, four-story hulk out the window behind her and across several rooftops. Grim and foreboding with the feel of a concrete bunker, the jail stood between the Broussard Center and Broadway.

"You'll need to get his story, and make sure he's eligible for the PD," she instructed.

City Jail was where arrestees were processed and held waiting to be arraigned. After arraignment, they became guests of the county, billeted at Santa Rita County Jail, twenty-five miles southeast of Oakland in Pleasanton, or at Glenn E. Dyer Detention Facility, North County for short, a block down 6th Street from where they were sitting.

Bobbi scanned the file. "Forms are pretty self-explanatory. You'll figure it out. Hispanic kid, Ruiz, charged with, mmm…" She frowned. "…stealing three hundred pounds of butter?" Slapping the file closed, she tossed it across the desk. "Yeah, well, we do get 'em all."

She rose and started out of the room to let him know the discussion was over. After years of endless lawyer prattle, she had the technique down. Right on cue, Noah's prattle began.

"But what do I ask?" he groped. "How do I know what we need to know?" The nausea was returning. "I mean… what if he—"

"Like I said," Bobbi told him without turning back, "you'll figure it out."

CHAPTER FIVE

The Alameda County Coroner's Office and morgue were in the basement of the records building, two blocks down Washington from the courthouse, west of the freeway. It was after noon when Martin Cheung, M.D., Deputy Medical Examiner, outfitted in his OR greens, emerged from the glare of the stainless-steel autopsy suite into the subdued light of an adjacent linoleum hall, leaving behind him a gore-covered surgical table on which the fluid and solid remnants of his patient awaited aspiration and scrubbing down by an ME Tech II.

Passing through the secretarial pool, he pulled off his surgical gloves, tossed them into a wastebasket, and lit a Marlboro. He took a deep drag as he walked, then blew out a cloud of gray smoke that followed him into his minuscule windowless office. It wasn't until he had taken a step inside that he noticed Detective Ned Swarth seated in the single gray-metal chair in front of his gray-metal desk. Cheung's eyebrows gathered behind his thick glasses. He wasn't up for chatting, as he had a mountain of reports to dictate, and besides, his heavily introverted personality didn't lend itself much to the bedside manner anyway, one explanation for his choice of specialty. The hurry-up autopsy that morning on Swarth's potentially high-profile case had already disrupted his day. Any time gang execution or organized crime was suspected, an effort was made to undertake the post-mortem on a priority basis to preserve evidence while the investigation was hot.

"What do you need, Ned? Let's make it quick, I got a lotta work stacked up."

"Just interested in the results on the sewage guy, that's all. Got a make on him?"

Cheung squeezed past the detective, who all but filled the room, then fell into his chair and propped his cigarette in a kidney-shaped, stainless instrument tray half-filled with butts. Piles of papers and forensic pathology journals were stacked high on the desk, surrounding the computer monitor and almost obscuring the diminutive doctor from the detective's view.

"We ran the prints. You're not going to believe this."

"What?"

"Name's Warren Van Zandt. Sound familiar?"

"Van Zandt? Not the money guy? The one that handles the county retirement funds?"

"That's him. Big-time stockbroker. Somebody said he's a denizen of the social elite." He squinted down at his notes. "But I wouldn't know about that."

"Shit." Swarth exhaled audibly. "Looks like the high-visibility dance, doesn't it. Did you get anything on cause of death?"

"You got choices. Whaddya want first?"

"Start at the beginning, I guess."

"Well, see, that's the problem. Everything depends on what came first. Can't tell just yet. He had four bullets in him, sewage in the anterior buccal cavity—his mouth—but not in his lungs or stomach. Bruising about the neck with a broken hyoid. Take your pick."

"Shot, strangled, and drowned in sewage. Somebody was makin' sure."

"All current possibilities, except the drowning part. It's clear he was dead when he went into the tank. Trick is to find out whether he was killed by the shooter or strangled first."

"So which do you make it?"

"Can't tell. Labs aren't back. With the bath he took in that sewage, we couldn't see how much he bled from the gunshot wounds. Also, we gotta check on the age of the hematoma in his sternocleidomastoid." He tapped the ash off his cigarette and took a drag as he glanced up at the detective. "His neck. Can't imagine strangulation after death by gunshot, but the neck could have been an earlier injury, I guess. Right now, my money's on strangulation, but we're not ready to call it yet."

"Did you get a bio on him? Where does he live? I need to get the techs out to his place, and maybe get started with some neighbors."

Cheung took another drag and blew out a lungful, causing Swarth to recoil, and then crushed out the cigarette. Used to be everybody smoked; now, maybe only one in ten in government work, less than that on the biomedical side. But it did make for short meetings, which wasn't lost on Cheung. He sorted through a few recently arrived files on his desk, selected one, opened it, slid his notes inside, and scanned the face sheet.

"Over by Lake Merritt. East Gate Plaza. Suite 1204."

"Thanks, Marty. Call me when those labs are in, willya?"

"You got it."

• • •

"I'm here to see Pablo Ruiz."

"Congratulations. Who're you?"

"Public Defender, here for an interview."

The female sergeant looked him up and down. "ID?"

"Oh yeah, sorry." Noah took out his temporary identification card, placed it in the metal tray, and slid it under the thick glass.

She scrutinized it. "Noah Shane, is it? You're new."

"First day."

"That'll qualify." She smiled. "I'm Christie. Welcome to Devil's Island."

In the ten minutes it took to get around the corner to the jail and wait his turn in line, Noah had consumed the three-page file labeled *People v. Pablo Ruiz* in its entirety. There was an intake and eligibility form, an arrest report, and a computerized rap sheet that appeared to be clean, if he was reading it right. According to the report, Ruiz had been arrested on a violation of Penal Code §459, burglary. The essential facts were: a Foremost dairy truck was parked behind a local Safeway at 2:30 AM while the driver was inside making a delivery and shelving product. He came back to find three hundred pounds of butter missing. No witnesses.

The defendant had been stopped by Oakland PD on routine night patrol after his 1992 Nissan sedan ran a stop sign six blocks from the crime scene. The arrest report contained the usual verbiage: "When instructed to exit his vehicle, the suspect attempted to resist," and "after reasonable and necessary force was employed to subdue the suspect, in the ensuing search for weapons attendant to taking the subject into custody, three hundred pounds of butter was discovered in the trunk."

It being his first case, first day, Noah accepted the narrative at face value. With a bit more seasoning, he would be convinced, like the other PDs, that OPD had the reports pre-baked on a word processor, complete with all the operant phrases neatly quoted directly from the language of the applicable case law on drop-down menus, available for easy selection. All the arresting officer had to do was fill in the name, the scene, and the contraband discovered. A real time saver.

Of course, had he been around just a little longer, another red light would have flashed with the phrase "resisting arrest." This was invariably a signal for the PD to expect at least facial bruising, and maybe other injuries, when he met the potential client. Sometimes the consequences were more serious, but any broken bones or internal injuries would usually mean the interview would take place in the jail ward at Highland Hospital. This being Noah's first outing, the subtleties were not yet apparent.

Inside the glass front doors of the jail building was a dark anteroom with green-gray, linoleum-tiled, institutional flooring and numerous wooden benches, all giving the place a post office ambience. A handful of mostly African-American and Hispanic women populated the benches, engaged in quiet conversation: mothers, wives, and girlfriends of inmates waiting to visit their men. Directly across from the front door was a clear-acrylic bulletproof window with a steel-framed slot at its base under which a sliding metal tray accommodated the exchange of visitor identification and entry badges.

Christie sat behind the window and communicated via an intercom that eerily detached her from her voice. Clad in the black Oakland Police Department uniform and tie, she was white, somewhat heavy, late forties, and reasonably attractive, her short bleached-blond hair dark at the roots.

"Heard the PD was signing a little new blood, without the beard, and hopefully without the attitude. Would that be you?"

"Could be. Don't know enough yet to have an attitude."

"I like that in a man. Think we'll get along fine."

Christie slid the ID tray back to him. "Your first lesson is that next time you come in you don't have to wait in line," she said, typing some information into the computer. "Lawyers I don't despise have priority. Just come to the front and I'll buzz you through."

She pressed a key on her communication console and said, "PD Shane to see prisoner number 374810, Pablo Ruiz." She printed out a nametag that bore Noah's name and the prisoner's name, which she slipped into a small plastic casing with a metal clasp, dropped into the tray, and pushed to him. "Clip this on your lapel, and come in through the door to your right. Go to the end of the hall, show the deputy your clearance, and don't forget to turn it in when you leave."

"Right, thanks."

"See ya on down the road, Noah," she said, again with the smile.

"Mos' def," he responded, as he stepped toward the door. Pushing it open when the buzzer sounded, he entered and walked down the hall to the end, where further ingress was blocked by a barricade of bars covered with pale green paint that was chipping away after years of deferred maintenance. An obese, bald guard at a metal desk, black jumpsuit with insignia, no tie, looked up from a recent issue of *Sports Illustrated*. None of the inside OPD personnel wore ties, metal badges, or shoes with laces, only sewn-in cloth badges and black leather, zippered boots. Noah would come to find out that all potential weapons were verboten.

After checking his nametag, the guard motioned him through the metal detector, then activated a switch on the side of his desk. A barred gate slid aside, providing access to a small antechamber, four-feet square, bars on all sides, with an identical sliding panel opposite.

"Report to the officer inside," the guard instructed, recognizing Noah's novice status. "He'll set you up with an interview room when your client arrives."

The barred door slid shut behind Noah with a low, metal-on-metal thud, leaving him caged. Dismissing the momentary queasy feeling as lingering flu, he forced his attention forward.

A younger guard inside threw a similar switch, opening the inside door. Noah entered a large room beyond, probably sixty-by-sixty, partitioned on three sides by steel bars. This was the Reception Center. Along a solid wall to his left were five identical gray-steel doors, four with square, wire-reinforced, glass windows, no more than eight inches on a side. A single guard was perched at an elevated desk in front of a console with a cluster of monitor screens that depicted various halls and rooms in the facility. The room seemed remarkably devoid of activity.

"Your man'll be down in a minute," the desk guard said. "Have a seat." He gestured to a wooden bench against the wall. Noah sat and, forcing the notion from his mind that he was now perma-sealed in the bowels of Oakland City Jail, began to scan the eligibility form.

Five minutes later, the barrier on the far side of the Reception Center slid open. A guard entered with a Hispanic man who immediately struck Noah as younger than he had expected. His longish, black wavy hair neatly combed, he was dressed in a creased orange jail jumpsuit, a clean white T-shirt showing at the chest. Laceless athletic shoes flopped as he was led to a visiting room, his attention riveted on Noah. Opening the door with a large brass key, the guard guided his charge inside.

"Ruiz," he announced in Noah's direction. Noah closed his file, rose, walked over, and entered the room.

Without a word, the guard closed the steel door with a mechanical thud, and the sound of the oversized brass key turning in the lock again prompted Noah's uneasiness to rise, more intensely this time. *No way this was the flu.*

He found himself in a small room, maybe five-by-eight, furnished with a gray-metal table and three chairs. A round, green, metal shade over a wire basket enclosed a single light bulb that hung from a conduit in the middle of the ceiling. The only window was the one in the door, above which a small video camera pointed down toward the table.

Noah's unease now grew into unmistakable agitation, with panic not far behind. Perspiration collected on his forehead; his hands were damp. His first instinct was to sit at the table and gut it out, but within seconds it was clear that he had to get out. Attempting to camouflage his oxygen hunger, he stepped to the door and rapped as he stared desperately through the little window. The guard who had just left him stopped, looked back quizzically, then returned and opened the door.

"Yeah?"

"Uh… men's room?" Noah struggled to steady his quavering voice. "Th—thought I'd take a leak before we got started."

Eyeing Noah curiously, the guard motioned to the last door at the end of the solid wall. "Down there."

Noah turned to his prospective client, who was already seated at the table. "Right back," he said, and walked by the guard, trying for nonchalance. The deputy turned back, closed the door, and locked it.

After several minutes of deep breathing in the tiny, windowless restroom, only a little buoyed by his ability to obtain maybe a particle of control with his excuse, Noah returned to be re-situated in the interview room. Following the closing and locking exercise, the dread once again began to rise. A second trip to the head was not an option, and since running screaming from the building would likely be frowned upon even on his first day, Noah yanked his focus forward and found himself slightly better at suppressing the apprehension. Stepping to the table where his client was seated, he stuck out a hand.

"Noah Shane. PD's office," he said, addressing his first client, his legal career now officially, if not somewhat awkwardly, underway.

"Pablo Ruiz, Mr. Shane. I guess you are my attorney." The response was fluent English. Focusing intently, Noah picked up the clipped-consonant hint of barrio, accompanied by a smile that seemed to contradict the surroundings, but it was the large, angry purple welt on the left side of Ruiz's face, yellow in the middle with a scabbed-over abrasion, that dominated his attention.

"Jesus," he said with a fleeting wince. "What happened to you?"

Pablo shrugged. "I guess the cops thought I was some kind of threat."

"Were you?"

Pablo smiled meekly, then scoffed. "Me?" he said. "I don't think so." The olive skin, dark brown eyes, and long, almost feminine eyelashes lent a Johnny Depp in *Pirates of the Caribbean* quality to his proportioned features. Two inches shorter than Noah, he was lean and trim, appearing even younger than his twenty-three years. Despite the discolored swelling on his face, the smile was definitely his gold standard, broad, engaging, infectious, and he clearly knew how to use it. Only ten minutes into his first City Jail experience, Noah's intuition nevertheless told him that this guy was at serious risk behind bars.

"Okay, technically I'm not your lawyer yet," he said. "But it's probably just a formality. I've gotta demonstrate that you're indigent if you want to be eligible for the Public Defender."

"That should not be difficult."

Shuffling the forms, Noah's outlook continued to improve as he became progressively more absorbed in the task at hand. He drew out the checklist and launched into the questioning.

"Ever been represented by the PD before?"

"No."

"Employed?"

"No."

"On welfare?"

"No. My mother is supporting us, mostly. I was parking cars at Spenger's Restaurant in Berkeley until several months ago, but now I am looking for work. Get odd jobs where I can."

"Educational background?"

"I went to Fremont High, but never graduated. I've worked a few jobs since. I guess I never thought it was important to get the diploma."

Moderately surprised with the articulateness of the first few responses, Noah looked up, studied him, then returned to checking boxes.

"Brothers or sisters?"

"No, just my mother and me."

A pause as Noah scanned the remainder of the questionnaire. Then Pablo added, "There is no money to afford an attorney, Mr. Shane. That is certain. My mother is a housekeeper."

"Okay. You're an adult. Why don't we just put down that you're out of work and not mention your mother. That might do it."

"Thank you." Pablo spoke softly, looking down at his hands on the table in front of him. The picture of humility.

"Just a few more vital statistics. Is your father living?"

"No, he died when I was ten."

"What was his job?"

Pablo hesitated. "He was a disabled veteran."

"I see. What kind of work have you done besides parking cars?"

"I have been a busboy, drove a delivery truck, helped my mother with the housekeeping. Nothing for very long, I am afraid."

"Okay. Address?"

"11601 Forty-Sixth Street, Oakland."

"Own or rent?"

"My mother's home."

"Does she have a mortgage?"

"I don't know."

"Any money in the bank? Other assets?"

"Nothing."

"Credit cards?"

"No. Canceled."

"Phone?"

"(510)639-8240 is my cell, but I lost the phone."

"Who is your next of kin?"

"My mother, Amparo Ruiz."

"Does she know you're in jail?"

"She has been here three times."

Another pause. "So I guess that about does it for the eligibility part. Let's get down to it." Noah closed the file, and slid it behind his yellow legal tablet. "What happened with this butter?"

Pablo began the story tentatively. Noah developed the details with a few interspersed questions, writing furiously. He had heard of these street busts, had read plenty of cases in the Search and Seizure section of crim law, but this was his first taste of the real world.

"So did you take the butter from that truck, Pablo?"

"No, I did not."

"Really. Where did it come from?"

"The butter was mine," Pablo said.

"Yours. I see. So, where'd you get three hundred pounds of butter?"

"I got it cheap from several different stands at the Fruitvale Flea Market."

"Why butter?"

"I was going to try to sell it to some of the people my mother keeps house for. They sometimes buy pastries and the things that she bakes, so I thought maybe I could make some money."

"Do you have any receipts?"

"No."

"Was anyone with you when you went to the flea market?"

"No."

"Do you know the names of anyone you got the butter from?"

"I really don't recall."

Clean rap sheet, but he seemed to have the drill down. Multiple anonymous sources. Couldn't be traced.

"What will happen to me, Mr. Shane?"

Noah looked up from his pad. "I really can't say, Pablo. But it'd definitely help if you had some information we could use to prove how you got the butter." He turned the tablet to a fresh page. "Let's talk about the bust. Did you run the stop sign?"

"I do not know. Does anyone ever really stop?"

"It says here you 'resisted arrest.' Did you?"

"What does that mean?"

"It means you fought against the cops, refused to do what they told you, tried to get away, something like that."

"I did not," Pablo said. "I got out of the car as they told me. They took my keys and opened the trunk and they found the butter. Then they hit me."

"Did they say you were under arrest before they looked in your trunk?"

"No."

"Did they ask for your consent to search the trunk?"

"No. They just took the keys out of the car and opened it."

"Well, at least that's something. Maybe we can suppress the search if we can show there was no probable cause for it after you ran a stop sign. If they don't have the butter, they don't have you, do they." Noah made a note and underlined, *check search.*

"Any prior convictions?"

"None."

"Ever been arrested before?"

"Nothing since I was a kid other than a couple of traffic tickets."

"Anything serious when you were a juvenile?"

"Just two petty thefts, some beer."

"Okay. Now I'm not sure exactly how this works, Pablo, but it says here that your case will come up for arraignment tomorrow morning. I guess you'll have to stay inside until then. In court we can see about getting you released on your own recognizance. Your record seems clean." Noah got up, gathering his papers. "I don't suppose you have any money to make bail?"

"My mother can probably come up with some, if it is not too much. Do you think we can win the case?"

"I just don't know."

Noah walked to the door, rapped several times, and looked out through the little window. There was no one in the room except the one guard seated at the video console. Hearing the knock, he turned toward the holding cell, raised a hand, and picked up the phone, apparently indicating he would call for someone to come get them. Noah felt his anxiety rising again. Pablo was speaking; something about what he should do in court, what he should say. Noah couldn't focus.

After what seemed like forever, the other guard again entered the Reception Center and went to the desk. Noah watched, heart pounding, as the two men apparently exchanged pleasantries. He could hear nothing through the massive door. *Dammit! The fuck were they doing?* He felt his face flush. The guards' banter continued as the second one backed across the room, talking while taking the key from his belt. He was laughing as he opened the door, but the smile disappeared abruptly as he motioned Pablo to exit the room. Noah struggled out, groping for composure.

Only when he left the jail and fell into a brisk stride down 6th toward Oakland Division did the tension begin to lift. As he breathed deeply of the winds of freedom, he slowly became aware of the returning muscle ache, fatigue, and a vague but familiar fluish queasiness. *What was with this claustrophobic bullshit? He'd never had anything like that before. Definitely no malady for public defenders who spend all their time in the lockup. What do the guys on the nuclear subs do, under the ice for three months at a time? Drugs? Gotta get used to this shit, or it could turn into one helluva long career… very soon.*

CHAPTER SIX

"I know, I know, but after the special assignments, I've only got forty-four lawyers to service thirty-six departments. We've got two each in the prelim courts, and should have four on each of the jail runs, but we're totally short-handed. Best we can do for you is two right now."

Bobbi paused for the response, and her gaze wandered across the desk to Noah, but she wasn't seeing him. He slid the Ruiz file toward her. No reaction.

"I can't help how long it takes to get through the interviews out there." The tone was stressed-yet-attempting-polite. "I understand, but I'm telling you I can't help you right now. We just got a raft of new people who'll be coming in. That should take some of the pressure off." A long pause, during which Noah could hear some kind of strident rant from the muffled voice in the receiver, and then, "Oh, don't mention it." The parting words dripped saccharine. "Any... time. Byy-ee." She slammed the phone back to its cradle.

"Sheriff's office," she said, as though some explanation for her affect was called for. "Whining about the scheduling. Say they've got a 'critical mass' of prisoners at Santa Rita waiting for hours to see the PD. Say they trade dope, get in fights. Now there's a news flash. Criminals actually trading dope and fighting. So what am I supposed to do? Go hire some more PDs myself? Give us a bigger budget, for god's sakes. I got my own problems." Pausing the diatribe, she suddenly realized she was justifying herself to the office's newest rookie, and her focus settled on Noah, who had been patiently awaiting her return to the here and now.

"Sorry," she said, picking up the *Ruiz* file. "So was it really three hundred pounds of butter?" She perused the completed eligibility form.

"Butter."

"Okay, so now you log on to one of the computers, and input your ID. Go to the PD program, *defenderData* it's called, and copy in the material from the interview and the stuff about his arraignment tomorrow morning. Department, charges, all that. It'll prompt you through."

"I'll give it a shot."

"So, did I give you a desk yet?"

"No."

"Then let's go get you one."

She grabbed a stack of papers and books from the credenza behind her and led him out into the pool. They passed several rows of cubicles before she stopped.

"This is it," she said. "Home, at least for now. But don't get too comfortable. Never can tell when they might send you down to Hayward, or over to Berkeley, even to one of the juvenile courts. You'd love Berkeley. Totally defense friendly. Only one trial in the last two-and-a-half months wasn't an acquittal. And that was a petty theft where the defendant didn't show up. They prosecuted *in absentia*, and it was still a hung jury." She laughed. "Gotta love those Berkeley juries."

Plopping her stack of materials on his desk, she went on, "Anyway, anything's possible except felony trial staff. Doubt you'd end up there very soon. But then, who knows?" She raised an eyebrow and playfully looked him up and down. "You might turn out to be a star."

"Yeah, well. Star pretty much seems light years away. Right now I feel a little more like ten pounds of glittering guano in a five-pound bag. Besides, I know less than zip."

"Everybody feels that way at first," Bobbi assured him, "but that part we can fix." She picked up a black binder from the top of her stack. "Here's a manual that gives you an overview of our local criminal justice system." She set it down, then thumbed through a long, flap-over card catalog. "And this's a compendium of all the cases you might need for search and seizure, evidence questions, exclusionary rule, probation, sentencing. A couple of our volunteer law-student clerks brief the new cases as they come out in the advance sheets. We put the cards that have their notes on them in your box, and you just clip them into the compendium."

Noah was impressed. "How do you know all this stuff? Are you a lawyer?"

"Much more qualified." She smiled, flattered. "Know more about the system than most of 'em, particularly the new ones. But you don't want to take anything I say too seriously," she said, shaking a well-manicured finger. "The minute you start to count on the law according to Bobbi, you could find yourself in some deep trouble."

Next she held up a thick, soft-cover tome and set it back on the desk. "Congratulations," she continued. "You also win a set of penal codes, criminal procedure statutes, and regs. Your phone extension is 5757.

Your inbox is up front next to Raylene's desk. Check it regularly for your mail, phone messages, and any written stuff from administration. Oh, and here's your name plate." She handed him an official-looking plaque on which 'Noah Shane' was spelled out in gold leaf.

"Looks like something for a loan officer in a bank."

"Yeah," Bobbi scoffed. "Better hang onto it. Your next job might just be in a bank. Loan officers make decent money, unlike us bottom feeders."

She went on to explain the computers, internet access, and the legal research software. When she'd finished, she put a finger to her cheek, pensively. "So," she said, "I guess that's it. If you need anything typed, get on your secretary's sign-up list. She would be Nina. Your permanent ID card, which you should have in a couple days, will operate the copy machine. If you have any trouble, click on 'Help' in the program, and if you're still drowning, click on me, but don't cry wolf, okay?" She turned to leave.

"Wait. What do I do now?"

"Well, after you input the *Ruiz* info, why don't you spend some time reading this stuff." She put a hand on the stack of materials. "I don't really have anything else for you today. Tomorrow we might start you with some more interviews over at the jail, and see where it goes from there."

"That's a happy thought," he mumbled, his mind going to the minuscule gray room with the tiny window in the door.

"Well, gotta go. Have at it, Noah Shane." She gave him an encouraging smile. "Like I say, if you need anything… don't."

• • •

Ned Swarth pondered his next steps in the Van Zandt investigation as he mounted the stairs that led from the bowels of the records building to the street level. When he reached his car, he called in a request for an FET team—field evidence technicians—then he stopped for a sandwich on Broadway on his way over to the victim's condo.

By the time he arrived at the top floor of the East Gate Plaza, it was nearly 2:00, and the crime scene people were already hard at it. He ducked under the yellow tape and strolled through the flat, noting the sumptuous decor. It was all dark paneling and deep earth tones, great views of the lake and the hills beyond. He wandered into the study. More paneling and floor-to-ceiling bookcases. A leather-topped oak partner's desk stood in the middle of the room, where a bespectacled officer in his early sixties, wearing a gray FET jacket and a department-issue baseball cap, dabbed at the center drawer with a small camel-hair brush, his face inches from the bristles. Behind him, a Nikon clicked and flashed as another gray-jacketed investigator systematically photographed the condo.

"Got anything, Phil?" Swarth asked.

The ball-capped tech looked up. "Oh… afternoon, Ned. A little, maybe." He returned to his brushing.

"So?"

Phil continued to daub methodically, letting the detective cool his heels. These lab guys considered their function the linchpin of the criminal investigation. Totally meticulous, they were the guys who built models as youngsters, who washed the immaculate jalopy three times a day as teenagers. Only when Phil had finished dusting, brush in one hand and vial in the other, did he deign to raise his head and look up at Swarth.

"Yeah," he said. "Front door was jimmied, probably a screwdriver. Latents all over the knob, the jamb, the door. A drawer in the bedroom bureau was ajar, and so was this one here in the study, both covered with prints. Gotta separate 'em from the ones that belong here, but based on where they are, it's pretty clear we got us an uninvited guest."

"Any blood? Signs of a struggle?"

"Negative."

"No slugs, nothing?"

"Not so far. Still at it, but I doubt we'll find anything like that. In this building, somebody woulda heard gunshots and reported. Can't imagine a sound suppressor. This was definitely not a professional job. Perp didn't even wear gloves."

"Can you say anything about when it happened?"

"Nah. Nothin' here but the latents and some busted wood."

"Okay, Phil. Run those prints and call me when you're done, wouldja? I'll be back in the office about three-thirty or four, but you got my cell. I'm gonna talk to some of the neighbors."

"Check. Who was this Van Zandt guy anyway?"

"You know, the broker who ran the county and city employees' retirement plans."

"Our plan?"

"Right, managed the investments, so I get it."

"Jesus, Ned. I hope the funds are okay. I got three more years, and the wife and I are outta here. We're gonna need all the money we can get."

"Yeah? What're you gonna do when you hang 'em up?" Swarth asked, turning to go.

"We bought an old place in the woods up near Shasta," he said. "I'm gonna fix it up, then do my HO gauge trains…" —wide grin, nodding for emphasis— "full time."

Shaking his head, Swarth snorted a chuckle as he ducked under the tape on the way out. "Figures," he murmured.

CHAPTER SEVEN

"Is this your desk? No way."

Glancing over at the neighboring cubicle, where a grinning Sandy had just arrived and was setting down a stack of files, Noah said, "Yeah. Just got here this morning." Somehow he'd missed Sandy's name plaque when he'd settled in. "Bet you set this up, didn't you," he chided. "Knew you couldn't survive without me."

Nearly the antithesis of Noah, Sandy was about 5'11", baby-faced, and slight. The wire-rimmed granny glasses and disheveled blond hair gave him the misleading look of a bookish high-school kid. Actually, he'd been a mediocre student all the way up, and through law school. His father, Howard Sutherland, was a successful agricultural lawyer in the Central California farming community of Modesto. Sandy had "polished up the handle on the big front door" at Sutherland, Marks & Cooper since he was ten. Totally one-dimensional, he'd wanted to be a lawyer as long as could remember. The old man was fond of saying that there was a lawyer locus on the Sutherland DNA.

After Modesto High, Sandy arrived at St. Mary's College by way of San Joaquin JC. He had to work hard for his Cs as an undergraduate, but his father's longtime acquaintance with the Dean of Admissions was enough to get him accepted to Hastings, Sutherland the Elder's law school alma mater. Howard trumpeted the news to *The Modesto Bee* and invited half the town to a gala send-off, upping the pressure exponentially on Sandy to succeed.

"I can't believe it," Sandy said. "Shane and Sutherland, side by side again. Kinda like fate, isn't it?" Sandy's comment went back to that first time Shane and Sutherland had found themselves next to one another.

• • •

The Hastings freshman class had been so large that it was divided into three sections; it would thin out substantially by the third year. They had all heard the old *Paper Chase* adage even before opening day: "Look to your right, look to your left. Only one of you will be here come graduation."

The Civil Procedure prof had been the dreaded Graham Kennedy, a small, wrinkled man in his late sixties with wispy white hair and a stentorian voice that dripped with sarcasm. Having fixated in the 1970s, Kennedy still wore dark horn-rimmed glasses that couldn't hide the piercing glare welded to his persona. A frustrated litigator, he had always wondered what might have been had he gone into practice instead of academia; as he aged, that curiosity hardened into bitter regret. The result was a mean streak that pervaded his classroom dialogue: "These rookie jerks carry fantasies of being trial lawyers? Well, they'll learn the price." He took an almost erotic delight in terrorizing every student unlucky enough to become enmeshed in his web.

One couldn't get through the matriculation process without hearing the rumors of Kennedy's draconian Socratic style. Ideally, this method of question-and-answer teaching, employed by many of the better law schools, taught young lawyers to think on their feet, preparing them for the public pressure they would face as professionals. That was the theory, but in Kennedy's case, it was unclear what possible educational benefit could be derived from the humiliation of being intellectually pantsed in front of 120 of one's peers by the Adolf Eichmann of law professors. Noah found himself somewhat tentative on day one; Sandy was a basket case by the time the thunderous voice had reverberated.

"Mr. Sutherland!"

No… possible… way. First day. First class. First victim called on. Sandy's first thought was that he was dreaming it.

Kennedy dialed it up: "Mr. Sutherland!"

Desperate to say something, respond somehow, Sandy was paralyzed. Even had he been able to manufacture a thought, his throat was too constricted to emit any sound.

Noah cast a sidelong glance to his right at the quivering mass seated next to him. *Was this the guy Kennedy was calling on?* He glimpsed the nametag, then the face. Sandy was staring down at his desk, crimson, rigid, motionless, gurgling.

Kennedy's voice filled the lecture hall. "Is there a Mr. Garren Sutherland?" The celebrated glare was fixed directly on Sandy. He knew full well where Sandy was; he had a seating chart in front of him.

"Come on Mr. Sutherland, speak up. We know you're here."

A few sniggers could be heard, muffled for fear of attracting the beast.

"Sutherland!" Kennedy boomed. He had seen the syndrome many times before. He was merciless.

"Yes, sssir." Sandy's voice was almost inaudible.

"Ah, Mr. Sutherland. You *are* with us," Kennedy cooed. "What I wanted to discuss with you today is this: is litigation a game?"

Silence. Then Kennedy asked again, "Mr. Sutherland, is litigation a game?"

Utterly frozen, Sandy was still staring at the desk, unable to fathom the meaning, what Kennedy was saying, what he wanted him to say.

Starting to feel his ire rising, Noah frowned and shook his head. *Was it a game? The fuck did that mean?*

Seconds ticked away. Thirty, forty-five. Not a word spoken. Kennedy let it intensify. He loved this. The awkwardness became electric. As it got worse, it got worse. Sandy couldn't speak; he couldn't *not* speak, and the dread was contagious. Labored breathing became audible around him. Tension closing in, Sandy felt himself crumbling. His mouth opened and closed like a gulping trout thrown up on the bank, but nothing came out.

Kennedy knew it wasn't just Sandy; they were all crumbling, just like so many classes before. He waited, glaring. No one dared look over, "… but for the grace of God."

Powerless to raise his eyes, Sandy saw nothing, couldn't hear the fidgeting, the shuffling, the throats clearing, but Noah could. His jaw jutted. *What an asshole. He knew this guy was dying. He was getting off on it.*

Sandy wasn't thinking about failing. He wasn't thinking about his future. In the end, he wasn't thinking at all. He simply had to get out. Full-on animal flight flooding through his system, the doomed gazelle inches from the claws of the pursuing lion. In a final act of desperation, he put both hands on the desk in front of him and pushed backward to stand. Suddenly there was a firm, steady voice from his immediate left.

"No, sir. It's not a game."

They heard it throughout the room. Heads jerked around.

"Who said that?" Kennedy squinted in the direction of the voice.

"I did, sir. Shane."

Kennedy frowned, studying the seating chart through the bottom of his trifocals. Midway through the S's, he pasted a condescending smile, and looked up.

"Mr. Shane. Thanks for volunteering. Now, I believe you said litigation is not a game. How *would* you characterize it?"

So it began. The bell had rung for round one.

Stay loose. Stay away from him. Don't get caught in the clinches, trapped in the corners. Keep a good distance.

Noah took a swing. "Well, it's a… it's a method of resolving disputes… that allows litigants their day in court."

Kennedy gazed curiously over his horn-rims, measuring Noah for a long moment.

"Is that so? Is it fair, then? Is it just?" The infamous glare was now riveted on Noah.

"For the most part, I would think. I mean... I'm sure mistakes are made, there are corrupt judges, maybe biased juries. But—"

"You think those circumstances are rare, do you, Mr. Shane? Error? Corruption? Bias? Then why do we need an appellate process? Why shouldn't we just accept the will of the trier of fact, judge or jury, if it's fair, 'for the most part'?"

Uh... oh. No good. Appellate process? Trier of fact? Stay out in the middle of the ring. "I would think that appeal increases the fairness. If there is the occasional error, it's corrected by the appellate court."

"Corrected, is it?" Kennedy sneered. "Do you know the percentage of verdicts that are appealed in California?"

"No, sir."

Sandy was virtually catatonic, staring blankly at Noah. He was still seated, his hands hung at his sides. Unable to comprehend what was being said. His chair remained pushed back from the desk.

"Twenty-one percent, to the Court of Appeals, and eight percent of those get to the Supreme Court. Does that surprise you?"

"No, sir," he said. *Dancing.*

"It doesn't. Good. It's gratifying to see a first-year student who isn't surprised by what he finds in the law. Now, have you any idea of the cost of appeal?"

"No, sir." *Keep dancing.*

"No. Of course not. Do you know what the litigation process involves, before it ever gets to verdict and appeal?"

"Uh... preparation, sir?" *A defensive jab.*

"Preparation. Yes, Mr. Shane. But what kind of preparation?"

"Thorough preparation, sir?" *A quick, Ali-like, counter.*

The rest of the section was silent. No one could believe he had stayed in it this long.

"Well, let's talk about that. Thorough preparation in this state consists of endless pleadings, interrogatories, depositions of every party and every conceivable witness and expert witness, non-binding judicial arbitration, mediation, motion practice, plus legal research and brief writing. All this before the case is ever close to trial. Would you call that 'thorough'?"

"Definitely, sir."

"And what is the role of the lawyer in all this?" Kennedy queried, changing direction.

Sandy was still gaping at Noah. As he began to realize what was going on, all he could think was, "How could the guy survive this?" Fuck the law. He'd sell insurance, maybe shoes.

"I—I guess to handle and present all the procedures you mention, the best representation possible."

"To be sure. But does counsel also have some responsibility for the preservation of his client's funds in this system of yours which is 'fair… for the most part'?"

Noah hesitated, knowing it had taken a nasty turn. *System of 'his'? He didn't say anything about a system. What were the options? He was clearly being totally set up for the combination, but nowhere to hide.*

"Yes, sir. I suppose he does," he conceded.

"Do you know how much this 'fair and just' system of yours costs litigants in California, Mr. Shane?"

Again with 'his' system. "I don't, sir."

"Up to ninety-one cents of every dollar recovered goes to fees and costs of litigation—pleadings and research, discovery, arbitration, mediation, and more research…"

Kennedy projected the unmistakable timbre of a man in love with his voice, rising to a crescendo, lingering on every word, accentuating each syllable: "Wri-ting, an-a-lyz-ing, mo-tions. Does this sound like a fair and just system which allows litigants their day in court, and a means of resolving disputes?" His head now thrust forward, arms outstretched on the lectern, veins bulging on his neck: this was what he lived for.

"No, sir—uh—yes, sir. Uh, no. I mean…" *On the ropes.*

Kennedy's tone was suddenly soft, supercilious. "Doesn't this sound a bit like a game to you, Mr. Shane?" He was staring over his glasses, pasting a tight, condescending smile, head cocked slightly, voice dripping with tolerance. "An upside-down game where the players get it all? The gate, the TV rights, the concessions, the luxury boxes, the jackets, the sweatshirts, even the T-shirts and funny hats? Management puts out all the bucks, and gets screwed."

"I don't know… Is there…?" *Definitely taken one square on the jaw. Struggling not to go down.* "Maybe… there's a better way?"

Kennedy's expression glowed with patience as he regarded Noah for what seemed an eternity. He had exactly the line he wanted. "You don't know," he said, followed by a long, uncomfortable pause.

"Well, you should consider whether there is a better way, before you decide you are pursuing the world's noblest profession, with all its prestige and financial remuneration. You and I will discuss that very question again—at length, Mr. Shane—at the end of the semester." The patient glow lingered as Kennedy looked from face to face, then finally back at Noah. Suddenly his countenance went blank, and he said abruptly, "That will be all."

Gathering his materials, he strode solemnly from the podium. Twenty-two minutes gone, and the first class was over. No one spoke. No one moved. Another year had begun.

Sandy idolized Noah from that moment forward, forever grateful for his rescue, forever admiring of his courage and presence.

• • •

"What're you doing right now?" Sandy asked. "I just got out of a prelim, and we're not due back until two-forty-five. Time for a late lunch?"

"You got a prelim? What're you talking about? You're here two days."

"I'm tellin' you, I just got out of a preliminary hearing."

Noah searched his eyes, reading the bullshit meter, then said, "Nah, it'd be malpractice. You got no clue what you're doing. They're not giving you any prelim."

Another beat. "Okay, okay. Second chair. But it's still a prelim."

"Ah," Noah said. "You spent your morning taking notes."

"I took some notes, yeah. But it was definitely a prelim. So you up for lunch?"

"Got nothin' but time, but I'll pass on the lunch." He put a hand to his stomach. "So far my biggest contribution to the office is not puking on it. I'd like to keep it that way."

"Okay. Lemme input the judge's order from this morning, then we're out of here."

They walked up Washington toward 9th, to G.B. Ratto & Co., a landmark Italian deli that had crafted world-class sandwiches in the West Oakland neighborhood for more than a hundred years. Sandy ordered pastrami; Noah grabbed a bottle of club soda.

Cutting over to Broadway, through Jack London Square, and along the Oakland Estuary, they settled onto a bench overlooking the water. Archeologists had determined that the Estuary, a narrow inlet separating Oakland from the island community of Alameda, was navigated as far back as 4000 B.C. by Native American tribes. It had become a hub of industrial activity and shipping in the late nineteenth century, and a landing for ferries that plied the San Francisco Bay in the early twentieth. With the advent of the Bay Bridge it lost most of its commercial function, and was now a picturesque home to a flotilla of pleasure boats, as well as a raceway for rowing clubs.

The sun was high in the sky, glittering off the water. Sailboats and the occasional cabin cruiser passed in either direction as Noah and Sandy soaked up the salt air and silence. Some distance from the crowds at Jack London Square, the intermittent laughing chatter of several Heermann's gulls circling overhead, and the occasional belch of a boat's air horn, were all that disturbed the quiet lapping of the water. A seventy-eight-foot Coast Guard cutter was moored across the way, virtually motionless despite the mild rise and fall of the water.

Noah breathed deeply, feeling the healing negative ions flooding his troubled digestive tract. "A guy could get used to this," he said, leaning back with his soda.

"So, you all set up?" Sandy asked, unwrapping his sandwich. "What'd they have you do this morning?"

"Goddamn jail interview. What's up with that? I thought you said they started everybody in court."

"I said I was in court. But they sent me for a couple jail interviews first. I guess most rookies spend a couple of weeks at the jail to get them familiar with the eligibility requirements. But I got lucky. Somebody was out, and they put me on a calendar department yesterday. Today I'm second chair on prelims." Sandy took a bite and squinted out over the water. "By the way, anyone tell you about the PD's Association?"

"No."

"You missed that at the orientation Monday. It acts for all the lawyers in the office."

"For what?"

"I guess they negotiate with the county about pay and benefits, working conditions, but maybe more than that. Claims to be trying to improve the office, maybe build a better product, better rep."

"Sounds like a union."

"Kinda. But they're the ones who put together the manuals and compendiums and stuff, do trainings. They apply for funds to send lawyers to continuing education if they can't afford it."

"Like not having to go into that bastille?" Noah rolled his eyes, recalling the coffin-like holding cell.

"Not sure we could get out of that."

"I don't know, man. I'm not much of a joiner. What's in it for you?"

"So, the president—this guy Mike Michelin?—pitched us on

Monday. Said there's a lot to fix, low wages, lousy investigation, not enough money for experts. That kinda stuff."

"What d'you care?"

"I don't know. He says there's not much respect for PDs. He was laughing about this dreaded line they get from clients: 'I don't want no PD, man. I want a *real* lawyer.' Says it's because salaries are low, trouble getting quality people."

"Maybe the clients are right," Noah mused. "How do they know who we are? I mean, we're paid by the same county that's payin' the cops who busted 'em, payin' the DA who has an office next door, the jail guards? And most of the PDs look like kid interns, or old hippies, or something, so what do you expect?"

"But don't you want to try to improve that image?"

"Jesus, man. We just got here. We're not on some kinda crusade. We came over to learn a trade. Maybe do something for these poor devils in the bargain. I think we oughta keep our eye on the ball. What's a union got to do with anything?"

"Seems like a good thing. That's all."

Silence.

"So what do you hear from your old man?" Noah asked, feeling a little guilty about shutting down Sandy's labor issue. "He must be lovin' that you're finally out in court and all."

"Calls me every day."

"He still want you out in Modesto where he can bring you into the firm?"

"Totally. Keeps askin' when I'm gonna give up this foolishness, come out to God's Country and make some money."

"What do you tell him?"

"Nothin'. Just that I need to learn the courtroom biz. Need some time to get up to speed."

"You gonna go out there and do your thing with him some day?"

"Would you?" Sandy gazed off over the water. "Really wouldn't be doing my thing. It's like it's totally about him. He wants to set up everything. Lunches to introduce me to clients, meet the judges, shadow him." He shook his head. "Guy eats me alive. Like I'm still fifteen."

"Yeah, well. At least you got an old man who knows you're alive."

"So, you hear from your dad lately? Does he know you're in the PDs office?"

"Sure, I heard from him. Last birthday. A card and a check for a hundred bucks. And I'll get one this year too, like clockwork."

"Bummer. You never said anything about that."

"Not something I think about much. Haven't spoken to him in three years. Haven't seen him in five."

"Do you write or anything? Tell him what's going on?"

"You mean like float a message in a bottle out into the void? Nah, I might be into pain, but not enough to stand on the beach waiting for that kinda mail."

Another interval of silence.

"So what do you think about Stark?" Noah asked. "Seems to think he's got it going."

"Couldn't say. He spoke at the orientation, but I haven't had any face to face."

"Strikes me as a small-time bureaucrat, the kind that uses his synthetic muscle to make people dance, all with this big shit-eating grin." A beat. "Worse. He's got his eye on Kate, which could definitely be trouble. You'd just as soon guys like that would ignore you."

"Yeah."

"Speaking of fathers, I need to have a little chat with her, make sure she's clear on the color of the caution flag."

"Right." Sandy went back to his sandwich. After a couple of chews, he frowned. "So what color is the caution flag?"

Noah shot him a look, then got up, stretched, and wandered off down the wharf, breathing in the salt air. A little after 2:00, it was time to get back.

Back at Oakland Division, Sandy gathered his files to return to court. He paused at Noah's carrel on the way out.

"You up for a cool one later?"

"I guess."

"So see you at the Oarhouse around six?"

"Sounds right."

"I'll let Kate know."

After struggling through entering the *Ruiz* eligibility data into the system, Noah read the chapters on interviews and calendar courts in his manual, pored over the compendium for a while, then decided to call it a day at about 4:30. As he was packing up, Bobbi paused at his cubicle.

"You still got that *Ruiz* file?"

"Yeah, I didn't know what to do with it."

"Okay, so hang on to it. You're gonna appear with him tomorrow morning. Just got the word from Stark that the regular calendar PD won't be handling the arraignment."

"What does that mean?"

"Well, Ruiz'll be arraigned in Department Sixteen, Judge McCormick. That's Chris Connelly's court. Why they don't want him to take it, I don't know, but it's your big chance, I guess. You up to it?"

"Okay with me."

"Nine AM. Be sure to read the chapter in your manual on arraignments."

"Already have. Ready to go," he told her, thinking he was.

"So have at it, Mr. Star."

CHAPTER EIGHT

Noah backed Captain America up to the curb on Ellis, three blocks from the Larkin, and disembarked. His rebellious gut had cut him some slack, to the point that he was actually looking forward to a beer.

Peeling off his jacket, he started up Ellis, falling in with the workday survivors from nearby government buildings. The Indian Summer sun hung low in the sky, still radiating warmth through the Tenderloin streets that were being cloaked in lengthening shadows.

Near Mason and Ellis, he dodged through an alley where a cacophony of TV, hip-hop, and the conversations of marginalized inhabitants filtered down through clotheslines draped between opposing walls of the tenement canyon. He turned down Taylor and strode the familiar half block to Eddy, and over a block to Jones. After grabbing a *Chronicle* from the machine on the corner, he ducked into the Oarhouse, an ancient dive whose clientele was about half law students and alumni from nearby Hastings, and the other half Tenderloin types from neighboring flats and hotels, the ones that could still afford the occasional beer or two.

The place was already engulfed in a raucous din. A long wooden bar ran down one side, behind which a massive mirror added depth to the otherwise narrow establishment. Crossed oars hung on the walls next to crew photos and other mementos of the once-popular Bay rowing contingent, originally launched in 1877 by John Wieland and his German immigrant brothers as the Dolphin Club. Two antiquated quad sculls were suspended from the high ceiling over a saw-dusted floor that was crowded with primeval oak tables. A handful of booths were nestled in the back. Circumscribing the room was a wooden Victorian picture rail on which more photos rested, autographed by dignitaries and celebrated customers. The front door brass was polished, and the windows were clean, creating the image of an oasis of respectability in an otherwise questionable neighborhood.

Noah swung a leg over a vacant stool at the well-lit end of the bar closest to the street, then spread the newspaper in front of him and paged toward the sports section. Growing up in Los Angeles had molded him into an avid Dodger fan, and he still followed them closely, enjoying frequent banter with the Bay Area fans when his team was out front in the standings.

He also relished the great American, mostly male, pastime of endlessly rehashing games and trades with the similarly inclined, vying for the superior insight. A fantasy sports enthusiast, he mapped out his teams in football and baseball seasons, and typically finished toward the top of the pack. Then there were also the occasional penny-ante bets through Stork, the Oarhouse bartender, so named for his long, bony frame. Stork fancied himself a bookie of some stature, though his gaming activities were limited to small stuff he took across the bar. As Noah scanned the front page, Stork drew a pitcher of Miller Lite from the tap and set it on the bar in front of him, along with an iced mug.

"Where y'been, counselor?" Stork drawled in a low, cigarette-rasped Texas lilt as he poured the amber into the mug and it formed a thin meniscus at the rim. Proud of his craftsmanship, he set the pitcher down and leaned forward on an elbow. Stork's bald head rounded into a face that was heavily lined from decades of cigarette smoke, making him look older than his fifty years.

Noah raised the mug in his direction. "L'chaim," he offered.

"Luck high-'em," the smirking barkeep echoed.

"Been lookin' forward to this one," Noah told him. "But I don't know if I'm up for a full pitcher tonight. Been havin' this all-out war with some god-awful Tenderloin bug since…"—his mind went back over the days of the flu—"…since Saturday now, I guess."

"Cold brew'll settle your stomach," Stork reassured him. "Besides, I'll help you finish it if it comes to that."

Thumbing through the paper, Noah glanced at the various segments as he neared the Sporting Green. As he passed the Bay Area section, something caught his eye that wouldn't have commanded attention before today: a story that mentioned Oakland police.

PROMINENT STOCKBROKER SLAIN

Oakland Police detectives are investigating the death of a well-known Bay Area man. The bullet-riddled body of stockbroker Warren Van Zandt was discovered today in the Emeryville Sewage Plant by an attendant who was repairing the mechanism. Active in civic affairs, Van Zandt was an avid benefactor of the arts, and also managed the Oakland City Employees' Retirement Fund and the Alameda County Retirement Fund. Oakland Mayor Rowland Murphy said he was "Deeply shocked and grief-stricken at the loss of my close friend." He went on to say that he pledged to marshal the full resources of his office, and that of the community, to bring the responsible party or parties to justice. Police reported that they currently have no suspects.

"So, Noah, you wanna put a buck or two on the Niners this weekend?" Stork asked, trolling for players.

Noah took a swig of his brew and looked up. "Niners? The season doesn't start until next weekend."

"Got some action goin' for the last round of exhibition games," Stork told him, as he drew a cold one for a customer a couple of stools down.

Noah went back to his paper with an inward smile that leaked externally just a touch. "A major clown act is what you 'got goin'," he said. "Those games are a total crapshoot. Coaches play the whole bench. I'll need more of a sure thing, Stork, maybe something on the qualifying rounds of the U.S. Open?"

Wiping a damp rag over the bar, Stork swept some peanut shells onto the floor, snorted, and changed the subject. "What're you readin'?" he asked, without looking at Noah.

"Stockbroker got whacked in Oakland. They found his body in the sewage treatment plant. Fortunately for him, he was already dead when he got treated."

Stork retrieved a nearly burned cigarette from an under the bar, tapped off the lengthy ash, ducked his head to take a deep drag, and crushed it out. San Francisco probably had the strictest smoking laws in the country, having banned the practice in almost every public place, including bars, as long ago as 1994, but there was no way Stork could survive longer than an hour without lighting up, and no way he could leave his post behind the bar long enough to grab a smoke outside. "I heard about that guy," he grunted, holding his breath like it wasn't tobacco he was smoking. He exhaled what little remained, and drew a swallow from his mug.

Noah looked up from his *Chron.* "You're kiddin'. Heard about this guy? Where?"

Stork leaned over toward the bar, eyes darting secretively. "Coupla guys from downtown were in here talkin' about it. Sounded like some kinda professional job to me," he whispered.

Noah pondered it a moment, and returned to the paper. "Well, while I certainly wouldn't want to question impeccable mob authorities, the *Chronicle* makes this guy seem totally clean. No links to the underworld mentioned. He's a longtime broker with Morgan Stanley, and keeper of the Oakland City, and Alameda County, Employees' Retirement Funds."

"See? Now there it is." Stork leveled a finger at him. "Guy's in charge of retirement funds. Everybody knows the big boys are up to their ears in union money. Eight to five I got it right."

"You're on, Stork. How much d'you want?"

"Want of what?" The female voice came from Noah's right. He turned as Kate Waverly climbed onto the stool next to him, with Sandy right behind her.

"Of nothin'," Noah said. "Stork was just pitching me some action I couldn't refuse. So how're the PD's heavy hitters?"

Noah and Sandy had studied together throughout law school. A reasonable symbiosis, Noah brought a sharp instinct that sliced through to the core of the issues in their sessions, and Sandy kept him motivated enough to pass. Others came and went from the study group; then, in their third year, it settled into Noah, Sandy, and Kate.

An attractive USC transfer, at 5'5" Kate was well-proportioned but slim, more athletic than voluptuous. Her shoulder-length wavy brown hair was often tousled. Soft, engaging, gray eyes were deep-set, intent, as befits a good listener, though her smile came easily, often playfully, projecting the sense that she knew something she shouldn't, a feature that Noah loved. Bright and practical, Kate had the mark of a promising and effective advocate, her style tending more to persistence than bravado.

The Oarhouse became the study group's hang of choice, a sanctuary in which to rework the day's tribulations. Noah and Kate also enjoyed a regular morning run. He would collect her at her place in the Western Addition at 6:30 AM Tuesdays and Thursdays, enduring the ire of her two roommates at the early intrusion. A forty-five-minute jog before class, usually up the hill into Pacific Heights and down through Cow Hollow, invariably got the juices flowing. Except for the gut-busting uphills, the conversation was continuous. Nothing deep, mostly school, restaurants that offered an edible meal for under fifteen bucks, her dogs and goldfish growing up, his athletic career. Sandy often lectured them about exercise taking years off their lives. His idea of a workout was a few rounds of shuffleboard, or a stint at the video arcade next door to the Oarhouse.

A survivor of a couple of serious relationships, both unsatisfactory, Kate had developed a discriminating eye and a healthy aversion to dangerous men. In fact, it was just such a recent disaster of the heart that had prompted her transfer north from SC. When Noah good-naturedly probed the potential for a romantic direction in their first few encounters, he soon discovered that she wasn't up for jousting. Still, over their last year at Hastings, they had grown close. Both felt a basic chemistry, and they enjoyed their ample time together. But for some reason neither understood, every time any real intimacy threatened, something would derail it, and the superficial status quo would be restored. Though occasionally dating others, both held out an unspoken hope that something between them might eventually blossom. Meantime, Noah's wisecracks and sometimes garishly predacious teasing became a cliché that was off-putting for Kate, given her history. She found him clever, humorous, and attractive, but pretty much only when he was authentic.

"Couple more glasses, Stork?" Sandy asked, as he scooped up the pitcher and started through the multitude toward the back of the room. The bartender withdrew two more iced mugs from the freezer and clunked them down in front of Kate, who grabbed them, and she and Noah followed Sandy.

They weaved among scarred oak tables that bore the carved hieroglyphics of generations of law students. Overhead, several ceiling fans circled lazily, like props in a Bogey flick. As evening descended, the crowd usually morphed from the hardcore afternoon regulars to homeward-bound commuters, mostly nostalgic Hastings grads stopping in for a couple of quick ones while reviewing the day with longtime mates, and fortifying themselves against the impending home-front ordeal.

Sandy found an empty table where things were quieter, put the pitcher down, and pulled out a chair. Noah turned one around and straddled it, then reached into the popcorn bowl on the table and grabbed a handful.

"Hope your day was better than mine," he said.

"Why? What happened to you?" Kate asked, pouring for herself and Sandy.

"Nothing, really. My great legal adventure began locked up in a City Jail that reeked of urine and Lysol. Then I had to use all my practice skills to cross-examine some petty thief about his butter fetish. Course the guy's a major public enemy, implicated in larceny from a major American corporation."

Sandy took his first swallow of the day and luxuriated. "Corporation?"

"Foremost, Incorporated," Noah responded. "He's accused of relieving the company of three hundred pounds of its finest product out of the back of a delivery truck. They busted him a few minutes later, a few blocks away, with a trunk full of butter, but believe it or not, he denies everything." He took another slosh and glanced at Kate. "Who the hell's idea was this job anyway?"

"Don't be looking at me," she protested. "I didn't twist your arm. Besides, Stark said I'd be spared the usual jail purgatory. They've got me assigned to the two-seventy calendar."

"Right," Sandy derided. "The two-seventy calendar. Whatever that is. Hell, I'd probably be trying felonies by now if Stark had the hots for me." Kate ignored it. So did Noah, who had been planning to get into that with her in private.

"So, Noah," Sandy said. "How much does this petty thief of yours weigh?"

"Weigh?"

"Yeah, weigh."

"Why?"

"There's this pool," Sandy told him, chomping a few popcorn kernels. "Everybody puts in five bucks, and there's a drawing at the end of the week. You get the weights off the jail intake sheets and you add them up. Whoever's total gets closest to the number that was drawn takes the pot. They call it 'Justice By the Pound.' The results are posted on the board at Oakland Division."

Noah looked down, shaking his head.

Kate wasn't smiling. "Oh, that's great," she retorted. "Why don't we bet on which prisoner's got the most zits? Lord, Sandy. This isn't a goddamn zoo. These are human beings, with families, mothers for god's sakes."

"Not bad," Noah mused. "Zits. But how would we count 'em?" He gazed into the distance, then shrugged. "Nah, not verifiable. Too subjective."

"You laugh, but I'm serious." Her disgust was gathering momentum. "We're dealing with suffering here, and you're making jokes. Guys who are supposed to be their lawyers betting on how much they weigh? How many zits they have? Why not how many years they'll get?" She turned away. "You're sick."

"Okay, okay," Sandy said, snickering. "People with tough jobs gotta do something to break the tension. Ever read *Catch 22*?"

"Do they?" Kate shot back. "You're responsible for defending indigent clients. You don't ridicule them behind their backs. Period. You can't justify it on any theory."

Casting a glance at Noah, Sandy tried to measure whether

reinforcements were on the way. Satisfied he was hanging out on his own, he continued to cajole. "You're getting all upset about nothing."

Noah emptied the last of the pitcher into Kate's mug and held it up to get Stork's attention. Finally Stork waved.

Noah tossed a kernel of popcorn at a still pouting Kate. "So what's this two-seventy stuff?" he asked, moving it in a safer direction.

"The criminal non-support statute," she said, sipping without looking at them. "Penal Code Section 270."

"Don't know it," Noah said.

"Nothing we got in law school. But talk about stupid justice. It's worse than your poundage pool."

"How so?"

"When a mother applies for welfare. Aid to Families with Dependent Children? She has to give the name of the father of the child. The application is automatically referred to the DA's support division to investigate whether the father can pay his legal support obligation. If somebody at the DA's office thinks he can, bingo, he's arrested and shaken down for whatever he has, in order to reimburse AFDC."

"Sounds perfect for you, Kate," Noah said. "Isn't hounding deadbeat dads one of your dreams?"

"Don't you take anything seriously?" she snapped.

He adopted an exaggerated smile. "Sure I do, honey. I take love seriously. I take life seriously. I even take you seriously."

She glared. This was the cocky façade she detested. "You can joke, but this is real for a change, you know? Not hypotheticals in a law school class. The only guys who are picked up are the ones who're working; otherwise the DA won't waste time with them. They're put in jail and then they can't work, which jeopardizes their jobs, jobs that are usually pretty shaky to begin with. So they lose the job, now definitely can't pay, they're arrested again for violation of probation, and the system has successfully totally cut off its nose."

Noah and Sandy were both now listening, definitely impressed with her insight after just a couple of days.

"Second," she went on, "the mother usually has no idea who the actual father might be, anyway. The name she tends to write on the application is someone she's been with who has a job, so she maximizes the chances of getting paid. Sometimes blood tests are given to establish paternity, but they're often inconclusive, and DNA's expensive, so they pretty much act on the mother's say-so as to who the father is, at least until there's a trial."

Stork arrived with a fresh pitcher and filled their glasses. "You guys want somethin' to eat? How about some calamari?"

"Sure. Bring us a coupla orders, lots of lemon," Sandy said.

"So why does the court enforce non-support where it costs guys their jobs?" Noah asked. "I mean where paternity's still in question?"

"Yeah. You might ask," she said. "It's because in Oakland the two-seventies are heard by Judge Renee Krousse, a tough sixty-year-old divorcee who represented exclusively women in domestic relations cases before she went on the bench. Story goes that her husband ducked out with someone a little more to his liking, and left her with two kids to bring up while putting herself through law school. The guy apparently never sent her a dime, and I guess she didn't take it too well. Now she thinks every man with a libido oughta be castrated."

"Whoa," Noah said, shuddering. "I'll remember that."

Kate described a few of the day's cases; the conversation then lagged until Stork arrived and set two plates of fried calamari on the table, along with napkins, red cocktail sauce, tartar, and a bowlful of lemons.

"You're a real turn-on when you stick up for these poor guys that let their *schwantzes* lead them astray," Noah mumbled through a mouthful of crispy squid. He washed it down with a slug of brew. "I gotta come down and watch you do your thing. What department did you say this happens in?"

"Twenty-one." Kate poked through the plate and selected a morsel. "Tough duty," she crunched, "but at least I'm in court. What're you doing tomorrow? Back in the jail?"

"Believe it or not," Noah told her, "I've got my first court appearance. For some reason they've got me doing the arraignment for this guy I interviewed today."

Although Noah loved the taste, his gut let him know that it wasn't happy. "Yuck," he murmured as he reluctantly pushed the bowl in Sandy and Kate's direction, and took a calming sip of the Lite.

Kate put a few golden pieces on a napkin in front of her, dipped one in tartar sauce, and popped it in her mouth. "How come the regular calendar PD isn't handling it?"

"Beats me," Noah said. "Do calendar people always handle the arraignments?"

"I think they do." Sandy injected his three days of PD know-how. "Unless there's some special problem."

"Like what?" Noah wondered what kind of special problem might have prompted the *Ruiz* arraignment to descend on him.

"Well, like this guy Cohen I'm doing prelims with? He had a 187 and ducked out to take the arraignment. Said he was personally taking all the appearances."

"Yeah, well, that's not it," Noah chuckled. "Just butter. No dead bodies."

By 9:00 an order and a half of the calamari was gone, no thanks to Noah, and their second pitcher was nearing the dregs. True to Stork's prediction, the beer had relieved Noah's gastric corrosion and lifted his spirits, but the small taste he'd taken of the tiny deep-fried cephalopods had wreaked some havoc, and he was thankful he stopped them when he did. He decided he'd had enough for one day, especially in light of his recent medical history, and tomorrow being his first day in court. Saying his goodnights, he made for the door. As he passed the bar, Stork handed him the remainder of the calamari in a white to-go box. Noah thanked him and stepped out onto the sidewalk.

The cool air felt soothing on the four-block walk to the Larkin. By the time he got home, his wellness gauge was nearing the green zone. Reaching the front steps, he leaned around the railing and called softly.

"Margaret?"

There was a stirring under the steps. A bottle clattered noisily.

"Mmmmm…"

"Got some calamari." He waited a beat, then set the box down and slid it under the stairs. It wasn't until he got up to the door that the gravel voice came from below.

"Bless you, Noah."

Closing the door to his "suite" behind him, he switched on the light and saw the papers at his feet. As he picked them up, the large boldface heading jumped out at him:

> **Notice of Dependency Proceedings Under Welfare and Institutions Code Section 361.** *"The Department of Child Protective Services of the City and County of San Francisco alleges that Lisa Sanders, by virtue of her addiction to controlled substances, is not a fit parent to retain custody of her minor child, Margaret Sanders…"*

He sat down in the overstuffed chair and scanned the supporting documents. *Lisa had her problems, but neither of them would last long with Maggie gone.* He resolved to call the County Counsel in the morning, maybe bring some special attention to the matter, try to keep them from dismissing it as just another faceless Tenderloin hooker.

He stood, tossed the Notice on the table, and peeled off his tie as he wandered to the bathroom. The warm shower felt great in his hair and on his back, and his thoughts returned to Lisa. *Might have even been a good thing. Might get her to turn her life around. She owed it to that kid.*

Later, crawling between the cool sheets in his shorts, he savored the sanctuary. For a long time he lay awake, his thoughts a jumble of the day's events, until they ultimately slowed, and his breathing became heavy.

Alone and naked, he was walking down a dark empty street. Suddenly he was aware of being stalked by some dreaded presence behind him, just out of sight every time he glanced back. He picked up the pace; it followed. He ran, thrashing this way and that, but the pursuit was relentless. Dashing around a corner into a dark alley, adrenalin pumping, he found himself facing a brick dead end. He whirled, and found that the way out was now also walled in, trapping him in an enclosure with only a small square window in the wall behind him. He ran to it and peered out. Darkness.

Unable to catch his breath, nowhere to run, he thought he saw movement above him and, looking up, he watched in horror as the green concrete ceiling descended slowly, inexorably. Panic engulfed him, consuming him, and he bolted upright.

Heart pounding, he gasped for breath and groped for the light next to the bed. Gradually his awareness returned, and he settled back into an off-and-on doze until sunrise.

CHAPTER NINE

Seriously? The guy was denying it? He was burnt toast. So how did this arraignment court thing work? The manual was pretty clear on the procedure, but not so much on the practicalities. Maybe if Ruiz wasn't the first case called, he could sit through a few others and pick up the drill. And what was up with this three hundred pounds of butter? Guy didn't seem like a thief, but three hundred pounds? Maybe there was some way to plead him out at the arraignment?

Questions loomed as Noah's strides fell into a rhythmic jog up McAllister. The air was crisp, the morning clear, the sun just beginning to cast a pink glow into the still gray streets. Trash collectors clanked cans and the first commuter buses headed downtown, carrying stockbrokers and other early risers to the daily grind.

After three, the more he had thrashed, the more the nausea invaded his twilight sleep. He surrendered at 5:15 and got up to take his run, alone. Kate had suspended participation when she started work, saying she wanted to get her schedule together, that she'd get back to it later. He remained addicted.

Setting out slowly south on Larkin, he adopted a brisker pace as he turned right onto McAllister, past the bronze American Renaissance dome of City Hall. He admired the majestic structure for the thousandth time as he passed. Its sheer strength was always uplifting, and he made it a fixture on his morning route. Reopened in 1915 after protracted repairs from the 1906 earthquake, the dome was the fifth largest in the world, forty-two feet higher than the Capitol dome in Washington. A memorial to sadder times as the site of the 1978 Moscone and Milk assassinations at the hands of a fellow politician who resented their refusal to support his reappointment to office, this grand Beaux Arts monument to the City Beautiful movement stood as a symbol of the resistance of steadfast social institutions to willfulness and greed.

By the time he reached Van Ness and turned north, his breathing was deep and regular. He hadn't run since the misery descended over the weekend, and he thought his Thursday flu remnants might be diminished by some forced physical activity. When the warmth surged into his quads and calves as he took the hill up Van Ness and started down toward the Bay at Clay, he knew he'd been right.

Ahead in the distance, the rising sun reflected orange and red on the hills of Marin across the bay. The circling lamp atop the main cellblock of Alcatraz was still visible above the morning mist that hung below it over the water. With every third stride, Noah filled his lungs with cool air, and he felt his resilience returning.

Turning east on Bay Street, he passed Galileo High, then proceeded south on Polk. His thoughts went to his intense reaction to the lockup the day before. *What was that about? Brand-new claustrophobia at his age? Perfect. A PD that freaks in the jail. So maybe everyone had a little of that at first. Maybe being locked up, totally out of control, with the uber-desperate and the criminally insane, grew on you.*

He pounded uphill past the Chinese groceries and Italian fruit stands that were beginning to receive deliveries, finally covering the last mile on a gradual downhill through the increasingly prominent dinge of the Tenderloin: early-opening bars, all-night porn houses, sex shops; and then a left on O'Farrell, a right onto Larkin, and home. By the time he'd showered, shaved, and dressed, he was surprised to find that he was actually looking forward to eating something.

Half an hour later, he picked up a *vente* coffee and a bear claw at the Starbucks on 4th and noshed as he guided Captain America over the Bridge to 880, then south to the Broadway off-ramp. Pulling the Captain into the half-full parking structure on Jefferson, he consumed the last of his coffee just as he selected a space on the second level. It was still shy of eight when he grabbed his herringbone blazer out of the back seat. He examined it critically, finding it sadly antiquated. This might be the first time he had ever worn it a second consecutive day, and he jotted a mental note to make a pilgrimage to the Men's Wearhouse with his first paycheck to find a mate for it, maybe even a suit. The main goal was to avoid the derogatory comments that were sure to come soon, were there no change of uniform.

The clear, crisp air was facilitating his continued recovery, and he sucked in several deep breaths. He hoped that an early arrival at the office might lead to some insight into how to negotiate a deal, were someone to turn up before court to break down the *Ruiz* appearance with him. *Even though Ruiz denied the charges, this case wasn't going to trial. He knew that much; this guy wanted out. Probation? Get him cut loose? Seemed reasonable, his record was clean, but what did he know?*

At this hour, there was no sign of humanity in the parking structure, but as he skipped down the stairs to the sidewalk and turned toward the Broussard Center, something caught his eye, or rather his ear. The sound was immediate, disturbing, urgent. He squinted down 6th toward Jefferson into the morning glare. It seemed to come from about half a block away. As he strained to make out the source, he could see an OPD black-and-white stopped, its red and blue lights strobing in that general vicinity.

Cocking his head, he could have sworn the sound was high-pitched screams, echoing off the concrete overpass. Maybe a young child? He turned and half-walked, half-jogged, down 6th, parallel to the freeway bridgework arrayed with gang tags, his eyes searching between the parked cars beneath, and to the street beyond.

As he drew nearer, he could make out a couple of OPD policemen who had two kids detained under the freeway on Jefferson between 5th and 6th. The larger officer, an overweight six-footer, held a tall, lanky girl, maybe sixteen, up against the squad car, yanking one arm up behind her, gripping the back of her blue-print dress at the nape of her neck with the other. The scarf over her cornrows was knocked askew as the cop thumped her head repeatedly against the cruiser's front passenger door.

"Owwww! Lemme go!" she howled. "Asshole mothafucker! Lemme go! You hurtin' me!"

"Simmer down, sister!" the obese patrolman growled.

His partner, of similar height but slimmer, was dragging a younger boy who wore a white T-shirt, jeans, and Nikes, toward the rear of the car.

"Leave my sister alone!" the boy squealed. "We didn't do nothin'!" He suddenly jerked, broke loose, and was on the back of his sister's tormenter, beating the big cop ineffectually with small fists, still hollering. "Let 'er go! Let 'er go!"

Reaching a muscular forearm around the boy's neck, the second cop wrenched him off his partner, a thumb gouging the pressure point under the child's clavicle. The boy screeched in agony, and the cop opened the back door of the patrol car and, in a single motion, thrust the diminutive youth inside. Bouncing in after him, he pulled both the child's arms up behind him, snatched a pair of wrist restraints from his utility belt, snapped them around the tiny wrists, and cinched them up until the child screamed again.

A few neighborhood residents glanced over silently as they walked down 6th on the way to their own lives, but no one intervened. Drivers falling into the morning commute slowed their cars to gawk, but no one stopped.

The boy continued to squirm and buck, despite repeated warnings and jerking of the restraints by the monster more than three times his size. Finally, the cop lost patience, grabbed the child by the neck, and smashed his face against a back seat window. He backed out of the car on the street side and slammed the door as blood oozed from the small nose and mouth, smearing against the glass.

Noah felt a sudden bolt of electricity fire through him; a high-pitched ringing filled his ears as adrenalin flooded his system. He sprinted across the street, ducking through stop-and-go traffic, shouting, "Stop! What are you doing? Stop!"

The beefy cop raised his head, turning to peer over his shoulder at Noah, eyes narrowing. He loosened his grip momentarily, and the girl jerked free, squirted around the front of the squad car, and darted into traffic. Brakes squealed as she dodged across the street, up Jefferson to 6th, dashed around the corner, and disappeared.

There was a fleeting uncertainty as the cop's eyes followed the escaping girl. Then he turned back, took two quick strides, and confronted Noah, who was approaching the patrol car. Leather creaking and utility belt jangling, he grabbed Noah by the jacket, dragged him toward the car, and threw him against the passenger side where the girl had been pinned a moment before. Reaching back, he pulled the cuffs from his belt and snarled, "Okay, smart guy. You're under arrest."

"Yes, sir," Noah grunted. "May I know the charge?"

"When I'm ready to tell you."

"Aren't you required to give an arrestee notice of the charge… if there's no emergency?"

The cop paused. "Interfering with a police officer," he said.

"Okay," Noah managed, cheek up against the squad car. "I'm sure my judge will love to hear about what you did to these two kids. I'll need your badge number, and your partner's."

The policeman slowly released Noah's wrists and re-stowed his cuffs. "Stand up and turn around," he ordered. "Let's get some ID."

A newcomer to street confrontation with police, Noah straightened and reached under his jacket. The officer jerked forward reflexively, then relaxed when he saw the phone emerge. Noah brought up his note-taking app and, enunciating the name on the black plastic nametag, "Fitz-ger-ald," he tapped it into his cell.

"I said show me some ID," the patrolman snapped.

Noah pocketed his cell, pulled out his wallet, and handed over his temporary PD card.

Fitzgerald studied the card, then smiled.

"We got a PD puppy here, Zach, just started yesterday." He returned the card to Noah. "For your information, counselor," he said, his tone returning to authoritarian, "you interrupted a detention of a couple of teens suspected of drug trafficking."

"Seemed to me it got pretty physical," Noah said.

"It's called ordinary and necessary force. Now I know you haven't been around long enough to understand how all this works, but you'll catch on. In the meantime, you might confine your defensive maneuvers to the courtroom. Interfering with the activities of a police officer is a felony in this state, so you'll probably want to read up on those sections."

"Speaking of the law, Officer Fitzgerald," Noah said, replacing the card in his wallet, "I'd like to know where in the Constitution it says that necessary force involves beating a handcuffed child." Noah's stare was now locked on the deep-set, piggish eyes.

All three stood motionless for a beat; then Noah added, "Maybe you guys want to think about turning this kid loose?" He returned his wallet to his pocket, and again withdrew his cell. Raising it, he pointed the camera toward the back seat of the police sedan, where the window was streaked with blood.

Fitzgerald pretended to ignore him, canted his ear toward his shoulder radio, and feigned attentiveness to a broadcast. "Copy," he said in a low rumble, deliberately audible, but what Noah couldn't see was that he wasn't depressing the talk key. "Clear my last with an HBO and show me en route to that call." He turned to his partner. "Stop over on MacArthur needs backup," he instructed, then jerked his chin toward the car. The second cop opened the back door, reached in, and snatched the boy out by his scrawny upper arm.

On seeing him close up, Noah thought he couldn't have been more than twelve, perhaps younger. His head hung forward as the blood dripped from his nose onto his T-shirt, where a damp crimson stain was collecting. The child looked up and fixed the officer with a silent stare that smoldered with hatred. No cry, no whimper, no sound. Noah flashed on Soweto.

The cop pulled a pair of clippers from his belt and cut the restraints. Then, shaking the boy a couple of times like a rag doll, he said, "Next stop, juvie, boy. Your mama's not gonna like that. Better clean it up while you can. Got that?" He let go, and the kid scurried up 6th, into an alley, and was gone, never looking back, like a fingerling wiggling away after being released into a mountain stream.

The two uniforms turned to Noah, their postures nearly identical, heads back, chests thrust forward, hands on belt buckles, Fitzgerald shifting his weight, straight out of *Saturday Night Live*, comical were it not the real world.

Still pumped from the adrenalin rush, Noah heard himself say, "Strikes me you guys might—"

"Strikes me you wanna be real careful who you're smart-mouthin', son," Fitzgerald snarled through clenched teeth, eyes now slits. In his early fifties, he had graying, close-cropped hair, thinning on top. His massive neck squeezed out over a black collar, continuous with large jowls.

"Way it looks to me, you just arrived on this block," Fitzgerald went on. "Y'might wanna try keepin' your fuckin' mouth shut until you got some idea what you're talkin' about. See, you got no clue who I am, or what I do, but I know who you are. Folks in law enforcement don't like interference when they're doin' their jobs." He looked down the street, then back at Noah. "Now, you got in the way here this morning, but I'm gonna cut you a little slack this once, because you're new and you don't know better."

Noah started to respond, then censored it.

"See, our job is to maintain some order in this fuckin' jungle. People can die if we don't. You keep this kinda shit up, you're gonna find that life gets very unpleasant, very damn fast."

Noah remained locked on for a beat; then he turned, crossed the street, and walked slowly up 6th toward Oakland Division.

It was after 8:15 when he passed the front desk. The attorneys' pool was empty, so he went directly to Bobbi's office and poked his head in, glad she was an early riser.

"How much would you charge for a little legal advice?" he asked.

Bobbi looked up then down again, distracted, not smiling this time. "Make it quick. I gotta be over to Main Office for a managers' meeting at eight-thirty." She glanced at her watch.

"Well, I think I got the arraignment procedure down, but I'm weak on the strategy. I mean, should this case really be set for trial? Can't we plead Ruiz to some kind of misdemeanor today and get him probation or something? He's got a clean record."

"In theory." Bobbi got up from her desk. "Depends how big a deal the DA thinks the butter is, whether they charge the burglary as a felony or a misdemeanor, maybe even grand theft. Burglaries and grand thefts are 'wobblers'." She was packing papers into a black leather messenger bag.

"Meaning?"

"Meaning they can be charged as misdemeanors or felonies. The DA usually charges wobblers as felonies first. Gives them more bargaining room on a plea." She threw the strap of the bag over her shoulder, grabbed her purse, and strode briskly to the door.

"Go on over to Department Sixteen," she said. "They'll have an extra copy of the complaint in the court file. Check how they've charged the beef and see what your guy wants to do." She walked out of her office and started down the hall.

"Yeah…" Noah said, starting after her. "But who do I talk to about dealing it? And when?"

She didn't break stride, didn't look back.

"Wait, Bobbi." He followed her toward the door. "What would a good deal be anyway? What are they gonna do if we don't deal it? Set it for trial?"

"Call Chip Feeney. He's the Deputy DA in Department Sixteen."

"How do I know what to ask for?"

Bobbi waved as she pushed through the glass reception-room door and disappeared down the stairs.

Noah went back to his cubicle and pulled out his manual. He dragged his fingers through his hair as he looked up the government extension number for the DA's office. When he punched it in, a female voice answered.

"Alameda County District Attorney."

"Chip Feeney, please."

"Mr. Feeney's in court."

Noah looked at his watch, feeling like the actor who blanked on his lines five minutes before curtain. "But… but it's not even eight-thirty yet. Court doesn't start until nine."

"Would you like to leave a message for Mr. Feeney?"

"Can't you check and see if he's still there? I mean, it's not time for court yet."

"Listen, I saw him walk out the door right in front of me not five minutes ago, okay? What do you want me to do? He's not here. You want to talk to somebody else? You want to leave a message? I got other calls to deal with."

"No, no, that's okay." Noah hung up and looked around the office. Empty except for the receptionist. He pulled a legal tablet from his top drawer, put it in his file, and started toward the front door. Passing the reception desk, he paused.

"Uh, Raylene?" he said hesitantly. She looked up from her newspaper and coffee wearing the 'can't-you-stop-pesterin'-me-for-a-goddamn-second?' scowl, her massive jaw grinding cud-like, a red glob of jelly doughnut clinging to the corner of her mouth.

Noah eyed her tentatively, considering his options. *Ehhh, why not? Everybody had more time in grade than he did.* "You know anything about whether they deal cases at arraignment?"

She stopped chewing and gaped through the black horn-rims, jelly lingering. Not a word, just a disbelieving 'I-knew-it, you're-not-really-a-smart-ass-Jew-boy-PD, you're-a-fuckin'-baboon,' stare.

"Mmm, yeah, that's what I thought." Noah opened the front door, then hesitated and looked back.

"Don't happen to know where Department Sixteen is, do you?"

Raylene stared after him, still punishing the doughnut, her expression fixed.

He nodded. "Okay… good. Thanks."

CHAPTER TEN

"You folks hold it down out here! It's only eight-forty-five. Department Sixteen will open at nine o'clock!"

The red-faced bailiff in his mid-fifties shouted over a sea of heads, holding the courtroom door firmly as it extended outward into the crowd. Just as he turned to close it, Noah stuck a foot out.

"Excuse me, officer." It had actually been Noah who had rapped on the door, prompting the deputy's response. "I wonder if I could see Defendant Pablo Ruiz before court? He's on calendar for arraignment this morning."

"Who're you?"

A crowd of nearly fifty was milling noisily in the hall. Standard for a Thursday morning. Against the wall, a few of the wooden benches were jammed; most in the crowd were standing. Those familiar with the drill checked the multi-paged list on the bulletin board to the right of the tall double doors, checking for the name of their case. These potential defendants and family members had been through the exercise before; they experienced little angst in the circumstances. Most of the faces were black. Some of the women held babies, one of which was loudly voicing its disapproval, oblivious to the solemnity of the impending proceedings.

"I'm his PD." Noah held up his temporary ID card like the cross before the vampire. "I'm representing him this morning, and I need a word."

The deputy took Noah's card, examined it, and handed it back. "I'm gonna let you in this time," he said, stepping out to block others from following as he allowed Noah to enter. "But don't ever bang on the door like that again. Could cause a riot. There's a door at the end of the hall, to your right as you get out of the elevator. Sign says 'chambers.' Go in there. There's a deputy just inside who'll check you in. Come down the hall in back of the courtrooms. Each department has a holding cell. Got it?"

"Yeah, thanks."

"So that brings you into our department in the back, over there," he said, indicating, "and I'll let you in."

"Have you got Ruiz's court file?" Noah asked.

"I don't, but the clerk might. Did you check the defendant list out front? You sure he's one of ours?"

"Defendant list?"

"Jesus, you are green, aren't you. There's a printout of all the defendants who're on calendar for arraignment this morning; it's posted out front next to the door. The same list is on a bulletin board just inside that door to chambers I told you about. Check when you come in to see if your guy's on it, and whether he's been logged into the holding cell. If not, you need to talk to the clerk and find out where he is instead of sitting around waiting for a matter to be called that's not on calendar. Could waste your whole morning."

The deputy sat at the bailiff's desk, just inside the bar separating the gallery from the well of the court, to the right of the jury box. "So ask Judy." He gestured toward a woman sitting in front of the bench, then went back to his newspaper.

Noah stepped to the clerk's desk, where Judy was absorbed in her computer screen. "I wonder if you might have the court's file on *Ruiz*," he said. She didn't acknowledge, her fingers working the keyboard. He waited.

"Excuse me," he repeated. "Are you Judy?"

"Yeah," she murmured without diverting her eyes.

"Pablo Ruiz? I'm his Public Defender. Do you have his file?"

"That stack there," she said, jerking her head, fingers clacking.

Noah thumbed through a pile of brown files on the edge of the desk until he found Pablo's. As Bobbi predicted, there was a complaint that charged him with a violation of Penal Code §459, burglary, a felony. Nothing else was new.

"Can I see him?" Noah asked the clerk.

"Ask him." She nodded again, still riveted, this time toward the bailiff, bouncing Noah back upstream in the attaché hierarchy.

"This way," the bailiff said, having heard the exchange. He led Noah to a door to the left of the bench and inserted an oversized brass key. As the door swung open, Noah could see that the wood on its courtroom side was a thin veneer: the door was actually three inches of steel, opening into a concrete-walled bunker. He stepped tentatively into the holding cell.

Inside, the brightly lit chamber was painted a pastel jailhouse green. A steel bench was bolted along three of the four walls. To the rear, a small alcove housed a stainless-steel commode, out of sight of the door opening into the courtroom, but otherwise devoid of privacy. A stainless-steel sink hung next to it. Beyond was another steel door to the hall behind the courtrooms, above which a wide-angle video camera peered down into the cell like an electronic alien eye from *War of the Worlds.*

The door closed behind Noah with the increasingly familiar metallic thud. Instantly, he again felt the rising anxiety. Nowhere to go, he forced himself to focus on the job at hand as he looked around for Pablo Ruiz.

The bench was occupied by fifteen to twenty prisoners of all colors, ages, and sizes, all clad in orange jumpsuits and sneakers without laces. A few were stretched out trying to sleep, unused to the early wake-up call. Another five or ten were engaged in conversation. Several were gathered around a young man with shoulder-length brown hair and wire-rimmed glasses who wore a gray suit and a wild blue tie. Noah walked over.

"Chris Connelly?"

Connelly looked up. "You must be Noah Shane. They told me you'd be coming in. Gonna handle one of the arraignments, I hear." He looked down at his list. "*Ruiz?*"

"Right. So how come they want me to take this one?"

"Beats me," Connelly said, shrugging. He turned and shouted over the cacophony of conversations: "Ruiz!"

"Yes?" Pablo answered from across the room. He'd been lying on the bench and hadn't seen Noah come in. As he sat up, the trademark smile spread across his face, like he'd recognized a long-lost mate from high school. He stood and walked over.

"Morning, Pablo. How y'holdin' up?" Noah asked, his internal disquiet temporarily at bay.

"All right, I guess."

"I called the DA, but no response yet, so we've gotta work out a game plan for this morning." Noah had no idea what that entailed, but he tried to sound confident. Apart from a search that might have been illegal, it seemed that the situation was about as hopeless as they must come. One option was to stall for time, see if he could find someone who had a few years in, and ask whether he should pursue a motion to suppress the butter before talking about a plea. The offer might get more reasonable if they didn't have the butter, but on the other hand, if the motion were denied, there'd be nothing left to negotiate about.

"Things are going to start to move fast out there," Noah told him, never having seen an arraignment, fast or slow. "I thought the best thing would be to put this over, and see what they'd be willing to do by way of a plea. You've got a clean record; maybe I can get you probation or something."

"Can I get out this morning?" Pablo's mind was still locked on a single track.

"I'll see what I can do. You need to give me permission to talk to the DA about a deal."

"But I told you, I did not steal the butter."

Noah stared at him. "I know, I know," he said, nodding his exasperation. "You got three hundred pounds of butter, all one brand, from a bunch of different people, and just happened to have it, still frozen, when you were stopped at three o'clock in the morning, six blocks from a store where, by coincidence, three hundred pounds of frozen butter, same brand, was stolen ten minutes before, and you told the cops you planned to sell it. I get all that, but I'm gonna say a jury might have trouble with it as a not-guilty story."

"But it's true."

"Uh-huh. So let me at least explore what they're thinking about. Then we can talk."

"I thought you said the police may have been wrong to open my trunk. Would that help to get me out of jail this morning?"

"Well, maybe. We'll have to see."

"You must try to get me out, Mr. Shane. It is very important."

"I'll do what I can."

"I guess if I have to plead guilty to something in order to have this over, I will do that, as long as I do not go to jail."

"I'll talk to the DA," Noah promised. "See you out front."

He returned to the heavy courtroom door and knocked. Seconds passed. He looked over his shoulder at the video camera, and waved his file at the lifeless, electronic eye. There was no way to know if he had been seen, or if anyone was responding. As the seconds ticked away, the panic rose, and he envisioned himself decompensating in front of all the occupants of the cell. His heartbeat escalated to machine-gun level. He glanced over at Connelly, who was still talking to a client about the upcoming morning's events, apparently unconcerned about being locked down in a concrete and steel crypt with a cohort of hardened criminals. *How the fuck was he so calm.* He suddenly hated Connelly for his composure, and rage displaced his growing panic. Just as he raised a fist to bang on the door again, more violently this time, it swung open. For a long moment the bailiff studied him as they stood toe-to-

toe, Noah's clenched fist cocked, face a mask of wild-eyed fury. Then the deputy's expression morphed into a slightly annoyed glower, as if he'd been interrupted in a particularly critical section of his sports page. Noah sauntered by him, attempting a nonchalant smile that came off more like a wild-eyed, semi-psychotic grimace.

The courtroom was now a buzz of activity. After the front doors opened, people had occupied every seat in the gallery. Spectators were standing at the rear. Fifty simultaneous conversations made the place sound like a Hong Kong fish market.

In front of the clerk's desk, a motley line of private defense lawyers, mostly men over sixty, waited their turns to check in. The clerk patiently wrote the name of each lawyer next to the case name on her docket. Judy had known them all, and for twenty years, she'd danced this tired dance several times a week with each of them. Many of these hacks were quiet and reserved. Others popped off about her hairdo or made off-color remarks about her weekend or her interest in a bailiff from another department. The picture was long-haul drivers at the truck stop ordering coffee, eggs, and hash browns to start their day for the ten-thousandth time. The well-worn waitress scribbling their orders had taken the job countless years ago 'just to tide her over' on the way to her dreams, but now, well past her prime, she had resigned herself to interminable boredom.

Seated at the counsel table, the deputy district attorney was almost hidden behind his stack of files, his short blond hair neatly coiffed in an ivy-league razor cut. Contact lenses did nothing to hide a pimply face that gave counsel for the People of the State of California the look of a precocious teenager. Rounding out that image was a high-pitched voice in which he now conversed with one of the fleet of defense lawyers who had paused to float a bail proposal. Noah approached.

"Chip Feeney?" he asked. The elderly and disheveled defense attorney, who had been occupying the prosecutor's attention, measured Noah for a moment; then, with a blank stare, he capitulated and shuffled off to a seat in the jury box like a thwarted zombie in a late-night horror rerun.

"Yeah?" Feeney squeaked, still engrossed in his files like everyone else in the room, girding for the onslaught that would ensue when the judge arrived.

"Noah Shane. I'm the PD here on *People v. Ruiz*."

"Yeah?" Feeney raised his eyes slightly to check out the new kid.

"So what can we do with it? Ruiz's record is clean."

Feeney paused, half his mind still in his morning files, the other half considering how he might take this neophyte's pants down in some way. "Y'know," he said finally. "I was thinking in terms of a 484." He glanced at Noah for some sign of recognition. Seeing none, he went on, "Petty theft. I thought we might refer him to probation for a pre-plea report to see what's going on, like drugs or something? Then this morning, this totally radical executive memo came down from the DA, Ben Owens himself, which basically says 'defer action.' There's to be no arraignment, no discussion, no deals, no bail, no nothing."

Noah frowned. "What does that mean?"

"No clue."

"So what do we do now?"

"Nothing, today." As he spoke, Feeney was opening and closing one file after another, making a note in each. "Let's just continue the arraignment, like to tomorrow? And I'll try to find out what's up."

"Well, uh..." Having reached the end of the script, Noah realized it was all ad lib from here. "Can I get him out?" Noah posed.

"Nah. Like I say, my instructions are no way on bail." The fleeting glance shot up again. "I mean, there's a complaint on file and everything, so I'm sure the judge'll go for giving it another day without arraigning him."

"Okay, so tomorrow you'll know whether we can deal him for a petty theft?"

"I guess so. I mean, like, I don't make this shit up, but I'll check into it. So we just chill until tomorrow, right?" Again with the somewhat furtive glance.

"Okay," Noah agreed. He walked over to a chair in the jury box, and just as he bent to sit, the bailiff called: "All rise!" which bounced him back to his feet.

So, here it was. First court appearance. A variety of competing feelings. In all the times he had imagined it, none had included the nagging apprehension that although he had no clue what was supposed to happen, everyone else apparently did. He'd run onto a field to a cheering crowd before. He knew the limelight. He was familiar with the butterflies, and usually had little trouble organizing them to fly in formation. All the practices, the review of the film, the strategizing, always resulted in a clear understanding of his job come game day. He was the guy, the quarterback, who led the army into battle. This was different. He had always expected that when the time came to walk up to the counsel table, he would know more than anyone in the room about his case. But now he was groping. Still, excitement and anticipation ran a reasonably close second and third to the trepidation as his eyes roamed the room and he drank in the reality of it.

The gallery fell silent as the bailiff continued: "Department Sixteen of the Superior Court of the County of Alameda is now in session. The Honorable Seth McCormick presiding. Be seated." Silence was replaced by noisy shuffling as a hundred congregants sat simultaneously. A specter in a black robe emerged from a door to the right of the bench, settled into the black-leather judge's chair, and looked up at the assemblage.

"Good morning, ladies and gentlemen."

"Good morning, Your Honor," came the chorus of responses, mostly from counsel.

"All right, Madam Clerk, call the arraignment calendar."

At sixty-four, McCormick was a brusque, humorless man who bore the pain of playing in the minor leagues on the downhill side of a career that had never included a stretch in the bigs. It had all begun with promise in the DA's office thirty-eight years ago, but now, sitting as a magistrate on the criminal arraignment calendar was his purgatory where he awaited retirement with full pension, the odds of getting another crack at the felony show as a trial judge being roughly in the range of zero. He was a short man, and his thinning white hair was combed back over his balding head. Metal-rimmed trifocals enlarged his eyes in a severe way, rather than achieving the hoped-for softening effect. There was a pasty look to his pink, clean-shaven face, an effect produced by after-shave talc, the powdery vestige of a bygone era.

McCormick enjoyed the luxury of that total ignorance of the harmonics and overtones of life that comes with fundamentalism. His religious, political, and professional worldviews were wholly convergent and entirely coextensive. The precepts were uncomplicated, few, and straightforward. He was the white master who brought the rule of law to a chaotic wilderness that needed only a firm hand to function smoothly, like a colonial governor serving in some third-world colony of the British Empire. Never in doubt, he dealt swiftly with the offenders and infantilized the victims. McCormick never made a ruling that was wrong, and he couldn't fathom where the problem lay with those who disagreed with him.

"Your Honor?" It was the soprano voice of the boy DA. "I wonder if we could call *People v. Ruiz* first, out of order? There will be no action on that matter today."

"Is defense counsel present, Mr. Feeney?"

Noah rose to his feet in an actual courtroom for the first time. He had no idea where he was going, but by God, heart pounding, hands clammy, he was going. "Yes, Your Honor."

"All right, state your appearances for the record."

"Deputy District Attorney Charles Feeney for the People, Your Honor."

"Noah Shane for Mr. Ruiz, Your Honor." So there it was. He had made an official appearance, in court, on the record.

"Are you a Public Defender, Mr. Shane?"

"Yes, Your Honor."

"You might so inform the court in future. It is useful information. Do you wish your client present for these proceedings?"

"Oh, uh—yes, Your Honor. Please."

The bailiff, who had been standing next to the holding cell door, opened it and leaned in. "Ruiz! Step forward!"

Pablo emerged to stand behind a waist-high, wooden rail that guarded the witness chair next to the bench. The clean white T-shirt was visible under his orange jump; his hair was combed. Though it did not occur to Noah at that moment, this was Pablo's first court appearance, too, a golden smile the talisman protecting him from formidable forces he didn't understand. His bearing was respectful, hands clasped behind him at "parade rest." He directed a pleasant look toward the judge.

McCormick didn't notice. "All right. Are the People ready to proceed with arraignment?"

"No, Your Honor," Feeney squealed. "My instructions are to continue the matter. We would ask the court to put Mr. Ruiz on tomorrow's arraignment calendar, if that's possible. The People would further request that the defendant remain in custody pending arraignment."

"Any objection?" McCormick, who had been scanning the file, now looked up and cast a meaningful gaze over his glasses at Noah, but it didn't register. This was an adversarial system, and McCormick wasn't about to argue counsel's defense release motion. Pablo looked on hopefully.

"No, Your Honor," Noah answered.

McCormick hesitated, offering Noah a brief chance to change his mind, then moved on. "Very well. The matter is continued to September sixth, nine AM, in this department. The defendant will remain in custody. Next matter, Madam Clerk?"

"*People v. Newton*," the clerk droned.

That quick, Noah's first court appearance was over, giving rise to a mental sigh of relief. *Not bad for a first outing. He might have been a natural.*

He looked over and saw Pablo being guided toward the holding cell, craning over the bailiff's shoulder, scowling. For the first time, the patented smile was gone. He was motioning vigorously for Noah to come over.

Noah strode the three long steps to the rail, and leaned over toward Pablo as the sheriff paused.

"I thought you were going to see about a deal?" Pablo whispered angrily. "Do I get out? I told you I have to get out."

"They weren't going to let you out before tomorrow, Pablo. The DA told me that."

"Why didn't you ask the judge? See about bail?" The whisper was getting louder, and the bailiff puckered his eyebrows and put an index finger to his lips.

"I'm going to try to find out what's going on. I'll see you tomorrow morning. Don't worry. We'll get you out."

"Bailiff, next case?" The judge's attention was now fixed on the conversation at the holding room door. "Bring Mr. Newton in, please?" Noah needed no further admonition. He turned toward the exit.

"Yes, Your Honor." The deputy briskly guided a gloomy Pablo back inside, then called: "Ridell Newton! Step forward."

Noah walked back through the swinging gate, up the aisle, and out the front door of Department 16, now most definitely a full-fledged lawyer, ardor for the courtroom flowing, only slightly dampened by a disgruntled client.

CHAPTER ELEVEN

Oakland Division was vacant when Noah returned. His first stop was Bobbi, but she had not yet returned from Main Office. Stark's door was closed. Pausing, he could hear a muffled conversation inside; apparently Stark was on the phone. Because it seemed like the Owens executive memo justified a consultation, he considered waiting, but then decided the crux of the thing was still how to plead a petty theft, a bit mundane to take up with the boss.

His thoughts turned to Kate and Sandy. He'd get with them about it. They were as inexperienced as he was, but maybe three incompetents were better than one. In the past, they'd always chosen the right way forward: like when they decided to come to the PD's office, for example.

• • •

Toward the end of their law school careers, students' thoughts inevitably turned to career options and fantasies about life beyond Hastings. The Shane, Sutherland & Waverly study group was no exception. At first the discussion centered on money, downtown firms, and Porsches, but it didn't take long for the speculation to set in that even if they got interviews in those hallowed halls, they probably wouldn't survive the call-back cut. They weren't law review; not even top half of the class. It was Kate who first broached the idea, over obligatory brews at the Oarhouse, of them signing on somewhere together. After all, they'd faced some pretty heavy pressure as a team. A united front would definitely ease the transition into professional life.

"Sure," Noah had said. "Only I've never really aspired to enlisting. Never looked good in a buzz cut. No Jewish guys do. It's the nose." He reached out for Kate's tresses. "Now, a buzz on you, on the other hand. Might actually conjure up the nun look. Whoooa," he said, with a mock shudder.

She shook her hair loose.

"There must be someplace that needs lawyers bad enough to take all three of us, short of an Indian reservation," she said.

"Won't work," Noah mused. "Not enough night life in the desert."

"My guess?" Sandy speculated. "The best we can do is some kind of civil service job. You know, criminal stuff. Those guys mostly don't come out to interview, but they might have some openings. I'll check in with the placement office."

It turned out Alameda County was hiring, so they signed up for the civil service exam. Their scores and questionnaires got them interviews with the County Counsel, the District Attorney, and the Public Defender. They decided the County Counsel was dry, civil stuff. The DA's office would be rigid cop types. If they got the offers for all three, the PD would be their first choice.

Kate's interview had been the first one scheduled. She was to see Stark, whom she later described as "...a middle-aged, single, self-important peacock who fancied himself Oakland's own legal Richard Gere, albeit a bit shorter on hair." The interview had been a "unique experience."

Stark held out a hand as Kate was ushered in. "Jim Stark," he said, looking intently into her eyes, grip lingering, hand warm, a hint of clammy.

"Katherine Waverly," Kate responded, smiling.

"A pleasure, Katherine." The stare remained fixed. "Guess you could say I run things around here. Delighted you've chosen to think about our office. You know, most of the really good people end up with the DA these days. It seems like it's just the idealistic twits and beardos that we see, so you're definitely a refreshing change."

She smiled as he motioned her to a chair. He was reasonably attractive, if you could get past the terminal personality defects. Definitely more the business lawyer look than Percy Foreman.

"I'd think you'd get a lot of good people, Mr. Stark." Kate let her gaze loiter. "Criminal defense work is all over TV and the paperbacks. It's really very romantic."

"It is, isn't it," he agreed. "And well it should be. It's the most exciting work a young lawyer can find, to my way of thinking. A chance to get into court and actually do something, rather than sit in a library for two years, writing research memos for those uptown clowns. I've been with the office twenty years, and I don't regret a minute of it."

"No kidding?" she said, fawning, as if he cared what she had to say.

"Tried eighteen murders, five with special circumstances."

"Eighteen? Really. And special circumstances," she purred, stopping just short of "My, my..."

"Trial work. That's the real surgery of the law. I remember my third

187. It was a rape-murder where my pervert had kept this young, beautiful co-ed locked in his garage as a sex slave for seven months. Committed every kind of act imaginable, then killed her with an ice pick." His gaze morphed into a faint leer as her eyebrows rose, and she recoiled slightly.

"Yeah, pretty gruesome, I guess, but exciting stuff. It's the real world." He paused momentarily. "Murders are pretty tough to win. Juries have no sense of humor. But burglaries and robberies? I've walked a lot of those out. And the rapes? No sweat. I've got a cross-examination for victims guaranteed to make my accused look like an innocent victim of a promiscuous woman scorned. Lots to learn. Course you don't get the heavy ones right away. You gotta cut your teeth."

Even as she continued to punctuate his monologue with the periodic "Um hm...", "No!", and "You're joking", Kate's mind was drifting with the dubious joy of being a rape victim with this guy cross-examining.

"A lot depends upon whose team you draw. I was lucky enough to get assigned to old Ryan Murdock, God rest his soul. Finest cross-examiner I've ever seen. He'd climb to his feet, pose what seemed like a lot of irrelevant, disjointed questions, pacing all over the room without a note. Drew a million objections, admonitions from the court to stick to the facts." Stark chuckled, reminiscing. "And all the time the noose was tightening, until, *bam!*" He banged the desk with his palm, and Kate jerked. "He'd have the prosecution witness in a lie, then another, and another. Pretty soon, the witness had no idea what was true, and the DA's case would start to disintegrate." He shook his head slowly, smiling. "Gotta warn you, though, the courtroom can be pretty intimidating at first." He studied her, measuring her level of admiration. She had "wide-eyed fascination" pasted. "But you strike me as having a lot of promise, Katherine."

He stopped abruptly and snapped his fingers. "Y'know? I just happen to have an opening on my personal team right now. If you're interested, I think I could hold it for you until you pass the bar. Most new PDs start on the jail run, interviewing prospective clients for financial eligibility, but I could work you into a calendar court immediately, get your feet wet. Of course, I'd train you myself. Maybe have you trying misdemeanors within six months or so. Who knows? With a few strings I'm in a position to pull, you could be in preliminary hearings a couple of months after that, even trying felonies within a year." The holy grail. "What do you say?"

"I'm sooo honored, Mr. Stark," Kate cooed, playing him like a

Guarnerius. "This is exactly what I wanted. I'd love to work here, especially for you."

"Perfect," he said. "Then it's settled."

Kate was beaming. "That's great," she said. "I'm really looking forward to it."

"So…" Stark rose to his feet. "Is there anything else you need to know?"

Kate hesitated. "Well, there is one thing."

"Nothing we can't work out, I'm sure."

"I hope so. I've got these two classmates," she said softly. "Very bright guys. You'd really like them both. The three of us applied for several county positions, sort of as a team? We studied together through our last year, and we wanted to work together in our first job. We really love the idea of the Public Defender's office, and we've kind of taken an oath of solidarity to all come together, or not at all. It seems kind of stupid now," she said, trying for sheepish, "but I did promise them." She could see that he was hesitating. "And I do think you'd find them to be excellent prospects," she added hopefully, uncrossing and recrossing her legs.

Stark looked doubtful, but before he could speak, Kate asked, "Do you think the Public Defender's office might have room for all three of us, Mr. Stark?" Just the right amount of innocence, eyes set on "stun." These guys never saw through the act. Their mammoth egos were factory calibrated to filter out any trace of insincerity when the adulation was directed at them.

"Y'know," Stark conceded as he moved closer, "I think we just might have a couple extra desks open. Not on my staff, but if they qualify, I think we could work them in. Give me their names."

The deal was sealed with an unspoken promise that Kate never intended to keep. That night she was toasted at the Oarhouse as the conquering hero. All three received offers in the mail the following week, to start work in September, subject to their passing the August bar.

The bar exam had been a continuing struggle to keep Sandy alive and breathing. He had grown a beard during the review course, and he actually began molting the week before the exam. Reddish facial hair fell out by the handfuls, revealing a scabbed-over stress rash beneath. This gave him a kind of leper look; when coupled with his recently acquired, Tourette-like startle response, it prompted Noah and Kate to seriously recommend medical attention. The anxiety syndrome continued until the exam was over, and then for several weeks thereafter, until all three had received notification that they had passed.

Of course, Sandy's good-news envelope was delayed for twenty-four hours after Noah and Kate received theirs, prompting a deep therapy session, mediated by rum, which went late into the night in Noah's suite. Alternative careers were considered: Peace Corps, military service, even the foreign legion. Sandy agonized about his father's reaction to his failure and, toward the end, he actually engaged in sloppy speculation on how to retain a contract hit man to "take care of" the old man.

Sandy was so hung over when he went to his post office box the next day that he carelessly threw the brown envelope from the State Bar into the trash barrel with the junk mail. Fortunately, Noah had seen it go in, and rescued it. When he realized what he'd almost cast into oblivion, Sandy dropped to his knees and sobbed uncontrollably, right there in the Federal Building.

• • •

Noah checked his watch. Plenty of time to take in a bit of Kate's shtick on the 270 calendar, then maybe some lunch, and a chance to go over the *Ruiz* thing together. But first, he'd make the call to San Francisco Child Protective Services for Lisa and Maggie.

Dropping the *Ruiz* file on his desk, he picked up the Notice of Dependency Hearing and dialed the San Francisco County Counsel at the number provided in the caption. He survived a bout of trial by secretary and wheedled a transfer to the deputy assigned to Lisa's case. A few lies about Lisa having been a former Alameda County PD client, then the pitch that he had "some information that might be material in the dependency proceeding," finally did the trick. Half an hour later, after a long chat with the lawyer in charge, he hurried downstairs to catch what remained of the morning 270 calendar.

CHAPTER TWELVE

"Mr. Buzbee denies paternity, Your Honor."

Kate's defense to the crime of failing to support was that her client was not the father. "He has not been with the complaining witness in more than three years. The child in question is only fourteen months old. It would seem that the complaint is unsustainable on its face."

Department 21, on the fourth floor of the Broussard Center, was almost identical to Department 16n, the scene of Noah's "triumph" earlier that morning. Recessed lighting in the ceiling reflected off the 1950s blond wood paneling of which the bench, bar, clerk's desk, and jury box were all crafted. On the paneled wall behind the bench was the Great Seal of the State of California from which the lifeless eyes of the Roman Goddess of Wisdom, Minerva, gazed down on the proceedings, the grapes of wrath strewn at her feet.

Judge Renee Krousse sat erect between flags of the United States and the State of California. Somewhat of an authority on wrath herself, she was a squat, square woman in her early sixties with a dyed dishwater-blond pageboy that hung raggedly to her shoulders, her face devoid of makeup.

Noah made his way down the middle aisle of the nearly full courtroom to the jury box, from which lawyers were permitted to observe, as Kate addressed the court from the counsel table. Almost imperceptibly, the judge's eyes flitted over as he slid beside several other attorneys. Kate followed the glance and hesitated when she saw him. At the prosecution side of the counsel table sat a large-boned, red-headed, fortyish DA, somnolent, her eyes cast down, ostensibly absorbed in her files. Due to the fact that Krousse ran the prosecution single-handedly, the DA might as well have dozed off and, truth be known, she sometimes did.

Noah recalled Kate's account of the ballad of Judge Krousse the night before, over the dwindling supply of beer and calamari. She had described how Stark explained the concept of judicial realism to her, and how, though not taught in law school, a judge's early years, and resultant psychodynamics, were often critical in understanding her rulings. Such knowledge, he explained, was crucial in fashioning a persuasive argument. By way of example, Stark had characterized Krousse's father as a self-absorbed drifter who had split without a trace, leaving her bright but dispirited mother to raise three daughters on the sparse compensation of an unfulfilled librarian. According to Stark, the judge had unwisely repeated her mother's mistakes as a young adult, marrying a carbon copy of her father, and with similar results. As a consequence, it seemed that every defendant who appeared on the non-support calendar unwittingly wore the composite face of the reprehensible father/husband archetype. In her two and a half days of experience, Kate had come to see Krousse's courtroom routine as the swift establishing of minimal facts, followed by the real fun: castigation rivaling the seventeenth-century pillory. The judge's current victim, Clarence Buzbee, a handsome African-American in his mid-twenties, stood patiently in the dock, turned out in the orange jumpsuit of a defendant in custody.

"On the dearth of facts, this case should never have been charged," Kate was saying. Of course, it was useless to argue the facts at this early stage, but PDs quickly learned that stating the case at first opportunity was nonetheless essential. Every irate basketball coach who moaned about a foul knew that if she let a bad call go unquestioned, the referee would think there was free rein to take her players down at will.

"On that theory, Ms. Waverly, why don't I just walk over and open that holding cell myself. We'll let all of these deadbeats out and spend the rest of the day at the beach. Would that suit you?" The sound of throats being cleared was accompanied by the shuffle of feet.

"And wouldn't that be awful," Kate muttered under her breath.

"Was there a comment, Ms. Waverly?"

"No, Your Honor."

"I take it you want to set Mr. Buzbee's case for trial? We will afford him the full-dress jury trial that is most certainly his constitutional right, all at the expense of the taxpayers of the State of California and the jurors of this community. We are anxious to please." (Translation: "If this son-of-a-bitch wastes my time and the public's funds walking him through the charade of a jury trial on this foregone conclusion, he's going to do mucho time in addition to paying through the nose when he's found guilty.")

"If his plea is not guilty, would the court entertain a motion to O.R. Mr. Buzbee so that he might return to work pending trial, Your Honor?"

"Not in light of his demonstrated irresponsibility. But I most certainly would consider bail, Ms. Waverly. We don't want useful citizens like Mr.

Buzbee languishing in jail. Bail would be set at twenty-five thousand dollars."

Right. How was this guy ever going to come up with the twenty-five hundred dollar premium on a twenty-five thousand dollar bond? He was living paycheck to paycheck as it was, and had probably already lost his job in the two days he had been in jail. Bail might as well be a million.

"A moment to confer with my client, Your Honor?"

"A moment only, Ms. Waverly; no more. We have a full calendar. Sin is rampant in the world. We will be in recess for five minutes." Krousse rose before the bailiff could instruct her flock to please rise; she plodded off the bench and exited, stage right.

Noah's gaze followed Kate as she went to the rail to talk to Buzbee. Shaking her head, her face flushed, she endeavored to explain the unexplainable. Noah was impressed. With only a couple of days under her belt, Kate was already running this calendar solo. Not only did she seem to know what she was doing, but she had a solid courtroom presence. After a brief, but animated, conversation with Buzbee, Kate turned and walked back to where Noah was sitting.

"So what do you think?" she said in a low voice. "As advertised?"

"Pretty much," Noah observed. "How long will you be? Up for a cup?"

"This is the last of the custodies. All the non-custodies are represented by private counsel, so we can go. Let me wrap Buzbee, and gather my stuff."

"Remain seated and come to order," the bailiff announced. Kate looked up to see Krousse settling back into her Black Widow's web.

"Have we made a decision, Ms. Waverly?"

"Yes, Your Honor. The DA offered one count of two-seventy, and referral to probation for arranging terms of child support, two years probation, no jail. That is acceptable to Mr. Buzbee."

Krousse now turned to the DA as if realizing for the first time she was present. "Is this correct, Ms. Frobisher?"

"Yes, Your Honor," the state's lawyer replied without looking up. So much for her contribution to *People v. Buzbee.*

"Very well," the judge said. "You may voir dire your client for the record."

"Thank you, Your Honor." Kate turned to Buzbee and glanced down at her notes to conduct the examination that would establish his full comprehension of the charges, and of his plea. In a week or two she would have it by memory, would recite it in her sleep.

"Mr. Buzbee, you understand that by pleading guilty you are admitting to the allegation of the complaint that the minor, Anfernee Simmons, is your natural child, and that you have failed in your lawful obligation to support him?"

There was no response as Buzbee dropped his eyes. "Yes or no, Mr. Buzbee?" the judge snapped.

"Yes," Buzbee said, resigned.

"Yes, what?" Krousse demanded.

Buzbee assumed she was trolling for tribute. "Yes, Your Honor."

Exasperated frown. "Yes, you understand you are admitting to the charges?"

"I understand, Your Honor."

"Good. Proceed, Ms. Waverly."

"Thank you, Your Honor." Kate turned back to the defendant and again consulted her script. "You understand that you have a right to a jury trial on those charges? You do not have to admit them. You can make the People prove beyond a reasonable doubt that you are the father, that you willfully failed to support your child, but you are giving up that right by pleading guilty. You understand?"

"Yes, Your Honor." Buzbee continued to address his responses to the court.

"You understand that you have the right to confront the witnesses against you, and have your attorney cross-examine them at trial?"

"Yes, Your Honor."

"By pleading guilty, you give up that right, as well. There will be no trial. The judge will find you guilty, and sentence you. You understand?"

"Yes, Your Honor."

"My client understands the plea, Your Honor."

"All right. Mr. Buzbee, you understand that your attorney, Ms. Waverly, and the District Attorney have agreed upon a recommended disposition, for probation and a support plan, but I am not bound by their agreement. You get that I can sentence you up to the maximum penalty: a year in the county jail and a two-thousand-dollar fine?" The judge was staring at him sternly.

"But I thought if I pled guilty—"

"You thought you would get out and run free to impregnate any number of other helpless women who succumb to your raging hormones, then abandon them again. I know what you thought, Mr. Buzbee, but I do not have to accept counsels' recommendation. By pleading guilty, you are giving me full authority to sentence you as I see fit, do you understand that?"

More throat clearing and shuffling feet from the gallery. Buzbee was now unquestionably caught in the headlights, looking to Kate for help. She regarded him sympathetically, knowing that not even Krousse would trap him in such a fiendish way, moving the goal posts after getting his agreement to plead guilty. Besides, they could set the plea aside if she tried to put him away after a negotiated resolution. But she ran this morality play on all of them as part of the "penalty phase," making them twist in the wind before bringing the gavel down. Kate had seen it several times, but Buzbee was new. She nodded at him.

"Y-Yes, ma'am, I understand," he managed. There followed a long silence, during which Krousse glared menacingly at him.

"And you nonetheless wish to plead guilty?"

"Uh… yes, ma'am."

Another long beat.

"All right," she said abruptly. "That'll be the order. Two years probation. The defendant is referred to the probation department for financial review and recommendation of support payments. The matter will be set over sixty days for probation report. You need not return to court if you agree with the recommended payment plan, Mr. Buzbee. May we have a date, Madam Clerk?"

The clerk looked at her computer screen. "November fourteenth, Your Honor?"

"November fourteenth it is. The defendant will be released from City Jail." She slapped the file on the growing pile on the right side of the bench, and reached for the next one from the dwindling stack on her left. "Call the *Jefferson* matter," she growled.

Buzbee breathed a long, audible sigh, shaking his head as the bailiff led him back into the holding cell.

"*People v. Jerronn Jefferson*," the clerk called.

Kate looked over at Noah, held up her index finger to indicate she'd just be one minute, and began gathering her files.

Noah nodded and turned his attention back to the proceedings. An immense man, dressed in a neon chartreuse jumpsuit and wraparound Gucci sunglasses, was struggling over the people in his row toward the center aisle. On arrival, he ambled forward affecting an exaggerated pimp roll, sauntering slowly, working the room.

Uh-oh. Noah had been in Department 21 less than half an hour, but he understood well enough that this was definitely trouble. He glanced up at the judge, who was locked on, becoming exponentially more steamed with each rolling step. *This guy's oblivious. He's gotta have been before Krousse in the past. Sat through the proceedings this morning. What could he possibly be thinking? He's history.* Krousse's narrowed eyes followed Jefferson's every move as he passed through the gate and approached the counsel table, unrepresented.

It was like the 'bait cars' they had studied in Crim Law on the issue of entrapment. Unlocked cars parked by the cops in high crime rate areas, filled with TVs, cameras, and leather jackets. The crooks and junkies knew they were traps, but they broke in anyway and got busted. Simply couldn't help it. There was nothing rational about it. Jefferson was plunging downstream toward the falls, and at some level he knew it, but no way could he resist. The gallery in this full courtroom was his public, and he was powerless to alter his course.

Krousse scowled down at her file. "Jerronn Jefferson?"

"Yes, ma'am." Unconscious, and no lawyer to at least take some of the heat, if not advise him about the abyss he was hanging over.

The judge didn't look up. "I want you to turn around to the gallery and say 'Thank you.'"

Jefferson had no clue. He eyed her quizzically, but having spent a good part of his life in court, he didn't question it. He shrugged, glanced over his shoulder, and said, "Thank you." No affect. No conviction. He returned his focus to the bench.

"We didn't hear you, Mr. Jefferson!" Krousse enunciated, in her high-pitched power tone. Everything in the courtroom seemed to stop.

Only a slight frown drew his countenance downward as he struggled to understand. He turned fully and repeated, "Thank you!" Considerably louder this time.

"Now," Krousse went on, glaring, "I imagine you're wondering why I asked you to say 'thank you'?"

A fair question. "Well, yes, ma'am."

"Because, Mr. Jefferson," Krousse's voice reverberated, dripping with mock patience, "each and every one of these citizens"—she pointed in turn to several members of the gallery—"these hard-working taxpayers, are supporting your wife and your child on welfare with their tax dollars while you're out buying chartreuse jumpsuits and sunglasses!"

Pondering this, Jefferson stood transfixed, staring at the judge through the orange lenses, and then a smile broke.

"Oh yeah?" he drawled, half-turning again to the gallery. "Well, thaaaaank you!"

The room exploded, and Krousse pounded her gavel. Riveted on her soon-to-be victim, like the puma eyeing the heedless rabbit, she glowered malevolently. Hands went to mouths. No one wanted to be

1 4

seen smiling. Sniggers and snorts were stifled by gallery, lawyers, and clerks, like the aftermath of an obscene noise in a high school assembly. The bailiff had his head down, biting his cheek.

"We'll see how grateful you are, Mr. Jefferson..." Krousse hissed, coming to a full boil, "...after you've had a little time to contemplate your contemptuous conduct. Bailiff, take Mr. Jefferson into custody. We'll call his case at the end of the calendar. Next matter."

Like the hook reaching out from behind the curtain, the bailiff took Jefferson, who went willingly, to the holding cell, still wearing a smirk, rolling into each step, basking in the moment that was destined to enhance his legend.

Kate, who had gathered her belongings and had stood watching the festivities, was now walking up the aisle toward the door. She motioned Noah to follow.

"Cafeteria?" Kate asked as they emerged into the hallway.

"I guess," Noah answered. "Haven't been there yet."

Snickering over a rehash of the Jefferson sketch, they walked down the hall and took the elevator to the basement. The doors opened into a brightly lit government-issue eatery with chrome-tube tables and chairs on a linoleum floor. Against the pale green wall across the room was a serving line offering sandwiches and hot entrees, pastries, and designer coffee. Kate ordered a latte, Noah a cappuccino, and they selected an empty table.

"Man, you really hit the jackpot," Noah said as they settled in. "Not only running your own calendar in your first week, but in Comedy Central, no less."

"Tell me about it."

"Gotta admit you seem to know what you're doing, lady. How'd you pick all that up in just three days?"

"Jim took me down on Monday and showed me the ropes, then I talked to a couple of PDs who've handled the two-seventies."

"Jim?"

"Stark. He and I went to lunch after the morning calendar, and he gave me some more notes. It's not that tough, really, once you get the point of the various procedures."

"So it's Jim and Katy, is it? Where else has he taken you? Felony Court? He's really got your career on the fast track, hasn't he? Let's see, 'buffoon.' Wasn't that how you described him?" It was more strident than he actually intended.

"He's not such a bad guy once you get to know him." She stirred the foam on her latte, not taking the bait.

"And you've sure had that opportunity."

"Come on, Noah. He's been a big help." She still didn't look up, her face impassive, secretly pleased with his reaction but not about to let him know.

"Not sure he'd be quite so helpful to me."

"Okay, okay. So how'd your first appearance go?"

Noah wasn't quite ready to leave it, but he did. "Quite a morning," he said finally.

"What happened?"

"Started with this amazing beef down the street, under the freeway at Sixth and Jefferson. These two thug cops were beating up on a couple of kids as I was coming out of the parking lot."

"You're kidding."

"I'm not. Two white behemoths kicking the shit out of two black kids, twelve-year-old boy and his sister, maybe fifteen, within spitting distance of the courthouse. Had thirty-five years and a hundred-and-fifty pounds on 'em. Luckily for them, the champion of the people arrived just in time."

"That would be you?"

"That would."

Though smiling, she didn't really know what to make of it. "So what did you do?"

"Held up the Star of David and shamed 'em into desisting, what else?"

"C'mon. Be serious. What did you do?"

"Well, it was serious, and things went downhill from there."

"What do you mean?"

"Got a little odd in court. Turned out they didn't arraign Ruiz. DA said he had instructions straight from Owens to do nothing. He told me he'd been thinking about a 484, but the orders from on high were not to talk about a deal."

"So what happened?"

"They put it over to tomorrow. What do you suppose it's all about?"

"No idea." Kate took a cautious sip of her steaming brew. "Did you get him out?"

"Out?"

"Yeah, did the judge cut him loose?"

"No."

"Did you make a bail-O.R. motion?" She looked up at him.

"No. The DA just said because there was a complaint filed, they had enough to hold him another day. They wouldn't agree to bail."

"When was he arrested?"

"Last Friday. Why?"

"Oh, Noah. They have to arraign him within forty-eight hours and set bail within five days of his arrest. Otherwise, you can get a Writ of Habeas Corpus and get him out. Remember from Criminal Procedure?"

He stared at her for a long moment, then dropped his gaze and shook his head. "Shit! So what do I do now?"

"I don't know," Kate said. "I think you've gotta wait 'til tomorrow. Probably couldn't get him back on the calendar or get a writ any faster than that anyway."

"Jesus." Noah looked away, then abruptly slapped the table with his palm, the anger and frustration breaking loose. "I tried to find someone," he said. "There was nobody around. How the fuck are we supposed to do this goddamn job without some kind of direction." *Course, if he had the luxury of some sleazoid bureaucrat sniffing around after him, answering all his questions…* "Somebody could get the fucking death penalty before I'd get an answer. I mean, it's only people's lives we're talking about here, right?"

Kate glanced around the room to see who was listening. A few heads had turned. She knew better than to mention right then that all the relevant procedures on bail and O.R. were there in his manual.

"There's a guy I met Monday named Roger Moreland who might be around right now," she said. "He's got about ten years in. I think he's working a prelim calendar. If they didn't have a full schedule this morning, he'd be back in the office. Let's go see what he says."

CHAPTER THIRTEEN

"Lemme get this. There's an executive memo from Owens telling the calendar deputy in arraignment not to deal this butter thing to a 484 on a twenty-three-year-old Hispanic with a clean record?"

Roger Moreland was tall, thin, and freckled, his skin the color of strong coffee with cream. Close-cropped, reddish hair was graying at the sideburns; a wide diastema separated his two front teeth. Kate sat on the corner of his desk, and Noah leaned up against the wall of the cubicle.

"Right," Noah said.

"Nothin' said to the deputy, just the memo?"

"That's how I get it."

Thick, round glasses gave Moreland a studious look, and his annoying habit of frowning his attention, not making eye contact while listening, somehow implied that the speaker had it wrong. Conversation with him was a bit disconcerting.

"Yeah. That's unusual. The head District Attorney of Alameda County getting off into a petty theft? But there's any number of reasons that might happen at this stage."

"Like what?" Noah asked.

"Could run from wanting to deport the guy, to thinking about some much heavier beef. Could be anything. No way to guess."

"Deport him?" Noah's eyebrows went up. "Nah. He's a citizen. Born in Oakland."

"So that rules that out," Moreland said. "All you can say for sure is there's clearly something lurking behind the butter."

"How do I find out what?"

"Okay, you'll know tomorrow. Nothin' more you can do 'til then."

Noah winced. "But even then I'll just know what they tell me, right? How do I find out what's really going on?"

Moreland looked past Noah, cast a quick glance into his face, then looked away again.

"Well, I guess you could call Becca," he said.

"Becca?"

"She's a file clerk with the DA. Everything that goes in their files goes through her. She might have something."

Even as he spoke, Moreland hesitated. "I take her out now and again, and she can be real helpful." A beat. "I guess you could mention my name... but be careful, dammit. She's been a good resource, and I don' wanna muck it up on a rookie. You feel me?"

"Great, Roger," Kate said, looking to Noah for some sign that he was encouraged.

"It's a start," Noah said.

"Yeah, well... Just don't press her, man. She's good people, and she needs the job. Two kids, y'know? It's tough." He looked in the top drawer of his desk at a list of numbers. "Her extension's 3871."

"I'm total discretion," Noah said.

Kate smiled at him. "Thanks, Roger. I knew you could help."

"Right." Roger wasn't smiling. "Just be cool."

Kate went to gather her files for the afternoon calendar. Noah returned to his desk, wrote down Becca's extension number, then picked up the phone and dialed.

"Becca," the childlike, Billie Holiday voice answered.

"Becca, this is Noah Shane, Alameda County's newest PD. Roger Moreland suggested I might call you."

"'Bout what?"

"He said you're the best-looking woman in the DA's office."

"He told you to call me and say that?"

"Nah. That was my idea."

"So, I don't know what you're really about, Noah Shane, but that's a nice way to start a conversation."

Noah imagined a short, ample woman in her mid-twenties and, for some reason, a clipped, bleached-blond Afro. In his mind's eye, she was sitting in a windowless back room in the entrails of a non-descript government building at a table piled high with files, lightly sanding her long, multicolored nails with an emery board, the phone balanced between her shoulder and ear. She would be wearing bright-red lipstick to match her nail polish, and she'd definitely have a lovely smile.

"Roger said you guys have a lot more fun over there than we do." He didn't want to jump into things too quickly.

"That's probably cuz we win a few of our cases."

"Right. I'm beginning to think I should've applied over your way instead of here. Takes a Trappist monk to enjoy this kinda beating every day."

"A what?"

"You know. Like a priest."

"A priest? If you're anything like Roger, you ain't no priest, honey."

"With the kinda day I'm having, I was starting to consider a monastery."

There was a lull. "So, Noah," Becca picked it up again, "did y'all just call to chat me up, or is there some point t'this?"

"Chatting's good, but yeah, I did have a favor to ask."

"I knew it."

"Nothin' much," Noah promised. "Just take a second."

"That's what they all say, shugah."

"So I got this hand-off. Ruiz is his name. Looked pretty routine. I mean, I don't know what I'm talkin' about here, this being my second day on the job and all." *Disarming enough.* "But it looked to me like this was a fairly minor beef, one we could deal. He was busted for stealing butter off a dairy truck."

"Wait, butter?"

"Yeah, three hundred pounds of butter."

"Now, see? That's what I'm tellin' you."

"What?"

"Why we win so many of our cases. Y'all got clients dumb enough to be toolin' around with three hundred poundsa butter on board."

"Right, you can't make this stuff up. Anyway, I was talking to the Deputy DA in arraignment court this morning, who said he'd seen it as one to deal too, til he got this memo from Owens telling him not to do anything with the case. He didn't know what the story was, and neither did Roger, when I asked him. Roger said you were really smart about these things, and he thought you might have an idea what was slowing things down." He left out the part about blowing the release motion.

"All right, lemme check. What'd you say his name was?"

"Ruiz. Pablo Ruiz."

"Hang on." She put the phone down. Thirty seconds later, she had something.

"Hmmmm…"

"What?"

"Well, the file's here, like you said. Didn't go down to arraignment as it usually would. There's a copy of a complaint on the 459 about the butter, and the police report that goes with it; then there's this memo from Owens that Feeney told you about. But it doesn't say much, just that he's not to plead Ruiz to anything, and he's to keep him in, no matter what."

"So what's that mean?"

"Hold on. Mmmm… wait now, there's a second memo here."

"From who?"

"Just a minute, Noah." She was reading. "It's from Ned Swarth, and it says—"

"Who's Ned Swarth?"

"He's a senior detective in homicide. Let's see…"

"Homicide?"

"…'please instruct DA's office'… Same thing as Owens says. 'No plea to be accepted and the defendant should not be released from custody…', but there's no explanation."

"What's it mean, Becca?"

"It means that your boy's obviously got the attention of the highest levels of the Oakland Police and DA. And here's something—"

"What?"

"The Swarth memo says at the top, 'Re: Van Zandt Investigation'. Does that mean anything to you?"

"Jeezus." Noah pondered it. "Isn't that that stockbroker who they found in the sewage plant? What's the connection?"

"Beats me, honey. Nothin' here to explain it. No police investigation report about Van Zandt. Nothin'. You say they're gonna arraign him tomorrow? Friday?"

"That's what Feeney said this morning."

"Then if there's something bigger goin' on, the paperwork is prob'ly ready, or nearly ready, by now."

"Where is it? I mean, how do I get it?" *What the hell? Van Zandt? Why wasn't Ruiz giving him anything about this?*

"I can't tell you any more, Noah. There's nothing more here."

"Who could tell me?"

"Well if anything's goin' down, the paperwork would still be upstairs with homicide, but you'll never get it there."

"Will you see it today?"

"Whoa, honey. Don't ask. You are the enemy, y'know. Besides, I wouldn't see it before the arraignment tomorrow, which is when you'd get it, anyway. Now, you got some 'heads up' with what I told you already. Hope that helps. I gotta run."

"Becca, you're too much."

"Yeah, I prob'ly am. Gonna get me fired one of these days. Lord, the things I do for love."

Noah hung up; with a pencil, he absently began sketching lines and boxes on a legal tablet. Nearby, ringing phones, clacking keyboards, several conversations, and intermittent laughter laid down a background track, but he was oblivious as he plodded through the facts. *Van Zandt? Homicide? What was Ruiz mixed up in? Did he witness something? Know somebody? And what did it have to do with the butter? What was the deal with stealing butter in the first place?* He had a clean record. *That in itself was pretty amazing given where he grew up, but a professional killing like this just didn't fit. Time to go to Stark with it? Maybe.* His pencil scrawled three question marks on the page, then an exclamation point. *No. He needed more information. Had to see what Ruiz would say.*

• • •

Ushering Noah into an empty interview room, the guard went to get Pablo. The door closed, lock clicked, and Noah returned immediately to the little window in time to see the guard passing through the sliding barred barrier and disappearing into the hallway beyond. *What's with the locked door? He didn't have to do that.*

The now-familiar glow once again started in his back and traveled north through his neck, his face flushing. He went to the table and sat, increasingly clammy, beads of sweat collecting on his forehead as his mind raced. *Was this about the Fitzgerald bust that morning? Could it have already gotten to these guys at the jail? Playing with his brains? Dammit. He didn't have to bolt the frigging door.* The lock clicked again, and Pablo came in.

"Sorry I had to lock you up," the deputy said. "I'm alone right now, and the regs say I can't leave you here unsupervised."

"Yeah…" *Course, he couldn't have said that before. Were there actually humans who had no problem with this lock-up business? Did you get used to it? How long did that take?*

The door closed, and Noah turned to Pablo, whose smile had returned since his unhappy court appearance earlier in the day.

"So, Pablo."

"Hello, Mr. Shane."

"Call me Noah."

Pablo sat down across the table without acknowledging the invitation to familiarity. "What happened in court this morning? You said you would discuss a deal."

"I did discuss it, but they stonewalled me. You need to tell me what's going on here, Pablo. It turns out that whatever it is, it apparently involves more than butter."

"What do you mean?"

Noah filled him in on the conversation with Feeney and, without revealing the sources, the information he'd gleaned from Moreland and Becca, and the apparent involvement with the Van Zandt investigation.

Pablo reacted with an unaccustomed frown and a rapid shake of the head. "What is the Van Zandt investigation?"

Noah searched his face for some sign that he knew something. Seeing none, he went on with the explanation, relating what the newspaper story had said.

"And they think I had something to do with that?"

Noah was still eyeing him. "Did you?"

The smile was gone, the delicate features now serious. "This is the first I have heard of it."

"So why would they have Van Zandt's name in your file?" Noah wanted to keep it alive a little longer, probing for any indication of a lie. He flashed on what probably had been countless visits to principals' offices, detentions by police, accusations by employers, all routine in the life of a barrio kid. Pablo doubtlessly had long since learned the art of evasion in such situations.

"I cannot imagine."

Noah's head was cocked, eyebrows furrowed.

"I swear, Noah. I do not know the man."

"Okay, you never heard of him. But what am I gonna hear from the DA? They obviously think you're connected to Van Zandt in some way. Did you see something they want to know about? Do you know someone who might be involved? Just play 'let's pretend'. Try to help me here."

The room went still. For just an instant, Noah sensed something more might be forthcoming. He kept silent, hoping that maybe Pablo would want to unburden himself. But when he finally spoke, he said only, "I just do not know. I cannot tell you what I do not know."

Noah stared a moment longer, then sighed and shrugged. "Yeah. So I guess we just play it by ear. But remember, you make it harder if you do know something you don't tell me. Harder on me makes it harder on you." He started gathering his file materials. "But like you say, you can't tell me what you don't know. I'll see you in court tomorrow morning."

When he reached the door, he turned back. "By the way, have the police tried to talk to you since you've been in jail?"

"No one."

"All right. They may, but if they come to see you, you don't talk to anyone, right?"

Pablo's soft eyes grew more intense. "Is this going to be okay, Noah?"

"Just don't talk to anyone. That's important. Got it?"

"I will not, but what is this all this about? Will I be okay?"

"I don't know yet. I could say more if I knew more. I was hoping you could clue me."

In the silence that followed, Noah could see that Pablo was on the verge of tears. There was a fleeting awareness that his focus on figuring out the drill, on not embarrassing himself, was outweighed by the pain experienced by this man-boy around his helplessness in the face of uncertain consequences over which he had no control.

He put a hand on Pablo's shoulder, nodded, and smiled. "We'll know more tomorrow, man," he said, trying for reassurance, shaking the shoulder.

Then, crossing the room, Noah peered anxiously through the little window as he gave six loud raps to the door.

CHAPTER FOURTEEN

FRIDAY, AUGUST 31ST, 2:00 AM:

Three members of the four-man skeleton crew remaining aboard the Chilean container ship, *Santiago Playa*, were asleep below. The fourth, twenty-two-year-old able seaman Alex Borbon, was standing the midnight to 6:00 AM watch, leaning back in his chair with his feet propped on the Formica table in front of him, staring fixedly at the TV in the mess lounge just aft of the bridge.

He took a deep pull on his cigarette and blew out a cloud of gray smoke. His eyes were bleary, occasionally closing, as he only partially followed the plot of a Spanish-dubbed B-movie. He took a slug of lukewarm black coffee and ran his fingers through his dark wavy hair in a vain attempt at resuscitation. Shaking his head, he forced his eyes wide, then stood and ambled out through the wheelhouse onto the bridge, into the cool, damp air. The last time he fell asleep on watch, it had cost him three days' pay, which was a significant piece of change on these containers.

He wandered over to the water side. Spread out before him were the bright lights of the Port of Oakland. Two berths over, on Pier Nineteen, another container ship was night unloading, flooded with orange halogen reminiscent of the alien ship in *Close Encounters of the Third Kind*. In a few hours, the longshoremen would arrive, and his own ship would be relieved of its cargo, primarily wood products and bottled wines on-loaded at Valparaiso. He took a deep breath, flicked his cigarette into the water eighty feet below, cranked his head back, and stretched. Turning to walk back across the bridge toward the wharf side, he filled his lungs in a further effort to fight off the inexorable somnolence.

Suddenly, the sound of men walking and talking on the pier below caught Alex's attention, as no personnel were authorized on the dock this time of night. He leaned forward silently and looked down over the rail. In the dim light, he could make out some kind of activity aft of amidships. He craned for a better look that might allow him to identify the source of the voices. Now fully awake, after watching for a few seconds, he hurried back to the lounge, slid into his rubber-soled deck shoes, then crept quickly and noiselessly down the interior stairs, out onto the deck and aft along the starboard gunwale. Nearing a point just above where he had seen the movement on the dock, he peered down from behind a large storage bin that was lashed to the rail, a vantage point from which he could observe the lighted wharf, but not be seen.

Two black men were standing behind a white Chevy delivery van parked with its lights on and motor running. Roughly equal in size, both wore dark sweats and navy blue watch caps, clearly distinguishable from the usual blue jeans and chambray work shirt attire of the crew. Their focus was on the deck above, where a third man of similar description emerged from behind a stowage deckhouse and went to the rail. Alex strained to make out his face, but didn't recognize him as one of theirs. The three men exchanged conversation in a low tone that Alex couldn't decipher. Within moments, the man on deck again disappeared behind the superstructure.

Slowly and robotically, the number three cargo winch ratcheted a pallet out of the *Santiago Playa*'s after hold. Alex ducked across the walkway and watched from behind a large ventilation funnel as the man on deck guided the winch from the after control panel, raising the pallet above the deck and gunwale, then deftly swinging it out over the side, and cranking it down to the rear of the waiting truck. The team members below scrambled to direct the load, steadying it to a position just behind the van, a task they had obviously performed before.

Once the freight was safely resting on the wharf, one of the men pulled a box cutter from his back pocket and sliced through the heavy-grade canvas, revealing a number of shoebox-sized, brown-paper-wrapped packages inside.

"Okay, let's move it," he said, sotto voce.

They hustled about loosening lines, freeing the pallet, and the winch slowly withdrew as the two below began loading packages into the back of the panel delivery.

Alex crept back inside the bridge castle, and up the stairs into the lounge, where he grabbed the ship-to-shore and dialed 911. Minutes later, an OPD black Ford Interceptor cruised slowly down Pier Seventeen with lights out, the wharf planks creaking and thumping as it passed over. When it reached a point some hundred yards from the white van, it silently braked to a stop. Two patrolmen in black uniforms emerged, drawing their nine-millimeter service semi-automatics, and began to work their way down the wharf, separating to a flanking approach about fifteen yards apart. Communicating by hand signals as they moved forward, they concealed themselves behind one canvas-covered stack of pallets, then another.

The collaborator on deck stowed the winch, glanced fore and aft, climbed over the rail and down the midships rope ladder, then returned to the delivery truck, where he joined in the loading process with the others. In minutes, the job was done.

When the older, taller, graying officer, Sergeant Meachem Wayne, was about twenty feet from the van, he was satisfied that he and his younger partner, Patrolman Jaime Esteban, had reached an appropriate engagement position. Esteban, a short, heavily muscled weight lifter, crouched behind a stack of empty pallets ten feet in front of the van to the driver's side. The move had to come soon; the loading operation was complete. Esteban looked toward Wayne, who raised his left fist, then jerked it down.

"Freeze!" Wayne barked, as the two stepped forward simultaneously, weapons extended in the two-handed ready position. All three perps responded instantly, whirling in the direction of the officers, the situation momentarily unstable as darting eyes scanned for possible escape routes. The one closest to the *Santiago Playa* started toward the edge of the wharf, as if planning an early-morning swim. Another took a quick step toward the pier warehouse.

"Hold it! Everybody stay calm!" Wayne ordered. "On the ground! All of you! Face down, hands out!"

Above, at the aft deck rail, Alex watched as the two patrolmen moved in, guns pointed alternately from one to another of the suspects, as the situation came under control. The officers quickly took positions on either side of the rear of the van, the three men on the ground between them.

Wayne pulled one of the rear doors of the van open and peered in, but in the faint light, he could make out little of the interior. He walked to the driver's window, reached in, and turned off the ignition as Esteban began to frisk the detainees.

"So what's all this?" he said to one of the young hoods as he quickly patted down both legs.

"Just unloadin' this ship is all," was the response.

"Up a little early, aren't you?" Esteban queried, moving on to the next one.

"We like to get an early start," the first arrestee said.

"I'll bet," Esteban popped back. "Guess you weren't early enough today."

Wayne returned to the rear of the van and began to open the other door to get a better look, his semi-automatic still in position should things begin to unravel. All six—five below, one above—were focused on one another, unaware of the two figures approaching in the shadows from the stern of the *Santiago Playa*.

"Nobody moves!" a voice snarled from just beyond the illumination. Heads jerked around.

The uniforms were definitely law enforcement, but not Oakland PD. Shirts were light gray, pants and ties dark blue, black fur-collared windbreakers, plastic brimmed hats, and silver shields. They stepped out of the shadows into the overhead light on the wharf, one African American, the other Caucasian, .45-caliber revolvers out front. As he moved forward, one of the recent arrivals pulled a leather ID case from his belt and handed it to a momentarily disconcerted Wayne, who took it with one hand, his other hand still gripping his semi-automatic.

"Harrison and Lutz. AMPPS. We can take it from here, Sergeant. We got the same call you did, but this is our jurisdiction."

Wayne studied the credentials suspiciously, looking from the ID to Harrison, and back to the ID. The card and badge confirmed Harrison as holding sergeant rank with the AMPPS, Airport and Marine Patrol Police Services, a division of the Alameda County Sheriff with authority over the Port. Wayne turned to Esteban, who was staring back, awaiting direction.

"All right," Wayne said. "You guys hold 'em here. I'll call dispatch and bring the car up." He turned and nodded to Esteban. "Stay with them, Jaime, I'll be right back."

Wayne holstered his weapon and jogged off down the pier. Moments later, the Police Interceptor, now with headlights on, rolled up within feet of the front of the van. Wayne got out and walked back to the others, the radio squawking.

"Okay," he said to Esteban. "It checks. We stand down and give it over to AMPPS." He turned to Harrison. "You guys need back up?"

"No, Sergeant. We're good."

"Okay, then. We're clear."

Resigned, but still a little uncertain, Wayne climbed back behind the wheel of the big SUV as Esteban eased into the passenger side. Wayne backed a few feet, then slowly cranked forward through the narrow confines of the pier as the two Port Authority police moved toward the three men lying face down behind the van.

Harrison glanced at the rail above where Alex Borbon stood watching, then shined his flashlight inside the van. "Awright! Stand up!" He kicked the shoe of the perp on the ground nearest him, and the man climbed to his feet. "Get 'em cuffed," he told Lutz, "then move that van to the other side of the wharf, and get a statement from him." He nodded up toward Alex. "He must be the wit that called this in."

The two moved quickly, handcuffing the three suspects; Harrison held them while Lutz started the van and drove it to the far side of the warehouse. When he had returned to the ship, Lutz shouted up to Alex.

"Do you speak English, sir?"

"Yes, I do," Alex responded with a thick Spanish inflection.

"Would you kindly step down to the wharf? I'll need a statement."

Alex moved toward the ladder as Harrison escorted the subjects at gunpoint around the warehouse to the van. Once out of sight of the *Santiago Playa*, Harrison glanced back over his shoulder, took a key from his belt, and started to remove the cuffs.

"Okay, you guys, get this shit outta here — now! Management hears how close you came to bein' busted by OPD, heads are gonna roll." He turned to one of the three. "'D'! You're in charge, man. You shoulda waited for us before starting to unload. You know the drill!"

"Yeah, yeah." Delmar Foster stretched his fingers to work out the kinks. At twenty-one, he had an eighteen-year-old attitude, testosterone often overtaking his brains from behind. "We did wait. Fuckin' half-hour, man. No harm, no foul."

D jumped behind the wheel of the van as the other two scrambled in on the passenger side. Popping the clutch, D laid a patch as the van jerked toward dry land. Harrison stared after them, shaking his head like the irritated father watching his teenage son peeling out in the family car. Then he turned and walked back to join his partner.

The white van was sufficiently nondescript, but D's waterbug driving through the vacant, early-morning streets of Oakland was hardly low profile. Squealing through the industrial area, he flicked his cigarette out the window as the van bounced into the driveway of a gated compound in East Oakland. D stopped at the guardhouse, where a uniformed security guard emerged, looked inside, and motioned them through. The van lurched forward under a black-and-gold sign overhead:

EBONY PROPERTIES, INC.

After winding among several warehouses, the vehicle stopped in front of a wide bay door. D pressed the electronic control on the visor, and the corrugated steel entrance slowly cranked up. He drove into the brightly lit interior, stopped, and all three got out. A thin man with a pale pockmarked face, dressed in black with white belt and shoes, approached, cigarette dangling from his lips. He flicked the cigarette out the bay door into the mist.

"Heard over the airwaves you guys almost stepped in it tonight," Leech Jaqua said. "That woulda ruined your whole evening."

"Shit, man. No thing," D grumbled. "Port cops have it easy. They'd moved a little quicker, we'd had no trouble."

"Awright, awright. Get this shit unloaded an' into the lab," Jaqua ordered. "It's gotta be on the street in forty-eight hours."

CHAPTER FIFTEEN

"So, we're early this morning, counselor."

Seated at his desk, the bailiff was already well into his second cup of Styrofoam coffee as he looked up from his sports page. "See you found the entrance round back for the help."

Department 16 was again beginning to stir into wakefulness. The clerk, like yesterday, was occupied at her computer, assembling the morning calendar.

"Is Mr. Feeney in yet?" Noah asked.

"Let's see… Feeney," the bailiff said, running the sarcasm as he glanced a mock search around the empty courtroom. "Nope, don't see him."

Before Noah could respond, the hormonally challenged DA hurried in through the back door, pushing a steel shopping cart loaded with the usual weighty stack of prosecution files for the morning calendar. He walked briskly to the side of the counsel table nearest the jury box, plopped the first few files down next to a nameplate that read "Prosecution," and slid into his chair somewhat breathlessly.

"Chip," Noah began.

"Morning, Noah."

"What's up with Ruiz? You guys ready to talk some kind of deal?"

Feeney eyed him earnestly. "Nope," was the response as he shoveled the rest of the files out onto the table. "No deals. In fact, I don't even have the file anymore. It's been reassigned."

"What do you mean reassigned? I saw it on the docket outside."

"Oh, it's on the arraignment calendar all right. But it's like a totally new complaint has issued. It's been reassigned to Marco Salem."

"Who's Marco Salem?"

Feeney continued organizing, layering the files out according to the line items on the docket for easy reference. "Chief trial deputy," he said without looking up. "Ranking senior trial dude in the office. Your boy must really rate."

Noah stood mute as this sank in. He didn't know much, but he knew this couldn't be good. "What's the new complaint about?" he asked.

The usual bedraggled crew of defense hacks had begun the trek through the back door, gossiping as they formed the usual check-in line, took their turn with Judy, then meandered, one by one, to chairs in the jury box.

"No clue. But you can ask Salem. He'll be here in a minute."

The typical chaos that began slowly with the lawyers broke into a crescendo when the bailiff opened the front door and the crush piled in. Within minutes, the room was once again packed, seething with the din of expectant conversations. Arraignment court was step one in the criminal judicial process. It was like this every morning.

Chris Connelly had arrived and seated himself on the opposite side of the counsel table behind the "Defendant" plaque. Like Feeney, he was scrambling to organize his armload of files in front of him, making a note here and there to remind himself of a plea or a bail pitch.

"Chris," Noah said.

Connelly glanced up. "Oh, hey Noah," he responded, and returned to his file collection.

"Feeney says *Ruiz* has been reassigned to Marco Salem. You know him?"

"Who doesn't?"

"So who is he?"

Connelly craned around to inspect the courtroom just as a tall, immaculately dressed, man in his late forties stormed through the door with an attractive, thirtyish woman hurrying in his wake. Noah followed Connelly's gaze to the flourish plowing through the crowd, down the center aisle. Waving a thumb over his shoulder, Connelly said, "Him."

Salem's premature gray, mixed with blond, lent his blow-dried and sprayed coiffure an amber hue, below which a tanned face was lined with middle-aged distinction, though just now somewhat flushed. The custom-tailored blue pinstriped suit, azure shirt with white collar, and deep red tie spotted with tiny white polka dots completed the image of six o'clock news anchor. Salem went nowhere without his female support staff, combination law clerk to handle his scheduling and calendar, and paralegal with the magic program that summoned up instant legal authorities for every occasion, all on a miracle laptop that was perpetually at the ready.

After a few seconds of blatant gawking, Noah started toward Salem just as the bailiff called, "All rise," and Judge McCormick took the bench, the herd thundering to its collective feet.

"Department Sixteen of the Superior Court of the State of California, County of Alameda, is now in session. The Honorable Seth W. McCormick presiding. Be seated."

Again the noisy shuffling as the throng, a hundred and fifty strong, sat simultaneously.

"Good morning, ladies and gentlemen," McCormick greeted them, smiling as he settled in.

"Good morning, Your Honor." As before, a smattering of the gallery, but mostly counsel, answered in dutiful unison, something out of a German grammar school. McCormick basked in the Teutonic quality of it, the regimentation.

Salem continued his march straight to the counsel table, where he stood next to Feeney, his all-purpose assistant behind him. Without waiting to be recognized, he addressed the court.

"Your Honor, if it please the court, I wonder if *People v. Ruiz* might be called out of order. I am appearing on that matter, and I'm in trial on a murder case in Department Two."

Salem's voice was resonant, commanding attention, his delivery evenly paced, confident. DA Benjamin Owens's fair-haired boy, Salem boasted a string of victories that outstripped his closest second in the office by double. Never missing an opportunity to remind the press of that fact, nor of anything else that might pump up his aura, he made no secret of his political ambitions, the only reason he'd signed on as a Deputy DA fifteen years earlier.

Looking up at Salem, the judge nodded, beaming. "Good morning, Mr. Salem," he said, his manner deferential, the over-the-hill "municipal-court" magistrate addressing the hard-charging, chief deputy prosecutor.

"Yes, I think we can accommodate." McCormick began sorting through his files. "Call *People v. Pablo Ruiz*, Number OM659331, line-item fourteen."

Noah was still standing next to Connelly on the defense end of the counsel table, still mesmerized by the Salem spectacle, and the veneration it commanded. In time, the name *Ruiz* seeped into his senses, and he took a step to his right, into an open space in the well.

"Um… Noah Shane, appearing for the defendant, Pablo Ruiz, Your Honor," Noah offered, still riveted on Salem, whose attention was fixed on the judge.

McCormick surveyed Noah doubtfully over his glasses, like he'd never seen him before. The aging synapses finally delivered their chemical message, and recognition spread across his features. "Ah, yes. Mr. Shane," he said. "The recently arrived Public Defender. I assume you would like your client present."

Noah was still locked on Salem.

"Mr. Shane," McCormick repeated, louder. "Do you want your client brought in?"

He slowly turned his attention to the judge. "Oh… uh… yes, Your Honor. Please."

"Very well. Bring Mr. Ruiz in," the judge directed.

The bailiff swaggered across the room in front of the bench, leather creaking, keys jangling, savoring the thirty seconds of center stage. As before, he turned the large brass key in the lock on the holding cell door, opened it on a collection of jumpsuited occupants, and called, "Ruiz!"

Pablo appeared in the doorway, once again a picture of neatness in stark contrast to the other prisoners. He stepped into the courtroom and assumed his position behind the rail, blinking in all directions like a diminutive bull just released into the glare of the corrida, groping to explore the length and breadth of his predicament.

"Your Honor," Salem intoned. "An amended complaint was filed with the County Clerk this morning in the *Ruiz* case. The People wish Mr. Ruiz arraigned on charges of violation of Penal Code Section 187, Murder in the First Degree, with special circumstances. As the amendment was filed only thirty minutes ago, Your Honor won't find the police report or other investigation in the court file as yet."

Pablo hadn't yet taken hold of the proceedings. He had no comprehension that what was being said related to him. But Noah knew, and was stunned. Already reeling from the news that he was pitted against the DA's Chief Trial Deputy, the murder charge staggered him, his mind racing. *Special circumstances? Jesus. What was he doing here? Third fricking day? What the hell? No way. Wait. Reconnoiter. How did the procedure go?*

McCormick was paging through the file. Satisfied he had the documents mentioned by the District Attorney, he looked up at Noah. "Mr. Shane, have you had a chance to review a copy of the Amended Complaint?" He watched Noah, waiting for an answer. Though not a paradigm of sensitivity, the judge knew numbness when he saw it, and didn't press for an answer.

"Bailiff," he instructed. "Take this copy of the pleading to Mr. Shane."

The bailiff reached up and took the document from the judge, walked it over, and dropped it on the counsel table.

Noah was fixed vacantly on the judge, his mind desperately thumbing through the syllabus of his criminal procedure class. Finally, he comprehended that the Amended Complaint was lying on the table in front of him. Stepping in front of Connelly, he picked up the stapled sheaf of papers and stared at page one.

The room had fallen silent. Section 187 was the Tyrannosaurus Rex of the magistrate's landscape. Noah glanced around to see all eyes forward, riveted on the bench, as if he were invisible. Minutes passed as the judge read the complaint intently. Noah paged through his copy but, never having seen a murder-one complaint, he couldn't pick up the thread. Slowing his breathing to stem the hyperventilation, he knew he had to somehow get the world to understand that this whole thing was a colossal blunder, that he'd been mistaken for somebody who had a clue. Finally, it was McCormick who spoke.

"Very well," he said. "I've read the amended complaint." He turned toward Pablo, who was standing next to the bailiff. "Mr. Ruiz," he began, reading from the file. "You are charged with a violation of Section 187 of the Penal Code of the State of California…"

As the arraignment droned on, it seemed to Noah that he was outside his body, somewhere above, looking down on a scene that was moving in slow motion. People and courtroom trappings were stretched and misshapen like a Dali painting. In the midst of the sluggishly grinding monsoon, the judicial voice seemed oddly banal. Was he the only one in the room who saw this as the opening salvo of World War Three? *It was like the judge was frigging ordering lunch: 'You're charged with murder… I'll have a ham sandwich'.*

"…in that on August twenty-sixth of this year, you did take the life of another human being, to wit, one Warren Van Zandt, with malice aforethought. It is further alleged that the taking of that life was with one or more of a category of special circumstances pursuant to Penal Code Section 190.2(a), to wit, the murder was intentional and carried out for financial gain, or the murder was committed while engaged in the commission of a burglary in the first or second degree in violation of Penal Code Section 460, which special circumstances render you subject to the death penalty if convicted. Do you understand the charges against you?"

Pablo was just beginning to get a glimmer that this torrent of words was directed at him, but the sense of it remained obscure. Gaping, his thoughts were running back upstream in a desperate attempt to locate the point where he last understood, and start forward again.

McCormick turned to Noah: "Are you ready to proceed, Mr. Shane?" Still ordering lunch.

Noah stared at the judge, trying to organize. McCormick tried again.

"Mr. Shane, are you prepared to enter a plea?"

Noah was still focused on the words "special circumstances." His only thought was that a life was at stake if he got the next two minutes wrong. It was clear that he had to buy some time, to get his bearings, but how to manage it?

"Your Honor," he stumbled, "this is the first we've heard of any of this. Uh… yesterday… this was a butter burglary." He glanced over at Pablo. "Um—may I have a moment with—with my client, Your Honor?"

"You may," McCormick assented. He glanced at an exasperated Marco Salem, and added, "But only a moment. We'll call the next matter." He picked up another folder and read the label. "Number OM384079, *People v. Harkens.*"

Inside the holding cell, orange-clad prisoners scattered to make room on the stainless-steel perimeter bench as Pablo and Noah sat down. Pablo was babbling as Noah tried to scan the Amendment to the Complaint.

"Noah, what does this mean? Murder? Murdered who? What are they saying? Death penalty?"

"Wait, Pablo."

"What is happening? How can this be? I know nothing about this… They cannot mean that I—"

Noah looked up at him. "Calm down, Pablo."

"Noah, you must do something." The smile was gone. His features were stretched tight in panic. "This is not possible."

"Okay, just wait, now."

Pablo sank down on the metal bench, and buried his face in his hands. "*Dios mio.*"

"They've charged you with the murder of this guy Van Zandt," Noah said. "The guy I told you about yesterday. It's obviously why the homicide detectives were on the case. Remember? We talked about this."

Noah had no idea where he was going. More than explaining, he was sorting, collecting his own thoughts. "Now, you need to tell me what happened. How do you know Van Zandt? I can't help you if you don't give me the facts."

"Nothing happened," Pablo insisted. "The police caught me with a bunch of butter. That is all." Head buzzing, his instinct was to keep talking. "I do not know this man. I swear. I know nothing about this. Please, Noah. You must believe me. I—"

"Okay, okay." Noah put a hand on his arm. "We'll plead not guilty.

They'll put it over, I think for some kind of setting. I'll get on it, get the police investigation, and see what they have. Then we'll talk. Meantime, you gotta hang in there, man. And you need to think about this. Why are they charging you with this murder? What would make them think you're involved?"

"Hang in? I cannot stay here. My mother… You must get me out."

"What about your mother?"

"I got to get out. She needs me."

"No way they're going to O.R. you now, Pablo. And McCormick probably wouldn't even grant you bail at this point, even if you could afford it."

"If I had the money to afford it, I would not be here." Pablo hung his head, not looking at Noah. "*Caray!* This is very big trouble. And I cannot afford a real lawyer."

Just like Sandy had said. Pablo wanted a "real lawyer." Of course he was right, but it still stung, getting that harpoon for the first time. It cleared his head a little.

"Yeah," Noah said, "you do need someone with more experience. Only right now you don't have many choices. We'll get this thing done today, and then I'll check on who they're gonna reassign your case to, now that it's murder one."

No response.

"So what is it about your mother?" Noah asked him. "If I'm going to make any kind of pitch for bail, you need to tell me what's going on with your mother." Had he been around even a little longer, Noah would have known that it virtually takes an act of Congress to get bail in a capital case, especially from McCormick.

"My mother needs—"

The holding cell door swung open, and the bailiff leaned in, pointing at Noah. "Judge wants you back in the courtroom."

"Needs what, Pablo? What does your mother—"

"Now!" the bailiff barked.

"Okay, okay," Noah said, passing through the thick steel door and into the courtroom as the bailiff gestured for Pablo to assume his place in the dock. There were now two additional deputies standing at the rail in honor of Pablo's new charges. One held a handful of steel shackles.

"All right, Mr. Shane," McCormick said. Having finished with the interim matter, he wanted to complete *Ruiz*. Salem stood waiting at the counsel table, his expression still dark, his "supporting staff" at attention. The room again fell silent as Noah and Pablo returned. McCormick continued, "Are you prepared to enter a plea?"

All eyes turned to Noah. This part came easily. "Not guilty, Your Honor."

"Very well, the defendant has pled not guilty," McCormick echoed.

The next part was not so easy. "Your Honor, would you consider releasing Mr. Ruiz on his own recognizance? He has no money to afford bail, but he has a clean record."

McCormick gazed at him tolerantly. "This is a capital case, Mr. Shane. There are virtually no such cases in which I would set bail, let alone grant an O.R. motion. Now, is there anything else?"

Noah flushed. Having dropped the ball on the release motion yesterday, he didn't want to let it go. "Well, Your Honor—" he began.

"Your motion is denied," the judge interrupted, "...without prejudice. The matter will be continued to September eighth at nine o'clock to set a preliminary hearing. Do the People wish to be heard at this time, Mr. Salem?"

"The People are in agreement with the Court, Your Honor," Salem said. "However, I should say for the record that the People would oppose any release motion for this defendant, whenever that might be made."

"I understand your position," McCormick said. "But we will take it up further at our next meeting."

Noah was staring, trying to puzzle it out. *Without prejudice? What did that mean? Should he argue it further?*

McCormick had been there many times and knew a raw PD groping in the dark for the light switch when he saw one. "It means that if you wish to renew your bail motion on the eighth, I will hear it at that time, Mr. Shane. But be advised, your burden will be substantial. The code provides that there is no bail in a capital case when the proof of the defendant's guilt is evident or the presumption great. The District Attorney does not file these kinds of charges willy-nilly. I take them very seriously. You understand?"

"Yes, Your Honor." *Right. Where there was smoke there was fire. The DA wouldn't be charging people if they weren't guilty.*

"Very well. September eighth, this department. That'll be the order. Madam Clerk, next case?"

Totally limp, Pablo was fastened into the shackles and led back to the holding cell flanked by his convoy of deputies, chains clanking. Noah reached him just as they got to the steel door. He leaned close to Pablo's ear and whispered, "I'll be over to see you later on, Pablo. In the meantime, like I told you, don't talk to anyone, okay?"

Pablo was vacant, ashen.

"Okay?" Noah repeated.

Weak nod.

Jeezus. Jeezus. Jeezus. The mantra rang through Noah's head as he left the courtroom, still behind in his respiration, like the intern alone in the operating room with his fingers in the patient's brain after the aging neurosurgeon keeled over with a heart attack.

• • •

"Come on in, Noah."

The voice was maple syrup. Before Noah said anything, Stark grinned. "So, you didn't want the jail run, how do you like your caseload now? Siddown."

Noah wasn't smiling. *Wait. What was that? Sounded like he already knew about this.* "Y'know?" he said, "I've got this case where the guy was accused of stealing a lot of butter?"

"Yeah, I think I heard about that." Stark's gaze dropped to his desk as he started writing.

"So, this morning they charged him with the 187 on that stockbroker they found in the sewage plant, Van Zandt." Noah awaited the reaction to what he saw as a screaming bombshell.

"Mmm hmmm…" Stark murmured, still writing, the husband engrossed in the morning paper at breakfast, only half-hearing his wife saying she'd run over a priest in a crosswalk. *That's nice, dear.*

"Don't you find that surprising, Mr. Stark?"

"Call me Jim." He looked up. "Find what surprising?"

"That they charged this Hispanic kid, no criminal history, picked up for stealing some butter, with the murder of this big-shot stockbroker, at an arraignment where I was hoping to plead him to a petty theft?"

"Not really, Noah." His expression was quizzical. "See, that's what we do here. We defend people accused of crimes, whether it's butter or murder."

Noah stared back, measured him, looked away, frowned, looked back. "Well, I know," he said. *Was he missing something here? Wasn't this monumental?* "But isn't this case just a little unusual?"

"I don't see why. What does the kid say?"

"He says he never heard of Van Zandt, had nothing to do with it. He's totally blown away. Keeps talking about having to get out of jail. Something about his mother."

"Yeah," Stark mused. "That's pretty much what they all say. Anyway, what can I do for you?"

What could he do? What the hell? "Well it's just that I think I have a rapport with Ruiz and so, whoever you're going to assign the case to… I'd like to follow along. Help out if I can. Who's going to handle it?"

Stark studied him for a beat, then said simply, "You are, Noah. It's your case." Flat affect. Matter-of-fact.

Noah heard it, but questioned whether he'd heard it right. He searched Stark's face and waited for some sign of clarification. Finally, he said, "I don't get it. What do you mean?" *His case? It had to be some kind of shorthand. Maybe he meant handle it through the initial appearances, then someone else picks it up when things get heavy.*

"What part don't you get? It's your case. You'll handle it to completion. What a remarkable opportunity for you. I'd expect you'd be salivating."

Noah's frown intensified, his head cocked to one side, now struggling to follow it.

"Just a fortunate situation for you," Stark repeated. "We're short-handed. I can't spare anyone to put on *Ruiz*, so you'll just have to run with it."

It was like scrambling to comprehend a critical piece of information in some foreign language. Noah's eyes dropped, then returned to Stark's. He cleared his throat and regrouped.

"Ahh… Mr. Stark. Seriously. This really isn't possible." He was reluctant to broadcast that he didn't understand it, but he was determined not to leave it this time until he had found a roadmap. "I've never handled a case of any kind, let alone a murder case. This guy's life is on the line here. I haven't the first idea how to proceed. I mean, we wouldn't be affording him a competent defense."

"Of course you can handle it, and you *will* handle it." Stark leaned forward, raising the volume a decibel. "You've been educated at an excellent law school. You're a member of the California Bar. You're licensed and qualified under the law to represent anyone, and dammit, that's what you'll do." His lock on Noah's eyes continued for effect, and then he softened, but only slightly. "We mustn't be diffident, Noah. Let's find out what you're made of here."

Stark shoved a legal tablet and a pen across the desk. "Now, get this down. For starters, make sure you've got the entire police investigation, and get a copy of the autopsy report and any other coroner's documents." He paused.

Noah remained incredulous. He picked up the pen mechanically and started to write, as though he were a recent arrival in the asylum, surrounded by psychotics, taking down directions to the Land of Oz.

"Then call Buzz Hoogasian," Stark continued. "He's one of our PD investigators. Get him started on witness contacts to nail down where this kid was at the time of the murder, whether anyone saw him. Ruiz is in custody, and time isn't waived. This thing'll come up like a rocket. They have to try him within sixty days of filing the information in Superior Court, so you'll want to consider a time waiver. We always waive time on 187s. It'll mean he languishes in jail, but it really doesn't matter, because he probably couldn't afford any bail McCormick would set in this kind of case anyway, if he'd ever set any. If you waive, at least it'll give you some breathing room. You'll need to figure out how you're going to handle the preliminary hearing, how full bore to go with it. Hoogasian's been around the block. He'll show you the ropes. If you've still got questions, come and see me. If the press asks, you can tell them the case is assigned to both of us." He took another beat, then added, "But just know that I'm expecting you to handle this thing. Okay, now you got all this?"

Noah stared, jaw grinding.

"And by the way," Stark went on. "Like I said, we both know what Ruiz is up against here. After you get things rolling, let's talk about how to approach a deal. This guy's better off with the devil he knows than the one he doesn't. If the facts develop right, we may be able to get him a voluntary manslaughter. He'll probably do the maximum because of the high profile, but you know how awful that needle can be. We need to plead him out early, before Christmas season is over up at the DA's."

Noah was still stuck back at "It's your case to completion."

Stark waited, watching him. "So," he said, ending the discussion. "That's it. Let's get on it."

After staring another few seconds, Noah knew there was nothing more to say. He rose, turned, and walked out. Mind churning as he wandered by Bobbi's office, he was oblivious to the balding man in his early fifties who stood, back against the wall, just outside her door. His eyes, behind metal-rimmed aviator's glasses, followed Noah as he passed, a mildly interested expression on his round, dark, Armenian features. He turned and peered into Bobbi's office.

"So?" he said.

"Yeah, okay, Buzz," she said, looking up from the usual chaos on her desk. "I'll see if he's in now."

"Right," he scoffed, then ran the sarcasm. "Why don't you 'see if he's in.'"

Bobbi rose, padded by him, and knocked on Stark's door.

"Yes?" was the reply from within.

She went in and closed the door behind her. Without actually putting an ear to it, Buzz leaned toward the door, listening. The conversation inside was muffled, but Buzz could make out a bit of Bobbi's side of it. "Buzz Hoogasian…" (*inaudible*) "…like a word with you." A beat. "…think it's about the *Mitchell* investigation." Another beat, and then some whispering, also inaudible. "No, he already knows you're here." Buzz sneered, shaking his head. More whispering and, "Okay, I'll tell him."

Bobbi stepped out into the hall and closed the door. "He can't see you right now," she said, as she walked by him.

"Why am I not surprised?"

"He says to leave a message on his voicemail. He'll check it out and get back to you."

Buzz pushed off and sauntered down the hall, delivering his parting shot without looking back. "Yeah, I know what he really wants," he said. "And God knows I try, but he's always sitting on it."

CHAPTER SIXTEEN

FRIDAY, AUGUST 31ST, 3:00 PM:

"So I laid up shy of the water at seventeen, put the wedge four feet from the cup, and sank the bird. Gotta love that new Mizuno wedge. Then on eighteen..."

Alone in his office in the penthouse occupied by Ebony Properties atop Lake Merritt Plaza, overlooking the water twenty-seven stories below, Freeman Mustafa gazed upward through long trails of swirling blue smoke emanating his slow-burning Cohiba cigar, his mind drifting as the voice from the speakerphone on the mahogany credenza behind him droned on about last weekend's round. Leaning back in his black calfskin and chrome chair, he blended in with his environment, his black-tassled Bruno Magli loafers propped on the glass-top desk that was bare except for a large, deep-red leather mat. At 3:00 PM, the collar of his white-on-white, monogrammed shirt was still buttoned, his tie still tight. A Sibelius symphony purred softly over the built-in 5.1 multiplex surround-sound system.

Behind him, the afternoon sun poured in, casting a sheen off the rich mahogany paneling, adding warmth to the back of his neck. Thick textured burgundy carpeting matched the color of the desk mat. In the middle of the room, the Ebony Properties logo was subtly emblazoned in the lush pile: a navy blue circular shield that depicted a blindfolded black Venus holding the gold scales of justice in her upraised right hand, all circumscribed by the company name. Across the room, a black leather sofa and three chairs were adorned with Zebra-skin throw pillows, the only hint of African roots. A coffee table, crafted from solid ebony, separated the sofa from the chairs.

Several of Mustafa's paintings hung here and there. An amateur artist, he executed his works in oils: vividly colored, attractively composed abstracts. Interspersed among them, framed photographs depicted Mustafa arm in arm with beaming black nobility: Stokely Carmichael, Congressman Ron Dellums, the Reverend Jesse Jackson, Eric Holder, even a candid shot where he shared a moment of levity with then-candidate Barack Obama at a Piedmont fundraiser. In one photo with Danny Glover at a Warriors game, the two looked enough alike to be brothers. Other luminaries represented included Senator Dianne

Feinstein, then-Governor George W. Bush, Chancellor Clark Kerr of the University of California, and Chief Howard Jordan of the Oakland Police Department. On the wall above the sofa were several rows of color photographs of the many Ebony Properties real estate projects, including a dozen mammoth low-income housing developments, several nursing homes, two sub-acute care hospitals, and a handful of restored Victorians converted into drug rehab units. Also prominently displayed were photographs of Mustafa posing with groups of black schoolchildren, their teachers, and coaches.

"You neva' laid up shy a nothin', Ben," Mustafa rumbled in the trademark deep-toned, semi-exaggerated dialect he reserved for the media and the brothers. Ben Owens, the District Attorney of Alameda County, was just such a brother from football days at Cal when Mustafa had been a 210-pound linebacker who could bench press 325 on a good day. He made up for a lack of size with strength and determination that were expressed in speed and aggressiveness. Definitely a hitter. Also undersized at 240, Owens had been a standout on offense as a quick, pulling guard.

Born Freeman Warrick, Mustafa had been a medium-radical black activist back in the day. At a Muslim meeting he attended with Owens and some other brothers in their junior year, he had been ignited by the positive energy, taken the pledge, and came out Abdul Mustafa. Though he had admired the discipline and structure, after seven months he could no longer deal with the abstinence, and he abandoned the order, returning to the original Freeman, but retaining the Mustafa. It carried a certain mystique, and perhaps even some aura of muscle, through all the years of warfare as a small-time local contractor, before Ebony Properties became a major player. In those days, Mustafa's bachelor's degree in business alone couldn't launch a career as a power broker. Contenders from his side of town still had to earn their spurs on the street.

"But, listen heah," Mustafa changed direction. "Somebody said you got a suspect in the Van Zandt case."

"Not a 'suspect,' I think we can safely say we've got the guy."

"What d'ya got on him?"

"We got prints in Van Zandt's condo; warrant turned up some of Van Zandt's valuables in the guy's place; and Van Zandt's gun's missing. We haven't found the gun yet, but we're assuming it's the murder weapon, and this guy had sense enough to lose it."

"Not bad," Mustafa rejoined. "Who is he?"

"Twenty-three-year-old Hispanic kid, named Ruiz. Probably a petty thief who got in over his head on an ambitious uptown home invasion. Looks like Van Zandt may have surprised him, and the 187 went down. Warren was shot three times. Guess you know his body was dumped in the Emeryville sewage plant."

"Yeah, I read that," Mustafa said. "Terrible. Drugs, you figure?"

"Don't know. No tracks. Kid's been in jail almost a week, and doesn't seem to be kicking. Could be pills, I guess. Denies any drug history. Funny thing is, he's got no record at all."

"Mmm. No matter. Sounds like you got a clean conviction on your hands, Ben. Can you deal it? Make him an offer he can't refuse? Way I see it, you wanna get the thing in the rear-view mirror." Mustafa's volume had ratcheted up just slightly, half a notch, the dialect almost disappearing.

"Well, maybe. Haven't been able to talk to the kid about the murder. We had him in custody on a small-time burglary, just got his prints into the computer when they came back with a match on Van Zandt. He was already represented by the PD, and a-course they told him not to talk to us. But maybe he'd deal. I don't know. He's lookin' at a lot of time and trouble for sure."

"Let's see if we can't plead him pretty quick," Mustafa repeated.

"What're you thinking?" Owens knew his friend well, but he often didn't have a good fix on the hidden agenda, and this was no exception. The "we," as in "we plead him," was an interesting choice.

"Well, you know how close I was to Warren." The dialect crept back. "Everyone who cared about Oakland loved that man. We were members of the Philharmonic board together. We cooked up that celebrity fundraiser for the museum last year, remember? That Mardi Gras ball? Warren was an outstandin' citizen and a warm human bein'. We wouldn't wanna see a trial go down that hashed over a lot of unimportant drivel. Might deface his memory. Know what I mean?"

"Yeah." Owens was still uncertain.

"Who's prosecutin'?"

"Marco Salem. You know him?"

"Know the name. You think he's the right guy for the job?"

"He's my Chief Trial Deputy. Been around more than fifteen years. Very solid."

"White guy?"

"Affirmative."

"Good, we don' want any sour grapes. Who's defendin'?"

"Like I said, it's the PD. This Ruiz doesn't have a pot."

"Is that good?"

"Freeman, I'm telling you this case is dead bang. A monkey could prosecute and Cochran defend. Wouldn't change a thing. Fact is, we're so sure'a this one, we decided not to charge the original penny-ante burglary, or the burglary of Van Zandt's condo."

"You think that's smart? To let those go, I mean."

"I do. We want the jury to keep its eye on the ball. Don't want them to convict on any lesser charge out of some kind of sympathy for a kid with a clean record."

"Okay, but like I said, I was hopin' a jury wouldn't be necessary on this one."

"So am I. But you never know."

"It's your call, for sure. Keep me posted, willya?"

"You bet I will, my brother."

"Awright. Give Twila a kiss for me?"

"Will do."

"And Ben…"

"Yeah?"

"Let's get out to the club so you can show me how you use that new wedge a-yours. Might cost ya' a few bucks, though." He clicked off the speakerphone mid-chuckle and started writing. Seconds later, his intercom buzzed. The secretary had been waiting for his line to clear.

"Mr. Mustafa?"

"Yes, Celia?"

"Mr. Jaqua has been waiting to see you."

"Send him in."

Leech Jaqua closed the floor-to-ceiling mahogany door behind him, crossed the room with an awkward gait, and sat stiffly in a visitor's chair.

"Afternoon, Mr. Mustafa."

"Right with you, Leech." Mustafa's back was turned as he completed the note in his telephone log about his conversation with Owens, then he swiveled around. "What's doin'?"

"Wanted to report that the most recent shipment from Chile arrived. It's being cut as we speak."

"Good stuff?"

"Two hundred and fifty pounds, pure. The best. It'll cut to at least twice that, maybe a little more."

"Good. I want you to provide it to the usual sources in the same amounts. Oh, and Leech?"

"Yes, sir?"

"Let's give an extra five to Terrence Farrell this time. He did a good job on that last shipment. Efficient. Good staff. You remember one of his runners was busted last time out, and Terrence cut him loose for the good of the organization. I like to reward that kind of loyalty."

"Yes, sir."

Mustafa leaned back in his chair. "So how'd the offload go down? No trouble?"

"Not really. Minor incident where we crossed paths with Oakland PD. Apparently one of the night crew on board called 911." Jaqua tried to slide it by, but this was the part he was dreading.

Mustafa leaned forward. Ordinarily, his signature features were the soft, disarming eyes, the endearing laugh lines, and a wide ready smile. The eyes could charm, and most often did, but they also camouflaged a ferocious streak that flared quickly, sometimes violently. Now they were narrowed, piercing, the forehead corrugations menacing, jaw clenched. He did not tolerate incompetence. Even a slight crack would allow a shaft of light to enter, light that could illuminate the project, destroy the entire operation. The mission was too important.

"What happened?" he demanded.

"Not much," Jaqua rasped, continuing the effort at nonchalance. "Our guys rolled a little early, is all. Before the AMPPS cops were in place."

"Aannnnd?" It was long, slow, head canted to the side, teeth grinding, eyes blazing.

"So nothin', really. I guess this deckhand on the morning watch musta heard somethin'. His call was routed to OPD dispatch, and a black-and-white rolls up. Makes the bust right as the offload finished. The Port Authority cops show up just after and get things under control. No harm done."

"No harm done," Mustafa repeated, nodding slowly, still locked on. It was precisely this kind of indolence, lack of concern for detail, that could destroy years of work. "Who was in charge?" he hissed.

"Delmar Foster." A bead of sweat collected on Jaqua's upper lip.

"Don't think I know that name."

"Kid from L.A. Smart, but a little cocky sometimes. Lotta balls, but young, y'know? I'm working with him. Makin' it clear he's not a loner no more, gotta fit in. I think he'll be okay."

Mustafa's stare continued to radiate heat. "Keep an eye on him," he growled. "We only have team players. Make sure he gets that. We're not gonna be so patient next time."

"I'll take care of it."

Mustafa looked down at the desk, manually gathering himself, breathing deeply through flared nostrils, jaw muscles still tensing. After nearly half a minute of effort, the storm broke, and he once again leaned back, the waters returning to placidity.

"So, what's the profit margin look like this trip?" he rumbled.

"It's hard to say exactly how much we'll get in street-ready, but I'd guess in the neighborhood of fifteen, maybe twenty million after everything's taken care of."

"That's very good, Leech." Mustafa's face was pleasant but emotionless. "Now, was there anything else?" The discussion was over.

"No, Mr. Mustafa. Just an update is all." Jaqua got up abruptly.

"Okay, thanks. Get back to me once you've got the final figures."

"Yes, sir."

Mustafa didn't watch him go. He turned back to the credenza and, when he heard the door close, punched the intercom.

"Metcalfe," was the response: swift, crisp, definite. Harlan Metcalfe was Ebony's CFO and Mustafa's right hand. His MBA was from University of Phoenix at night, but he had the right mix of financial wherewithal and street smarts. Fourteen years with the Oakland City Administrator's office, leaving as a senior analyst to join Ebony six years earlier, rounded out his credentials with not only the financial wizardry Mustafa needed, but excellent contacts at City Hall, as well.

"Good news, Harlan. We've got the funding to go forward with the Fourteenth Street Preschool project. We gave that contract to Century Construction here in Oakland, didn't we?"

"Yeah, Century. Right."

"Seemed like the damn thing'd never come through. Who you talkin' to over there?"

"Well, it was their project manager, Rico Otis."

"Yeah, I remember. Otis. Are they ready to start demolition? I wanna get movin' on this thing. It's been hangin' a long time now."

"I'll check, but I don't think they can tee it up immediately. Last time I talked to Rico was over a month ago. The delay cost us our primary position. Seems like he said they were spread pretty thin right now. You wanna go with someone else?"

"Well, what's your take on that? They were our only local bid. Thought you said they were pretty tight with the city, didn't you?"

"They are. Century's by far the leading minority contractor with the folks downtown. They go all the way back to the Cypress Structure project after the earthquake, so they been around a while."

"Then I wanna stay with 'em. Their history may not be totally critical for a private project, but seems like the permitting and approval process tends to slide a little easier when our contractor's a known quantity. What do you figure it'll cost us to get back on their radar?"

"I don' know, I'll check. Might be another twenty percent."

"That much."

"Probably. They'll be way above the low bid once we add that kind of premium."

A beat.

"Let's do it," Mustafa said. "We go with Century. And jumpstart it, will you? I wanna get this thing off the ground as soon as we can. It's key that we get the doors open by May first, so we're operational by the time school's out. Lotta teenagers stayin' home to babysit durin' the summer. We wanna be the ones to be carin' for the little guys so we can put the teenagers to work. You with me?"

"Right."

"Oh, and Harlan?"

"Yeah?"

"Get me those plans, would you? I've got some ideas for the computer room I wanna work on."

"They're on their way."

CHAPTER SEVENTEEN

"What in *hell* are you thinking, man?"

Noah was furious. Across the table from him, a dazed Pablo sat hunched, head down.

After leaving Stark's office, Noah had stormed back down to Jack London Square where he and Sandy lunched the day before. It was nearly an hour before he began to slow his heart rate. He found himself pacing, down one way along the waterfront, then back, wrangling with the inner diatribe. *Simply no choice. He had to go back to Stark and lay it out. He'd say there was no way he could risk this guy's life dumping him on a novice. They couldn't dance that close to the death penalty. Course he'd be canned on the spot. Insubordination. Cowardice in the face of enemy fire. And maybe it was. No, really? Could anyone survive this kind of nuke in their first week? How many others in his graduating class at Hastings were thrashing about with a murder case right now?*

He turned again, walked down to the marina, then looked back out toward the open bay. *No way this was a fair fight. It was a flat-out litigation meat grinder. You couldn't just catch a death penalty case on your third day as a lawyer. It was that goddamn simple... wasn't it?*

The more he obsessed, the more convoluted it became. He was tangled up in doubts, but one thing was clear: no way he could take this kid out on a high wire with him. *Ruiz could die from this. Then of course there was the annihilation of a budding legal career, his own, and the obliteration of a reasonably good mind, also his own, by way of guilt. No... No chance. No matter what Stark was willing to risk. But wait... Ruiz totally denied it all. What if there really was some bona fide way out? Mistaken identity? Mix up on the paperwork down at OPD? Then what? He dumps the case back on Stark, quits, and they find out they had the wrong guy? That would definitely involve some facial egg. Best at least to gather up the police and coroner's reports before packing it in? Deal with specifics? Yeah... At least that.*

By 1:30, Noah had found himself in the court clerk's office requesting the full file. When they told him it was not back from court yet, he had gone up to Department 16 to run it down, and found the courtroom locked up and empty. The deputy at the checkpoint told him that the Department would be dark all afternoon. Returning to Oakland Division, he had called the DA's office and asked for Becca.

"Is this gonna be a daily thing, honey?" Becca was a total bright spot in a sea of havoc. "'Cause if it is, you definitely oughta be thinkin' about sendin' over some flowers pretty soon, and maybe some Almond Roca."

"Would you be able to check if the paperwork is in yet on *Ruiz*, Becca? I can't seem to get it through the court."

"Well now, aren't we all serious and distracted?"

"Yeah, guess I am. Sorry. It's just that this thing has morphed into a total catastrophe, and I can't seem to get any traction on it from anywhere."

"Okay, then. Take a few deep breaths. I'll have a look." She was back in thirty seconds. "No, I don't even have the file now. Must be with the calendar deputy."

"You think? It's been reassigned to Marco Salem."

"Salem?" Her voice dropped an octave. "What have you gotten yourself into, Noah Shane?"

"Thought maybe you could help me with that very question. All I know is my little 459 has grown up into a big, bad 187. Van Zandt was the victim, just like you said yesterday."

"Whoa now, honey. Let's get somethin' straight. I didn't say nothin' yesterday. I was just lettin' you know we had a file on the case."

"So where do I get the paperwork?"

"Whole thing's gotta be down at Main Office now. You know, over on Fallon Street?"

"No. I really don't know. Where's that?"

"Man, you are all fresh and new, aren't you? You know where the main courthouse is?"

"No."

"Lord. You even gotta fix on what city this is? Somebody needs to, like, draw you a map. I'm terrible with directions, but if you got one'a those GPS gizmos on your phone, that might be good. The main DA's office is on the ninth floor in the old courthouse. Now hang on a minute. Let me call over there and see what they got."

She put him on hold and came back in a couple of minutes. "Yeah, they got it. But they say they're instructed not to give it to anyone, not even anyone in the office."

"Is that routine?"

"No. But not much routine about this case'a yours so far, is it. I ain't seen 'em playin' this close to the vest in the eight years I been here. Orders seem to be comin' down from upstairs."

"So what's it all about, Becca?"

"Beats me."

"How do I get the paperwork?"

"See, now I really don't know what to tell you, but it'll for sure be in the clerk's office tomorrow."

They were both quiet for a long ten seconds; then, Becca said, "Listen, Noah, I could probably get copies for you this afternoon if it's really important."

"That'd be great. I'll be right over."

"No, no. Don't do that. Better let me fax it. Gimme some time. I'll call you when I got it. You can stand by the fax machine so no one gets to wavin' this stuff around. Then keep it under wraps, y'feel me? It's gonna have the DA fax header on it. If there's any way to get that off, I don't know it, but I don't need all this to come back to me. When you get the official discovery, you wanna dispose'a these copies."

"You're great, Becca. Hope I can return the favor sometime."

"You'll get your chance, honey."

• • •

With each page of the police documents he consumed, Noah had become increasingly livid. By the time he had finished, going back to Stark was no longer on the radar. He stormed straight to the jail. Now he was pacing around the holding cell, laying into Pablo, giving voice to frustrations that were finally bubbling up out of the bog of his own ignorance.

"Goddammit, Pablo, what do you think this is?" He held up a sheaf of papers, shaking them. "They've got your prints in the Van Zandt condo. You tell me you were never there. They find a bunch of his jewelry at your place. You say you never heard of the guy. Christ, you think this is some kinda guessing game? Ruiz commits a class A felony, and Shane tries to guess what it is? This isn't butter, dude. They got you charged with special circumstances. You know what that means?" And so it went...

When he had pretty much punched himself out, he stopped pacing, took a deep breath, exhaled, pulled out a chair, and straddled it, having decided to shut it down and let Pablo speak next. Two full minutes of silence passed with one sigh after another from Pablo's side of the table. Then eventually he began, tentatively, without looking up, voice quavering.

"I thought that if I told you everything, you would not work hard for me. I did not know what to do." He raised his eyes until they met Noah's. "Would you have worked hard if I had told you?"

"Told me what?" *Oops. Wrong answer. Should have been something like, "Of course I would."*

"If I had told you all of those things you just said."

"I'm your lawyer, Pablo. I work for you no matter what."

"But not as hard if you think I am guilty, right?"

How was he to answer this? They had talked all this through in Legal Ethics class, what your duty was to your client, but what did he say to a twenty-three-year-old Hispanic kid from the barrio who was searching for anyone he could trust, who was accustomed to deception from all authorities. This was the real world now.

"Look, my job is to protect you, no matter what, like I said. I can't let you lie under oath and still represent you, but short of that, I'm here to protect you, do everything I can."

"But suppose you—"

"Listen, Pablo. Suppose you just tell me everything you know, then I can maybe help you find the best way to deal with all this." *Sounded great, but what did he know about the best way?*

Pablo held his eyes for a long beat, then said, "I didn't tell you because I thought if you were sure I was innocent, you would be stronger." It was softer now, contrite. "And the problem is that I have to get out to take care of my mother."

"Okay. Now what's going on with your mother, Pablo? Time to lay it out for me."

Straightening, he reached into the left breast pocket of his jumpsuit and removed a worn, creased paper. He unfolded it carefully, probably for the hundredth time, and flattened it on the table. Turning to Noah, he inclined his head toward the computerized document, inviting him to read.

Noah leaned in and examined it: the last page of a Highland Hospital Discharge Summary bearing the heading, *Patient: Amparo Ruiz.* His eyes soaked up a handful of grim snippets: "...*breast biopsy disclosed invasive ductal carcinoma...*" "...*wide excision lumpectomy...*" "...*exploration of the axilla revealed eight lymph nodes invaded...*" "...*pathology on the sentinel node reflects highly aggressive triple-negative tumor...*"

Noah looked up.

"My mother has cancer," Pablo began. "She has cancer in her breast, and it has spread already and is going to spread to the rest of her body.

The doctor said her only chance is some kind of special chemotherapy, but they are afraid that it will kill her before the cancer does. She has had a lot of chemotherapy already, and her body is weak. She has to have an operation they call a bone marrow transplant." He stopped. Inhaled. "It costs more than fifty thousand dollars, Noah. The doctor says the regular chemo is not really helping anymore, that nothing else will help now. This operation is what she needs so she can have the treatment…"—he looked down at the fading print on the heavily creased paper, tears welling—"…or she will die."

"Doesn't she have any health insurance?" Noah asked, knowing immediately it was a ridiculous question.

"No. She has MediCal—welfare—and they will not pay for the transplant. They say it is experimental." Pablo leaned back and looked toward the ceiling, again breathing deeply, then returned his attention to Noah. "I will not let this happen," he said. A simple, straightforward statement. Determination, for sure. But motivation for murder?

Another half-minute passed before Pablo started again, softly. "My mother and father were married as kids, not much older than me. My dad was a gardener's apprentice… for the city. He was drafted into the army and they sent him to Saudi Arabia. He finished his tour and he came home, but then they sent him back. My mother was pregnant when he left, but they did not know. She told me that he wrote every week. I was a baby when he…" Pablo paused. "He was in a wheelchair when I first remember. He was blown up in Kuwait when his Humvee ran over a bomb they call an IED. A piece of shrapnel went into his spine. I never saw him walk.

"My mother says he was very handsome, but all that I can remember is bad burns on his face, his chest, his legs. He got some money from the government, and we were able to buy a house." Another sigh. "It was not enough. My mother worked as a housekeeper." He hesitated, closing his eyes, then his focus returned to Noah, trying to gauge his reaction.

"She changed his diapers every day. I remember that part, because his bladder and bowels did not work. She dressed him, helped him with the bath. She put the medication on his scars when they would bleed." He glanced at Noah and quickly added, "But she never let him feel he was not a man. She cooked for him. She put him at the head of the table in his wheelchair. She would make parties with their friends, and put him at the center of everything. She refused to let him believe he was just a cripple. She talked to him… about everything.

"I was just a little kid. I was embarrassed about his ugliness, that he was different." He winced. "I remember when he would look at my mother, his smile twisted by the scars on his face. He always said to me: 'You need only one thing in life, Pablo. You must find a woman like your mother.' But we both knew there was no woman like my mother."

Noah's thoughts strayed to his own experience growing up, how totally different it was from this family. *His mother's angst was having to wait until next week for a mani-pedi appointment.* While he didn't see what all this had to do with the case, it was obviously front and center for Pablo right now, so he was willing to let it flow, finally getting some back story.

"When I was ten," he went on, "my father got an infection in one of the wounds on his face. They tried to treat it for several months, but they could not cure it, and it went into his blood. He was in and out of the hospital, and he got weaker and weaker. My mother stayed with him whenever she was not at work. We would eat dinner in the bedroom. I think she knew he would not get well, but she never let us know that. And then he died.

"She was very sad. She would do nothing but work and come home, and make dinner. She never smiled. She saw no one. I could not make her happy anymore. I did not know what to do. I was only ten, then eleven." He drifted with it, then said, "But she finally came back to life. Somehow she managed to keep me in school, keep me from becoming a *cholo*." Pablo paused, then added, "I did not deserve such a mother."

Noah waited, not sure if there would be more. Once again, the jail was silent except for an occasional muffled thud, and footsteps somewhere upstairs. Pablo dropped his head, elbows leaning heavily on his knees. Noah couldn't see his face, but he heard his breathing deepen. His shoulders began to wrack as he sobbed silently.

Finally, he pulled himself to an erect position, dragged a sleeve across his nose and eyes, and said softly, "The doctor told us that the bone marrow transplant must happen within the next couple of months, and the treatment six weeks after, or there will be no hope. I have only twenty-three hundred dollars saved. That is why I had to get out. I will do anything to get her the treatment."

"Anything?" Noah repeated. It was irreverent in the face of such angst, but maybe it was time to get back to the business at hand.

"I did not kill him," Pablo said.

Noah heard it. He was thinking that there would be sympathy for sure, but the downside was that the cancer and desperate thrashing for money would also provide motive. Salem would never let that pass.

"Okay," he said. "Let's start at the top and walk through it... the whole thing this time." He turned a fresh page on his tablet. "For openers, what do you mean you only had twenty-three hundred saved up? You say all you did was penny-ante stuff, but this burglary, with you in Van Zandt's place, we're talking upwards of ten thousand in jewelry. And how'd you know he wouldn't be there that night?"

"What I meant was that up until then I only had twenty-three hundred. My mother has been getting worse all the time. She is very tired now. She goes to bed without eating. She tells me nothing. A week ago, I found some tissues in the bathroom with blood on them. I panicked. I thought to go to the big apartment building down by the lake where people would have more money. It was late, about eleven-thirty, when I went into the garage. I found a work door into the basement that was open. I thought that the richest people would live at the top, so I went up there in the freight elevator. I tried several doors and found one that did not have a deadbolt when I rattled it. I rang the bell several times, and there was no answer, so I jimmied the door."

Noah was scribbling. He didn't look up. "You went in, took the jewelry, and the gun."

"I did not take any gun. I did not see a gun."

"So what happened to it? They say the guy had a gun that's gone missing. They say you shot him with it."

"I know nothing of any gun."

"Like you knew nothing of Van Zandt?"

Pablo's shoulders slumped. "Please, Noah," he said. "I admit I have not told you everything, but I know nothing of any gun."

Noah searched his eyes for a sign, something to get hold of in the murkiness of another human being who was utterly unknown to him until a few days before, one he had seen only a handful of times under impossible circumstances, one who had every reason to deceive. *He wanted to buy it, but the prints, the lies, the jewelry, and now the motive? But even so, could this guy pull it off? Shooting? Dumping the body in the sewage plant? So far as he knew, he had never met a murderer; somehow, though, it didn't seem that a guy who could do all that would walk and talk like Pablo. The story was right out of the midnight B-movies, the ones with the motorcycle-lawyer ads.*

"So what they're gonna say is the guy comes home while you're there and surprises you. You'd found his loaded gun, and you were taking it. You panic when he comes in, and you shoot him with it. Then you dump the body in the sewage plant to cover your tracks, and you dispose of the gun."

"No. No one came while I was there. I took the jewelry out of a box in the bedroom. I looked in a desk in another room. Then I left."

Shaking his head, Noah blew a long exhale through fluttering lips, groping for a game plan. Only an hour before, he had been determined to walk away.

"Okay," he said. "I'm going to get with an investigator and see if we can firm some of this up."

"Then you believe me?"

"I don't know. I don't not believe you, Pablo. I just don't know. We'll have to see. Incidentally, has anyone from the police come to talk to you?"

"Yes, two men came to the jail. They asked me if I would talk about the murder."

Noah leaned forward. "What did you tell them?"

"I said that you told me not to talk to them."

"Did you say anything at all?"

"Nothing."

"Good. I'll call the DA and tell them not to talk to you anymore."

Noah gathered his notes and stood to go. As he walked toward the door, Pablo looked up.

"Noah?"

"Yeah?"

"I know you will make this all right."

Sure. Just wave a wand. The smoke blowing never quits. "Yeah, well, we'll see what happens. For now you just gotta hang in there. I'll try to get back to you tomorrow."

Rapping on the door, he looked out, saw no one. Again, it seemed like an eternity before the guard arrived. Finally the lock clicked loudly, and the door opened.

Retracing the catacombs toward the lobby, his mind was scrambled with the tasks ahead. As he entered the lobby, there was a low female voice from his left.

"Excuse me."

He turned. "Yes?"

A slender Hispanic woman in a long dark coat addressed him. "I am Amparo Ruiz. I believe you are the lawyer for my son." The face was pale, but remarkably unlined, feminine, only the hint of a smile. She extended her hand.

"If your son is Pablo Ruiz, I'm his Public Defender. I just left him. My name is Noah Shane."

"Yes, I know. I am pleased to meet you, Mr. Shane. Pablo and I are grateful for your help." Under her coat, she wore a plain, flowered cotton dress, and she had on athletic shoes. A dark blue bandanna covered her head, no visible hair. "I wonder if we could speak for a moment?"

"Of course," he said.

"Thank you." They walked to the first row in a sea of wooden benches and sat down. Then she said, "I am hoping that you can straighten out this misunderstanding and get my son released."

"I'm not sure it's that easy, señora. It's much more than a misunderstanding. I'm very concerned about the evidence they have against Pablo. He's in a lot of trouble."

"He is a good boy, Mr. Shane. He has killed no one. But he is no match for these people. That is why he needs you."

He didn't want to undermine her confidence with a protest, but he was definitely becoming uncomfortable with the ever-increasing web of expectations. "I appreciate your feelings," he began the disclaimer, "but, like I say, the prosecution has a mountain of evidence, and their case is growing as we speak. The stakes are very high. I can't promise anything."

Now she smiled more fully. "I am sure that you understand what my son was trying to do," she said. "That you know as I do that he was only trying to help me."

"He told me that you have cancer and you need a bone marrow operation."

She hesitated. Things had progressed to a discussion of sensitive matters more quickly than was comfortable, but then, there was little time for formalities. She nodded. "I do not know how well he understands, but I have what they call triple negative carcinoma of the breast. It means that the tumor does not respond to certain hormones that could be used to treat it. I have had a lot of chemotherapy that has damaged my bone marrow and my immune system, so that now they have to try something much more powerful. But with already little immune system, this would be very dangerous. The surgery is to put in new bone marrow, which would build up my strength and make my immune system stronger. Without it, they refuse to try the powerful chemotherapy."

"I understand," he said. "But I hope you can see that they will claim this expensive treatment, being so important to you, gives Pablo the motivation to engage in criminal conduct. You can see that, can't you, Ms. Ruiz?"

Her composure was unwavering. "They may say what they like. Pablo would never kill anyone. That is what I see."

Okay. Cue the violins. Unfortunately, 'he's a good boy' wasn't a defense to homicide in California. "I'll do the best I can," was all he could think to say.

She tilted her head back slightly, still smiling, her eyes admiring him. *As if a blithering incompetent rookie PD was the only lawyer in the world she would ever have chosen for her son's murder case.* Then she nodded, reached out, took his hand, and grasped it in both of hers. Her touch was soft, warm. "I am honored to have met you, Mr. Shane. I am glad you are representing my son."

CHAPTER EIGHTEEN

"Buzz Hoogasian," Noah said, poking his head into Bobbi's office. "How do I get hold of him?"

"Oh, hey Noah." Bobbi finished the sentence she was writing, then looked up. "Yeah. Buzz was here a little while ago. Too bad you missed him. He works out of Investigation Division at the old main office over on Fallon. If he's not in the field, you can reach him there. Phone first and ask for Melissa Downey. She keeps his calendar"—her eyebrows went up—"such as it is. I guess she'd know where he is if anyone would."

"And the number is?"

"It's in the manual," she said, shaking her head. "Sheesh, you want me to do everything for you?"

"I wish you could," he said. "Wouldn't wanna try a 187, would you?"

"Yeah, I heard about that." She gave him a sympathetic, pained expression. "Never heard of anyone getting such a heavy case so early. See? Now I told you you were star material."

"Right, the kind of star that implodes into a black hole," he said, turning toward his cubicle.

He looked up the number, dialed Investigation Division, and asked for Melissa.

"Who did you say you were?" Melissa asked when she came on.

"Noah Shane. I've got a murder case, and I need to get with Buzz Hoogasian as soon as possible."

"You're in luck. He happens to be in the office this afternoon, dictating some reports. He stepped out for a minute, but I'm sure he'll be back soon. Why don't you come on over."

"Great. Ah, how do I get there?"

"Are you new?" Melissa asked.

"Nah. My third day."

"I see," she said, snickering. "Well, just come on up Seventh to Jackson, then left. That's the easiest. There's a high-rise parking structure called the Alcopark. You can't miss it. Park and take the elevator down to the basement. You'll find a tunnel to the old courthouse. We're on the second floor."

"Got it."

Noah parked the Captain on the third floor of the Alcopark, which was emptying out early for the weekend. He went down to the tunnel, under the street, and through security, then took the stairs from the basement two at a time to the second floor, and finally ducked into the men's room.

As he stood at the last of the six porcelain urinals, Noah was mulling Stark's instructions in preparation for his meeting with the investigator. Suddenly, he became aware of an arrival on his immediate left. He always felt a little unnerved when someone picked the urinal right beside him instead of another, unused choice. This guy was puffing like a steam calliope, and Noah lengthened his gaze, out through the wall, out to the horizon, trying to maintain his focus through the snorting and grunting. *What the hell?* He glanced over surreptitiously and winced. His neighbor was digging in his nose like a man with a mission. The mission accomplished, his pinky emerged, trailing a viscous string that the guy then twisted onto the tile in front of him. Noah exhaled forcefully, rolled his eyes, looked away, and zipped up. After hurriedly rinsing at the sink, he hustled out, not looking back.

The sole occupant of the waiting room was a receptionist, seated behind a dark-oak desk, absorbed in the obligatory fashion magazine.

"Noah Shane to see Buzz Hoogasian?"

She paused in her reading to look him up and down. "He's around here somewhere," she said. "Saw him just a couple of minutes ago." She pointed to a door down the hall. "Why don't you go down to that conference room on the left, and I'll page him for you."

"Thanks."

Noah meandered through the lobby toward the hall. This was the old PD's office that had been its nerve center until the Main Office was moved out to Lakeside Drive. Now it housed the eighteen PD investigators. The public didn't come in often these days, so at 4:30 on a Friday afternoon, it was virtually deserted.

As a consequence of funding finding its way to higher priority departments, the high-ceiling 1930s splendor had pretty much gone to seed. Dingy white plaster in the waiting room bore the scratches and smudges of years of clients and their kids. The once-lustrous dark wooden trim was now well-worn, the carpets threadbare. An unmatched hodgepodge of furniture mixed dark beige fabric upholstery, stained here and there, with a few older, scarred, leather pieces. Oak doors to once-sumptuous offices bore the unrepaired screw holes of nameplates long since removed, harkening up the ghosts of PDs past. Why did he think that the DA's investigation facility was in a lot better shape than this?

Wandering into the conference room, he surveyed his surroundings. An aged chandelier encircled by painted filigree adorned the ceiling, illuminating a long mahogany conference table below, around which stood twelve leather chairs. Occupied more by specters than humans now, the room was only a vestige of high-level meetings passed. On the walls, above bookshelves laden with papers, textbooks, and a scattering of out-of-date legal tomes, was a row of gold-framed portrait photographs of Alameda County Public Defenders dating back to 1938. All of another age, and definitely showing the miles, the place nonetheless exuded a sense of soul that was lacking over at Oakland Division.

Noah dropped his briefcase on the table, walked toward the back of the room, and pulled an issue of the *American Criminal Law Review* from the shelf. Now that he had some paper from *Ruiz* to put in it, he had reclaimed the old zippered leather folder, fraying around the stitches, he had used in law school. Scanning the periodical, he failed to hear the door open and close at the other end of the room.

"Buzz Hoogasian," the voice said.

Turning, Noah nearly gasped as his gaze fell on a smiling, overweight, 6'0", bespectacled, bald man who extended a hand as he crossed the room.

Christ! The guy from the urinal. Noah looked down at the outstretched hand and hesitated, but there was no way out. Hoping the hand had been washed since he last saw it, he shook tentatively, trying to avoid the pinky.

"Noah Shane," he managed, stifling a grimace.

"Welcome to purgatory," Buzz said, pumping and gripping.

Pulling out a chair near the end of the table, he motioned Noah to the one opposite. The ensemble was postal clerk: dark slacks and a short-sleeved dress shirt with several pens in the pocket. The tie was thin, short, and gray, with a light-green, leafy design. His oversized glasses partially eclipsed a dark, well-seasoned face.

"So, how long you been in stir?"

"Since Wednesday," Noah said, taking a seat slowly, his disgusted frown not yet dissipated.

"Whoa. You are the total bluc, aren't you?"

"Blue?"

"Yeah, 'blue.' You never been in the service?"

"Actually, no. Not yet, anyway, but given the last few days, I'm thinking about it."

"Don't rush off into anything. It gets better. Yeah, 'blues' were what we used to call the rookies. I don't know where it comes from. Color of guys' heads after their first buzz cut or something. Anyway, you're not loving it so far?"

"Aside from the fact that I'm fitted up with a special circumstances 187 on my third day in the office, it's peachy."

It went right by Buzz, who was drifting with the concept of newcomers to the office. He scratched at the black fringe arching over his right ear, eyes distant. The generous laugh lines engaged as he reminisced.

"PD I used to work with was fond of saying he remembered driving home drunk from a party one night, lights coming at him, a grinding head-on, then nothing… and he woke up in the PD's office." He hooted, trying to sell it, then suddenly jerked back in a classic double take.

"A 187?" he said. "Jeezus. How'd they stick a blue with that heavy shit?"

"I don't know. You been around a while. Tell me this isn't at least a little off the chart."

"Totally. Most guys are still waiting for their first 187 after five years. Some never get one. They must think you're some kinda hotshot. That, or they figure your man's dead meat. They got somethin' in mind for sure. Definitely no accident."

Noah was silent, reflecting.

"Anyway," Buzz said, "might as well lay out what you got."

"Twenty-three-year-old Hispanic kid named Pablo Ruiz," Noah began, pulling the file from his briefcase and opening it. "Lives in the barrio. Hard-working family. Mother has serious cancer, needs expensive treatment she can't get through MediCal. Ruiz has a clean record, but embarks on a major crusade of hustle, trying to raise like fifty-thousand for mother's bone-marrow transplant any way he can find it. Got busted a week ago for lifting three hundred pounds of butter off a Foremost truck outside the Safeway over on Market at three AM." He paused for the usual butter response. Nothing.

"No sooner do they book him and put his prints in the system than they bounce back a match with prints found in the Van Zandt condo. You heard about that stockbroker they found in the sewage plant?" He paused again. Still no response. "Strangled. Three gunshot wounds in his head?" Nada.

"Cops get a search warrant, search Mom's house, and find ten-thousand dollars worth of Van Zandt's jewelry in Pablo's room." He stopped again for a reaction.

"So?" Buzz said after an undue stretch of silence, the Coke-bottle lenses accentuating the wide-eyed look.

"So it doesn't look so good for him, would you say?"

"I don't know," Buzz said, shrugging and jutting his lower lip. "Doesn't sound so bad to me. He stole some jewelry. His mom needs surgery. What's the big deal?"

Noah regarded him doubtfully, marveling at how everyone found these facts to be routine. *Why didn't anyone think this was cataclysmic? Was he missing something?*

"Jesus," he said. "The owner of the jewelry, the guy that lived in the condo where Ruiz's prints were lifted, goes missing. They find him a couple days later, full of bullets, face down in the sewage plant over in Emeryville. You don't see this as a problem?"

"Well, like I say, he seems like a pretty good kid. No record. Trying to help his mother. Doesn't sound like he'd do something like that." Raising his eyebrows, he shrugged again and shook his head slowly.

"You don't even know him, for chrissakes," Noah snapped. *What kind of investigator was this? What was he thinking? Maybe the DA just cuts Pablo loose? Let bygones be bygones? Firm handshake and all. Although maybe Pablo's not so wild about the handshake part with this guy.* "Look, why don't we just assume for the moment that the DA thinks he's got a pretty good case, and take it from there," Noah said. "You know, see if we can contact some witnesses? Work on turning up some defenses?" *This for sure wasn't starting well, but good God, here he was, way out on this limb that was being sawed off behind him, and the guy out here with him who was supposed to know what he was doing pitches a total whitewash.*

Buzz looked up, locking onto Noah's eyes, obviously ruffled by the sarcasm. "We gotta do our job," he said. "I just don't see that we start from the place that this kid is public enemy number one, that's all."

"Right," Noah said. They sat for a couple of beats, averting their eyes in the awkward silence.

"Yeah," Buzz said finally, turning abruptly to pull a yellow legal pad off the shelf behind him, selecting one of the pens from the assortment in his shirt pocket and starting to write. "Okay, we give it the full-court press."

Launching a barrage of questions but not waiting for any answers, he began writing furiously. It was like letting go of a fully coiled wind-up toy. "I take it you've got the entire police file? Investigation report? Coroner's protocol? Arrest report? Wait, there is no arrest report for the 187, right? He was in custody when that came through. Okay. You've got the arrest report on the 459. They did charge the butter as a 459?" On automatic pilot, he blasted through a mental checklist, jotting down the to-do list, informed by hundreds of previous investigations. Then, pausing, he held out a hand. "So let's see the file."

Noah handed it over. Grabbing it eagerly, Buzz began to devour it. They spent an hour on the few pages, going through it together, then through it again. Every possibility. Every nuance. Noah was amazed. The transition was astonishing, like the eighty-seven-year-old musician, bent and shriveled with arthritis, who hobbles to the piano, sits down, and comes alive with graceful movement when he starts to play.

"Okay. The first contacts are at the condo," Buzz said. "Neighbors. See if they heard anything. DA thinks we've got gunshots fired in the middle of the night in an uptown apartment building. Without a sound suppressor on the weapon, the likelihood that no one heard anything is remote—but then, the likelihood of this kid using a silencer is nil, especially if the theory is that it was Van Zandt's gun."

As Buzz thought out loud, his pen moved like a seismograph tracer during the Loma Prieta earthquake. "We hook up with building security to see where the gaps are. We check them against Ruiz's story as to when he entered, when he left, what he did, how much noise he made. We interview every friend of the victim. Last contacts. Enemies. Possible criminal activity. I've heard of Van Zandt. He managed the Public Employees' Pension Fund. That's a lot of money. A lot of temptation. All we gotta show here is reasonable doubt, that somebody else could have done this as easily as our boy. And we start with a clean record. That's better than we get with ninety-nine percent of our clients."

Noah was taking it all in. Slowly, he felt a glimmer emerging. This was Stan Laurel morphing into Sam Spade before his eyes, and it didn't take him long to get on board.

"We gotta establish TOD with total precision. That's huge for alibi."

"Wait, TOD?"

"Time of death. You say he went into the sewage on the night of the murder? See, there's no way we're going to get anything with lividity or any other studies that rely on the level of bodily fluids at rest—that is, unless he went into the soup a fair amount of time after death. The body would have been moved continuously by the stirring mechanism, so nothing could settle out by gravity, you follow? But there are ways of getting PMI anyway." He looked up, and beat Noah's question with his answer. "Post-mortem interval. The time between death and discovery."

"So what are you thinking?"

"Maggots."

"Maggots?"

"Right. *Calliphoridae* and *Sarcophagidae*. Blowflies and flesh flies. The forensic examiner's ace in the hole, so to speak—or holes, more specifically. The holes in question are the natural orifices of the body, eyes, nose, mouth, whatever... and any wounds, which is where these little devils lay their eggs, in the case of the blowflies, or deposit their larvae, in the case of flesh flies."

Noah wrinkled his nose as Buzz's eyes flashed. "My favorite's the *Calliphora vomitoria*. That sorta says it all, doesn't it?" He grinned, nostrils flared, slurping and wiggling his tongue like Hannibal Lecter.

"Anyway, turns out the flies arrive almost immediately after death, do their thing, and the larvae grow at a very predictable rate through their several molting stages. With blowflies, the eggs are laid at a day. The first molt—an 'instar,' they call it—happens after one-point-eight days. The second means it's been two-point-five days. Like that. The expert consultant mixes all the data through ambient or artificial temperature, and can get very close on the estimate of PMI. That's how they get to the time of death." A quick nod for emphasis. "Nifty, no?"

"Nifty..." Noah was imagining the flies and maggots crawling around the eyes. "How do you know about all this?"

"Not my first rodeo, Blue. Done more than a few murders where ID of the perp depended on time of death. Testimony comes from forensic entomologists. Wait'll you meet some of those guys. Real gregarious. Guys you'd love to have a beer with."

"I bet."

"Sometimes they can even get DNA from the blood of a suspect that was bitten at the scene by adult bugs, and make an ID that way. Put the guy at the scene. That's pretty rare. But most of the time, they can get the time of death within hours."

"Wait. This guy was in sewage. Wouldn't that kill the bugs?"

"I don't think so. I'm told the only thing that does 'em in is freezing or burying the body, and even then it has to be pretty deep underground. But you may have a point. I don't know whether sewage might at least change the growth rate. The little buggers may feed on that rich organic stuff in addition to the body fluids, and do their thing a little faster... or even slower, maybe. We can probably do some studies to standardize the process, and find out what the effect of sewage might be, if any."

"Hold it. The PD's office is gonna do all these 'studies' you're talking about? This isn't Genentech."

Buzz smirked. "Not to worry. I got lotsa friends. Like Farley Whetmore, a retired tech from Western Labs. Western does all the forensic lab work for the county, and virtually every other county in Northern California. Farley dabbled in some day trading on the side when he was at the lab, got on board with Apple early, and rode it up through a bunch of splits. Pitched the day job, and now he runs his investments full time. Still stays up with all the latest technology in the forensic business, though. Once a techy, always a techy, I guess. Anyway, he'll be able to tell us what can be done and where. Might even be able to do it himself. He's got a pretty cool lab at his place." He looked at Noah. "Okay?" The smirk widened into a grin.

"Okay…" Noah nodded, his wonder turning to full-on admiration.

"Next, we get out to the Emeryville Treatment Plant. Talk to the security people out there." He was scribbling another entry on the list. "Find out what it takes to get past the guard. You'd think they might see through a Hispanic kid ringing the bell in the middle of the night in a beat up old—what?" He paged through to the arrest report.

"Nissan." Noah filled in the blank.

"Yeah, Nissan, askin' can he please come in, he has some sewage to dump."

Continuing to percolate along in a semi-hypomania, Buzz chewed up the last few paragraphs of the file, point by point, note by note. At about three pages of listed tasks, he began to slow; then he finally stopped and leaned back in his chair.

"So," he said. "I guess that's it… for now, anyway. Time to pick up the hammer and nails. I'll get started this weekend."

"I can't believe it." Noah's eyes were wide. "How're we gonna get it all done?"

"We'll do it. All good. It's when there's nothin' to do, no leads, no contacts. That's when you gotta worry. I see way too mucha that. What's your cell?"

Noah gave him his mobile number; Buzz reciprocated. Noah began packing his papers, and they both stood to go. It was almost 6:00.

"You'll need a copy of the file, Buzz. Where do we do that?"

"There's a machine in the back. Lemme have it. We can do it on the way out."

Buzz led him down a hall, around several corners to the mailroom, switched on the photocopier, and waited for it to boot.

"God," Noah marveled as they stood in the green reflection of the warming machine. "I can't believe how much there is here. I came in thinking Ruiz was screwed. But, now? Maybe we got some direction."

"Yeah, well." Buzz seized the opportunity to pontificate. "You just gotta remember. The key to this business isn't courtroom antics or even legal precedent. It's info. You know, data. You paper the wall with it. You line the cupboards with it. You go get so much you can use it for bunwad. Then you bend it, shape it, paint any picture for the jury you want, if you have enough of it. So our job becomes getting more info than the DA has. That's all. Then *we* control the vertical. *We* control the horizontal, until we convince that merry little band that our story's reality."

"I hear that, but they're still pretty stacked with facts. The truth is—"

"No, no, no," Buzz interrupted. Having finished the copies, he handed the file back to Noah. "You gotta get over this 'truth' thing. Truth is only an illusion in the courtroom. You got as many versions of it as you got witnesses. The real 'truth' is over. It's happened. It's history. There's only evidence. That's that info I was talkin' about. The fire's out, Blue. The ashes are all that's left. That's what we're sifting through. Ashes. But those ashes seem a lot like truth if you don't look behind the curtain. That's where you come in. I gather the ashes, and you orchestrate the illusion we paint with 'em."

Buzz gathered up the copies and stapled a set. "See, the bad guys on the other side of the table got all the clout on their side, all the political poundage. The PD who hired me, old Donovan Pulansky, used to say 'Where the fix is equal, let justice prevail.' 'Course the fix is never equal, is it. So if we want justice, we just gotta have more ashes. Gotta know more than they do. That's where we're going. Find a whole lotta ashes."

He presented Noah with the duplicated file and said, "So, anything else?"

"Nope," Noah said, smiling. "I guess that's pretty much it." Then he remembered. "Oh, wait, there is one thing. These reports have the DA's fax header on them."

"I noticed that," Buzz said. "What's that about?"

"This girlfriend of Roger Moreland in the DA's office faxed them to me so I could get a running start. Really good lady. So keep 'em under wraps, and chuck 'em when we get the originals. She'd catch hell if anyone picked up on her sending them, maybe lose her job."

"Guess she would at that."

"Sole support of her kids, y'know?"

"Right. So what else?"

"Well, there is one more thing," Noah said, as they walked out together.

"What's that?"

"I guess I'd like some clue about why this whole thing's crashing down on me from somewhere upstairs. Y'know? Like, what am I doing with this case in the first place?"

"I hear it. Well, we'll keep our eyes open. You never know. Some'a that might be lurking in the ashes too. You just never know."

They had arrived at the front door.

"Buzz…" Noah stuck out a hand without thinking, his whole hand this time. "It's great to be working with you. Thanks for putting a little semblance of shape into this thing. It was looking pretty ugly, but it feels a lot better now."

"Roger that." Buzz nodded, smiling. "Stay in touch, Blue."

PART TWO

LOSS

"Every experience is a lesson. Every loss is a gain."
—Sathya Sai Baba

CHAPTER NINETEEN

As Captain America pointed back over the bridge toward the safety of the Oarhouse, Noah found himself riding a natural high, fresh from Buzz's game plan. But as the old sedan rumbled on, over the four-and-a-half mile span, across the back of San Francisco south of Market, and down the 9ᵗʰ Street off-ramp, he began to visualize himself in court, trying to find his way through the morass of a high-level criminal trial with a life at stake, and an old familiar obsessiveness began to percolate up from the self-doubt locus on his Hebraic DNA. It commenced to nibble at his optimism.

A capital murder case clipped to the first day employment forms? Like teeing up a rookie quarterback to start in the Super Bowl. No wonder PDs have the reputation of losers. How could even a veteran be expected to figure anything out if his client tells him nada? And this client came equipped with a no-way-my-son-could-ever-do-any-wrong mother. Was he supposed to pull some kind of rabbit out of a hat? This was people's lives, for God's sake. So, what was the call? Play it out and see if Buzz could help with the rabbit? Maybe. But Buzz hasn't ever tried one of these things. How to pull that off? Then what? Quit? Maybe.

It was after 6:30 by the time he arrived in the cloister of the Oarhouse and swung a leg over the stool next to Sandy, who was already nursing a brew.

"Don't say anything until you listen to my day," Noah said.

"Shhhh, wait." Sandy threw a hand across Noah's chest, squinting a "shut-up" grimace, his eyes locked on the TV.

Stork, also absorbed, an elbow propped on the bar, leaned over and whispered, "It's that murder we were talking about the other night." Noah's attention drifted up to the screen, where a local reporter was mid-interview on the KXTV *Six O'Clock News*.

Slowly he recognized the backdrop as the front steps of Oakland City Hall, a smaller rendition of its San Francisco counterpart with an attached seventeen-story high-rise. This was another Beaux-Arts landmark not far from the main courthouse where he had met with Buzz forty-five minutes earlier. Across the bottom of the screen, a panel identified the interviewee as "Rowland Murphy, Mayor of Oakland."

Noah was struck by how young he looked for the mayor of a major city: compact, dark, handsome, athletic, and mid-forties, max.

"This has been a true tragedy for the City of Oakland," Murphy was saying, "and a great loss to our community. Warren Van Zandt was one of our most respected citizens. He was a friend of the arts, a friend of this community, and a close friend of mine."

Though the words were the clichéd rhetoric, it occurred to Noah that somehow the delivery seemed to stretch beyond the routine political drivel. Definitely an air of sincerity; definitely seemed shaken.

"What's the status of the investigation, Mr. Mayor?" the talking head queried.

"I'm informed that we have a suspect in custody," Murphy answered. "This man was apparently in Mr. Van Zandt's home on the night of the murder. I want to assure the people of Oakland that my office is at the disposal of law enforcement and the prosecutor of the County of Alameda. We will assist with the mobilization of all local resources in whatever way necessary to bring the guilty party swiftly to justice. Following a vigorous prosecution, the person responsible for this brutal attack will pay with the full measure of the law."

"Holy shit," was all Noah could say, running nervous fingers through his hair.

The cut to commercial broke Sandy's hypnotic focus, and he turned to Noah. "You seen this thing about the guy that got dumped in the sewage plant over in Emeryville?" he asked. "That's gonna be in our court when they catch the perp."

"That's my case," Noah muttered, still mesmerized by the TV but oblivious to the sexy blonde who was now touting Viagra. "...if your doctor agrees that you are healthy enough for sexual activity..."

"Yeah right," Sandy said, returning for a gulp of his beverage.

Stork was addressing his row of spigots, drawing Noah his usual. He put the frosty mug down in front of him.

Forcing his attention from the screen, Noah looked over. "No, really," he said. "It's Ruiz they're talking about. The butter guy. That's my case. They amended the charge to a 187 at the arraignment this morning."

Slowly Sandy's head rotated, mouth agape, probing for the routine signs of a put-on. He'd known this guy for years, through any number of moments like this in which he'd pitched some kind of absurdity. This seemed a little different, but... "Nah," he said finally, with a dismissive chuckle.

"I'm serious," Noah told him. He summarized the arraignment, the charge, the evidence of Pablo being in the condo, the jewelry, his meeting with Pablo, the discussion with Stark making it clear that there wasn't going to be any senior lawyer involved. Sandy sat rapt, then aghast, the blood progressively draining from his face. He removed his glasses and cleaned them with a bar napkin, twice, a long-established habit when stressed. Finally, he said, "Jeezus, man. What is Stark thinking, putting you on this kind of shit?"

"Beats me," Noah responded. "Says he's short-handed." He took a long pull of the brew.

"Well, I know… but it's not just some back-alley vagrant dust-up we're talking about here. I mean this guy's a… I mean… it's all over the news." He shook his head with a bewildered look and removed his glasses again, exhaled forcibly on them, and massaged them with the napkin. "Jeezus," he repeated. "What's he thinking?"

"Tell me."

More silence.

Sandy restored his glasses to their usual position. "You know what I think?" he said, groping for some hypothesis.

"Now lemme guess…" Noah touched his temple with an index finger. "Nope, don't know what you think. But I have a feeling you're gonna tell me."

"I think this has something to do with Kate. Stark told her he wasn't too crazy about you, so he's playing with your brains. He's gonna have somebody else take it over eventually, but meantime he rings you up, right? Tries to make you look tentative. Maybe thinks you'll panic and quit, and he comes off as the tough trial dude."

Noah sat motionless for nearly a full minute, pondering it. That hadn't occurred to him. Finally, he shook his head. "No way," he said. "Even a jerk like Stark wouldn't hang a client that far out over the edge for some piss-ant romantic bullshit." But he wasn't so sure.

"Maybe. I'm just spit-balling here." Sandy looked down the bar, then back at Noah. "But I mean, Jesus. It doesn't compute."

More silence, then Sandy shook his head again and murmured, "Shii-it. A 187."

"Really."

"So what're you gonna do?"

"Exactly what you said Stark wants me to do."

"Meaning?"

"Meaning, quit." It came out on reflex; Noah hadn't decided anything yet. Like the first suit that catches the eye in the clothing store. The customer always slips into the jacket, looking it over from all sides in the three-way mirror, before making up his mind.

Sandy was accustomed to this drill. He'd heard the "Q" word countless times, and, as always, the general quarters red lights flashed and the alarms sounded. Time to fall back and regroup. "Quit" was the magic button Noah routinely pushed when things went seriously south. The first time Sandy heard it, it had petrified him. He couldn't imagine Hastings without Noah, or *life* without Noah, for that matter. In time he had come to realize this was some kind of ego-defense mechanism that Noah used to externalize, to examine and work through the challenge in the space between them. It was his imitation of the oyster, trying to rub the grain of sand into a pearl, or at least get a somewhat smoother shell around it.

Over time, Sandy had assembled a catalogue of pep talks for all contexts of "quit." Change the names and events to fit, hunker down and practice containment as Noah ventilated, and let him punch himself out. This time, he had to admit, was pretty cataclysmic, no doubt. A freakin' 187. Still, he dug deep for the old voodoo.

"You're not gonna quit," was the straightforward opener. Step one was always to cajole.

"Why not? Wouldn't you?"

Okay. Just an opener. Step two was to pump up the anger with a challenge. Get him into they-can't-do-this-to-me mode.

"See?" Sandy said. "What if I was right? What if that's exactly what Stark wants you to do? All part of his grand design on Kate."

"Well, then fuck him," Noah snapped. "If he's running a shop where he sends people to the needle to chase some love fantasy, I'm out anyway. And by the way?" He looked over. "Maybe you guys wanna be thinking seriously about whether you're up for being part of that kinda death camp, too. I mean, if we got Oakland's own Dr. Mengele here, you sure you wanna go down the road of life with that?"

Sandy regrouped. Mengele? Hmmm. Might have stoked things up a little more than the game plan called for. Press reset and proceed to step three. Play to his narcissism. "But this is what you do best. Two weeks ago, something like this would have been your wet dream. Jesus, Noah. This case is custom-made for you. It'll make your career."

"Yeah, make it short."

Okay. That's a little better. Less volume. Run with it. "C'mon, you're a natural at this stuff. You know you are." Now straight into step four, eliminate the alternatives.

"And what're you gonna do instead? Sell used cars? All the law jobs are taken by now. Not many options out there. So you plead this guy, you got a murder-one arrow in your quiver. No worries."

"Don't know if it's that easy. The guy says he didn't do it."

"Wait. You're not saying you seriously think he's not guilty? I thought you said they found his prints in the condo and the vic's jewelry on him."

"The facts are stacked for sure. But there's something about the guy, you know? Something about his mother." He looked up at the TV, where the KXTV news had rolled into the Forty-Niner Watch segment. Then his attention went back to his brew. "It'd be malpractice for me to try this thing. Three month frickin' rookie, for chrissakes."

The TV droned against a backdrop of bar sounds, animated conversation, intermittent laughter, clanking shuffleboard pucks. Finally Sandy could stand the uncertainty no longer. "You are gonna stay in this thing, aren't you?"

A couple of beats. "For the moment," Noah said. "But not because it's a great line item on my resume."

"So, why?"

"Because the guy doesn't have anyone else."

Okay. That was totally unexpected. Not the Noah for whom 'quit' was a routine refrain. Sandy pondered it as he squinted at Noah's distant image in the mirror behind the bar, detached, gazing into his brew.

Just then, Kate climbed onto the stool to Noah's right, driving a frisky elbow into his ribs. "Lord, am I glad this week is over!" Her late arrival—due to Krousse's propensity for finishing the calendar before closing up shop—was becoming de rigueur.

Noah shook his head without looking up. "I hear that," he muttered.

"At least we got through it," she said, flopping her purse and briefcase under the stool. Spotting Stork, she waved and pointed to the line of taps. He nodded. She said, "So, we're still on for Bodega tomorrow?"

"Bodega?" Noah turned to her. He had totally forgotten.

Shortly after their acceptance to the office, the three had fantasized, then planned, a trip to Bodega Bay to celebrate their survival of the first week. None of them had ever been there, but a weekend in the diminutive fishing village, seventy-five miles up the coast from San Francisco, had been a bucket list item. Among the anticipated thrills was the massive San Andreas Fault that ran directly under this settlement of 1,077 souls. Cutesified over the decades since its starring role in the Hitchcock rendition of the Du Maurier thriller, *The Birds,* it had become known for a couple of gourmet restaurants, a handful of good bars, great crab, and world-class whale watching.

Noah dropped his head and exhaled. "Oh, shit..." he said. Given the present precariousness of his decision on whether to hang in, he needed to work with Buzz to begin finding some of those ashes he'd mentioned if he hoped to build the confidence that would help him dig out of his funk.

Kate's reaction was immediate, unyielding. "No way, Noah. No flaking this time. We put this together three months ago. It's gotten me through some very tough spots."

"Jeezus, Kate. I would, but..."

"No way," she repeated.

"God..." Another big sigh and head shake. "I gotta get going on this case. I was gonna start tomorrow."

"What case?"

"The *Ruiz* thing."

"Why? What happened? I thought that was going to be a plea to a 484."

Noah went over the day's events again, this time to a stunned Kate, who sat speechless.

When he had finished, she said, "I don't get it. Jim Stark knows what he's doing. What could he possibly have in mind?"

"Yeah. You won't be too surprised to learn that that question actually occurred to me, too."

She mused a beat, then said, "I'm sure he's going to put somebody senior on it soon. He's got to."

"Well, thanks for the vote of confidence. You sound like Ruiz. Maybe they'll get him a 'real lawyer.'"

"C'mon Noah, you know what I mean. It's preposterous."

"How about this," Sandy interrupted. "We go up to Bodega tomorrow morning, we eat some crab, drink some wine, break some bread, and we talk through the whole case, right? We come back early Sunday. It leaves you a whole day, and you get the full benefit of expert advice from the old study group. You know you're not gonna get anything done tomorrow anyway. It's not like it's goin' to trial Monday."

"Really," Kate said, piling on. "I wanna hear everything."

"But I told the investigator that I'd—"

"You got plenty of time," Kate said. "And besides, things won't get any easier if Jim does keep you on it. If we don't go now, Bodega's history."

He looked at her, digging deep for resolve, and then he relented. "I guess..." he said.

"Great, we'll take my car," Sandy announced.

"The Honda?" Kate said. "Too cramped for that drive." Kate drove a Miata, so that was out.

"Guess it'll have to be the Captain," Noah said, finally finding something to smile about.

"No, it won't," Kate protested. "I'm done with that nasty old thing. Had to shower for an hour last time, and bury my clothes."

Attempting to recover a glimmer of good humor, Noah cast her a sideways leer. "Why don't we just save the time and trouble, and bury your clothes first this time?"

Leaning around Noah's back, Sandy stage whispered, "Do we really have a choice?"

Kate shivered in disgust.

CHAPTER TWENTY

Grassy, sunburned hills dappled with clumps of oak floated by as Noah piloted the Captain through West Marin County, past cattle ranches, dairies, and then the truck farms out beyond Valley Ford. A warm mid-morning breeze gusted through the open windows, and the big Dodge meandered toward the coast, Crosby, Stills and Nash streaming a soft background over the ancient radio.

Despite his hope that this outing would bring him shelter, Noah grimaced as he thought of the week's events, the burden of responsibility he now felt for the life of another human being.

He glanced at Kate, dozing next to him: her light-brown hair blowing gently, strands wafting over her face, her head nestled comfortably into her baggy blue sweater that served as a pillow. Then he cast a quick look in the rear-view mirror at Sandy, snoozing in a similar pose in the back. Noah was suddenly mindful of their history, his warm feelings for them both, and he was glad he had come.

As the close harmonies of "Helplessly Hoping" played with his senses, his focus returned to Kate, and he was struck by how beautiful she was. On impulse, he reached over and gently laid a hand on her knee. She stirred, opened her eyes, smiled at him sleepily, then repositioned herself and drifted off again. The Captain lumbered on toward the Pacific, and Noah found his thoughts wandering back to Spring Quarter, a scant six months before, but now a lifetime ago.

• • •

"Does this trial stuff panic you guys too? Or is it just me?" Kate said. "I don't know if I'm really ready for this."

They sat around a table in a private study room in the law library, agonizing over the finishing touches on the mini-trial that would be their final exam in senior Trial Practice. A small institutional clock on the wall read 1:35; the proceeding was set for 3:00. There had been trials all day for two straight Saturdays, and theirs was near the end of the schedule. As the event approached, the conversation went to the pressure: not just to pass, but to make it a stellar performance.

"Nah. It'll be great," Noah told her. "Everybody gets the shakes in the locker room. Once we tee it up and kick it off, you'll be fine."

"Maybe," she said. "Worst of it is, I gotta max this thing if I'm gonna graduate this time around. The transfer requirements were brutal, so I gotta total a three-five my last year. That means an A on this project, or it's 'kkkkkk...'" She dragged a thumb across her throat.

"Yeah," Sandy said. "I gotta ace it too, if I'm gonna get out in June."

"So it's not like the heat's on or anything," Noah said. He wasn't at the top of his class, but it didn't have to be an A. He sensed that they were somehow both expecting him to bring it home for the team.

The project du jour was a personal injury trial with Graham Kennedy, the Civil Trial Practice prof. They were defending. Kennedy sat as judge and jury, employing his usual Attila-the-Hun curve, with grades being given on how well the students were prepared, and how they exhibited their skills in the course of the mini-trial. The class was divided into teams of three, and all members of a team received the same grade. A handful of law review students served as witnesses. The hook was the "Smoking Gun Award," some well-hidden secret piece of evidence that they had to ferret out of the facts they were given. If they found it, their grade would be substantially enhanced. If they exploited it in their presentation, they were well on their way to an A.

The Kate-Sandy-Noah group had spent hours preparing every aspect of the case, searching high and low in their evidence packet for the hidden peanut in the manure pile. Now it was down to the wire, and still nothing. They went over their various roles repeatedly; then, at ten minutes to the appointed hour, they marched down to the field of battle.

At Hastings, the Moot Courtroom was a high-ceiling, wood-paneled, windowless chamber, smacking more of funeral chapel than seat of justice. Perched high on the bench in his black robe, Kennedy had the look of presiding undertaker as he relished the lofty position from whence he had come to judge the quick and the dead, mostly the dead. One had the sense that at any moment he would cue the organ music.

Kate led off with pre-trial motions and opening statement. A bit stilted, but thorough. Probably a B minus. Sandy cross-examined the plaintiff's accident reconstruction expert, and put in the defense's technical evidence. He'd rehearsed it a hundred times, and he delivered a journeyman performance. Maybe a B. Noah had the hammer: cross-examination of the plaintiff, and closing argument.

As he wrapped up his cross, Noah returned to the counsel table and flipped through the exhibits one more time, mostly photographs of the scene and the accident vehicles, in a last-ditch quest for the hidden Holy Grail. He looked over at Kate, shrugged, and shook his head in resignation. *Still nothing. Time to just sprint for the finish and hope for the best.* He started back to the lectern… *Wait, what was that?* He took two quick steps back to the counsel table, grabbed the Exhibit Book, and squinted for a closer look. A slight smirk appeared, then quickly vanished. He turned back to the witness.

"Now, Mr. Ray-gun," Noah said, holding up one of the photographs already in evidence. Kennedy loved the little names for his trial practice characters, mostly denizens from the seventies where he'd fixated. One of the supercilious law review jerks was playing the role of the plaintiff, Ronald Ray-gun, trying everything to foil the cross-examining defense attorneys, fancying himself as pretty cagey. "You say that Exhibit Six is a photograph of the interior of your 1989 VW Beetle, taken after the accident?" Kennedy leaned forward with interest.

"That's right. And you can see that it looks like ground zero. Everything I owned was scattered everywhere, and the seat in which I was riding when your client struck me violently from the rear was torn completely off its moorings. If the impact sheared the seat bolts, you can imagine what it did to the muscles and joints of my back." Jerk was milking it. The 8x10 glossy photo depicted books, clothes, groceries, and God knows what, strewn across the interior of the Volkswagen.

"Thank you. Now, you've testified that all of your current pain and disability is from this traffic accident that is the subject of your case?"

"That's right."

"And that you had absolutely no back pain in your life prior to this accident, is that correct?"

"That's what I said, Mr. Shane. It all came from this accident."

"You're quite certain of that?" Noah was determined to back him into a corner from which there was no escape.

"Most definitely. I think I would know."

"And, no one drives this vehicle but you, isn't that correct?"

"I said that too, didn't I?"

"Then perhaps you'll be kind enough to tell me what this is, here in Exhibit P-9?" Noah held out the photograph, pointing to a smallish, but unmistakable, metal and fabric pad, peeking out subtly, but clearly, just behind some clothes on the tipped-over driver's seat.

Jerk examined the photograph. "I… I don't know what you're referring to."

"I think you do, Mr. Ray-gun. I submit to you that that is an orthopedic support. A pad, usually prescribed by physicians to ease the chronic low-back pain of their arthritic patients on those grueling, long drives. Isn't that what it is, Mr. Ray-gun?"

Jerk didn't answer. Noah glanced up at the bench. Kennedy was actually smiling. *Bingo.*

"Thank you, Mr. Ray-gun." Noah turned and walked back to the counsel table. "Nothing further."

In closing, Noah argued that plaintiff was a liar, that though his client's car had obviously struck the rear of the VW, plaintiff's testimony with regard to his injury, and all his other claims of damage, should be viewed with suspicion because he clearly had long-standing back pain before the accident, pain that he categorically denied. He quoted the Jury Instruction: "A witness willfully false in one part of his testimony is to be distrusted in others."

At the end of the day, Kennedy announced that Noah, Sandy, and Kate had the A; that they were the only team to find the "Smoking Gun." All three left the courtroom beaming.

In the hall, Kate threw her arms around Noah's neck as Sandy slapped him on the back. "You are something else," she bubbled. "Talk about victory from the jaws of defeat."

"That car didn't look half as bad as the Captain," Noah demurred. "I'm used to finding stuff in that kinda chaos."

She looked up into his eyes. There was a brief flash in which the joy of a shared victory momentarily seemed to be something more, but it quickly vanished. Another swing and a miss, and, as usual, Noah buried it under a genial change of subject.

"So, how about a couple beers for my co-counsel? Always like to share the fee with the litigation team."

"Man," Sandy moaned. "I'd like nothin' better, but I'm doin' the weekend at the haunted castle in Modesto. Dinner's at seven, and if you knew Mom, you wouldn't wanna be late for that command performance. Her broom gets airborne right after game time."

"Guess it's just you and me, Kate," Noah said. "You up for a cool one?"

"Why not?"

"Let's do it." He threw a forearm around her neck in a playful chokehold as he told Sandy, "Hang in there this weekend, dude. What's on the agenda? Polo? Croquet?"

"I wish. It's my youngest sister's first communion. Big do on Sunday."

Noah rolled his eyes. "You'll figure out something. Treat one of those Central Valley belles to a little too much champagne, and who knows? Eminent trial lawyer like you?"

"Wouldn't wanna come down and see if you could make that case for me, wouldya?" Sandy said. "You of the golden-tongued closing argument?"

"Be careful what you wish for, m'boy."

By the time Kate and Noah settled into a booth at the Oarhouse, the place was already three-quarters full. He ordered a pitcher, and the conversation returned to his favorite subject, the day's heroics.

"You're good at this stuff," she was saying. "You know that, right?"

"Right. The F. Lee Bailey of the Hastings Elementary School of the Law."

"You joke, but you do feel it, don't you?"

"I don't know, Kate. It's okay, I guess, 'til something better happens. What about you? You did a pretty nifty opening yourself. All this make you think you're gonna be a litigator when you grow up?"

"Yeah. I don't know either," she mused, considering. "I guess I'm thinking about it, but I was a little panicked going in."

"You never get over the nerves, but you do get used to them," he said, speaking from the experience of his years of quarterbacking. "If something's important enough, you're bound to be nervous before you go out there. And you did great, by the way."

"Maybe."

"You gotta go for the brass ring, no? The only legacy of a Cal Tech math prof? Your dad must have some pretty high expectations."

"I suppose."

"So why the law biz in the first place? I'd have pegged you for music, or drama. Here we have this tooo-tal starlet wasting away in a law library." He drew his fingers back through his bountiful kinky hair, shaking his head like a preening ingénue.

"That was actually something of an issue in my family. My mom and dad met at SC, but she never graduated."

"Bet she's a knockout."

"She's beautiful."

"I knew it."

She scoffed.

"Why didn't your mom finish up at SC?"

"I've never gotten a very good answer to that, just a lot of rationalizations: she didn't need it, she wasn't interested, always just wanted to be a mom. But then, there was the fact that she got pregnant with me."

"So she was the one who was into your seeing it through and becoming a lawyer lady? Do all the things she hadn't. Is that it?"

"Not really. In fact, kind of the reverse. It was Dad who was all over my career, and when he'd harp on it, I know it made her feel like she'd come up short. She never said anything, but she'd withdraw, bail out of the conversation, even got tearful a couple of times. I mean, I'm sure she knew he was proud of her. He always said how gorgeous she was, but she never pursued anything particularly intellectual. Like, she wasn't much of a reader."

"Sounds like my mother."

"Yeah, but the wife of a Cal Tech professor? She finally stopped going to his academic functions altogether."

"So, what was she interested in? Did she work? Outside your house, I mean."

"Never. She was heavy into the club set in Pasadena. Dragged me into being a deb, talked about my settling into the women's auxiliary."

"No way. The deb scene? You actually came out?"

"Pasadena Women's Club."

"My God. You never told me about that."

"Yeah, and not by accident. I'm not wild about the image. So now you're one of the elite too."

"Me?"

"The inner-circle that shares embarrassing information from my childhood."

"What did your dad think about all that?"

"He pretty much tolerated it, except for when he had to squeeze into a tux."

Noah chuckled. Never having met her parents, he conjured an image of her father as a handsome, middle-aged, academic long-hair, chafing in a tight bow tie and cummerbund, and hiding out in the women's club library with a book and a martini while the champagne and canapes were served downstairs.

"But the books always came pretty easy for you, didn't they?" he said.

"Actually, I had to work pretty hard, and I did, to please my dad. It meant a lot to him."

"He must've been proud when you went to law school."

"Definitely."

"And were you proud, too?"

"I guess."

He thought for a minute, then said, "Does it matter?"

"Kind of." She studied him, thinking how easy he was to talk to. Was it the beer? "Seems like it wasn't just about making him proud."

"No?"

Her voice dropped. "As I look back, it was probably more about him being prouder of me than he was of her."

"Mmmm." He nodded.

"He was all: 'this is what a real woman should be.' I knew it was really about comparing me with my friends, other kids my age, his students, saying that women should be on the same path as men these days. I didn't think he ever meant to imply Mom was a disappointment, but it was pretty clear she didn't hear it that way. I don't think they ever talked about it." Pause. "Probably because he sensed it was too raw for her."

He nodded again.

"I would have thought she'd have resented me." She raised one eyebrow, speculating. "And maybe she did. She never showed it."

"Does that bother you?" He found himself enjoying the growing intimacy.

She sat with it a while, considering, then she said, "I'd almost rather she'd have hated me, and been obvious about it." He could hear the emotion.

His instinct was rescue. "You gotta live your own life, Kate."

"Right. That's what I said, but it wasn't really like I was living my own life. If I'm honest, I gotta say what I cared about was winning."

"Ah," he said, "so maybe that's where the competitive spirit comes from. The mark of a litigator."

"I never meant to hurt her. I mean, after all, what were her choices? I'm the reason she drops out of school, then I proceed to get all the accolades for a life she couldn't have. And I secretly love it. Is that living my own life?"

"But it was sort of the hand you were both dealt, wasn't it? You didn't make it up."

"It wasn't even like I ever wanted law school." Her eyes descended to the table, then scanned the room. Tears were welling as she murmured, "Not much of a daughter."

Another "Mmmmm," was his only response, this time with a frown, mostly because he had no insight to offer, but he hoped it sounded wise.

They were quiet for a beat; then she winced and turned her damp eyes to him. "Where's all this coming from? We have a great win today, and I get off into my painful childhood."

He put a finger to her lips. "Your secrets are safe with me. Psychotherapist-patient privilege."

"Yeah," she murmured, with several quick shakes of the head, and a snuffle.

He reached out and covered her hand; she looked down at it. "We all have our little crosses, I guess," he said.

She had suddenly had enough of the self-pity. Dabbing her eyes with her napkin, she cleared her throat, straightened, forced a composed façade, drew her hand from under his, and reached for the pitcher.

"So," she said, draining it into their glasses. "You told me getting into the law was kind of a frat outing for you, but here you still are after all these years. What's your excuse?"

There had been a handful of moments in their history when, like now, he had experienced her growing investment in him. Every time, it had come home to him how much he cared for her, and yet he would slowly find himself growing uncomfortable. It distressed him, and he didn't understand it.

It seemed he had always tended toward the short-term flings, favoring the flashy types who would engage him in frisky repartee. Comfortable with their narcissism, he relished the sparring when they tried to get close, to break him to the spurs. Such trysts would often become physical for a time, in a superficial way. A few dates, then a mutual parting of the ways.

Kate was different. She was incapable of vanity, of guile. In the rare moments of increasing closeness, like now, he felt her genuine interest, but no effort at entrapment, no attempt to change him. Tonight he could sense her willingness to trust him. He relished it, but somehow he knew the discomfort would follow.

From the beginning they had shared a lot, studying, running, end-of-the-day brews at the Oarhouse, and a lighthearted humor that they both savored. But she made it clear from the outset that, in the wake of a recent relationship that she learned too late was grounded on dissembling, she did not find clever banter, or charming bullshit, amusing. The disaster was that these were pretty much the only arrows in his quiver, his go-to defenses in the face of impending awkwardness. He hated awkwardness.

Wait. What was the question? Why did he go to law school? Was this about feelings?

"Hold on now," he said. "Shrinks don't tell their own secrets. Rule One of the code of ethics. If I get off into all that, we're talking serious boundary violations. You could sue me for malpractice."

"So I bare my soul, make an idiot of myself, and you get a pass?" She was only half kidding.

"That's what I do best."

"What?"

"Passes." He faked a leer, walking his fingers up her arm.

She hesitated just long enough that he knew he was nearing her cheap-bullshit tolerance line. "C'mon, Noah," was all she said.

"Okay, okay. How did I get into this legal purgatory? An aversion to the real world, I guess. Seemed like law would be the last thing I'd do. A few of the guys from the house were sitting in the sun out at the Alpine Beer Gardens behind Stanford spring quarter senior year, and the subject of careers, fuuutures…"—he rolled his eyes—"…came up. They were taking the LSATs the next morning, and they shamed me into going with them."

"What do you mean? You hadn't signed up for it or anything?"

"Or anything."

"How did you manage that?"

"Registered at the door. Told them I'd lost my entrance certificate."

"Why did you do it?"

"You know? That very question plagues me to this day. I guess because they told me I couldn't, and I was just far enough into the Bud to take the bait." He scoffed. "They had it all worked out that they were going to Hastings together, room together in the City."

"So?"

"So it got pretty blurry out that night, and next morning? Yuck." He made a face. "A test-your-whole-knowledge-of-the-world excursion didn't seem like the best option at that point, but I'd shot my mouth off and really had to brazen it through."

"What happened?"

"You wouldn't believe it. I somehow maxed the thing."

She shook her head, smiling. "And you decided the law must be your destiny."

"Shocking."

"Yeah."

"Turned out I was the only one that got into Hastings." He shrugged. "I don't know. Seemed like the thing to do. I wasn't going back to L.A. to sell insurance, so I set up solo housekeeping at the Larkin, and in three short years became the hero you now see before you." He took a sip of brew.

"But you always did really well, didn't you?"

"My grades were okay, but it was mostly pretty boring. I thought about packing it in a few times. Fortunately, I guess, Sandy always got on my case." Her gaze was fixed, intent, a hint of admiration. He took her hand again.

"You have a gift, Noah," she said. "You must know that. Not only the way you found the Smoking Gun today, but how you crossed the witness, and argued it. No real preparation for that. It's instinct, right?"

"Mmmm…" He shrugged.

"No. You gotta pursue that. If I had it, I would. Anyone would. You could really be something special."

"I get lucky sometimes, but not often enough to justify trying to make it into some kind of classical art form."

"I'm serious. Your kind of talent is really rare. I think you've got an obligation to develop it."

Obligation?

"I could say I knew you when, that I made you everything you are."

"Wouldn't you rather just know me now?"

"No, really. How could you ever respect yourself if you just blew it off?"

Respect? Expectations? The awkward meter was starting to climb, entering the yellow 'Failure Possibly Visible' zone. He leaned back and momentarily closed his eyes. *How to stop the nasty little needle from rising farther.*

She nestled a little closer, wanting him to dip into the deeper feelings, make himself vulnerable, for once.

His eyes opened, and he looked at her.

She turned her head to the side with a half frown, a lovely caring look that sought to shine a light into the recesses. "Seems like there's something wrong, something holds you back. Don't you feel that?"

Something wrong? The indicator was definitely into the orange band, 'Failure Likely Visible.'

"C'mon," she said, still smiling. "I made my confessions." She was wading into the inner swamp. He had no way to deflect it.

"What is it? You think you're afraid of success? Afraid to really go for it?"

Total red-line. *Caught in the open. She knew. He reached to his quiver for an arrow, a line, something that would raise them out of the mire. 'I'm all about success, sweetheart, the big money, that's where we're going, you and I…' No way. So what was he supposed to say? 'You tell me, Kate. You obviously have the insights. Tell old Uncle Noah how you see his personality defects. Maybe he can fix them, then he'll be totally perfect… After all, you're about to see what's really down there, then we'll both know I'm totally empty.'* Abruptly, he checked his watch.

"So listen," he said. "If you want something to eat, we better get on it, because I probably oughta get in early. Told some guys I'd fill in at a high-level roundball game in the morning."

"Roundball?" The sudden loss of connection took her by surprise.

"Yeah, basketball. We got a game over at John Swett gym. Starts early. You hungry?"

"I guess…" she said, eyeing him. "But it's not even eight o'clock." She'd definitely had more in mind for the evening.

"I know…" He raised his mug and forced a smile. "Here's to victory," he said, fumbling for a way back. "Better than the alternative, no doubt."

They stumbled through burgers and fries under a cloak of small talk. She made several attempts to rekindle the closeness, but all were unsuccessful.

By 9:30 the food was gone, the glasses empty, and Noah circled back to the early-morning basketball story. Standing, he pulled on his windbreaker. She got up slowly, and he helped her with her jacket. They dodged through the crowd, out the front door, and onto the sidewalk. He continued the small talk as he tapped the Uber icon on his cell and it scanned for their location. "What was she doing with her weekend?" "Supposed to be nice, isn't it?" "Did she have to study?"

She wondered what happened to the guy who had carried her standard into battle that afternoon and won the day.

A green Prius pulled to the curb, and the young Asian Uber driver waved a hand. More idle chat on the ride to the Larkin. When the driver stopped at the corner of Eddy, Noah climbed out; Kate stayed put for the eight-block ride to her place, across Van Ness in the Western Addition.

Holding the door, he looked back, searching for a wrap-up line. "Nice job this afternoon, lady. You up for a run sometime? Sunday maybe?"

"Maybe…" she said. "Call me."

"Yeah." He slammed the door, and the diminutive hybrid sedan moved silently down the block.

• • •

As the Captain bounced into a packed parking lot near the Bodega Bay wharf, Noah glanced at Kate, who was stirring into wakefulness, shaking out her hair. He managed a smile, still wrestling with the baffling swings and misses, the inexplicable awkwardness that seemed to loom between them at those critical times. *Why does it have to be so damned complicated?*

CHAPTER TWENTY-ONE

"I'll say this much, I don't think I ever learned more in a week."

Sandy was battling an enormous claw as the early afternoon sun reflected off the water, through massive bay windows, and onto a table spread with Dungeness crab, drawn butter, a basket of Bordenave sourdough, and two bottles of Carneros Chardonnay, one dead, the other moribund. Outside, fishing boats moored to the dock rode gently up and down on the soft surge of Bodega Bay, which stretched a mile to the southwest, where a sand spit separated it from the expanse of the Pacific. There were two reasons for the large crowds at The Bayside: the crab was fresh, and the wine list long.

The last hour was spent wandering through the entire *Ruiz* scenario. What possible explanation could there be for Noah getting the assignment? What could Stark conceivably be thinking? Why was Ruiz withholding the facts? Did that point to his guilt? And what about his mother? Was this a burglary for her sake, one that turned into murder? Had the vic come home and surprised him, and now he can't let his mother know he was a murderer? Through it all, the centerpiece was: no way this was a case for a first-week rookie.

Noah sopped broth from the crab platter with a hunk of the brick-oven sourdough, devoured it, wiped his mouth with the outrageous "Kravetz the Krab" bib the waitress had secured around his neck, and took another slosh of Chardonnay.

"So what have you learned?" he asked Sandy. "The seven methods of carrying a PD's bag to a preliminary hearing?"

"Come on, Noah. Seeing a guy like Harvey Cohen do his thing is an education you don't get in law school. Cohen's a twenty-eight-year vet."

"What's he like?" Kate asked.

"From New York," Sandy told her. "NYU Law. Kind of a hard-ass who could care less what happens to his clients. He brags about never prepping. Goes home at five and dives into wine and TV without a thought for the next day, until the next day."

Kate crunched a leg with her crab-cracker, her face flushed by an hour of Chardonnay. "I don't know how he does it." She had read each file, and mapped out what she was going to say, the night before, even though it was only a calendar department.

"He's got an assortment of defenses for all occasions," Sandy said. "Treats his clients like shit, but the irony is, it's like he gets better results than most, assuming it's not anything that has to be heavily worked up, researched."

"Why wouldn't they all do better with a little creativity?" Noah mused.

"Yeah, so it would seem, but Harvey says most of 'em are guilty. Says by and large the cops aren't out there busting people who didn't do anything. So damage control is the name of the game. Not much creativity in that."

"Maybe Cohen's the guy for the dirty defendants, but what about the rest?"

"Beats me," Sandy said. "Law of averages, I guess. But it's his bag of tricks I'm interested in."

Kate took a sip and launched into her own show and tell. "So the take home for me was that the system affords bigots like Krousse so much power to destroy lives—the ones who can afford it least. Total eye opener."

"Now that's what Mike Michelin was talking about," Sandy told her. "We might be able to do something about the Judge Krousses if PDs had more respect. We make more money, and the caliber of lawyers goes up, the brand of justice goes up. The way it is, a lot of the PDs are second-and-third rate."

"So let's see," Noah said. "That would make us what? Second-rate? Or maybe third."

"You know what I mean."

"Yeah. I know what you mean. Your association's answer to everything is more money. Can I live with that? Maybe."

"Just sayin'," Sandy continued. "It's not only image, but ability to do the job. Like, we've got eighteen investigators for forty-five hundred clients. Most of 'em are retired cops and sheriff rejects. A couple are on-and-off rummies, and one is this wacko, Hoogasian. Practically certifiable, Harvey says. So if there was more money available—"

Noah's reaction was slightly delayed by the Chardonnay, but it had definitely landed. "Wait, wait," he said, waving a piece of bread at Sandy. "Say that again?"

"I said that if there was more money, the brand of justice would be—"

"No, no." Noah dropped the bread in his plate and wiped his hands. "The part about Hoogasian."

"The other day, Harvey told me to get some investigation on a case. I called down to Investigation Division, and they said the only guy available was this Hoogasian. Cohen said never mind, it's hopeless."

"How so?"

"Cohen made him sound like kind of a nutcase. Says before he came to the office, he was working patrol for OPD and was heavy into the sauce. Apparently he shaded facts for defendants. He actually got some psychiatric treatment, meds, but was supposedly still worthless. Mucked up busts. Couldn't track his way out of a trash bag with a flashlight. So they canned him, and now we've got him." Noah's interest suddenly dawned on him. "Why, you know him?"

"Well, yeah. He's working with me on *Ruiz.*"

Sandy absorbed it, then said, "No shit? That can't be helping the cause much."

Noah's head dropped in exasperation. "You know what?" he said, and looked up. "It's not just the PDs. The whole system's fucked. I'm defending a goddamn 187 my first week in the office. Nothing belittling about that. In fact, if I thought I was up to it, it'd be a total ego dance." The wine had dampened his inhibitions, and now he could feel the rise of frustration. "But it's not about me. I don't know if it's intentional, if it's not enough time, not enough personnel, or not enough fucking give-a-shit."

Kate cast an uneasy glance around them. Heads were starting to turn towards Noah's volume, and it wasn't lost on her that a third bottle was on order. "Noah…" she stage whispered, her features tightening.

But he was already well down the runway and nearly airborne. "Who cares what's driving it. All I know is Ruiz is getting fucked, and the PD's office is doing the pimping. Now, what's your PD's Association gonna do about that?"

Continuing sotto voce, Kate put a hand on Noah's arm. "Any chance you could hold it down a little?"

"Might be there's nothing the Association can do for Ruiz," Sandy said, picking up his glass. "But maybe a few changes could help some future Ruizes. I mean, the Association's making another push for better money as we speak, and if they don't get a positive reaction this time, there's gonna be some kind of collective action."

Noah's head snapped around. "Collective action? What? You mean a strike?"

Sandy made his usual effort to feather the brakes. "Well, I don't know how it will play out exactly," he said. "Could be some kind of strike."

Noah's face morphed into a sarcastic sneer. "Perfect," he said. "Ruiz is gonna love a strike." A majority of the surrounding Marin-Sonoma yuppies was now following the conversation. "So will all those future Ruizes. Pablo might wonder why the court appointed some seventy-five-year-old, bourbon-soaked, street lawyer to represent him while his PD's out marching around on a picket line. Course he might be getting a better deal with a rummie than a rookie, but at least I give a shit what happens to the guy."

"Come on, Noah. You know they'd make some kind of arrangements for people in trial," Sandy retorted.

"Sure, and when he puzzles over why he got sent to the joint, or worse, I'll just tell him to check out how much fricking money it's making me. 'I know it seems harsh, dude, but after all, your kids might get a better brand of justice.' He'll understand. That is, if he ever has any kids. He'll probably spend the rest of his reproductive years in the lockup." One of the onlookers spontaneously applauded, and several others picked it up, enjoying the moment.

Kate could stand no more. She stood abruptly and excused herself, saying she was going to wander down to the beach. She'd see them later.

Noah regarded her curiously, then, finally getting the message, he glanced around at the sea of faces, some bemused, a few annoyed. He raised his eyebrows, then waved an apologetic hand to the spectators.

"Okay, okay," he said. "Show's over." He busied himself in the crab platter, muttering "Sorry" to Kate. Sandy shrunk into his wine glass.

Kate gave them both a sidelong stern look, shook her head with an exasperated sigh, and slid back into her chair.

They started into their third bottle over continuing, more modulated, discussion, but on Kate's urging, they soon paid up and left. The conversation suspended, they walked along the beach for an hour, savoring the cool sea breeze. Shoes and socks in hand, they strolled in and out of the foam as gulls hovered overhead and several disappointed surfers settled for short rides on squat, frothy rollers.

Returning to the Captain, they rekindled the shop talk as the trek continued up Highway 1, along the coast toward Jenner, a seaside village nestled on a bluff overlooking the mouth of the Russian River. Kate tried to interrupt the argumentative flow by reading from a North Coast tourist guide that described Jenner as a town with a population of 136 that bore the name of the writer, Charles Jenner, who had settled there in the late nineteenth century. She went on to narrate that the picturesque vistas and quaint ambience managed to overshadow a moderately alarming history of the Jenner double murder case of 2004, in which the bodies of a teenage couple were found on Fish Head Beach, a stone's throw north of town. The unsolved mystery failed to deter a year-round stream of visitors.

Far below the road, the river current churned up roiling white spray as it collided with Pacific tidewaters. The deep blue of the ocean, together with a brilliant white where the surf crashed against the rocks, were etched in vivid color that was almost overpowering to eyes accustomed to urban haze.

On reaching the little settlement, Noah swung Captain America into the driveway of the Sea Change Inn. The wind was picking up as they alighted and, ducking inside, they welcomed the warmth of a floor-to-ceiling, fieldstone fireplace that adorned the homey living-room lobby. After a reasonable time to thaw, the focus again turned epicurean, and they nestled into a table next to a window in the dining room. This time it was clam chowder, a couple of platters of mixed seafood fry, and yet more Chardonnay, against a backdrop of the sun disappearing below the horizon and casting an orange, then pink, then gray-pink, glow over the Pacific.

The conversation meandered from the sunset, to the huge beach, to how much it would cost to buy a place out there, and to how pointless it was to consider such things on a PD's salary. When Sandy started to revive the labor issues, Noah cast him a withering look. Sandy shrugged and excused himself to the men's room, returning to announce that there was a C and W band warming up in the bar.

"Why don't you guys come on in? We'll show the local talent that city folks know how to two-step." He held out a hand to Kate. "Ma'am?"

"I don't know, Sandy," Kate said. "I'm not really up for dancing." She looked out the window at the deepening colors. "Thought I'd take a stroll on the spit, out next to the river."

"That's for me," Noah said. "Let's get a couple of glasses of brandy and wander down there."

"Yeah, well, there's a not-so-bulky red sweater in there that caught my eye," Sandy said. "Reckon I'll mosey over and check it out. Be sure to be in by late now, hear?"

With the sun all but gone, it was turning chilly. Noah and Kate zipped up parkas and strolled along the spit that was formed by the confluence of the Russian River and the Pacific. An onshore breeze whipped around them, blew the fog against the trees, and blasted it dramatically upward to the cliffs beyond, giving the beach an eerie sense of enclosure as darkness settled in.

They stopped and sat, huddling in the lee of a dune and leaning together for warmth behind a stand of cypress that had been stunted and misshapen by the incessant wind. The fog cascaded over the sandbank behind them, swirled between the small trees above, and wafted inland.

Grateful for the brandy, Kate took a sip of the antifreeze. "Cozy," she said.

Noah didn't respond, and she wondered what the preoccupation of the moment might be. "The beach is wonderful in any kind of weather, don't you think?"

"Mmmm."

She waited for him to add something. When he didn't, she said, "Something troubling you?"

"I'm okay." He took a nip of the brandy.

"Yup," she said, arms around her knees. "Mr. Charming gone totally silent, but he's just fine."

No reaction.

"Still about the case?"

After a couple of beats, he said, "Fuckin' Stark."

"Stark?"

"He knows exactly what he's doing."

"I still have to believe he thinks it's so dead-bang that whoever has the case will just have to plead it."

"It's bad, Kate. Ruiz says he didn't do it. Somebody could still get into it and give him a fair shake, win or lose." He sifted a handful of sand through his fingers. "But that's not me. I've told Stark that."

She shivered and nuzzled closer. "I know you feel helpless, but there's really nothing anyone could do."

"Somebody with some experience could punch up the thing about his mother being sick, maybe sell that whatever he did, he's not public enemy number one."

"I suppose," she said. "But there're gonna be lots of cases like this, aren't there? Isn't that the reality?"

"Only one I've got."

"And you'll probably get more that'll make you feel helpless as things go along. We all will."

He considered it. "They're such a caring family, so devoted and everything. Nothing like what I grew up with. It's something worth preserving, you know?"

"Yeah."

"If I was arrested for murder, my mother's reaction would be embarrassment. Guilty or not wouldn't much matter. 'How could you do this to me?'" he mimed in falsetto.

She giggled. "Pretty much all about her."

"PhD in narcissism."

Kate dipped her freckled nose into the snifter, inhaled a hint of the biting vapor, then raised the glass to her lips. "It's still great experience for you."

"Give me a misdemeanor trial, even a routine felony. That's great experience. Worst that happens is the guy goes away for a few years, but at least he comes back. This is like… I mean, how do the stakes get any higher?"

In their silence came the moaning of the wind and the surf booming softly in the distance.

Turning her head slightly, she glanced at him. In the moonlit semi-darkness she could see that his eyes were closed, and it dawned on her how deep this went. Taking the snifter from him, she buried the bases of both glasses in the sand and reached a comforting arm around his shoulders.

He turned and searched her eyes. Brushing her hair to one side, he gently kissed her, and they slumped back against the dune behind them, their warmth shielding them against the sea air and the fog. He opened his bulky parka, pulled her inside, and kissed her again, letting himself dissolve into her embrace.

His hands traced her curves, feeling the silk of her back up under her flannel shirt. Her lips lightly caressed his cheek as he unzipped her jeans, and his hands reached inside, fingers softly stroking.

She pressed herself down on him, nibbling at his ear. "I think I've always loved you," she breathed. For just an instant he felt a fluttering apprehension, but he smothered it, burying his face in the fragrance of her hair.

Struggling out of his parka, he threw it over them, coaxing her jeans down. She unzipped his, dropped a knee on either side of him and they began moving together, slowly, urgently, after all the fantasy and forbearance.

Afterwards, she lay on his chest for a long time before she lifted her head, propped her chin on her hands, and looked at him. He smiled.

"You always frightened me, Noah," she murmured softly. "I wanted to trust you, but—"

"Trust… *me*?" he said, eyebrows raised in feigned astonishment. "Mr. Dependable?"

"I wondered if you were just playing."

"Playing how?"

"Kind of with everything serious."

His expression morphed to mock suffering. "Now, you know me," he said. "I'm nothing if not totally serious."

"See, that's what I mean," she said, looking pleadingly at him. "I need to say something... and I want you to hear me."

"Go for it," he said, trying for nonchalance. He felt the awkward meter rising again, and would have given anything to avoid what was coming next.

"I couldn't... I guess I just couldn't let myself go. I've been hurt... you know?"

At first he thought it was rhetorical, but then he realized she wanted an answer. His reflex was for another punchline, but he knew it wasn't an option. He found himself at an utter loss for what to say, given the significance of the moment. "I could never hurt you, Kate," he finally murmured. "You know that. I..."

She waited a beat for him to finish. When he didn't, she said, "I wanted to tell you that I loved you, but I needed you to..." She paused.

He put a finger to her lips. "Shhhh..." he whispered.

She took his hand, gently removed it from her lips, and went on softly declaring her feelings for him, trying to wrap him in her longings, engage him in a way that he would reciprocate.

He couldn't hear her anymore. Across the growing distance between them, he wanted only to be the man she desired, to heal her wounds, to take care of her. He knew what she wanted him to say. He wanted to say it, but he couldn't bring himself to make the promises he would fail to keep. And then she would know the truth, that he was an imposter, not the confident doer who could mend everything that was broken.

"Sometimes we don't mesh," she was saying. "I know that. But I've always felt this connection. From the beginning, I knew that there was something special..." Her words were engulfing him, rendering his thoughts a self-loathing jumble. *He wasn't what she thought. He didn't deserve her. Not worthy.*

Her head lay on his chest as she gently stroked the mound of hair under his shirt. "...but when I felt the closest, you always seemed distant. I thought there was something wrong, and I couldn't get what it was."

Something wrong.

"But tonight I can see that I was the one who was wrong. I was wrong to doubt you—"

Suddenly his impoverished defenses, stretched to breaking, fractured, fragmenting him, and he jerked into a sitting position.

"No, dammit, you weren't wrong! You were right."

She flopped onto an elbow, stunned. "Wh—what?" she stammered.

"I'm no good for you, Kate. I'm no good for anyone… I don't know what made me think I could be." He stood, tugging at his clothes, pulling on his parka.

"Noah, I…"

"No! Just leave it. It won't work. You were right all along. There's definitely something wrong with me." He turned and started back down the beach.

"Noah, wait." She was wriggling her jeans up, zipping. "What are you talking about? I don't think you understood what I was trying to say. Noah… listen to me." She was brushing the sand off, staggering after him with no idea of what had just happened.

"Time to get back to reality," he muttered.

They slogged back in silence, she several paces behind him. With each step, he was increasingly consumed by an unbearable remorse, but he trudged on, hopelessly twisted inside, struggling for control.

When they reached the inn, Sandy was out front nursing a fourth margarita and a damaged ego.

"What happened?" Noah asked, fixing the composed-caretaker mask, number one in his toolbox of personas, precariously back in place. "Thought you said that less-than-baggy sweater was a sure thing."

"I did," Sandy slurred. "Bu'this cowboy had th'same idea. An' she seems t'go for the barnyard set." He waved an erratic thumb over his shoulder toward the dance floor, where a young woman in a tight red sweater was laughing through the two-step with a hatted, booted monster.

"C'mon," Noah said. "I'll buy you a little more pain relief." He pushed Sandy into the bar, unable to look back.

Kate's eyes followed him, brimming with tears. Then her jaw clenched, and she shook her head in disbelief. "What in the name of God is his story?" she rasped audibly.

Had she been in her own car, she would have been on her way home right then. Mindlessly, she strode into the lobby, picked up a magazine, and sat by the fire, flipping pages for a solid thirty minutes without seeing a thing, trying desperately to erase the last two hours from her life. Failing, she took herself to the registration counter and rented a room.

CHAPTER TWENTY-TWO

"Frank, you old fox, where did you find this lovely woman?"

Mustafa seized the hand of the heavyset, gray-haired man, as he smiled at his comfortably proportioned, elegantly assembled wife. It was intermission at the Oakland Philharmonic Sunday afternoon concert.

The Oakland Paramount Theater on Broadway, where the Philharmonic performed, was a remnant of the Art Deco 1930s. Among the last of the cinema-castle extravaganzas to be built, it opened in 1931, and was declared a National Historic Landmark in 1977. Its ambience was sometimes compared to the grandeur of Radio City Music Hall in New York. In recent years, it abandoned its heritage as a grandiloquent movie theater, and moved inexorably toward the sophistication of symphony, ballet, and legitimate stage, paralleling the cultural evolution of the city whose name it bore.

As the house lights gradually came up, Poseidon, horses rearing on either side of him, looked down from the spectacular bas-relief sculpture over the orchestra pit, arms outstretched, as if inviting the assemblage below to arise and rejoice in the musical refinement that had just concluded. Obediently, the black-tied patrons stood and slowly left their seats, milling toward the lobby and clucking over the "magnificence" of the Bartok concerto.

Mustafa reveled in his celebrity. He stopped intermittently to chat as he made his way up the aisle and through the lobby, working the room like the president leaving Congress after the State of the Union. Pumping the hands of friends and admirers as he locked in the eye contact, he introduced them to the beautiful twenty-six-year-old woman on his arm. Her shimmering brunette curls were casually fastened atop her head with the exception of a single whorl that hung to one shoulder. The red-sequined dress she was almost wearing rendered stark contrast to Mustafa's immaculate tuxedo, as did her porcelain skin to his deep brown hue. Despite the twenty-five-year difference in their ages, they were definitely a striking couple.

"Afternoon, Freeman. Great to see you." Frank Gordon was a prominent minority contractor and long-time business friend.

"How 'bout our Cal Bears, Frank. Are they stacked this year or what?"

"I don't know. They could still use you." Gordon squeezed the powerful bicep as they moved slowly through the lobby. "You seem to be stayin' in shape. Bet you haven't lost a step."

Mustafa beamed. "Well, maybe a step. Emily, you look ravishin', as always. How do you put up with this degenerate husband of yours?" He turned to his date. "May I present Cassie Miller? Cassie, Frank and Emily Gordon, some old and very dear friends. Cassie works for the Housin' Department of some second-rate city across the Bay, but we won't hold that against her, will we?"

The banter continued as the throng pressed into the lushly carpeted foyer, up the gold-banistered stairs, and fanned out into the spacious, gilt-adorned mezzanine lounge where champagne was being served.

"Freeman!" a male voice called from the stairs behind them. Mustafa turned to see a man in his early forties, tall with dark wavy hair, extending a hand through the crowd, with a somewhat round, blonde woman in tow.

Grinning, Mustafa stretched out a hand in return. "Hello, Dan. Great to see you. Why don't you and Rhonda join us for a drink?" There wasn't a name that escaped him. His internal card catalog was infallible, a genetic gift shared by few.

Mustafa and Cassie passed in front of the long, linen-draped, serving table, selected flutes of champagne, and took up a position with the Gordons to one side, next to a marble wall bedecked with curvilinear, frosted-glass sconces that magically radiated a soft green light. Within moments, they were joined by Dan Whittington and his wife.

Mustafa smiled into the face of the taller man, grabbing his forearm as they shook hands. "Afternoon, counselor," he said. "Cassie, meet Dan and Rhonda Whittington. Folks, this is my friend Cassie Miller, from San Francisco." He crinkled his face in mock revulsion, then went on. "Dan is one of the fine young lawyers in this part of the world, Cassie. Saved Ebony Properties from the vultures… more than once, I can tell you."

"So what's new over at the nerve center, Freeman?" Whittington asked.

"Well, our latest project is the Fourteenth Street Preschool." He faced the whole group, raising his voice so the Gordons and Cassie could hear. "I think you know about it, Dan. Your office got us the permits and administrative clearance."

Dan nodded, taking a sip of champagne. "Oh, yeah. I do remember."

"This new preschool is somethin' special. We'll have the largest enrollment in Northern California. Five hundred youngsters with a staff of eighty-five." Mustafa looked from face to face, launching into the bullet points he had run so many times. "Fifty teachers, ratio of ten to one, the remainder recreational staff, a full-time librarian, a computer guru, full-time nurse, office staff, and janitorial. We're gonna house it in a twenty-thousand-foot structure on grounds coverin' a full city block. It'll have a state-of-the-art computer lab and a full children's library. This school," he paused, smiling, "is gonna be a showplace."

"Wow," Gordon marveled.

"You said it, Frank. You know, our people have been comin' in dead last forever. Used to be we'd buy and support our schools with a property tax base. Course, we lived in the poorest part of town, right? From property with the lowest tax base come the least taxes."

Heads were nodding.

"So you had the poorest schools, which turn out poor students, poor workers, and poor adults, not to mention addicts, delinquents, and criminals. They lived in the poor part of town, and the schools their tax dollars supported were the poorest again for their kids. That's changed some now, what with quotas of the local property tax revenues going to the state, and the state keeping the distributions to various school districts a little more even."

His focus roamed from one to the next, like a barrister addressing a jury. "But that's not where the action is in education. See, we got to get these kids in the first few years of their lives if we're gonna make a difference. Studies show that by the time they get to kindergarten, it's too late. Now, there are head-start programs here and there, but they're hit and miss. If we're gonna break into this cycle, we gotta look to ourselves, start with our own preschools. It's the only way to get the job done." He looked benevolently at Cassie, who was gazing back, adoring. "That's the goal of Ebony Properties."

"Sounds simple enough." The forceful voice came from behind Mustafa, and he turned.

"Rowland! M'man. How are you?" Throwing an arm around the newcomer, he drew him into the group. "You folks all know the mayor, Rowland Murphy? The Gordons, the Whittingtons. And this is my friend, Cassie Miller."

"Sure," Murphy said. "Hello Frank, and Ellen, was it?"

"Emily."

"Of course, Emily. And the Whittingtons." The mayor shook hands all around. "Cassie Miller. It's always a pleasure to meet a friend of Freeman's. He has excellent taste in friends."

Murphy had a strong public presence that captivated assemblages, but in this instance, approaching solo, he seemed oddly awkward. He turned to Mustafa.

"Freeman, I wonder if I could have a word with you before the music starts again?"

Mustafa eyed him, smile lingering. "Sure," he said. "Will you excuse us for some high-level municipal business?" He turned to Cassie. "Back in a minute, Sugar."

Mustafa took Murphy's arm under the elbow affectionately, and they strolled, chatting and nodding at well-wishers, to the end of the salon, where they turned down an empty hallway carpeted richly in hues of green, beige, and brown. Once alone, they stopped.

"So, what's up?" Mustafa asked.

"Have you had a chance to be in touch with Ben Owens on the Van Zandt thing?"

"Just that I got another two calls from the media this morning, and I'm concerned that things are stretching out, is all. Warren was a popular guy with important sectors of the city, with virtually everyone in this room." He waved a hand toward the crowd in the adjacent gallery. "He managed a big piece of change, a lot of retirement funds. Folks need confidence in the stability of such things going forward."

Mustafa smiled and acknowledged an acquaintance who passed by the end of the hall as Murphy continued his monologue.

"We need closure," Murphy was saying. "I'm trying to assure the community that everything is under control, but they're asking questions I can't answer. My job is to maintain some semblance of calm, wouldn't you agree?"

"Can't disagree with any of that, Rowland. But, like I've told you, it'll be taken care of. All in good time." Mustafa's smile didn't waver. "So, what else is on your mind?"

Murphy stared at him, frown deepening. "I think it deserves your full attention, don't you, Freeman? Rather than your becoming distracted by some more non-essential matters."

Mustafa's smile still did not falter, but his eyes were now locked on those of the smaller man. "I said that everything is under control, Rowland. But since you asked what I think, I'll tell you. I think you need to maintain your composure if you're goin' to preserve some semblance of calm in the community. Now, it's been nice havin' this little chat."

He broke the stare and stepped around Murphy, moving back toward the lounge. Agitated, Murphy grabbed him by the arm as he passed.

"What I'm saying is I need some action on this thing, and I'm talking about immediately."

Mustafa, taller and broader, turned on him. The sometimes explosive temperament, ordinarily kept hidden at great emotional expense, was now very near the surface. Glaring menacingly, he seized Murphy's wrist in a vice-like grip and slowly removed the hand from his arm. Then, holding it between his two larger hands, he softened, and the smile returned.

"Now, Rowland," he rumbled. "We've been together a long time, haven't we?" He pumped Murphy's hand to punctuate his delivery. "And I've always appreciated your public interest. I still do. You know that." With an exaggerated deliberateness, he returned Murphy's hand to his side.

"But I would ask you to remember who put you where you are, and at whose pleasure you serve. We mustn't lose sight of the larger picture here, am I right?" He paused, staring meaningfully into the face of the smaller man. No response was forthcoming.

"Now, I'm gonna give Ben Owens a call tomorrow and check on how things are goin'. You call me Tuesday for an update. Will you do that?" The overhead lights flashed, signaling that halftime was over.

Murphy's face remained taut, jaw still flexing, but he still said nothing.

"Good," Mustafa rumbled. "And Rowland, in the future, if you have matters of a civic importance to discuss with me, call my office, will you?" A hint of the savage countenance returned as Mustafa leaned close to Murphy's ear and hissed, "Don't you ever try to corner me in public again." The smile reappeared as Mustafa stepped around him and returned to his entourage.

CHAPTER TWENTY-THREE

Noah plodded into his suite at the Larkin, exhausted and hung over. He winged his duffel onto the bed and instinctively reached for the remote, flipped on the TV, surfed briefly, and settled on a Dallas/Rams pre-season game.

After dragging Sandy back to the bar the night before, he'd bought a couple more rounds, trying to drown the self-hatred, Sandy just trying to drown. It was 1:30 when they staggered to the front desk and were told that Kate had rented a room. They got one of their own, lurched in, and collapsed.

Next morning, all three had stumbled through coffee and orange juice in monosyllabic silence. Kate was wishing she was anywhere else on the planet. All the way home, Noah had been lost in obsession, feeling like death, and overwhelmed by guilt. *Find a private moment to explain. 'Totally sorry about last night. I was a complete jerk. It wasn't you. I'm just bonkers. I really don't know what happened. I'll fix it. I'll get therapy.'* It all made him sound like a whack job, or worse, a weak wuss. Nothing worked. *She was probably done with him, and why wouldn't she be?*

Unable to comprehend the stony silence, Sandy had tried several times through his own bleak haze to pump up the conversation. No chance.

Once insulated in his sanctuary, realizing there was nothing he could do at the moment to make things better, Noah groped for the defense du jour: firm denial. He cracked a beer to nurse his bottle-fatigue, flopped down on the ragged overstuffed chair, opened the sports page, and punched voicemail for messages. There were two. The first was Buzz, midmorning Saturday, reporting that he'd picked up the remaining investigation and further autopsy paperwork after their Friday meeting. There was some interesting stuff. He was going to the jail to see Pablo. The next message, also Buzz, came in late Saturday. He'd seen Pablo. More interesting info. Call him. Time to get together. Rams scored, and the crowd roared.

When Buzz didn't answer his cell, Noah left the message that he was on his way. He'd meet him at the kids' zoo on Grand, next to Lake

Merritt, at 4:30. Call with a better place, better time, if there was one. He left his cell number again, just in case.

Noah's pace was slow as he descended the stairs. When he got to the second floor, he cast a fleeting glance down toward Lisa's apartment. After a brief inner debate, he took the detour, and rapped on her door.

"Just a minute…" was the response, a beat, and the door opened.

The jeans, untucked white shirt, no shoes, no makeup, were not the usual 4:00 ensemble, but he liked her light years better this way.

"Noah, hi." Definitely more upbeat than Wednesday.

"So what's up with Maggie? You been over to see her?"

"Twice a day. Met a social worker from CPS up there. You nailed it about the foster home thing. Placement looks like a sure thing, but the lady said if I complete a program, get a job, I can probably get her back."

"How do you get in a program?"

"The social worker said there's county money. I picked up an application and reserved space at Hampstead House for their twenty-eight-day program. All I need is to get the application in for the funds."

"Lemme see it."

She went to her dresser, sorted through a stack of papers, pulled out an application for the San Francisco County Medical Fund, and handed it to him.

After scanning it, he said, "Tell you what, Lees. Lemme take this and fill it out for you."

"Really?"

"I can give you a recommendation. I don't know. It might help."

"You've done so much already."

"Nah. Glad to do it. Let's get Maggie home." He checked his watch. "I'll get this together and get it back to you, then you can walk it down to social services. The sooner the bureaucrats get these things, the better."

As he turned to leave, she threw her arms around his neck, and hugged him. "Come down later, when you get back?"

He could feel the warmth of her breath, her breasts against his chest. He slowly pulled her arms down, combing the toolbox for an expression that said compassion.

"Thanks, Lees, but let's not complicate things right now. We gotta stay focused," he said, as the night before flashed back to him fleetingly. He smiled. "We'll see. You never know. I might just stop by some evening, when things get sorted out."

"You know the brandy's always open."

"I know," he said, and squeezed her shoulders.

Making his way down to find the Captain, despite his efforts to maintain his denial, his thoughts involuntarily coalesced around Kate. He ran the disaster film over and over, but had no luck with the editing. The ending was always the same. *How could he keep screwing things up? What in hell was wrong with him? And what were the options now? Play the sympathy card? Call and say he went crazy? That he was crazy? Well, wasn't he? But not exactly the most desirable image. Besides, it would all come out the same way, wouldn't it? She's still hurt. She still finds out he wasn't what she thought. 'You're a nice guy, Noah. Call me after you finish your treatment, maybe in ten years or so.'*

Locating the old gray Dodge, he slid into the driver's seat, turned the key, and fired up the aging power plant. The inner wrangle continued on the way to the East Bay. *So, what now? Just leave it? Let her move on? The only upright thing to do, but lose her completely?* He fiddled with the radio, trying for any distraction. Within minutes, the obsessing continued. *What in hell was all this about? He'd never had any trouble relating to women. But here was the only one he ever really cared about, and he comes up a fricking emotional cripple. Totally out of control…*

By the time he pulled up in front of the Children's Zoo and parked, it was 4:20, and Buzz was already there, grinning and waving down by the front gate.

"Hey, Blue," he called. Then, when they got closer: "Man, you look a tad under the weather."

"I been worse. So, what's up?"

"Let's walk," Buzz said.

They started down the asphalt running path that surrounded Lake Merritt. Passing joggers were beginning to seek early atonement for the weekend's evil deeds.

"Coroner's already done the insect studies for us. We may want to confirm them, but for now, those guys are way out in front. The preliminary report isn't as accurate as they'll get ultimately, but it places Van Zandt's death two days before Pablo says he broke into the condo. Better yet, the lung studies show the cause of death wasn't gunshot wounds to the head at all, but asphyxiation by strangling, and the flies establish that he didn't go into the soup immediately after death. The body was exposed to the air, at least for a short time. Conclusion? Someone strangled him, then drove him to the treatment plant, put a couple of slugs in his head, and dumped him, all about two days before Pablo says he went into the condo."

"Wow. That's all good, isn't it?"

"Wait. Now the bad news. The bullets were from a forty-five, and the police investigation said that Van Zandt's missing gun was thought to be a forty-five. Still, without it, no positive ID of whether it was the murder weapon."

"Taken together, I'm not sure if it all helps or hurts," Noah said. "I mean, as long as it was a shooting, we had some doubt from the fact that nobody heard anything at the condo. Now, I don't know."

"Neither will a jury," Buzz said. "The whole thing has a strange flavor. By itself, I grant you the strangling seems to fit the scenario of Van Zandt surprising Pablo in his condo with a burglary going down. But you know this guy. Would he have the wherewithal to put some slugs in the DB, drive it to the treatment plant, and dump it, alone? And police interviews confirm no unusual goings-on at Van Zandt's building that night. Like you say, no shots heard. How does Pablo get the body out by himself, without being seen? And how would he get access to the plant? All possible, but this starts to look like one hell of a stretch to me."

Noah eyed him, thinking about Sandy's comments, the propensity to whitewash, the initial blasé reaction when he told him about the case. As if all these prints and other evidence didn't point to murder or anything.

"I don't know, Buzz. We gotta keep an open mind on this thing. It's only Pablo's word about when he was in the condo. Nobody's turned up who'll alibi him around the time the coroner says Van Zandt died. He's bright enough to say he was in the condo two days after the death if he had killed him. And if he did it, he'd know what date it happened. There's no way we can put a time on when he was there. Nobody saw him. No witnesses. It isn't any kind of a real alibi."

"Yeah, well, I ran the date of death by Pablo, and he said he couldn't remember where he was the night Van Zandt died, but he thought he was home."

"Any witnesses to that?"

"Not that he recalled. But we ought to be able to find someone."

"What about his mother?"

"When I asked about her, he said maybe he wasn't home after all."

"Yeah. That's his M.O. It's always soft the instant we try to get something we can verify, particularly where his mother's involved."

"Wait, wait, Blue. Maybe it's drugs. Maybe he was swacked and really can't remember. We shouldn't automatically put the worst spin on this. We'll find someone to place him that night."

Noah stopped and turned to him. "Jeezus, Buzz. Let's don't make it into something it's not. Bottom line? No alibi." His tone was severe, expression to match.

Still reaching for the best reading possible, Buzz said, "We don't know that yet. We still might turn up an alibi witness. You want me to talk to his mother?"

Noah resumed walking. "No, I'll handle that. You get out to the sewage plant like we discussed."

"Won't be much out there. OPD's been over that territory pretty carefully... and it didn't turn up anything incriminating, by the way."

Nothing incriminating? Yeah, well, nothing exculpating, either. Noah couldn't stand any more. This would be awkward, but it had to happen at some point. He stepped in front of Buzz so they were face to face.

"You know what? I gotta clear the air here. I've heard some shit about you over the weekend that worries me. I need a few paragraphs about Oakland PD, booze, this story about seeing metaphysical defenses where they don't exist. I mean, I like your style, Buzz, but I've got concerns. If we're goin' down the road of life together, I need some reassurance."

Their stares were fixed and locked; then Buzz said, "Look, if you don't want me on the case, there's always other guys. Parker's available."

"I didn't say that. All I said is I gotta have some reassurance. Talk to me."

Buzz's stare continued, like he was about to tell him to go to hell. Finally, he took a deep breath and blew it out, looked down at his shoes, and gazed off down the lake, nodding slowly and pressing his lips together, staggering under the burden of dealing with it... again. For what, the hundredth time? He looked back at Noah, the dark Armenian eyes resigned, head shaking. Then, sighing again, he nodded.

"Okay," he said. "Here's how it goes." He sucked it up, started slowly down the running path, and began at the beginning.

"I always wanted to be a pilot, since before high school. That's where the 'Buzz' comes from. So, after I graduate from Cincinnati in Law Enforcement in '86, I enlist for Army helo flight training, but I'm washed out because of my vision. I'm god-awful nearsighted." He tapped the thick glasses. "They sent me for mechanic school, and I serviced the helos for as long as I could take it, maybe five years, then I'm reassigned to M.P. school at Fort Leonard Wood, because of my college degree. When my specialty training was finished, I was deployed back to Fort Stewart, Savannah, where I worked a few years, then out here to Fort Ord, and up to Fort Lewis in Washington. I'm breakin' up bar fights, runnin' down PX thieves, but after that they ship me out to Baghdad."

"When was that?"

"In '03, shortly after the invasion. Anyway, my job is to track down AWOLS. Doesn't sound so bad at first. In fact, I'd done it over here before I left, but it turns out that ninety percent of these combat runners are scared kids, seventeen, eighteen, nineteen years old, who've seen unspeakable horrors, buddies blown up by IEDs, fire fights, things that no kid should ever have to see." He winced, shaking his head.

"My job is to return them to duty. Problem is, I get to know them while I've got them in custody, taking them back to their unit. Sometimes we're together for a few days. They spill their guts. Sometimes I have a partner, sometimes not, but I try to listen, calm them down. Course, once I get them back to their unit, my job's done. I don't see 'em again. At first I don't think much about it, but later I find out that the Army's not as sympathetic as I am. I find out that on return, they're sent into forward positions, given high-risk assignments to make examples of them: 'Here's what happens when you rabbit.'"

Buzz stopped, looked over at Noah, searching his face for some sign of compassion. "Just teenagers, Blue." He nodded to a bench at the side of the path as a couple of runners jogged by, and they sauntered over and sat. Buzz cleared his throat and continued.

"Anyway, in checking around, I hear that most of my charges don't end up making it, and the ones that do…" He paused. "It was awful." His voice was unsteady and hoarse. "But I hang in, knowing that if some of the assholes I work with take over my job, these kids don't have anything. I hate it, but I tell myself I'll get used to it if I gut it out. Well, I don't get used to it. I start drinking heavily. I get pretty low, figuring it's weakness that I can't seem to come to grips with the goddamn job. Like an idiot, I re-up for a second tour to prove to myself I can bust through it." He shook his head.

"Then, toward the end of my second tour, I guess I kind of went bug-fuck. They found me walking naked in a high-density neighborhood outside the Green Zone. I have no memory of it, but they tell me I couldn't seem to get in touch with who I was or what I was doing there. Talking gibberish. 'Confabulation,' they call it. They shipped me back to Walter Reed for five months, then I got my separation. The regimental staff took pity on me and ended up giving me a medical discharge rather than a dishonorable." He scoffed. "Man, those were five fuuucked-up months. Couldn't think, couldn't concentrate. Couldn't eat. Couldn't sleep worth a shit. They gave me every drug they could think of. All pretty bleak." He exhaled through flapping lips, shaking his head. "Never actually tried to do myself in, but I thought about it enough times."

"Jeezus, Buzz."

"When they let me out, I went home to my mother's place for a few months. She was divorced, living in Detroit on unemployment. She didn't have anything. I couldn't find a job. That's when I got pretty deep into the sauce. Got busted a few times. Ma always ran bail for me, but I was draggin' her down lower than she already was. I had to get outta there. Went to Cleveland and worked security guard mostly, special officer duty at football games. That kind of thing. I was pretty heavily medicated. Only problem was my drug of choice was vodka and grapefruit. No-shows and showin' up loaded lost me more jobs than I got."

"Did you try to get some help?"

"Sure. VA was there. And it did help. I stopped drinking a bunch of times. Every once in a while, things would really get to me, couldn't get out of bed. Then they started me on the SSRIs, Prozac, Zoloft. Total wonder drugs. Changed my life. Gave me back my ability to function, pretty much."

"So that's when you went to OPD?"

"Yeah. I was out here looking for an old buddy from the M.P. unit, trying to find work. Never found the guy, but I saw an ad in the *Tribune* that OPD was hiring, and I put in an application. They liked my undergrad degree, and my military creds. I did reasonably well on the exam, so they hired me, apparently without making many calls. They put me on the street, then black-and-whites, but I always was a wannabe detective. I guess I bungled a few busts, misplaced some evidence, particularly when young kids were involved. I don't know. I didn't mean to, really. I just couldn't seem to get it together." He paused, reflecting.

"So they wrote me up for compromising a crime scene, and mislabeling some evidence bags. OPOA went to bat for me."

"OPOA?"

"Oakland Police Officers Association. You know, the union. They said that to save my job, they had to claim I had a disability. It worked, but the department said I had to get into therapy." Another long beat.

"And?"

"And so I went along with it, but at some point I left a medical claim form for my shrink in the copy machine by mistake. Some asshole found it and circulated it around the department. The one-liners started to fly. Big joke. Three partners dumped me in something under a year, and the department ended up reinstating the disciplinary proceeding, and they let me go.

"The next two years, I went from one job to another, mostly security again. The SSRIs chased off the demons, but the trouble was I went back to the vodka, and those two don't go too well together. Finally, I saw another ad and screwed up the guts to fill out an application for investigator with the PD. Donovan Pulansky, one of the world's great guys, was the head public defender then. He interviewed me. They had a lot of reasons to shit-can my application, but he took a chance on me."

"Pulansky. What happened to him? Where is he now?"

"Department Twenty-seven of the Superior Court, County of Alameda."

"He's a judge?"

"He is. Damn good one, too. No-nonsense guy."

"So now we get down to it. How've you done since you've been here?"

"I'll give you that there were a handful of cases early on, when I was still on the ropes, that I troweled it on a little thick. Some of my evidence didn't pan out at trial. But Pulansky laid down the law. Told me this was a job that required total honesty, reporting the long suits—and the short suits. I think I've turned it around, but you know, once you get a rep, you just end up wearing that shit.

"I've heard the stories," he continued. "I'm nuts, neurotic. I stack facts. They can't believe me when I report the positive stuff about defendants." He looked up. "It's bullshit, Blue. A lotta lawyers in this fucking office are doomsayers. I'm not. That's all. They're burned-out assholes who just wanna put in their nine to five, and plead everything that moves until retirement time. I guess there've been times I've said we kick ass and take names when the lawyers wanted to fold. That, coupled with my history, has earned me the wonderful legend you heard."

"So…" Noah cast a sideways glance. "What about the hooch?"

"Got my five-year chip last February. Four meetings a week. I'm not gonna tell you that a single day goes by that a vodka and grapefruit doesn't loom pretty large around nightfall. I think once you been on the sauce, it's just that way, is all."

"You know, I gotta say, it seemed to me you were a little overly optimistic about our chances on this *Ruiz* thing."

"I don't say I don't get enthusiastic about my cases now and again. But shit, Blue. Wouldn't you rather have that than some hack who gives you all the reasons to pitch it in every time? Hell, if you just wanna plead 'em, have at it. You don't need me."

Noah took a beat, considering, then nodded tentatively. "Sounds right." Mentally, he was still rolling his eyes a little. *Right. First case a dead-bang murder, a mountain of miserable facts, a client who says they got the wrong guy, a boss banging on him to plead, and here he was, out arm in arm with some moon man who says it's all under control. Perfect. But still, there was definitely something solid about the guy...*

"Okay," Noah said. "Get out to the sewage plant in the morning. I'm in court tomorrow to set the prelim, but I'll get with Amparo Ruiz as soon as I can. We touch base tomorrow afternoon."

Buzz looked away, hiding a faint smile. "Roger that, Blue."

• • •

Noah guided the Captain up Harrison from the Lake, toward the 580 Freeway and the Bridge beyond, his mind still ruminating on the exchange with Buzz. *Any facts were good, weren't they? All those ashes were important. But how would he know if the guy was ginning things up again? Maybe just take a quick look at that Coroner's Report, then go on home. Make sure? But Christ, if he had to check out everything the guy said, what good was he? Maybe just this once, see if the report really is as advertised, if it justifies some trust. Couldn't hurt.*

He hung a U and pointed the Captain back downtown. The sun was low in the sky, casting the usual pinkish glow through the late-hanging smog. The sunset brought back the nightmare of the night before once again, and he wondered where Kate was, whether she was thinking about what had happened, too; whether she would ever be able to stand him again.

He headed down Broadway, turned right on 6th, pulled into the parking structure, and chose a space on the first floor of the nearly empty building. On arrival at the Broussard Center, he flashed his ID card, and a slightly surprised security guard opened the front door.

"Working Sunday night?" he said.

"Can't stay away from this place," Noah responded.

Unlike the downtown firms, where associates burned the oil twenty-four hours a day, the PD's office was pretty much always deserted late Sundays.

Proceeding directly to the mailroom, he sorted through the incoming faxes and found the Coroner's Report near the top. He fed a dollar into the soda machine, extracted a Coke, grabbed a handful of packaged crackers from a bowl next to the microwave, and took the report to his cubicle, where he sat down and began to thumb through it.

First was the Autopsy Protocol, a grisly stroll through Van Zandt's earthly remains, organ by organ. It was largely medical jargon, but Noah understood enough to be a little queasy after his recent bacchanal. He pushed the crackers aside.

All seemed to be like he said. That was encouraging. Insect studies, gunshot wounds. Resulting cerebral and pontine damage, but little blood loss. Circumferential cervical hematoma. The hell did that mean? Cause of death listed as asphyxiation. Okay. Like he said, it actually didn't sound like anything Pablo could pull off, shooting the body several times after strangling him. Trying to make it look like an execution. Even if he was clever enough to think of it, which he probably wasn't.

He went to the conference room and picked up a copy of *Dorland's Medical Dictionary*, then returned to his desk to translate. Scribbling the English meaning above each medical term, he plodded through the report, page by page. When he was almost through the first section, having finished the Coke and rethought the crackers, he checked his watch. *Jesus. He'd been at it an hour. Might as well borrow the dictionary and finish up at home.* Snapping off the lights, he headed downstairs, out the front door, and down 6th.

His footsteps echoed off the concrete walls of the darkened parking structure as he made his way to the space where he'd parked the Captain. On reaching the big gray sedan, he opened the door, pitched his file and dictionary inside, and was about to slide in after them when he realized he'd left the other half of the report with the deputy coroner's investigation notes in the copy machine. Only the autopsy portion was in his file. He glanced at his watch, then headed back to the office at a jog, mumbled an excuse to the guard, and went up to retrieve the missing pages.

On returning to the garage, he plodded up the stairs again. Arriving at the second level, he heard a car door slam. As he rounded the bulkhead, a glare of headlights illuminated him in the frame of the stairwell, and he froze. Squinting into the light, he could make out an OPD black-and-white stopped behind his car. The old Dodge's trunk was open, and a silhouetted figure was leaning in, turning over the contents.

"Well, if it isn't the baby PD hero," a low voice growled.

Noah had no idea what was going on, but he knew the voice immediately. "Officer Fitzgerald," he acknowledged, stepping out of the beam of the headlights. "Some reason why you're searching my car?"

The cop with his head in the trunk stood, looked in Noah's direction, slammed the lid shut, and walked over to the passenger side of the cruiser. Fitzgerald, on the driver's side, was directing his flashlight into Noah's face.

"This piece of shit your ride, hero?" Fitzgerald said.

"What are you doing in my car?" Noah repeated, shielding his eyes.

"What're you doing in the building on a Sunday night?"

"Do you have a warrant or any probable cause to be searching my vehicle?"

Fitzgerald ignored it. "Any criminal activity going on here?"

"That seems to be the problem with you, Officer Fitzgerald," Noah shot back. "Your only tool seems to be a hammer, so you see criminal nails everywhere. But you can't just be sorting through cars looking for those nails."

Fitzgerald chuckled, his light focused on Noah's eyes. "And you still got that smart mouth, don't you. Wonder what makes you think you got all the answers right outta the box." He took a step closer. "You gotta earn your spurs in this rodeo, son. You didn't know that?"

It was out before he could censor it: "And I guess you musta earned yours riding teenage calves?"

Fitzgerald again moved forward, now definitely in Noah's personal space, the searing shaft of light blinding him. Noah held up a hand in front of his eyes.

"Mind shining that somewhere else?"

Fitzgerald instantly slapped the hand away and barked, "I asked you a question, Shane. What were you doin' in the building this time of night?"

Still struggling with the light, Noah said, "Well, I actually work here. I was cleaning up a few loose ends from last week." Then he added, "I might ask you the same question."

Eyebrows menacing, Fitzgerald took a long beat, then snarled, "Awright, lemme see some ID."

Noah turned his head quizzically. "You know who I am."

"ID!"

Noah reached into his back pocket, produced his ID card, and handed it to him. Fitzgerald examined the card under the light, then handed it back. "You got some proof about these 'loose ends' you were tending to?"

"Proof?"

"Yeah. You got any proof you were working in the building rather than engaging in some kinda illicit activity?"

Noah couldn't believe it. "Proof I was working?"

"You heard me."

What the hell was this? "Well, I've got the Coroner's Report in a case of mine."

"Get it."

Noah handed him the pages of the report. Fitzgerald looked them over.

"I thought you said you had a Coroner's Report. This isn't a Coroner's Report."

"Actually, it is. It's a few pages I left in the office that I went back for."

"You're makin' this up. What were you doing in that office?"

"This is ridiculous," Noah said. "Wait a minute and I'll show you the rest of it."

He turned to open the front door of the car but, as he grasped the handle, Fitzgerald shouted: "Stop him, Zach... he's trying to get away!"

A boot came up violently between Noah's legs from behind, and the breath exploded from his lungs. His knees buckled inward, pitching him forward. His face slammed against the side of the car, and he slid down the door to the ground. As he rolled onto his right side, both hands went to his groin, the nausea and pain coursing up through his lower abdomen, and he tucked into a fetal position.

Fitzgerald stood over him. "See, you need to learn to do as you're told." The piercing light came down inches from Noah's face, spittle and foul breath radiating from right behind it. Noah closed one eye, recoiling. "You're gonna have to understand," Fitzgerald rumbled, "that around here you fit in." He paused, then, "You get to grandstanding, and the animals think they run the zoo." He straightened. "You get that?"

Noah didn't speak, didn't move.

"Am I makin' all this totally clear?"

Silence. Boiling rage. Blood oozing from a cut under his right eye. Noah had a fleeting image of the small boy who had received the same treatment earlier that week. The light beam bobbed and swam as both men backed slowly to the black-and-white, leather creaking. Doors slammed, and the patrol car lurched forward, squealed around the bulkhead to the 7th Street entrance, and bounced out into the street.

Groping painfully in his pocket, Noah extracted his cell phone and aimed it in the direction of the disappearing police cruiser, clicking a string of photos, but it was too late.

CHAPTER TWENTY-FOUR

MONDAY, SEPTEMBER 3RD, 8:30 AM:

"Christ, what happened to you?" Stark asked, grimacing.

"What happened to me was two Oakland cops," Noah snapped, the left side of his face black, blue, yellow, and green, rounded like a half-grapefruit over the cheekbone. "They apparently didn't appreciate me breaking up their sadistic attack on two little kids damn near in front of our office last week, so they gave me a taste of the same routine last night in the parking structure."

Stark leaned forward in his chair, frowning. "What do you mean?"

Noah related the story as Stark shook his head intermittently.

"Have you reported this to anyone?" he asked.

"Not yet, but I'm on my way to Oakland PD this morning after the hearing on *Ruiz*. I was wondering if you knew anyone in Internal Affairs, maybe give me a referral. I'd hate to report this to some grunt who might be sympathetic to those goons and bury it."

Stark's eyes dropped and his brow wrinkled. He inhaled and exhaled deeply. "Listen, Noah…" he said. "I know how you must feel about all this, but, you know? This is a little bigger problem than you might think. Let's just—"

"What do you mean?" Noah interrupted, staring incredulously. "You think these hoods are entitled to—"

"Wait." Stark raised a hand. "Hear me out. The real problem is that these guys think they're warriors, risking their necks out there on the street with little thanks and less pay. They see themselves as urban combat troops. After you've handled a few more cases, it'll dawn on you that most cops don't look at an arrest like you do, as a legal case where a defendant's got constitutional rights and all. They see it as a single skirmish in a bigger battle that's part of an endless war of good against evil. Us versus them. That leads them to think, '…if the bad guy didn't do it this time, so what? He would've done it next time.' They figure they know he's the enemy. They're gonna load up the evidence to put him away. And they're gonna intimidate him in the process, so everybody like him'll think twice about it. They don't see this as one bust, one case, innocent until proven guilty. It's an endless chain of skirmishes in a war, and you're not gonna convince them otherwise by raising hell about one single hassle."

"Single hassle? This was *me* they were kicking the shit out of."

"No, I mean those kids you told me about. You've seen that these guys resent anything they consider to be interference. They think it threatens their mission, and they think that threatens their lives."

Noah's eyes descended, his teeth grinding, jaw flexing, pulse red-lining. He shook his head slowly.

"I know, I know," Stark continued. "Don't get me wrong. I'm as incensed by this incident as you are…"

"Probably not."

"Okay, I get it. But we've gotta be careful how we handle this. It's complicated. The last thing we want is the appearance of some kind of turf war between PDs and cops."

"Are you saying we let these assholes get away with this?" Noah glared in disbelief. "No way. It'll just happen again. They'll try to intimidate me, all of us, whenever it suits them. We're supposed to let some army of vigilantes run the streets, beating and killing whoever they think are the bad guys? What the hell kind of a justice system is that?"

"I'm not suggesting that at all." He slowed it down, his tone indulgent. "There are protections, and, yes, the system is critical. When you think about it, it's that attitude by the cops that makes a living for us in court. There's lots we get thrown out, cross-examine on. That's why we've got an exclusionary rule. I've argued a million motions to suppress evidence that was obtained by cops running that kind of number. It makes them crazy that guilty defendants get cut loose where the rules weren't followed, but it's the only real leverage we have to prevent the strong-arm stuff."

"So doesn't the exclusion of all their bad evidence just make them think they're justified in ginning up facts, and in kicking the crap out of me in the bargain?"

"I have to admit that it often prompts them to pump up their testimony some. Look at Mark Fuhrman in the OJ case. But what I'm telling you is we have to deal with the evidentiary issues in court, not through some all-out war."

Noah fidgeted, exhaled heatedly, and murmured, "No way."

"Now," Stark went on, "I'm agreeing that what happened to you last night can't happen. I'm not saying we do nothing when they get physical like that. Something definitely has to be done. I'm simply asking you to let me handle it. I actually do know the deputy chief in charge of IA. I'll take this up with her in a discreet way. We'll make sure those guys are brought down." His look was sincere.

Noah was staring, still grinding.

"I agree with you," Stark repeated, "but we've gotta be careful." The smile was supposed to be reassuring. "I'll take care of it, okay?"

Sure. Fine with it. The jerk who was willing to get him killed in the courtroom was now gonna take care of his ass-kicking in the parking lot?

Seemingly telepathic, Stark changed the subject. "And by the way," he said, "did you get with Hoogasian on *Ruiz?*"

"Yeah, Friday... and again yesterday."

"You guys got a game plan?"

"He's out at the sewage plant this morning."

"All right. Keep me posted, okay?" His expression was benevolent. Noah was still seething. After a beat, he said, "So, you have their names and badge numbers?"

"I've got them."

"Good. Then leave this with me, Noah," he said, holding the understanding smile. "I'll take care of it. Trust me."

Suddenly aware of the throbbing in his half-shut eye, Noah slumped his shoulders. *Yeah, right. Trust him.*

• • •

"Okay, Arlen," the truck engineer barked through the ear angel, "three, two, one... rolling."

The hall outside Department 16 was thick with press and rubberneckers long before the doors opened. *People v. Ruiz* had become front-page news, and things were unusually tumultuous. Two local TV stations dominated corners of the hallway with hand-held sun guns, taping lead-in for their segments that would air on the evening news. The TV reporters wore the usual dark suit jackets, ties, and makeup, but were Saturday-afternoon casual from the waist down: Levis and Nikes. Arlen Gates of KXTV News held a microphone as he stood facing the camera while a crowd of onlookers gaped.

"We're outside Department Sixteen of the Alameda County Superior Court," Gates began, "where, in the next few minutes, Judge Seth McCormick will preside over another chapter in the prosecution of accused murderer, Pablo Ruiz, the alleged killer of prominent stockbroker, Warren Van Zandt. Ruiz has pleaded innocent, so the case will now be set for preliminary hearing, in which it will be the District Attorney's task to put on sufficient evidence to convince the court..." — he glanced down at some notes — "...that there is probable cause to believe a murder was committed, and that Mr. Ruiz committed it. If the magistrate is convinced, Ruiz will be bound over to the Superior Court, an information filed, and the case will proceed to trial. Of course, if the District Attorney fails to carry its burden, the defendant would be released, but we are informed that that is rare in these instances. The onus on the prosecution is not great at this stage, and it is expected that Ruiz will be held to answer.

"Our legal analyst anticipates that the preliminary hearing will be set within the next week. Mr. Van Zandt was a well-known member of the Oakland community, and his brutal murder has therefore attracted significant attention here in the East Bay. We look forward to further events and will be following the case closely for you. Arlen Gates, KXTV News."

The lights switched off, and the TV crew began to disband just as Marco Salem made his way through the crowd to the front door of Department Sixteen. KXTV's tripod-mounted camera immediately swung his way, and the taping resumed. Salem could have used the rear door in the chambers hall, but the presence of press out front afforded the opportunity for an informal press conference that a Senior Trial Deputy with political aspirations could never resist. Moreover, it didn't hurt to slosh a little early poison into the jury pool.

"Marco? Marco Salem?" a reporter chirped as the lawyer wended his way through the throng. "Marco, can you give us a minute?"

Reaching the front door of the courtroom, Salem paused and looked back with a smile that left little doubt of his intentions. "Good morning, ladies and gentlemen," he said.

One question rose above the rest. "Do you anticipate any difficulty with the preliminary hearing?"

"No, certainly not," Salem answered. "Of course, you realize that we're only here this morning to set the prelim. The actual hearing will proceed sometime in the next ten days. But in my view, there will be no problem getting this defendant held to answer. The evidence against him is substantial." DAs rarely used the defendant's name. It would unduly personalize him.

The barrage began again.

"Mr. Salem…?"

"Marco, how do you…?"

Salem had now turned fully to face them, working the group like an organized press conference.

"Yes… ah… Herman," Salem said, pointing to a tall man with a

trimmed mustache. Herman Stout was the *Oakland Tribune's* eyes and
ears in the courthouse.

"How strong is the evidence against Ruiz, and what is the defense's
case?"

"Well, as you know, it would be improper for me to comment on the
prosecution evidence at this juncture. We certainly wouldn't want to
do anything that would jeopardize our anticipated conviction. As to
the defense, I'm sure I don't know what that could be." Gracious smile.
"Perhaps you're better off asking defense counsel."

"Who is the defense attorney, Mr. Salem? What do you think of him?"
The voice belonged to Nancy Maxwell, *Contra Costa Times.*

"It's a young man from the Public Defender's office, Nancy. Ummm…
Name escapes me just now." He glanced at his watch. "You know, folks.
I'm going to have to break it off for the moment. I'm needed inside,
but I'd be glad to chat with you later on. Maybe we can discuss all this
further at the preliminary hearing. Thank you all."

He pulled the door open and disappeared into the courtroom just
as the judge was taking the bench, and the bailiff was barking for the
assembly to rise.

"Good morning, ladies and gentlemen." Judge McCormick was
scrubbed as usual, wearing a bow tie for the occasion. He was enjoying
the celebrity that was rare in the cattle-call calendar world he occupied
these days.

The response was the usual chorus, "Good morning, Your Honor."

"All right, Madam Clerk. Call the first case."

The clerk pulled a file off her stack as Salem strode down the center
aisle. Before she could announce the case, Salem once again grabbed
center stage.

"Your Honor," he called as he passed through the swinging gate.
McCormick looked up.

"Ah, good morning, Mr. Salem," he said, trying for some semblance
of surprise calculated to suggest that he hadn't fully expected him at
exactly that moment. All well-choreographed courtroom ballet.

"Good morning, Your Honor. I'm here on a setting matter in *People
v. Ruiz.* As I informed the court at the arraignment, I'm in trial in
Department Two and, though I hate to impose, I would request that
the *Ruiz* matter be called out of order again this morning."

"I think that can be arranged," McCormick acquiesced. "And would
you ask Judge Hoover to call me when you get back to Department
Two? I have some administrative matters to discuss with him."

"I will most definitely pass that along, Your Honor."

"Fine. We'll call *People v. Ruiz*. Is defense counsel present?"

"Noah Shane, Public Defender, for Mr. Ruiz, Your Honor." Rising from his seat in the jury box, Noah stepped forward to the counsel table. Though he had often worn the marks of battle with a degree of pride during his football career, this particular morning he was definitely feeling self-conscious about the large purple abrasion on his left cheek. "May Mr. Ruiz be present?"

"Certainly, Mr. Shane. Bailiff?"

The sheriff opened the door to the holding cell and called for Pablo, who emerged tentatively at first, then briskly, as he walked to the dock, neatly put together as usual.

"Good morning, Your Honor," he said.

The judge looked up, his gaze lingering ever-so-briefly on Pablo, who knew instinctively he had scored a point or two, however minimal. Every point counted.

"Good morning, Mr. Ruiz," McCormick responded; then, looking back down at the file, he continued, "All right, gentlemen. Let's see. The defendant has been arraigned and has pled not guilty. Motions for release and to set bail have been deferred. The defendant is in custody; time is not waived. Are we ready to set a date for preliminary hearing?"

"The People are ready, Your Honor."

"Yes, Your Honor," Noah answered.

"Very well, the matter will be set for Friday, September fourteenth, at ten-thirty AM in this department. The defendant will remain in custody. Is there anything else?"

"Yes, Your Honor," Noah spoke up. "Last week, you invited me to renew my bail motion today. I would like to do that now."

"Very well, Counsel." The judge looked down at Noah, frowning, his eyebrows furrowed. "However, I also recall telling you that your burden would be great in convincing the court that bail should be set. With that in mind, you may proceed."

Undaunted, Noah began the upstream swim. "Thank you, Your Honor. Pablo Ruiz is a local resident, born and raised in Oakland. He lives here with his mother. The family is poor, and Mr. Ruiz is looking for work to assist his mother, who is a housekeeper, with their expenses." He elected not to mention her cancer. They would find out soon enough.

"He has no criminal record. As Your Honor mentioned at our last meeting, the court has discretion to grant bail unless proof of guilt is evident. It is far from evident in this case. This is a purely circumstantial case in which the only allegation is that the defendant was present in the victim's condominium—"

"Ah... please spare me the details at this time, Mr. Shane," McCormick interrupted. "I trust we will get into all that at the prelim. We wouldn't want to spoil the suspense, would we?"

Noah regrouped. "Very well, Your Honor. We would ask that the court consider releasing Mr. Ruiz on his own recognizance." Even Noah knew there was no chance that McCormick would O.R. Pablo, but he thought if he went for the brass ring initially, McCormick might be disposed to cut the baby in half and give him a bail order that was within Amparo's reach. It was worth a shot.

"If the court is seriously considering bail," Salem interjected, "I would like to be heard on the matter, Your Honor."

"No need, Mr. Salem."

Hmmm. Not a good sign.

McCormick turned to Noah. "Your statement that Mr. Ruiz has no criminal record may be technically accurate, Mr. Shane, but I see that your client was in custody on another charge, an alleged burglary, when he was arrested on the current charge. There appears to be ample justification to retain him in custody. Your motion for bail will be denied." Before Noah could protest, McCormick had moved on. "All right, gentlemen. See you back here on the fourteenth. Next matter, Madam Clerk."

CHAPTER TWENTY-FIVE

"Quit lookin' at me like that, dammit!" Buzz snapped. A beat, then, "I know what you're thinkin'."

The 1976 silver Porsche 912e intermittently roared and braked down Broadway, stopping at signal after signal, gears grinding as it pointed toward a right turn on 7th, still eight blocks away. A one-lung radio blared C and W at a volume designed to drown out the lawnmower engine in the rear. Windows open to keep the air moving, the interior nonetheless reeked of a gas-rich exhaust mixture. The only passenger, a diminutive yellow rubber duck, swung from the rear-view mirror as the car weaved in and out of traffic. It was almost 3:05, and Buzz had promised to meet with Noah at the office at 3:00.

Caught at yet another light at 11th, Buzz drummed his fingers on the steering wheel impatiently, then cast a long, sideways look of displeasure at the swinging duck. The light changed, and the Porsche ground forward in a low first gear.

"Shuuuut uuup!" Buzz moaned as he reached up and flicked the duck with his index finger before shifting into second. The neoprene fowl swung wildly from its moorings.

A block farther down Broadway, the bird was still gyrating, its painted eyes vacant, as Buzz launched into a diatribe. "We are not gonna gin up any facts! He's not gonna plead this one anyway. No, dammit. We're doin' this one straight. No way that kid gets into the sewage plant. Fuckin' sealed up like Ft. Knox with a guard on duty twenty-four seven."

The Porsche powered through the yellow at 9th. "I know, I know," he said. "We could make him smell clean as a French whore, but I said we're gonna play it straight! How many times I gotta say that?"

He glanced back at the bathtub figurine, whose movements had slowed. It seemed to be staring back. "Okay," he said. "So maybe we could find some stray prints in the condo that match some petty thief junkie with a giant rap sheet. Maybe we could—"

Another beat as Buzz downshifted, then shook his head definitively. "The fuck am I saying? No way, Daff, goddammit." He hit the brakes and banked into the turn onto 7th.

"And no," he said adamantly. "We are not gonna have a drink!" The steering wheel spun as the Porsche completed its right and accelerated up 7th toward the Broussard Building. "What we are gonna do is call our sponsor... right after this meeting." Buzz batted the bird again, sending it swinging.

• • •

Less than a mile away, the Oakland PD black cruiser eased down the Jackson Street offramp from southbound 880, turned right, then right again onto 3rd, backtracked to Adeline, and swung through the large entry gate into the Port of Oakland. Nearing the Matson Terminal, it turned left into a vast parking area densely populated with bob-tailed semis, and proceeded into a staging sector that was piled high with seagoing containers and cordoned off on three sides by chain link. An AMPPS beige-and-white patrol vehicle with a single occupant waited, engine running, next to the fence. The OPD car pulled up next to it and stopped side to side, headed in the opposite direction. Fitzgerald rolled down his window and greeted the AMPPS sergeant.

"So," Harrison said. He exhaled a lungful of diluted smoke into the light breeze and flicked the nub of his cigarette onto the pavement. "Do any good?"

"Nah. Nothin' there but the arrest and coroner's reports, and the investigation we already have."

"Shit," Harrison groaned. "Thought sure we'd pull something. We gotta stay ahead of these clowns if we're gonna make this thing go down right."

Harrison had known immediately that Ferguson was the man for this job when he saw his email posted on the interdepartmental police listserv. He had been carping about a run-in with a new PD, name of Shane, who needed his wings clipped, and he was giving his fellow officers a heads-up. Local cops shared thoughts, impressions, tips, even ads for sale of professional equipment, on the widely circulated electronic information distribution app.

For his part, Fitzgerald really couldn't care less about the intrigue of the *Ruiz* case. His beef was with Shane, who was rapidly becoming a major burr under his saddle, and he promptly agreed to the off-the-record assignment when Harrison pitched it.

"What about you guys?" Fitzgerald asked.

"Not much better. I guess I told you that we went through that dip-shit investigator's old Porsche on Saturday. Picked up a copy of the full arrest report. That might be something."

"So? We already have that, too."

"Not this one."

"What do you mean?"

"This copy's got a fax header from the DA's office on it."

"Meaning?"

"Meaning how does an investigator for the PD get official documents from the DA's office?"

"What are you saying?" Fitzgerald still didn't get it.

"Either he makes an unauthorized visit, or he's got a mole over there."

"Wait, wait," Fitzgerald said. "Nothing particularly secret about a police report."

"Well, maybe not. But it's interesting that this fax is dated September 7th. It had to be sent to Hoogasian before the reports were even over to the Court."

"And that means what?"

"Like I say. No way he has access at that time except under the table."

"And that means what?" Fitzgerald repeated, getting exasperated.

"Well, maybe nothing. But like I say, Hoogasian's a bleeding heart with a record as long as your arm of cutting corners, pumping up evidence. Begins to look like that might be what's going down here. Now, whether this Shane kid is in on it, I don't know, but it looks like Hoogasian's flying under the radar, and that apparently includes some kind of pipeline to the DA."

"So what are you going to do with that stuff?"

"Brass says do nothing with it for the moment, but it'll probably come in handy at some point. Meanwhile, our orders are to neutralize Hoogasian before that kind of bullshit compromises the case."

"I wouldn't put it past Shane to take things way beyond kosher to make this 187 come out the way he wants it," Fitzgerald said. "What's 'neutralize him' mean, exactly?"

"For now, I guess it means we keep an eye on him, see what kind of evidence these guys are putting together, whether it's legal, what they're up to. But the brass is definitely concerned about Hoogasian, and they want us to level the playing field if there's anything dicey goin' down."

"I don't know, man," Fitzgerald said. "There'd be hell to pay if any of this went public. We got sideways with Shane last night and had to get a little physical, so I'm a feeling a tad sketchy already. All I need is an IA investigation."

"Physical? What happened?"

"Nothin' much. He came back to the parking lot when we were

checkin' out his car, and he got a little mouthy. Had to show him a bit of the stick."

"Did he see what you were doing?"

"No doubt, but we told him we were checking for criminal activity. I think he bought it. We didn't find anything anyway. He doesn't seem to have much street smarts."

"Whatever. But don't worry about getting the wrong end of this assignment."

"It's just that I got twenty-one years in, and I don't want my retirement, pension and all, goin' down the dumper."

"Yeah, well, these orders are coming from some high-level, heavy hitters. Trust me, nothing's gonna come back on you guys. And besides, the anytime-hour overtime you're gettin' has got to make it worth it."

Fitzgerald had no idea who the 'heavy hitters' might be, and he didn't want to know. The extra cash was meaningful, but so was giving that arrogant Jewboy some humility. The PD was lousy with them, and someone had to take a stand at some point. "So what's the duty look like for Zachary and me?"

"Nothing right now, I guess. Just stand by for further orders."

"We can do that." Fitzgerald put the cruiser in gear. "Later," he said as he rolled up the window and slowly accelerated back toward West Oakland.

• • •

Noah was heavy into the material by 3:30 when Buzz, can of Pepsi in hand, found him in the conference room at Oakland Division. He was seated at the far end of the long metal table, surrounded by stacks of transcripts of prior preliminary hearings, trial practice texts, file materials, and a couple of yellow legal tablets. Buzz swung the door closed behind him.

"You rang?" he affected with a deep Lurch growl, then took a hit of Pepsi and swirled it around in his mouth like Listerine.

"Yeah," Noah said, not looking up, but Buzz immediately noticed the battle scars.

"Christ. What happened to you, Blue?"

Noah recounted the events of the night before, yet again.

"Fitzgerald? Yeah, I know him. Fat, arrogant fuck with more than twenty years in. Pissed off he never made detective."

"Figures," Noah said.

"Sounds like more than a chance encounter in the garage, though. What do you think's going on?"

"I don't know, but Stark promised to 'look into it.' Pretty reassuring, wouldn't you say?"

"Probably best to stay off the guy's radar. Fitzgerald's a snake. I don't know what could be eating him with you, but it's probably not gonna get any better. You think it's just your butting into that bust of the kids?"

"Unclear, but right now my priority is *Ruiz*. McCormick set the prelim for Friday."

"Okay."

"I been over all these other transcripts, but it doesn't feel together yet."

"What transcripts?"

"Bobbi gave me a bunch of old prelim transcripts. I been goin' through 'em."

"Suit yourself," Buzz offered. "But there's really not a lot to a prelim. You been over to see one?"

"Not yet. I was gonna do that next."

"That'd probably do you more good than wading through a lot of testimony." Buzz pulled up a gray-metal chair, set the Pepsi can down, and tipped back, hands behind his head. "Look," he said. "I don't wanna tell you your business, but you don't actually have to prep for a prelim, Blue. It's really just a charade. Especially in cases like Pablo's. No way you'd ever walk him out. Only thing it gives you is a chance to get a snapshot of the prosecution case, that is, if you're good."

"What do you mean, 'if I'm good'?"

"Well, you know. Since defendants never get sprung at this stage, judges and DAs only worry about prelims from the standpoint of a 995 motion to dismiss, or an appeal, you know, reversible error."

"Remind me about a 995 motion?"

"Yeah, it's a motion to dismiss when the defendant's been bound over on a felony after prelim, usually on the ground there was no probable cause for a holding order."

"Oh, right."

"And if the case went to 995 to test probable cause, or up on appeal after a conviction, and the court in one or the other was looking for a way to cut the defendant loose, it might come up as to whether the procedure was all bulletproof, whether there was enough evidence put in at the prelim to get probable cause."

Noah gazed at him briefly, then shook his head, exasperated. "Non-responsive, Buzz. What did you mean, 'If I'm good'?"

"I'm gettin' to that." Buzz picked up the Pepsi can, swigged, swirled, and swallowed. "I was trying to say that their only motivation is to put on enough probable cause to withstand a later review, so if you cast a little doubt, they come forward with a little more evidence, and if you press 'em a little more, maybe they show you little more than that, and pretty soon, you got at least a snapshot of what they got, where they're goin'. That's really the best you can do. *Comprende?*"

"Sooo...?"

"So, figure out a few probing questions and see if you can draw Salem out a smidge. That's all. You don't put on any evidence yourself. You don't call any witnesses. Nobody ever wins a real murder case at a prelim. You're there to listen. The only point of your cross is to ask enough questions to get a little more to listen to."

Buzz belched mindlessly and wiped his mouth with a shirtsleeve that had been white in the distant past. "And maybe you also get your feet a little damp in preparation for trial?" The aroma of second-hand Pepsi and something fried wafted toward Noah, who made a face, shook his head, and blew out sharply. Buzz was oblivious.

"You think they'll give us anything?" Noah asked him.

"Not much. Salem's cocky for sure, but he's been around a while. He won't tip a lot. I'm just sayin', the game plan is get as much as you can and get out. But there's no big prep for it. You just play it by ear."

"How many of these things have you seen, Buzz?"

"In seventeen years? More than a handful."

"Okay. So did you get out to the sewage plant?"

"Twice. Once mid-morning. Once at one-thirty AM."

"And?"

"And the place is guarded like an Israeli ammo dump. There's a locked front gate with a guy in the kiosk, night and day. No way our boy gets past that army without some big-time clearance, even if he wasn't draggin' a body behind him."

"That's good stuff. How about witnesses? Anything there?"

"Nah. Like I told you. Pablo doesn't give us anyone he was with the night they say Van Zandt died. Maybe you get something from his mother. Have you talked to her yet?"

"Not yet, but I will. Probably not 'til after the prelim. We'll know more by then."

CHAPTER TWENTY-SIX

"Were you able to identify the body as that of the decedent, doctor?"

Marco Salem stood in the well of Department 16, head cocked to one side, trying to appear interested.

"Yes, I was."

It wasn't routine for Dr. Nathan Farnsworth, himself, Medical Examiner of Alameda County, to testify at a prelim. At his age, he was only working about half time, but he needed the money that half time provided him and his aging wife. So, though he usually had little left in the tank for these minor shows of force for the press, when Salem insisted, he succumbed. He was the People's first witness.

A gaunt man with a sallow complexion and thin, spidery white hair, the doctor's eyes appeared large behind the thick glasses he had worn since his cataract surgery. Into his late seventies, he was nearly as cadaverous as his patients.

Department 16 was jammed with spectators for the 10:30 prelim calendar, and Salem was reaching deep to make an otherwise uneventful proceeding newsworthy.

"How did you go about that?"

"Identity of the body was established through fingerprint evidence and dental records as that of Warren Van Zandt." Farnsworth had been there a thousand times and could do his taxes while testifying in these things.

"Was an autopsy performed?"

"It was."

Salem handed the Post Mortem Protocol to the clerk. "Ask that this document be marked for identification as People's next in order, Madam Clerk?"

"Let's see," the clerk said loudly. "People's one is the doctor's curriculum vitae, two (a) through (n) are the autopsy photographs. That would make this... People's three." Everyone had her little moment in the sun. She stamped the document and wrote in the exhibit number, gave it back to Salem, and he returned to the witness.

"I show you what is marked People's three for identification, doctor, and ask if you recognize it."

"Yes, this is our Protocol for the autopsy of the decedent, Warren Van Zandt."

"Is this your signature on page four of the report?"

"Yes, that's my signature."

"Did you perform the autopsy?" Salem knew he hadn't, but was cutting off all lines of defense inquiry before they materialized.

"The autopsy was performed by Dr. Martin Cheung, a Deputy Medical Examiner in my office. I reviewed and approved its content."

"Is that routine, Doctor?"

"It's the typical way we do things, Mr. Salem."

"Ask that People's Three be admitted into evidence, Your Honor?"

McCormick glanced at Noah. "Any objection?"

Noah looked at Buzz, who shook his head almost imperceptibly. "No, Your Honor," he said.

"The Autopsy Protocol will be admitted," McCormick intoned.

"Now, moving ahead to the bottom line..." Salem went on.

McCormick silently thanked God that someone was interested in the bottom line.

"...did you establish a cause of death with reasonable medical probability?"

"I did."

"And would you be kind enough to tell the court your opinion in that regard?"

"Yes. It was my opinion that the decedent died of asphyxiation due to strangulation at approximately two o'clock in the early morning of Sunday, August twenty-sixth."

"On what have you based that opinion, doctor?"

"It was a bit more complicated in this case than in most..."

Salem never liked his experts to talk about how difficult or complicated their tasks were. It just put a bookmark in the testimony for the defense cross-examiner to come back and attempt to pry open their conclusions, establish that the "difficulty" was reason for doubt. God knew, any little particle of doubt would be blown into nuclear proportions. But the years of feeling these little thorns jabbing at his flesh had deadened Salem's sensitivity and numbed his reactions. His face remained impassive as he appeared to be listening intently.

"...because Mr. Van Zandt's body had been agitated for a number of hours in a vat of sewage, which was continuously mixed by immense circulating blades. The usual indices of temperature and gravity—lividity and the like—were therefore called into question. Accordingly, we proceeded to biological evidence."

"Biological evidence?"

"There are several species of flies that infest human remains very shortly after death. These blowflies and flesh flies lay their eggs in body orifices. By microscopically inspecting the eggs, larvae, and various developmental stages of the insects, we can establish the post-mortem interval, because their rate of growth and development is remarkably regular and predictable for a given environment. All this has been well documented by scientific investigation. We can therefore extrapolate back to the time of death with a high degree of accuracy."

"That's extraordinary, Dr. Farnsworth." Salem had heard it many times, but tried to appear amazed by the doctor's scholastic acumen and cleverness, pumping him up as a master of the "complications" he had mentioned. The judge had heard it more times than Salem. This was clearly not to persuade him at a prelim, but rather, it was a near-trial performance, all for the media and its market.

"And please tell us the name of these exceedingly intelligent insects."

"The major biological families would be *Sarcophagidae* and *Calliphoridae*."

"Now, do you personally perform the measurements and calculations to arrive at the time of death?"

"The measurements and calculations are outsourced to forensic entomologists, but I am schooled in the science, so we collaborate on the conclusions." This was his report, and as long as his participation could be documented, the opinions and conclusions could be attributed to him. Again, Salem was closing a potential door before it could be opened.

"Would you inform His Honor as to what those measurements and calculations were in this instance?"

"If I could see the Biological Laboratory Report, Mr. Salem, I would be happy to go over the forensic entomological evidence with the court."

Salem extracted the document from his file and handed it to the clerk. "People's next in order?" he said.

Perhaps the only person in the courtroom paying close attention to this dance was Noah. Locked on every word, he was writing furiously. Beside him at the counsel table, Pablo sat in his orange jumpsuit looking down at his hands, detached from the proceedings. To Noah's left, Buzz doodled with a pencil on a yellow pad, sketching bugs with razor-like teeth and huge eyes behind giant glasses. Their antennae resembled the wispy hair of the witness. Under them was scrawled '*Attack of the Calliphora vomitoria*'.

Salem went on to establish that the victim's asphyxiation was caused by strangulation, with the doctor pointing to marks on both sides of the decedent's neck that were clearly visible in the autopsy photographs. The pictures were pretty grisly, the body having languished in sewage for a couple of days. Any cleaning might have disrupted the evidence — and made the body less likely to inflame a jury in the bargain. Definitely to be avoided.

Salem confined Farnsworth's testimony to the actual findings at autopsy, and conclusions drawn from them, and from studies conducted by his office, leaving the circumstances of the discovery of the body for other witnesses. Having obtained what he needed from the Medical Examiner, he asked that the most recent exhibit be moved into evidence, then abruptly terminated the direct and walked back to his position at the counsel table.

"Your witness, Counsel."

Even though he had been completely focused on the proceedings in front of him, when the moment came, Noah was startled. He stood tentatively, rooted in place, to examine his first witness in an actual courtroom. Behind him, fifty butts fidgeted; a hundred feet shuffled.

"So, Dr. Farnsworth," Noah began, trying to pitch himself into the flow. "There was an autopsy performed on the decedent?" Pause.

A wildly auspicious beginning. The savvy doctor tilted his head to the side and frowned, looking for all the world like he was groping for some deeper significance hidden in the opening question. With the experience that had come from sparring with defense attorneys for forty-five years, he played the moment, delaying his response, allowing the inanity of the question to hover and sink in.

"An autopsy, yes," he answered at length. "I think that is what I have said."

Noah hesitated, gathering his thoughts. More shuffling of feet. Although he had tried to map out the course he would take as he listened to the direct, it now came slowly.

"Well, it is a fact, isn't it, doctor, that Mr. Van Zandt had been shot with a forty-five caliber weapon four times in the head and upper torso, after death, and dumped in the Emeryville Sewage Treatment Plant?"

"Objection, Your Honor." Salem, who was writing something, didn't even dignify the question by looking up or stating his ground, which of course was that the question was compound.

McCormick had the business section of the morning *Tribune* open in front of him, concealed from the gallery by the six-inch privacy panel that rose above the work surface of the bench. His gaze came up sluggishly, a tolerant smile on his face, as he glanced at the magic screen in front of him that actually displayed the rough transcript as the court reporter recorded it. Having entirely missed the exchange in real time in favor of his stock quotes, he found the passage, scanned it quickly, and made his ruling.

"Ah… yes, Mr. Shane. Please try to ask one question at a time. And unless you have established some foundation to indicate that this witness has any knowledge of where the body was found, you really are calling for speculation at this point. The objection will be sustained. Proceed."

"He was shot four times, wasn't he?" Noah began again. The question was fine as far as it went, but then he mucked it up by continuing, like the young amateur on the first green at the US Open who knocks the three-footer twenty feet past the cup on sheer adrenalin, "…in the head and torso, after he was dead?"

"Your Honor?" Salem affected some exasperation this time.

"Mr. Shane…" McCormick looked up again, still patient. There were voting constituents in the gallery and many more who would read the press account. "You see, that's four questions. Please break them down so that the doctor can respond to them one at a time."

"He was shot, wasn't he, doctor?"

Farnsworth looked at the judge before answering, to see whether there would be any further admonitions. There being none, he responded.

"Yes. Four bullet holes were found in the body."

"Where were the bullet holes?"

"There were two in the head, and two were found in the upper torso."

"They were fired at close range after Van Zandt was dead, weren't they?"

Salem rose to his feet this time. There really was no damage in letting the witness answer these compound questions, only two questions at once this time. In fact, experienced lawyers often questioned in this manner initially, to save time on preliminary matters over which there was no dispute. But Salem didn't want to waste any opportunity to pull Noah's very newly forged chain, particularly in a high-visibility situation like this one.

"Objection, Your Honor."

McCormick was now becoming a bit annoyed. He didn't have time for neophytes, or prosecutors who wanted to laugh and point at them, and he resented the repeated interruptions from yesterday's closing market statistics. "I think we can cut counsel a little slack here, can't we, Mr. Salem? Is there any dispute about the matters under interrogation?"

"No, Your Honor."

"Very well. Please move on, Mr. Shane. And do try to ask one question at a time."

After a struggle, Noah was able to establish that the body had been shot at close range with a .45, after death, and was then immersed in sewage. Farnsworth testified further that, although a search was made, there were no substances found or marks on the body that would tend to identify the murderer, because sewage contamination made finding any such evidence virtually impossible. Noah paged back through his notes while a heavy silence hung over the room. Then he sat down.

"Anything further of this witness, Mr. Shane?" McCormick asked.

Noah looked up. "Oh... uh, no, Your Honor."

"The People have nothing further of Dr. Farnsworth, Your Honor."

"May the witness be excused?"

"Yes, Your Honor," Noah said.

"Thank you, Dr. Farnsworth. You may step down. Call your next witness, Mr. Salem."

"The People call Vincent Spunelli."

Salem's direct established that Spunelli was the Emeryville Sewage Plant manager who, on Wednesday, September 5th, observed that the mixing system in Number Three Effluent Vat had malfunctioned. The rotating blade had frozen, and efforts to free it had failed. He had to drain the tank to repair it and, when he did so, he discovered a human body wedged in the blade. He summoned police.

With Buzz's whispered prodding, Noah managed to elicit from Spunelli on cross that there was a guard on duty at the plant twenty-four hours a day who was in constant radio contact with a private security headquarters in Oakland. The only way one could gain access to the facility in an automobile would be through the locked electric chain-link gate at the front of the plant. The gate kiosk was at most times during hours of darkness manned by an armed night watchman, whose duty it was to check credentials of any person, unknown to him, trying to gain admission.

"So, could the defendant, Mr. Ruiz, have gotten past the guard, Mr. Spunelli?"

"Objection, speculation, calls for a conclusion, lacks foundation," Salem droned in a soporific monotone.

McCormick again checked his transcript screen. "Sustained," he said. "Anything further, Mr. Shane?"

"No, Your Honor." Noah sat down.

"Mr. Salem?"

"Nothing further, Your Honor."

"You may be excused, Mr. Spunelli," McCormick said. "Next witness, Mr. Salem?"

Salem turned to the gallery. "Call Detective Ned Swarth."

"Detective Swarth," the clerk echoed.

Swarth stood and strode forward from the third row, through the swinging gate, and into the well. His well-tailored brown suit and red power tie seemed to cast him as a business type. The black leather portfolio he carried enhanced the image. He walked straight to the witness chair and turned to face the clerk, raising his right hand to be sworn. Obviously not his first time at bat.

"State your full name and occupation please, officer?" Salem began.

"Edgar Emmons Swarth, Senior Detective, Oakland Police Department, Homicide Division." He settled into the witness chair.

"How long have you been a member of the Oakland Police Department, Detective Swarth?"

McCormick looked at Noah, expecting him to stipulate to all this drivel, which just served to underline the officer's credentials for the press. When he said nothing, the judge interrupted as Swarth began his answer. "I think we can dispense with the preliminaries, can't we, Mr. Shane? I'm familiar with Detective Swarth's background and qualifications."

Noah again glanced at Buzz, who gave a slight nod. "Yes, Your Honor," he said.

"All right, Mr. Salem. Let's get to the meat of it." The pun was unintentional in this instance, but it was almost impossible to avoid stepping in such verbal muck occasionally in the course of murder proceedings. A few throats were cleared, but no laughs.

Salem brought out the investigation at the sewage plant and put in the photographs of the body stuck in the mechanism. He walked through the establishment of the victim's identity and the search of the Van Zandt condo at the East Gate Plaza on Lake Merritt Place, the latent fingerprints lifted from the door, the desk in the study, the bedroom bureau, and the jewelry box. When run through the Central Identification Bureau, the AFIS, Automated Fingerprint Identification System, turned up a high-reliability match with the defendant, whose prints had just been entered into the system.

Swarth went on to describe a search pursuant to warrant the day after the body was found in which several gold bracelets, two diamond rings, and a gold Rolex watch, total value of over $10,000, were discovered in the bedroom occupied by the defendant at the Ruiz residence in East Oakland.

Noah listened with interest to Swarth's testimony about a conversation with Van Zandt's cleaning woman in which she identified the jewelry as belonging to the victim, not noticing Buzz's facial contortions until he finally elbowed him in the ribs. When Noah looked over, Buzz nodded down to his tablet, where he had gouged the word *HEARSAY!!* into the yellow paper. Noah jerked to stand, but Buzz put a hand on his arm. Too late. It was in. They would have called her anyway. Salem sat down.

On cross, after more Salem objections and resultant backtracking, Noah was able to establish that there was no evidence of blood, shooting, struggle, or violence in the Van Zandt condo, though a highly trained FET team had searched diligently for just such evidence. In fact, apart from the jimmied front door, nothing had been disturbed. Ticking off each point on the list he prepared with Buzz, Noah also brought out that, though many neighbors and staff at the East Gate Plaza had been interviewed, there were no shots, nor anything else unusual, heard or observed in the early morning hours of August 26th. There was no evidence of a body having been dragged out. There was no gun found in Pablo's possession. The Van Zandt gun was never found. Swarth had no evidence to link any shooting to Pablo. With a growing sense of competence, Noah waded into the turbid water just a bit further.

"Did the defendant admit to anything that would place him at the scene of the murder, Detective Swarth?" Buzz looked down and winced, palm to forehead, covering his eyes.

Swarth didn't drop a beat. "No, Mr. Shane, but of course we couldn't interview him, could we? He was already in custody on a burglary arrest when we learned the facts of this murder. He was represented by you on that charge, and when we advised him of his rights and tried to discuss the murder with him, he refused to talk to us… on your instructions."

Apparently believing that he now had ample evidence in the record upon which to make a ruling, McCormick didn't wait for another question. He knew full well about the burglary arrest, he had cited it as a reason for denying bail, but it was now in evidence, and would bulletproof his ruling of probable cause against reversal on motion or appeal should the question ever arise. "Anything further from the People, Mr. Salem?"

Absent the testimony about the prior burglary that put an end to things,

Noah might have gotten enough from Swarth on cross that Salem would have felt it necessary to put on some additional evidence. The abruptness with which McCormick cut Noah off after that revelation clearly told Salem that the judge was now hovering, ready to hold Pablo to answer. He had been down this road often enough to know to leave it there. "No, Your Honor, the People rest."

"Thank you, Mr. Swarth. You are excused." The judge's attention turned toward the defense side of the counsel table. "Anything from the defendant?"

Noah was still standing. His first instinct was to say that he hadn't finished his cross. He glanced down at Buzz, who didn't look up, but shook his head slightly. "No, Your Honor," Noah responded.

"Do the People wish to address the court?"

"Just briefly, Your Honor."

Salem rose, buttoned his jacket, and moved into the well, in front of the counsel table.

"Your Honor, this is a simple matter. The People have established that the life of this very prominent man, Warren Van Zandt, was taken by foul play. He was strangled, his body then shot four times with a forty-five caliber weapon, ostensibly to make this seem like a professional killing. Then the body was dumped into the Emeryville Sewage Treatment Plant. It has been demonstrated that the defendant was unlawfully in Mr. Van Zandt's condominium at the time of the killing."

"Objection, Your Honor." Noah was on his feet. "There has been no evidence as to when my client was in the Van Zandt condo."

"Simmer down, Mr. Shane." McCormick waved him off. "Your time will come. Overruled. Proceed."

Salem continued. "The defendant had unquestionably stolen a significant quantity of the victim's valuable jewelry. He was identified by his fingerprints at a time that he was in custody on another arrest, for yet another burglary," he said, taking full advantage of evidence that never would have come in at this stage had Noah not stepped in it. It would undoubtedly seep into the evening news in a few places.

"This man is clearly a burglar. The facts are susceptible of the reasonable inference that he was involved in a home invasion, burglarizing Mr. Van Zandt's condo on the night in question. Mr. Van Zandt undoubtedly surprised the defendant, who strangled him, then shot his dead body and dumped it into the sewage plant to cover his tracks. The People have established motive, means, and opportunity. We submit that there has been proof of premeditated murder, or at the

very least, the taking of a life in the course of a burglary, either of which
would give rise to first degree murder. Moreover, there is probable
cause to believe that this crime was committed by the defendant."

Long pause for effect. "Thank you, Your Honor."

"Thank you, Mr. Salem," the judge responded. "Mr. Shane?"

His confidence flowing, Noah stood and buttoned his herringbone
jacket, like Salem had.

"Your Honor, this case is no more than a patchwork of innuendo,
devoid of substance." Buzz had warned him that argument was futile,
but Noah simply couldn't resist. "There isn't a shred of evidence
to link Pablo Ruiz to this murder. There were some fingerprints in
the Van Zandt condo. It may be that the prosecution has made out
probable cause for an illegal entry. Some items of jewelry were found
in my client's possession. It may be that he could be held to answer
for burglary. But murder? There is no evidence of violence, no shots
fired, no sign of any struggle at the condominium. This man was shot
and dumped into a sewage treatment plant that was guarded like
Pelican Bay. There is no way that Pablo Ruiz could have gained entry
to that compound.

"All the prosecution has proven is that Mr. Ruiz may have burglarized
the home of a man who was later murdered, Your Honor. It is pure
coincidence of fact. There is no probable cause to believe that Pablo
Ruiz murdered Warren Van Zandt."

Noah paused to look down at his notes, and McCormick seized the
opportunity. "Submitted, gentlemen?"

Before Noah could answer, McCormick plowed ahead. "Thank you.
The court finds that there is probable cause to believe that a murder
has been committed, and that it was committed by the defendant.
The defendant, Pablo Ruiz, will be bound over to Superior Court
to answer the charge of murder in the first degree, a violation of
Section 187 of the Penal Code. The matter is set for 'Arraignment and
Trial Setting' before Judge Simon Erhardt, Department One of the
Superior Court, at nine AM, Tuesday, September eighteenth. This
court will be in recess."

"All rise," the bailiff announced. McCormick hurriedly rose and left
the bench; the gallery stood and began to shuffle out. A sheriff sitting
behind Pablo took him by the arm, and he followed meekly toward
the holding cell. Noah put a hand on his shoulder and promised to be
over to see him that afternoon. As they walked out of Department 16
together, Buzz glanced at Noah and smirked.

"Well, counsel, your feet are gettin' damp and the area behind your ears is gettin' drier by the minute. How does it feel?"

"I can do this job, Buzz," Noah said, grinning and chortling with a major post-trial high. "Dammit, I can *do* this frickin' job."

CHAPTER TWENTY-SEVEN

"It's in the works, Rowland. I checked with Ben. The Ruiz kid has been bound over to Superior Court. He'll be charged Tuesday."

Leaning back in his chair, Mustafa was turning over a small, ebony female figurine in his hand, stroking the smooth surfaces as he gazed out his office window toward the hills to the east that were bathed in late afternoon sun. He mused about how beautiful the hills were in that light, burnt umber fading into a yellow ochre, then alizarin crimson toward the crest, with just a hint of titanium white, mixed with cadmium yellow light—was it?—no, cadmium yellow-orange, as highlight.

Although the term "Oakland Hills" was in common usage for these gently rolling prominences, they were actually part of the larger, ancient, Berkeley Range. Seemingly placid under Mustafa's observation, in reality the hills had experienced countless catastrophic geologic events over the eons, thanks to the Hayward Fault, a branch of the monster San Andreas Fault system that had fashioned the entire west coast.

Unrelated to the ongoing tectonic upheaval was the most recent disaster—the Oakland Hills fire of 1991—that took twenty-five lives and over three thousand dwellings. Insurance funds had rebuilt much of the destruction, creating the embarrassment of enormous replacement homes that stood naked on the burned-out ridges, mocking their verdant history. Mustafa's eyes traveled analytically over the scars left by the inferno, as well as the gauche structures now perched upon them. Blight, to be sure, but this was the white man's blight.

Across the desk behind him, Harlan Metcalfe's posture was more erect as he listened to Murphy's voice come back over the speaker.

"Good. What does Ben think of the chances for a plea? I'd like to see this thing ended before it does any more damage than it already has."

"Ben said his contacts were tellin' him that a plea is likely, very soon, now that Ruiz has been held to answer. They're gonna offer him a deal no sane person could refuse."

"When?"

Mustafa sighed and rolled his eyes. "Well, my guess is it'll come in the next week or two, somethin' like that."

"With this heat from the press, anything you can do to shake it up would be good."

"Oh, I don't think I can add anythin'. Ben's solid. You know that. He'll follow through."

Mustafa sat up, leaned forward, and repositioned the figurine in its place on the credenza. "Listen, man," he said. "I gotta bounce, but I'll keep you in the loop."

"I'll give you another call first of the week."

"Do that. And have a good weekend. You gonna play some golf?"

"Nah... I'm down in Carmel. Speaking at a mayors' symposium. The national association puts it on."

"That's great, Roland. What're you gonna talk about?"

"'Early Educational Intervention: Its Effect on Urban Juvenile Crime Statistics' is the title they've given it. I'll be talking about our experience here in Oakland. Margie Kassel over at the school district put some numbers together for me."

"Really?" Mustafa's interest was piqued. "I didn't hear about that. I'd like to see those numbers. You got a syllabus?"

"Not an actual syllabus, but I've got some PowerPoint eyewash. Y'know, a few graphs and charts, a short bibliography. Tell you what, I'll email a copy over to you before I take off."

"Perfect. Appreciate it. Hey, break a leg down there."

"Thanks, Freeman. You have a good weekend, too."

"Will do, m'man."

Mustafa punched the speaker button, ending the call, and swiveled his chair back toward Metcalfe, who was slowly shaking his head.

"He's weak," Metcalfe said.

"Rowland?" Mustafa shrugged. "Nah, he's okay."

"I don't know. His kind of skittishness could be dangerous. He's had almost two terms. Why do you keep him on?"

"He's a bright guy, and a hell of a hard worker. He's known around the country as an innovator. Race relations, education. You heard about his gig this weekend. That little meeting will get some cross-country play. Rowland has a way of makin' those things happen. Might even get his butt into a witness chair before some Washington legislative committee. You can't buy that kind of ink."

Mustafa pulled a stack of documents over in front of him, drew the fountain pen from his desk set, and began signing. "He projects the right image, and he's still popular with our local electorate. You know that voters don't always turn out strong for the intellectual types, but Rowland's got a pretty good combination of flavors, I'd say."

"Yeah, but can you trust him? He's pretty shaky sometimes."

"I've known Rowland Murphy for twenty-five years, Harlan." Mustafa continued signing. "Nope, probably more'n that. We were at Berkeley together during the Civil Rights and Anti-War Movements in the seventies. He was a BMOC, led a bunch a marches. Radical motherfucker." He chuckled, looked up, eyebrows raised, and pointed the pen at Metcalfe. "But he was also dean's list in political science." Returning to complete the last signature, he said, "We were close in those days. Roomed together for a year and a half."

"That was a long time ago."

"Yes, it was." Mustafa turned and pitched the stack of documents into the outbox on his credenza, then turned back. "But not to worry. That man would never, ever, cross me. No matter what his emotional state."

"How do you know that?"

Mustafa smiled broadly, leaning back in his chair again. "Let's just say I know."

Metcalfe looked doubtful.

"Besides, he fits in perfectly with our solid lineup at the county level."

"Maybe," Metcalfe said. "Don't get me wrong. I'm definitely on board with having a good team in place." As a former government functionary, he knew the value of grease in the seat of power. "It's just that Murphy seems to be the weak link in all that."

"Well, it's not just about political capital. We need some major dedication to fairness after all the years of favoritism. That's where Murphy gives us some juice."

"Don't you think Marty Silver over at Education gives us enough of that kind of juice? He gets us qualified black teachers in the city schools, and access to enrichment programs at Park and Rec for the kids. That's fairness, isn't it?"

"That's part of it, for sure."

"Well, we've also got Phil Lewis at Public Works making sure our businessmen get equal treatment, and Henry Barnes at the Port Authority? Seems like we got it pretty well covered, with or without Murphy."

"Yeah, but it's really Rowland who pulls 'em all together. He's our front guy who sells the whole program. And all those other guys respect him."

"I admire your loyalty, Freeman, but the way I see it, he's unstable, egotistical…"—he hesitated—"…and he's white. I mean, you know what direction he'd go if everything ever hit the fan, and he'd likely be believed, not us."

"Harlan, Harlan." The tone was patronizing, the smile condescending. "You underestimate me. Do you seriously think those thoughts haven't occurred to me?"

"Have they?"

"Well, sure. It's because of those very kinds of concerns that I've assembled a sort of database over the years that contains, what shall we say—'intimate'?—information that'll keep all the brothers, both white and black, on short leashes should it come to that." He leaned back and extended a loving hand to pat the locked black-steel two-drawer file cabinet under the credenza.

Metcalfe had always seen his boss as an influence broker in addition to a tough businessman and a charming, masterful political force in the community, but this was the first inkling he'd had of the depth, and source, of his power. He had no idea what lurked in that cabinet, but surely it had to be potent. A smirk played at the corners of his mouth as he reflected on the level of trust he was enjoying from Mustafa at that moment, but then it hit him that there had to be a dossier in that cabinet with his name on it. He knew this was a time to project only total confidence, so he continued to nod pleasantly. "You'll have to give me a tour of that gallery sometime."

Mustafa instantly darkened. "No one enters the gallery but me," he rumbled menacingly.

Now Metcalfe was certain that the cabinet held some humiliating, if not seriously incriminating, features of his history. There were plenty of matters during his years with the city that he would pay to keep from public scrutiny. But didn't everyone have to make compromises to be successful? Lord… what about the handful of weak moments in his personal life? Any of those would most definitely threaten his family, not to mention his status as an elder in the Missionary Baptist Church. But how could Mustafa possibly know about any of that? He couldn't. Could he? Metcalfe sat in silent turmoil, hoping his apprehension wasn't visible.

Mustafa's agreeableness returned. "As much as I rely on you, Harlan, neither you, nor any other human bein', gains entry to those hallowed halls. Might diminish the mystique, know what I mean?"

The intercom buzzed. Mustafa answered without diverting his gaze from Metcalfe. "Yes, Celia?"

"The first-grade class from Freeman Mustafa Elementary is here for their photo session, Mr. Mustafa."

"Thank you. I'll be right with them." He rose and beckoned to Metcalfe. "C'mon. You gotta see this."

Opening the right side of the mahogany double doors, Mustafa stepped aside as twenty-eight rambunctious, dark-skinned six-year-olds burst, squealing, into the room.

"Afternoon, boys and girls," Mustafa said, beaming, as they spewed past him, followed closely by their teacher and three members of the PTA, who were trying in vain to bring them under control. The teacher, an attractive woman in her early thirties, stopped in front of Mustafa.

"I'm sorry, Mr. Mustafa," she said, harried. "They're not always this crazy. They been looking forward to this for two weeks."

Mustafa smiled, holding out a hand to her. "Tell me your name," he said.

"I'm Latisha Cormier."

"A pleasure, Ms. Cormier," he said, taking her hand warmly as her cheeks flushed. "Not to worry. We'll manage."

The photographer came through behind the children and began setting up his tripod. "Max Reynolds, Mr. Mustafa," he announced. "Where do we want to shoot?"

"I thought over here, in front of the Wall of Fame." Mustafa motioned the photographer to the paneled wall bearing many of his celebrity photographs.

A short, slight man approached and extended a hand. "Alan Zucker, Mr. Mustafa. From the *Tribune*. Brought my photographer, too. This is Allen Holt. Your secretary let us know about the event."

"The two Allens, eh?" Mustafa greeted them affably. "Great to have you."

Mustafa was in his element, chuckling as he tried to help Ms. Cormier herd the raucous group of darting kids, grabbing arms, hands, jackets, and sweaters, like a farmer trying to snag a hen for Sunday dinner from a scurrying flock of chickens in the barnyard. Finally he put two index fingers between his lips and whistled at such a piercing pitch that several children winced and covered their ears.

"Okay, gang," he said. "Let's give Ms. Cormier a break, and all form up over here to have our picture taken." The chaos began again, though somewhat diminished. "Right now, boys and girls. Understand?" Firm, but fatherly.

With some effort, the photos were completed; then Ms. Cormier asked the children to gather in front of Mustafa's immense desk, as he leaned against it and observed the proceedings. Twenty-eight diminutive bottoms nestled into the thick carpet as the youngsters sat cross-legged, whispering, elbowing, and pinching each other, the adults struggling to quiet them. Metcalfe observed from the wings.

"Now, then," Ms. Cormier began. "T.J. Hayes? Will you come forward?"

A neatly dressed six-year-old, small for his age, stood up and stepped tentatively to the front of the still-fidgeting group.

Mustafa raised a finger to his lips. "Shhhhh," he admonished, then pointed, and the kids became silent.

"Do you have something to present to Mr. Mustafa?" Ms. Cormier asked, as one of the PTA moms handed the boy a framed painting.

"Missah Mustafa," he whispered. "This f'you."

Mustafa reached out, bowed, and ceremoniously accepted the picture from the child, the *Tribune* camera clicking.

"Now let's see, T.J.," Mustafa said, holding at arm's length a watercolor that was executed in primary colors. "Did you paint this?"

"Yes, sir."

"It's very good. Tell me what it is."

The small voice was almost inaudible. "It's FME."

Mustafa glanced at Ms. Cormier quizzically. "Freeman Mustafa Elementary," she enlightened him, smiling.

"Ah," Mustafa said, practically glowing. "And who is this?" He pointed to a great brown giant standing next to the school, as tall as the flagpole from which the American flag stood straight out to one side.

"It's you..." the boy murmured.

Mustafa stared at the child, then scooped him up in his arms as the shutter continued to click. He winked at Ms. Cormier. "Well, thank you, T.J. Do you like FME?"

"Yes, sir."

"What do you like about it?"

"My daddy says it's the best."

"Your daddy says that, eh? I bet you love your daddy, don't you?"

"Yes, sir." The child made a face, exposing a missing front tooth, as he scrunched his shoulders up around his ears.

"Tell me, T.J.," Mustafa asked. "What do you wanna be when you're all grown up?"

The boy looked down, back at Mustafa for just an instant, then down again. "I'na be like you..." he murmured.

In the silence, Mustafa nodded slowly, clearly moved, clamped a thick forearm around T.J.'s neck in a mock choke-hold, then gently set him down.

It was Ms. Cormier who finally spoke. "Okay, class. Time to get back to school." The PTA parents rose and began steering the youngsters out as they resumed jabbering like magpies.

After saying his goodbyes, Mustafa closed the door behind the throng, and turned back to Metcalfe, who was settled on the couch.

"Y'know? That little T.J. reminds me a lot of myself as a kid." He pulled two Cohibas from a humidor on the bookshelf, chopped the ends, handed one to Metcalfe, and lit them up. "But thanks be to God he'll have some chances I didn't have in that cesspool that was the West Oakland projects in the sixties."

He walked over to one wall, opening a panel to expose a wet bar. "Yep, those kids are gonna be just fine," he said, as he poured two snifters of Courvoisier. He walked back and handed one to Metcalfe, then dropped onto the couch next to him.

"You an' I? We're doin' fine, too." Mustafa stretched one leg over the other on the ebony coffee table. Leaning back, he drew on his cigar, luxuriating, and blew the gray smoke toward the mahogany ceiling.

"But it's the T.J.s that this is all about." His eyes closed as brought the goblet to his lips and savored a taste of the burning amber liquid. "We never forget that piece, right?"

• • •

Noah returned to his suite feeling more confident than any time since becoming a PD. He knew there had been a few stumbles at the prelim, all of which Buzz had had the decency to point out, but he was nevertheless riding a sense of competence. Moments after he closed the door behind him, there was a knock. He opened to a bubbling Lisa Sanders.

"Look who I got," she gloated, with a hand on her hip and a half-frown, half-smirk.

"Maggie!" Noah swept the seven-year-old into his arms, and she squealed. "How'd you do it?" he asked.

"I didn't. You did," Lisa told him. "Like you said, they've designated a couple to be foster parents. Maggie goes over tomorrow, but that lawyer you spoke to at the County Counsel let her come home with me tonight."

"Lemme look at you, squirt." He hoisted Maggie above his head. She was tiny for seven, only forty pounds. "So whaddya think? Glad to be out of stir?"

"They made me go to bed at eight-thirty every night. Only an hour of TV. Mommy doesn't make me have a bedtime."

"No more of that, young lady," Lisa said, waggling a finger. "If they say eight-thirty, then eight-thirty it is. And it's almost that now. So give

Noah a kiss and run downstairs. Brush your teeth, and I'll be there in a minute."

Maggie wrapped her arms around his neck. "G'night, Noah. Will you come see me at the foster place? Mommy says it won't be very long 'til I can come home for good."

"Don't I always say your mom's right about everything?" he said. She kissed his cheek, and he squeezed her. "And you can bet I'll come see you. All the time. Now get to bed," he said, setting her down and giving her a playful swat.

She ambled to the door, opened it, spun around with a phony grin that framed her missing front teeth, and curtsied. "Byyyee, Noah." He grabbed a pillow off the sofa and faked winging it at her as she ducked out, giggling, and slammed the door.

"I have you to thank for all this, Noah," Lisa said. "The County Medical Fund reviewed the application you filled out for the rehab program, and they said I've got a good shot. Like I told you, the social worker at CPS says if I get a job after rehab, they'll review things again, and maybe Maggie comes back right then."

"These foster parents, they good people?"

"Haven't met them yet. Good news is they're only a half a mile from here, in the Western Addition. I can see Maggie all the time." She started toward the door.

"That kid's worth whatever you gotta do, Lees."

"Don't I know." She turned back and gave him a flirtatious smirk. He smiled and nodded.

"Gimme the address, and I'll get over there, too."

"Soon as I get it," she said. "Maybe we can go over together."

"Maybe…"

CHAPTER TWENTY-EIGHT

"Peeveluvtha Shdada Calivornia vurzuge Pavlorueege, Zberior Courd Nummer OS 659331!"

The high-pitched, barely intelligible voice of the elderly female clerk reverberated off the marble walls and through the vast expanse of antiquity.

At first glance, Department One of the Alameda County Superior Court looked more like the Sistine Chapel than a courtroom. The vaulted ceiling was painted with Renaissance figures. Along the east wall, narrow twelve-foot-high windows, guarded by rich red-velvet drapes, stood nestled between marble statues of the male form, evocative of Michelangelo. The well of the court inside the carved gold rail was immense; within it, the desks of the clerks and bailiff were set in thick royal-blue carpet. A deeply stained Rhodesian teak podium, center stage, matched the two counsel tables on either side to its rear. Each was long enough to accommodate four large chairs, upholstered in dark brown leather.

The bench was six feet high, also crafted from Rhodesian teak. Its front panel was adorned with an enormous gold leaf seal of the State of California. On the marble wall behind hung a ten-foot oil of the blindfolded gossamer figure of Justice holding her scales, executed in dark colors with lacy white accents, reminiscent of the dreamlike style of Gainsborough. To the right of the well, along its full length, a spacious jury box held sixteen brown leather chairs. The gallery had seating for three hundred.

The proportions were heroic and the ambience solemn, hallowed, aspiring to the spiritual. This chamber was designed and constructed, as all such sanctuaries are, from the depths of the unconscious, the soul. They are refuges where members of human communities have gone since Cro-Magnon men gathered in the spectacular caves in Lascaux to address the unsolvable problems of mortal interaction that confronted them: when the dead could not be restored to life; when the innocent fetus should not be aborted but the young woman should not be required to bear the product of violent rape; when a tortured mind has blown up a building full of defenseless people, psychotically believing it to be occupied by the killers of his wife and children, long since dead in a highway tragedy; when there simply was no just solution.

It is in such places that the elders of all cultures have donned their black robes, and chanted their incantations, calling on the ways, the rites, the laws, of their ancestors. When human efforts at resolution are so inadequate that all that can be done is say to the grieving individuals involved, and to the suffering community at large: "This is important… utterly, profoundly, important." But in the last analysis, over the eons, that has usually been enough. It has allowed the aggrieved to go on, to return to the living. It has provided closure to the community, and it has restored a faith in the future. Such places are holy.

And the effort had been to make Department One holy. But here, the effort had fallen short. The art and solemnity was arguably equal to the task, but the acoustics were abysmal. The marble walls generated impossible echoes. The sound was more high-school-gym-shower than hallowed temple. Countless studies were undertaken, and an elaborate public address system installed, in an effort to dampen the reverberation, but all had failed. The voice of the lawyer addressing the court from the podium resounded back to, and around, him or her in a manner that was hopelessly distracting. Outside a radius of ten feet, the words of the judge were unintelligible mush.

Useless for any lengthy proceeding that involved interactive communication, Department One fell into disuse as a seat of justice, and was relegated to a ceremonial chamber. Cases were never tried there. Mayors and judges were sworn in, visiting dignitaries were welcomed, but no judicial business was transacted. There was one exception, however. Each Monday and Tuesday morning, Department One stirred, rose from the dead, and came alive for the criminal trial calendar. Monday mornings, trials were called and assigned to departments to begin the week of litigation. Tuesday mornings, trial dates were set.

Noah had fidgeted continuously through the first two matters called. Now, hearing the garbled call of his case, he hurried forward from a sparsely populated gallery. It was his debut appearance in the daunting surroundings of Department One, and he felt it, profoundly.

"That matter is ready for the People, Your Honor. District Attorney Marco Salem appearing," Salem boomed as usual. His one-woman entourage stood next to him at the counsel table, also as usual. Both were well-dressed and well-coiffed. This was Salem's element.

"Ready for the defendant, Pablo Ruiz, Your Honor. Assistant Public Defender Noah Shane." Noah stood behind the other counsel table, thirty feet from Salem.

Before them sat the Honorable Simon Erhardt, all jurist. His dense white hair was orderly, his aura erudite, his manner dignified, distinguished. His voice exuded power.

"All right, gentlemen, we are here this morning for the arraignment of Mr. Ruiz and to set a trial date. An information has been filed by the District Attorney. Is the presence of the defendant waived, Mr. Shane?"

"Yes, Your Honor."

"Is reading of the information waived?"

"Yes, Your Honor."

"Very well. Probable cause having been found by the magistrate to believe that the defendant has committed the crime with which he has been charged, he has been bound over to Superior Court for trial on the charge of murder in the first degree, with special circumstances. Are the People ready to set a trial date?"

"We are, Your Honor," Salem responded.

"Defendant?"

"Yes, Your Honor."

"Time is waived?"

"Time is not waived, Your Honor," Noah said.

For the first time, Erhardt paused, and regarded Noah with a frown. A criminal defendant had a constitutional right to a speedy trial. In California, that meant within sixty days of arraignment on the information in Superior Court. The defendant could waive that right in order to have more control over scheduling, and more preparation time. In fact, if the defendant refused to waive time, the court, viewing control over its calendar as crucial, and its God-given prerogative, often reacted punitively.

Noah had tried to convince Pablo to waive time, but he had failed. He had to get out to help his mother, he said. He wanted trial as soon as possible, he said. Noah told him that was crazy, that if he went down on this beef, he'd never get out. All the same, Pablo's mind was made up. Noah explained that it would be at least ninety days until the case could even be close to ready for trial. There was a lot to do. Investigation. Experts. Trial preparation. But Pablo wanted the trial as soon as the court would set it if he couldn't be OR'd.

The judge was looking down at his calendar.

"Have counsel discussed a date?" he asked.

"We have not, Your Honor," Noah said. "But the defense was thinking of a date in mid-November."

"November of what year?" Erhardt asked, drenched with the sarcasm that was also his divinely mandated prerogative. Yet another bad judicial omen; Noah ignored it.

"This year, Your Honor, sixty days from now?"

"This case will be tried and completed by... Halloween, gentlemen." Erhardt was looking back at his calendar. "Trial date in... five weeks. Twenty-second of October. Pre-trial conference on the nineteenth. Motions will be completed by October twelfth. I will entertain applications to shorten time on any motions, should that become necessary."

Noah was shocked. There was no way he could be ready to try this case in five weeks. He had to figure out how to try a case, period.

"Y-Your Honor," he stammered. "I couldn't possibly be ready by October twenty-second. I'm attempting to retain experts and complete my investigation."

"Your client has now been in custody almost three weeks. I would assume he would be as eager as I am to move this case forward. We will begin picking a jury on October twenty-second." Erhardt commenced sorting through files for the next case.

"Thank you, Your Honor," was the reply from Salem. He closed and snapped his briefcase, the legal assistant zipping up her laptop. Truth be known, Salem's trial calendar was jammed. He was already set on October 22nd, but he'd find a way to deal with the calendar conflict in a high-profile case like this one.

Noah's forehead furrowed, his anxiety flaring into an anger that would never have found its way to the surface prior to the prelim. His voice was raised, defiant.

"Your Honor?" It echoed off the ubiquitous marble.

The judge slowly returned his gaze to Noah. "Yesss, Mr. Shane?"

He didn't think it through. "This is a serious capital case," he said, glaring. "I don't have to remind the court of that. This kind of rush to judgment simply does not permit adequate preparation. It's a denial of the defendant's Fifth and Fourteenth Amendment rights to due process, and his Sixth Amendment right to effective jury trial. Absent the setting of a reasonable trial date, Mr. Ruiz will seek immediate appellate review by way of a writ."

Erhardt didn't hesitate for an instant. "What did you have in mind?" he asked, giving no sign that he had perceived any kind of a threat. No weakness. No intimidation.

"I had in mind a trial date in sixty days, Your Honor," Noah answered quietly.

Engrossed in his calendar, the judge said, "I'll give you... fifty-four," he said, not looking up. "Trial on November twelfth. Pretrial the ninth. Motions by the second." He raised his attention to Noah. "Now, is there anything else?"

Nothing from Salem. He'd live with any date.

Oh, what the Hell. "Yes, Your Honor," Noah said. "As the court points out, my client has been in custody for three weeks, his mother needs him at home, and—"

"Denied. Call the next case. *People v. Barnett.* Number OS967550."

Noah returned his pen to his pocket, zipped his briefcase, turned, and left the courtroom as the next pair of lawyers hustled forward. He stepped into the hallway to find Salem waiting.

"A word, Shane?"

Surprised, Noah paused. This was the first time Salem had addressed him outside the courtroom.

"Let's talk over here…" Salem nodded to an alcove near the end of the marble hall.

"So, now that we have a trial date, things are going to happen fast," Salem began, his tan, pancake-makeup face serious, his manner brusque. No cordial lead-in. *What happened to: 'You enjoying your job?', 'How's the family?'* Clearly any cordiality would be a significant tactical error. He was in control, and he knew it. Anything to make Noah feel awkward.

"Right," Noah said. "I wonder if we could agree to compare discovery as soon as possible? I'm not sure I have everything you have."

"Listen," Salem snapped. "The case against Ruiz is airtight. I'm sure you know that. But in light of your client's lack of a heavy criminal record, and in the interest of getting this case closed, I've been authorized to offer a plea of involuntary manslaughter with a recommendation of five to fifteen." He paused to let it sink in. "The offer remains open exactly four days, until Friday. If it's not accepted, we proceed to trial. No further negotiation. We seek the death penalty."

His newfound confidence having just evaporated, Noah was again mystified. He studied Salem's face. *Jesus. They had him by the cojones, so why the offer?* He hated that phrase, 'death penalty.'

"Yeah, well, Ruiz had nothing to do with any murder," Noah managed, "and I don't think you can get a jury to buy that he did. But you know I've got to take him any offer, so of course we'll discuss it."

"Better not discuss it too long," Salem said. "This isn't my idea. Truth is, I'd love to try this case. So you'll wanna move before the match burns out."

"I'll get back to you."

Salem's attention drifted off down the hall, then returned to Noah, as he smirked. "This is as good as it gets, Shane. If you're confused about that, you might want to consult one of your supervisors. They'll explain it to you."

Noah held the stare a beat, and then, turning on his heels, he terminated the conversation without response. When he reached the elevator, he entered behind several other lawyers. Once inside, he faced the front and saw Salem still standing in the alcove, still with the smirk. Their eyes met as the doors closed.

On the way down, Noah reflected on it. *This only upped the ante. Pablo would never go for it. Just meant there was a whole lot more to leave on the table now. What if the worst happened after Pablo turned down a plea? What then? He hadn't had this much fun since his bris.*

●　●　●

Returning to Oakland Division, Noah went straight to Stark, who listened to the events of the morning, the trial date, the offer. Again, inexplicably, he was not surprised.

"They always make a pretrial offer," Stark said, "but I didn't think it would go this low. You've got no choice, and neither does Ruiz. He'll never see anything better. And take my word for it, he'll go down like a rock at trial."

"Why are they doing this?" Noah asked. "And what's with the dynamite? Why should Ruiz have to take the deal by Friday?"

"No idea," Stark said. "But don't even think about it. They might withdraw it. Five to fifteen is nothing. This guy'll be out before he's thirty."

"I don't know," Noah said. "Is there something they know that we don't? We've searched for an alibi, but we can't find anything, no one who can say where Ruiz was the night of the murder. And we don't have anything close to a guilty story from him. It does matter what he wants to do, doesn't it?"

Stark regarded him for a beat, then stood abruptly. He stepped out front and sat on the corner of his desk, three feet from Noah.

"Look," he began, with a solicitous smile. "If you're going to have any kind of future in this office, there're a few things you need to understand." He darkened and pointed a finger. "The first is that you need to do as you're told. Now, I've discussed this case extensively with Chuck Tolliver. He agreed that we'd go for murder two if it was offered, and he's the boss. Neither of us dreamed they'd come down to an involuntary. We'll look like idiots if we try this case against an offer like that and lose it. And you *will* lose it. This isn't a time to try to be a hero. You talk to your client and tell him whatever you have to, but you get him to take this plea. Then come back to me and confirm it."

"But…"

"No buts! You do as I say."

Noah's stare radiated insolence. Stark's words projected him to another galaxy, another time, three hundred miles to the south in the Tehachapi Mountains east of Santa Barbara.

"Time out! Time out!" Ballard screamed. Noah raised both hands in the time-honored 'T' sign, and the whistle blew. He trotted to the sidelines to where the coach was standing.

"All right," Ballard said, tugging nervously at his cap and looking up at the scoreboard. "Third and four. We're down three. Seventeen seconds left. Here's what you do."

Noah unsnapped his chinstrap, pulled his helmet off, and shook his sweat-soaked curly black mop. Behind him, the crowd was going crazy. His adrenalin was flowing. The girl with the squeeze bottle squirted water into his mouth, a stream that ran out the corners, down onto the front of his blue jersey and the big red seven on his chest. His high-school career at Ojai Prep had come down to this. Seventeen seconds for the CIF championship, the last game of his senior year, all on the line against Chadwick. History repeating. They'd played Chadwick for all the marbles three years running, and lost the last two.

Ballard looked up into Noah's dripping face. "You give it to Silvan," he instructed. "Tailback off left tackle to center the ball between the hash marks. We got one timeout left. When the whistle blows, call it. If Silvan makes the first, we got one shot at the end zone, maybe two. If not, Heinz takes the twenty-nine-yard field goal."

Noah's attention had been on the field, but now he turned, frowning. "Wait, Coach," he said. "We don't have to run it. Lemme go for the six right here. We can win this thing. What're we gonna do with a tie?"

"We're gonna bring home the hardware, that's what. Co-champs is better than runner-ups, hero. Now, get out there and do it."

"But…"

"NO BUTS! DO IT!"

Slowly, the trappings of the present reassembled with Stark standing in front of him.

"Look, Noah," he was saying—oily but insistent. "There's nothing to be ashamed of here. This is a sensational result. Maybe a lot of the reason they're making the offer is because they're concerned about you. Sure, you're a rookie. But you're an unknown quantity. And you obviously believe in your guy. That all adds up to an unstable situation to them. They don't like that."

"Neither do I."

"It'll rocket you way ahead of your class." He looked away and exhaled forcefully. "God, I wish something like this had been dropped in my lap when I came aboard. No one'll believe you pulled it off."

"See, the problem is I won't have pulled it off," Noah responded. "I don't know why they're making the offer. Pablo tells me he didn't kill the guy. Well, maybe he didn't. And maybe they know that. How am I supposed to advise him if I don't have a clue?" He paused, pondering. "Maybe we just have to try it." *What was he saying? Was he really suggesting that he try it?*

Stark was starting to pace. "Goddammit, Shane, you don't 'advise' him. This isn't some fucking downtown corporate firm. You tell him. You tell him in poker big pots are sometimes lost with good hands, and won with lousy ones. He can have the best hand going and still rot in the joint, or worse." He stopped behind the desk and put both hands on the top of his leather chair. "You tell him he does what he does because it's the best fucking choice he has. He's not interested in making a point, and for chrissakes, neither are you. The DA's stacked here. That's all there is to it."

Noah trotted back onto the field, snapping his chinstrap. "Okay, huddle up!" he yelled. The offense gathered around him as he bent in and kneeled to call the play. "Balanced line, power I, double tight end," he said. He looked up; there was no hesitation. "Fake to Silvan off left tackle." He turned his head and looked sidelong at Mark Sandifer, the tall, strong wide receiver who would line up at tight end in the double tight end run set. "Mark, block down on the end, then slide over the middle and look back at me. I'll pump as you come free, then you haul ass to the flag. I mean HAUL ASS! The ball'll be there. Got it?"

"Got it."

Pulling out his chair, Stark slid in behind the desk and leaned forward. His delivery was slow, syncopated, strident. "Now you listen to me. I kept you on this case because I thought you could handle it. Don't prove me wrong. You *will* get this guy to plead."

Noah took the snap. Time went haywire. There was only silence as he pivoted and buried the ball in the belly of his tailback, who was churning by on his left. It was all slow motion. Silvan dropped his head and doubled over, crossing both arms in front of him. At the last instant, Noah snatched the ball out of his gut and turned his back as the big tailback powered forward and blasted into the line behind the tackle. Noah retreated ten, then fifteen yards, giving Sandifer time to clear. In the eye of the storm, he turned again and saw his wideout break into the secondary, slow, and glance back. He pumped once, just as Sandifer sold the inside move, cut sharply, and sprinted for the corner of the end zone, leaving his man completely turned around. Noah let the ball go, and the wide-open receiver ran under it a few yards from the goal line. For an agonizing second Sandifer juggled, then gathered it in for the six. Game over.

In the bedlam that followed, Noah trotted to the sideline, remarkably composed under the circumstances. He slowed as he passed Ballard, who was glaring at him. Noah shrugged, and walked off the field.

Returning to the here-and-now, he looked up to find Stark still glaring. "That's all, Shane," he snarled. "We're finished here."

Noah stood, shrugged, and walked out of the office.

CHAPTER TWENTY-NINE

"Welcome, Mr. Shane. Did you have trouble finding the house?"

Amparo Ruiz greeted him warmly, wearing the same colorful scarf as when he first met her at the jail.

"No, señora," he told her. "No trouble. Your directions were perfect."

The home was a modest, wood-frame bungalow built in the 1920s that stood on 46ᵗʰ near Melrose in East Oakland's run-down San Antonio Neighborhood—the heart of the barrio. One of the more than 14,000 craftsman structures constructed as part of the First Bay Tradition architectural movement, like its many fellow bungalows, it had fallen into disrepair as original owners followed the urban exodus to the more upscale Oakland Hills and Piedmont.

Here and there, abandoned trash littered front yards and driveways of the aging residences; a derelict car sat on blocks. In contrast, the Ruiz home was cared for, though it, too, was in obvious need of paint and the other repairs that would address long-deferred maintenance. A diminutive front lawn was neatly trimmed, though somewhat faded.

That morning, Noah had explained the DA's offer to Pablo, who was moved to tears of relief when he thought he was no longer facing the death penalty. When it was explained that if he turned it down, took the case to trial, and lost, he could still get a death sentence, his spirits sagged, and he became quiet, withdrawn. Finally he said, "I don't know what to do, Noah. They want to kill me. Why do they want to kill me?"

"I know it must feel like that, Pablo, but it's really not about killing you. There's some other reason that we don't know."

Pablo looked up, bewildered. "Like what?"

"Yeah, that's what we don't know."

"I could end the risk of them killing me if I said I did it, couldn't I?"

"Yes."

He looked away and said, "I am so scared." Then, seconds later, "No, I could never let my mother down that way." He looked into Noah's eyes, pleading. "You have to help me."

Noah felt his desperation, and some of his own around the inability to help. "I'll talk to your mother about the offer," he said, "if you give me permission."

Just for a moment Pablo had looked tentative; then he said, "Yes, of course. Talk to her."

And so he had come to the Ruiz home. "Please come in and sit down," Amparo said. She led Noah into a dimly lit living room and directed him to a threadbare, overstuffed chesterfield.

Photographs, portraits, and group shots, of men, women, and children of Hispanic descent, decorated the walls. The dark wood furniture was ancient, but looked comfortable. A faded oriental rug, once of vivid reds and blues, added to the ambience of another time, another culture.

"I have made some coffee. Will you take some?"

Noah wasn't an afternoon coffee drinker, but he speculated she had hurried home from work to make it especially for his visit.

"I'd love some," he said.

"Good." Amparo smiled. "I will be just a moment."

Alone, Noah surveyed a room cast in diaphanous shadows from afternoon sun filtered through lace curtains. The photographs were mostly black-and-white. Some bore the artificially intense hues and washed-out pigments from the early days of color photography. He reflected on the faces of the men and women who sat around tables and stood organized into rows, family members from long-ago gatherings, all gazing tolerantly into the camera while children mugged and pinched one another in the foreground. In a darkened corner behind the front door was a shrine, a crucifix mounted on dark wood. A ceramic statuette of the Virgin Mother stood next to it, her countenance gentle, maternal. A votive candle flickered faintly.

Amparo returned, carrying a tray on which a gleaming silver coffee pot, two china cups and saucers, and a plate of crystalline sugar cookies were arranged next to a polished silver creamer and sugar bowl. Noah marveled at their elegance.

"How beautiful," he said.

She looked up at him as she set the tray on the heavy oak coffee table. "Oh, the tea set," she said. "Yes, thank you. It has been in my family for generations. One of the few things my mother managed to bring with us from Mexico." She observed the pieces with reverence. "I remember so well my mother polishing them when I was young. There were many years we had nothing. We sold everything, but she refused to sell these."

She filled their cups. "Cream and sugar?" she asked, extending the plate of cookies to him.

"Just black, thanks," he said, noticing the gracefulness with which she poured, bringing to mind a ritual ceremony as the aroma of rich, dark coffee wafted up to him. He took his cup and a cookie, and sat back. Amparo settled into the heavily upholstered chair next to the sofa and regarded him anxiously.

"Tell me, please, Mr. Shane."

Noah nodded, and began. "We're working very hard on the investigation, señora, but so far it's turned up very little that's encouraging." He outlined the prosecution's evidence that placed Pablo in the victim's condominium as Amparo digested every word in silence, looking down into her coffee cup.

"We haven't been able to establish when he was there," Noah told her. Replacing her cup on the tray, she clicked her tongue, drew a deep breath, and shook her head slowly.

He went on. "Of course you know that when the police came here and searched Pablo's room, they found a lot of valuable jewelry that has been identified as belonging to the murdered man. None of that looks very good."

She looked up. "I did not want to let them in, but they had papers. Should I have turned them away? I did not know what to do."

"You did what you had to do, señora. They had a warrant. They would have searched whether you consented or not. What they don't know, yet, is… is about your illness, your treatment, and Pablo's desperate need for money."

Again she reflected a hesitance, about her secrets.

"If they knew about that, it would probably give them even more reason to suspect Pablo. They would try to show that he would do anything to raise fifty thousand dollars."

She folded and refolded her hands in her lap.

"But right now, it looks to them like Pablo had a clean record until just recently, when he stole some butter, which clearly doesn't seem like something an experienced thief would do."

He paused, watching her, wanting to be sure she followed. She was nodding, her eyebrows again rising hopefully.

"I think it's his clean record, more than anything else, that prompted the District Attorney to offer a plea to a lesser offense, involuntary manslaughter. It usually carries a sentence of only a few years in prison, but they say they want Pablo to serve five to fifteen years." He waited for a response, but she was impassive. *Now came the hard part.*

"Pablo has to consider this option very carefully, señora. The DA says he is willing to accept the plea for only a short time. They're very serious about the case. This Van Zandt was a well-known man in Oakland,

and his murder has received a lot of attention. The deputy DA who will try the case hopes to become a politician and would welcome the opportunity to further his career at Pablo's expense."

"What does Pablo say?"

"He says he's confused... about what to do. He's very concerned about what you think."

She reflected on this. "Why are they so eager for Pablo to say he is guilty?"

"The truth is that we really don't know. Like I said, this is a pretty high-powered crime for someone with no criminal record. But I can't say exactly why they offered the involuntary manslaughter. They're very busy at the DA's office. Maybe they're willing to avoid the time and the cost of a trial in light of Pablo's good record. The most important thing is that there's a high degree of likelihood that he'll be found guilty of first-degree murder if the case is tried. Do you know what that means?"

"A sentence of death," she said softly. She knew.

Noah tried to think of something to add, but there was nothing more to say. He sat quietly, determined to let her speak now, to let her react.

Amparo took her cup from the tray and cradled it in her lap, without drinking. At length she raised her eyes to meet Noah's. "I have made mistakes in my life, Mr. Shane. Some of which have come to hurt the people I love. I will not repeat those mistakes with Pablo."

"Mistakes?"

She inhaled deeply, exhaled, and began, quietly but firmly. "I was born in Mazatlán. My father was a very proud... a very religious... man. He actually studied to be a priest." The hint of a smile appeared for an instant, then dissipated under the weight of her memories. "But when his father died, he went to build the adobe houses, like his father had. You know the ones? The big thick walls? Very cool inside in the hot weather." He nodded, and she returned to her narrative. "And for most of my childhood, he was able to provide. My mother tended our garden and cleaned at the large hotels when work was available. I took care of my little brother, Oscar." She paused again, another glimmer of recollection crossing her face. "My baby brother...

"Then, in my teenage years, times got very bad. There was no building. There were no tourists. There was no money, no food. It was a terrible depression. Many people were sick and dying. There was violence. Many stole. Some were even killed for the little they had." She sighed, knitting creases into her forehead, as if those times were so long ago that she could hardly believe they were real.

"My mother had no work, and my father traveled great distances to do whatever he could, and returned with a little money. There were times we had nothing to eat. Finally, my brother was able to get work on a fishing boat, but it did not pay enough. The fishing was not always good. The church brought us food sometimes." Her eyes were glistening.

"But you see? We never begged. My father taught us that it was better to die with the grace of God than to live by taking what belonged to others.

"We were a religious family, Mr. Shane. Not like so many now. So much religion has become just convenience. But my father prayed for guidance, and he thought to bring his family here, for a new chance. We had to wait for the immigration papers, but it was much easier then. Many who stayed in Mazatlán died. We were delivered."

"Is Pablo's uncle here in Oakland? He never said anything about him."

"My brother Oscar? He died in Mexico."

"Oh, I'm sorry."

"Yes, thank you. And times were difficult here, too, but there was always work to be done. We never had much, but we had our faith… and our good name." Again her eyebrows arched, this time with the reconciliation that had evolved over the years. "I guess that is really all there is." Her eyelids lowered, and she went inward.

Stillness pressed in through the gloom. Noah became transfixed by the rays of sun that shimmered off the tiny dust particles drifting silently around her, and soon he couldn't take his eyes from this image: part sacred, part Victorian tintype, dazzling. Minutes passed, it seemed, in which neither spoke. A car passed quietly out front; in the distance, a mother called to her children.

Amparo opened her eyes, and her attention came to rest on a photograph across the room. Noah looked over to see a framed picture of a young soldier with a dark moustache and smiling eyes, dressed in desert camo fatigues, standing in front of a military half-ton truck.

"My Jose, Pablo's father, went to war for this country." A beat. "My parents, my brother, Jose, all are gone now." Once again her eyebrows bespoke her feelings, as her gaze dropped to her hands. "And I am ill." It was diminished, resigned. "Pablo… is the last of our family."

She looked up abruptly, straight into Noah's eyes. "Pablo did not do this thing, Mr. Shane. He did not kill this man. We have shared our lives, and I know him as I know myself. He is not capable of such a thing." The words were soft, but delivered in a measured cadence, reflecting their gravity. "It is evil to try to make him say he did something so terrible that he did not do. The Lord knows the truth, and the Lord will protect him." She breathed deeply, replaced her cup on the silver tray, and added solemnly, "No, Mr. Shane, Pablo will not say he killed when he did not, as a convenience to anyone."

Noah suddenly understood the depth of Pablo's predicament, the Gordian knot in which he was enmeshed. He was terrified of the consequences that confronted him, but obviously powerless to betray his mother, his family, his tradition.

Amparo's smile returned. "But the court will understand the truth," she said, "because you will tell them." For her it was a simple assertion of fact. "The Lord has sent you to us; my son will be delivered through you, and will be returned to me in my last days."

Wait. What? Sent by God?

"I would like to tell you that there was some hope with my cancer, but it is clear that I am beyond treatment now." She shook her head slowly, a stoic smile appearing. "You see? The money would not have helped..."

Noah's mind raced as he felt the same Gordian knot tightening, and he groped for rationalizations that might extricate him. *Savior of this family? Miracles? He had to help her with the reality that her son had a rookie PD who never should've been saddled with his case.* He searched for a way to say it without her seeing the self-doubt that would undermine her confidence. He would tell her that he would make sure the defense got to someone else, someone capable, someone experienced. *But wait... there was no one else.*

Amparo's gaze never left him. Gradually, he felt his focus externalizing, and the turmoil began to subside. As he allowed himself to be drawn into her, his thoughts slowed, and his doubt was slowly replaced by the glow of... something... what?

Presently, Amparo Ruiz spoke again. "Did you say this terrible thing happened on August twenty-sixth? Pablo was in Mexico with friends that whole weekend."

CHAPTER THIRTY

"So how's the guardian of the people, Ben? Crime under control, I trust?" Mustafa beamed as he grasped Owens's hand and rolled it over into the brothers' handshake.

"Under control," Owens assured him.

Owens had arrived early and was seated at Mustafa's usual table at Giovanni, an exclusive Italian eatery on Broadway, a block from the lake and two blocks from Ebony Properties. Mustafa slid into the dark leather booth across from him.

"Campari, Mr. Mustafa?" the waiter inquired.

"Please, Harold," was the response. Owens had a Diet Coke in front of him. He never indulged in anything stronger at lunch.

"And the linguini puttanesca?" Harold asked.

"Mmm. Let me have a menu, will you? Might be time for a little variety."

"Certainly, sir." The middle-aged waiter lifted the white linen napkin from the table and laid it in Mustafa's lap, drew a leather bound menu from the stack under his arm, placed it in front of him, and then stepped away.

"So you goin' to the game tomorrow?" Mustafa asked.

"I'm not," Owens lamented. "My daughter's in from Boulder, and Twila got tickets for Berkeley Rep. Guess I'm stuck."

"Man," Mustafa commiserated. "You're gonna miss a good one. This kid from Oregon's a great passer, and they got a back that's second in the Pac-12 in rushing."

"Right."

"But if our Bears get past this one, we're in pretty good shape for a Pac-12 North title."

"Don't I know. I'll be taping and watching tomorrow night."

"Like I'm always sayin'"—Mustafa chuckled as he opened the menu and scanned the Northern Italian delicacies—"there are definitely fringe benefits to bein' single."

"Don't start, Freeman. You know anyone who might want my tickets for tomorrow?"

"Nah... " Mustafa said. Then he looked up. "Wait a minute. Harlan Metcalfe in my office might. He's not much of a fan, but he actually said something about the game this week, and I need to get him a little more community exposure as my second-in-command. I'll check with him." He returned to the menu.

"Yeah, let me know before close of business," Owens said as the waiter set the Campari in front of Mustafa. "If he's on board, I'll leave them out front, and he can pick them up on his way home."

The waiter had returned for their orders and stood silently next to the table. "I was thinkin' about the tutto mare, Harold," Mustafa said. "You recommend it?"

"I do, Mr. Mustafa. Had a couple of rave reviews already today."

"Great. Book it then. Let's do it over fettucini. Oh, and bring me a Caesar too, will you? The romaine chopped, the way I like it?"

"My pleasure, sir. And for you, Mr. Owens?"

"Just a cheeseburger. The cheddar, I guess. Medium rare."

"Thank you, gentlemen," the waiter said, and left them.

Mustafa returned his attention to Owens. "So what's the big mystery?" he asked. "You call this meetin' to discuss golf scores? Compare wedge sizes again?"

"I thought we needed to chat about this *Ruiz* case," Owens said.

"What about it?"

"Well, I think I mentioned that we'd offered him an involuntary like you and I discussed?"

"Right."

"We don't have a response from him yet, but I'm told he's likely to turn it down. Last night it came through that he thinks he's got an alibi. He's gonna say he was in Mexico when Van Zandt was killed."

"Mexico?" Mustafa frowned, mid-sip of the Campari. "He got any witnesses?"

"Well, that's it. This new PD kid I told you about who's representing him. Shane? He's applied for funds to send that bumbler investigator we talked about down to Baja to drum up witnesses."

"Damn. You sure about all that?"

"Managing PD at Oakland Division is the one I've been working with on this. Member of our regular foursome? We were talking, and he said—"

"No, no. That's okay," Mustafa interrupted, waving a hand. "No specifics. I'm sure you got it right. We're just gonna have to roll with it."

Owens' look was exasperation. It irked him that Mustafa never wanted the details, handing out the instructions and leaving him to do the leg work, then clinging to his "plausible deniability."

"Well, it's beginning to look like there's gonna be a trial," Owens said.

"Shit..." Mustafa growled. He thought about it a beat, then said, "So can you jam it out right away? Before we get into all this extraneous investigation?"

"Well, see, it's set in a little over six weeks. Probably can't get it out much sooner than that no matter what we do."

"Okay. Then we'll have to live with it. Now can we keep the thrashing around to a minimum? They can't prove any alibi without witnesses, and they'll never put that kid on the stand with all you've got on him. Nobody's gonna buy this Mexico bullshit without corroboration, are they?"

"I think we can minimize the investigation, but you gotta understand, this is a capital case, and courts don't feel good about cutting the defense's preparation short," Owens said. "Judges get reversed on that kinda stuff. But I'll get with the PD on it."

The lines in Mustafa's face seemed to intensify as he labored to maintain his equanimity. "This thing is serious, Ben," he rumbled. "We're doing a lot of good things in this town, and this has the potential to jeopardize all that."

"Just because of Van Zandt?"

For a moment, Mustafa considered getting further into it, but then he decided to let it go. "Well, yes. Warren was an important piece of the landscape, and things like this are totally unsettling, disruptive to our agenda. That means we're all about containment, damage control. It's already front page, but we'd like to stifle it as much as possible. Can I count on you?"

Owens frowned his lack of understanding. He knew there was something at the bottom of it that his old friend wasn't willing to share, but he also knew about the unfortunately documented history between them that had to be protected at all costs. Given the length and depth of the friendship, he could not imagine any of that would ever see the light of day; then again, Freeman was definitely driven, so he had never been willing to test it.

"We're clear, aren't we Ben?"

"Well, sure, Freeman. I'll do what I can."

"Good. So keep me posted."

Harold brought the entrees, and the discussion turned to lighter subjects, the 14th Street Preschool, city politics, golf scores, and a bit of reminiscing about the old days at Berkeley. As they were finishing up and settling down to cappuccinos, a young man in Levis and a tie appeared at the table.

"My apologies, gentlemen," he said. "I'm Arlen Gates with KXTV News." Mustafa and Owens looked up simultaneously.

"Don't know if you remember me, Mr. Mustafa. I've covered a couple of your recent projects, that permit squabble about the preschool?"

The waiter hurried up behind the intruder and addressed Gates stridently. "This is a private luncheon, sir. You'll have to leave."

"That's all right, Harold," Mustafa said. "I know Mr. Gates."

"Sorry, Mr. Mustafa," Harold fawned. "I was in the kitchen."

"Don't you give it another thought," Mustafa told him. He turned to the newsman, all smiles. "Of course I remember you, Arlen. How are things over at the Bay Area's media nerve center?"

"I guess my kind of rudeness comes with the territory, but I'm covering the *Ruiz* case, and I'd appreciate an interview with Mr. Owens when you finish your lunch." He turned to Owens. "If you could see your way clear. I have a truck out front, and we could use the restaurant as a backdrop. Twenty minutes of your time, tops."

"I don't know" was Owens's reaction. He didn't need this just now, for a host of reasons. "I've got a busy—"

"I'm sure Mr. Owens would be delighted to oblige," Mustafa interjected. "I've gotta run, anyway." He turned back to the reporter. "He'll be along in a few minutes."

"Thanks," Gates said, not giving time for further protest. "I'm right outside the front door when you're ready."

Owens was now completely confused. Wasn't he just talking about containment?

"This is perfect," Mustafa said after the newsman left.

"I don't know, Freeman. I hate to get mixed up in this kind of crap. It never gets us anywhere good. And weren't we just talking about trying to keep it quiet?"

"Yeah, we want to contain it, but see, a lot of it's already out there. Nothin' we can do about that. This guy is going to tell the story anyway, so we gotta bend it our way if we can. Try to float the Mexico angle a little. We want the public to start to get used to it now, what a stretch it is. Diffuse it early. But be careful, okay? Push the envelope a little, but don't overdo it. We don't want to blow the whole thing by givin' Ruiz grounds for a venue motion."

Owens's irritation returned. Now it wasn't just plausible deniability, he was going to force a TV interview, and even hand out legal advice. "I'm not really worried about that," he said. "Venue motions are pretty tough these days."

Mustafa paid the check and guided Owens to the front door. The black Mustafa limousine was waiting, double-parked, motor running. He spurned walking in public, even the two blocks between Ebony Properties and Giovanni. Spontaneous meetings could be managed in the office, but were more troublesome on the street.

Smiling, he shook Owens's hand, then grasped his bicep. "Stay in touch, man. Go Bears."

"Right. Thanks for lunch," Owens responded, and turned reluctantly toward the camera crew.

• • •

The secretary handed Mustafa several phone messages as he strode past her desk. He paused outside his door to scan them. Two, from Commissioner Barnes, were marked *Urgent.*

"Get Barnes for me, will you, Celia?"

"Right, Mr. Mustafa."

The phone was already buzzing by the time he had shed his blazer and reached his desk. He hit the speaker button as he sat.

"Henry!" he boomed. "How's everything down at the waterfront?"

"All right, I guess, but—"

"Good," Mustafa interrupted, wanting to take control before the news came, whatever it was. "You know, I want to congratulate you on our recent success over your way. You should feel damn proud of the work you're doin'."

"Yeah, but, uh, Freeman…"

"Yep. The Fourteenth Street Preschool is gonna be ready to open early, probably late Spring, thanks to you. Might even be able to get started on the drug rehab conversion over on MacArthur. That's next."

"Great, but…"

"Isn't it? Now then, you had somethin' on your mind?"

"Well, it was brought to my attention this morning that there was another breach of security at the wharf last night. A call went in to OPD from a witness again before our Port Authority guys were on hand. I wanted you to hear about it from me, before any other reports came in."

Mustafa's tone was suddenly foreboding. "Didn't this happen once before, very recently?"

"It did. This time it wasn't a major shipment, so it wasn't the same concern, but I'd really like to come up there and discuss a solution with you. Do you have some time this afternoon?"

"Tell you what." The voice was still severe. "You stay where you are and I'll come to you. I been meanin' to get down your way for a while anyway."

"You sure?" Barnes didn't like the sound of this. It was never comforting when Mustafa came into his neighborhood to lift his leg on the hydrants, the fence posts… and the docks.

"You bet I am. Be there in a half hour." He clicked off and punched the intercom.

"Celia?"

"Yes, sir?"

"Have Raymond bring the car around front, will you?"

"Yes, sir."

He tapped the intercom again. "Harlan?"

"Yeah?"

"Come in a minute, will you?"

"Right there."

Mustafa was sliding into his jacket when Metcalfe arrived.

"Get your coat. I'd like you to come with me to see Henry Barnes down at the Port Authority. I want you to hear this."

"What's up?"

"I'll tell you on the way."

As the black Lincoln limo cruised down East 14th, through West Oakland toward the waterfront, Mustafa described the security breach.

"This young punk has to be dealt with," he said. "Fuckin' grandstander from L.A. gettin' his endzone dance in the way of the operation. Twice, now." He flashed on the early days when he was personally responsible for the discipline on the street. It came back to him that there had been a satisfaction in that, a certainty about how things would play out. "We need to hurt this guy," he told Metcalfe. "We're not gettin' his attention, and that kind of disease can spread."

After the appropriate interval in which he hoped things had cooled down, the accountant began an update on the preschool project, but Mustafa remained preoccupied as they passed through the slum of West Oakland on the way to the Port. He hadn't been down this way in a long time, years maybe, and not by accident. As he took in the blight, he was once again staggered by the magnitude of the problem, and he interrupted the financial briefing.

"See this fuckin' wreckage, Harlan?" he said, waving a hand at the devastation outside. "Looks like a goddamn A-bomb hit this neighborhood, doesn't it."

"Yeah…" Metcalfe stared out the window absently.

"How could anythin' worth shit happen down here?" He looked around at Metcalfe, who remained inert; then his gaze returned outside. "I'm serious. How could anyone create something beautiful in a sewer like this?"

"I don't know. Wouldn't be easy." Metcalfe became uncomfortable when it wandered too far from the numbers.

"Nothin' happens here. Beatin'. Stealin'. Whorin'. That's what. All of it fueled by crack. People tryin' to wipe out reality with any kinda fuckin' feelgood they can buy." He shook his head. "With good reason, right?"

"I guess."

"Yeah, with good reason." He drifted with it, then said, "This is where I grew up, Harlan. Couple blocks over, behind the theater. Marcus Garvey Projects. Thirteenth and Market."

"No shit?" Metcalfe knew he'd come from somewhere in town, but hadn't realized it was the West Oakland Projects, the heart of the hood.

"No shit."

"Bet it was in a little better shape then, wasn't it? Those buildings were relatively new back in the seventies."

Mustafa looked over at him for a beat and scoffed. "Matter of fact, it was about the same nightmare you see now." Then, on impulse, he abruptly punched the intercom. "Raymond. Pull over up here," he barked. Almost before the limo coasted to the curb, he thrust the door open and was out.

"Stay here, Harlan," he instructed. "I'll be back in a couple minutes." He slammed the door and started briskly up the sidewalk, past an abandoned store with broken, boarded windows, then a narrow-fronted liquor store with worn wood showing through peeling gray paint, its windows protected by steel security screening. When he reached the alley, he was almost running. His feet knew the way.

Emerging into 13th Street, he stopped and stared across at the three massive, twelve-story, concrete edifices, the Marcus Garvey Memorial Apartments, current home to some 3,000 human beings. Countless others had been born, lived, and died here in the last fifty years, some more violently than others.

As he crossed and hurried up the concrete walkway to Building Three, his two-toned monogrammed shirt and Armani tie drew curious stares. He pushed through the cracked-glass front door that was surrounded by painted gang tags and other graffiti, then turned left, down the first-floor hall, stepping over a beat-up bicycle and squeezing past a stack of cardboard cartons. Papers, bottles, and other detritus littered the floor, but he didn't see any of it. He was riveted on the green pockmarked door on the right at the end of the hall. It was then that he heard the voices. He glanced back up the hall, then down the other way again, as the images and sounds flooded back, still indelibly etched after all the years. Yes. He'd been standing right here…

• • •

"That's it, you fuckin' punks! Give it up!"

The deep authoritarian shouts had come from outside. Within seconds, the front door banged open, and two teenagers dashed through, pushing by the runty thirteen-year-old, knocking him to the concrete floor, then sprinting down the dingy hall and disappearing around the corner at the end. One of them had been wearing the same black Raiders sweatshirt he was.

He picked himself up and was on his feet just as the first of the two burly OPD cops burst in and charged down the hall in his direction, nightsticks raised. Panicking, he started to run, but didn't get more than a few steps. A monstrous hand grabbed his sweatshirt from behind. Before he knew what was happening, a beefy leg swept his feet out from under him, and he went down hard on his back, a forearm landing heavily on his chest.

"Okay, you little asshole! You're done!"

His eyes flashed upwards in terror. The giant round face with the black clipped mustache hovered just above him, barrel chest heaving, nostrils flared, lips stretched tight over clenched teeth.

"Where's your partner?" the cop demanded, as the second patrolman lunged through the front door.

"I didn't do nothin'!" The voice was pre-pubescent thirteen-year-old, a squealing baby pig. "I didn't do nothin'! Warn't me!"

"Bull fuckin' shit! We saw both a ya' over on Eleventh, gettin' outta that hot Camaro." The policeman jerked him violently. "Don't guess you rabbited cause y'didn't do nothin'." The cop shook him again. "Now where's your fuckin' partner?" The other patrolman dropped a knee onto his legs, mashing them into the cement floor.

"Owwww!" he screamed. "I didn't do nothin'!"

Several doors opened, faces poked out. Toward the end of the hall, a heavy woman in her early forties, dressed in light-blue warm-ups, head covered with rollers and a hairnet, stepped into the hallway from behind a green door. The small wooly head of a five-year-old peeked around the jamb at her legs, searching for the source of the shrieking. The woman turned back and said firmly, "Tyler, you stay here!" She half-jogged down the hall toward the officers.

"That's my baby you got! Turn him loose. You leave him alone!"

The youngster was still crying. When he heard his mother's voice, the volume increased. Again he screeched: "I didn't do nothin'! Lemme go! Owwwww!"

By the time the woman got there, the two policemen had the boy on his feet. One held him while the other strapped his hands behind him with polyethelene wrist restraints. She stopped next to the officers, a foot from her child, but made no move to reach for him.

"What's he sposta done?" she demanded. Both cops ignored her.

"I said what's he sposta done?" she repeated, louder, as the boy sobbed, gasping spasmodically.

Now the cop, who had his hands on the child, turned and sized her up, his face devoid of affect. She was every bit of 5'9" and well over 200 pounds. He returned his attention to the boy, going about his business without responding.

The instant the two cops started to drag the child, limp and sobbing, down the hall toward the front door, the woman took two steps forward and laid a fleshy hand on the forearm of the one who was pulling him by the restraints.

"Did you hear me, officer?" she growled in the low tone of a mother tiger. "I axed you a question. What's he sposta done?"

The response was now immediate. The cop that held the boy dropped him, and both rushed the woman, knocking her backwards. She careened against the concrete wall across the hall and, before she could react, a fist struck her full on the mouth, dislodging several teeth. Blood gushed.

Down the hall, onlookers gasped and shouted as the boy, struggling to his feet with his hands restrained behind him, wailed, "Nooo! Don't! Momma!" He took a step toward her and stopped, terrified. "Please!"

As one cop held the woman, the other hit her two more times. At last, she went down. The youngster she had told to stay put was now running down the hall toward her, wailing. One cop looked in his direction, and the nearby heads disappeared and doors slammed. Collapsing to his knees, hands bound, and powerless, the scrawny thirteen-year-old wept uncontrollably at the atrocity before him that he was certain had been, in some incomprehensible way, his fault.

• • •

Despite the bright sunlight, Mustafa shivered as he walked the two blocks up 13th, past the corner of Market where the old Jewel Grocery had stood, now replaced with a convenience store run by a Korean family. The boarded-up hulk next door had been the Moonlight Lounge, where he and his boys smoked in the alley and watched the white men pull to the curb in their new cars to pick up hookers. He turned and stood for nearly a full minute, squinting back up 13th toward the projects. After thirty years, he still hated this place. Buncha fuckin' losers, goin' nowhere. He turned his back and retraced his steps to the car.

Climbing back into the limo without speaking, he settled into the back seat, the turmoil lingering. As the car resumed its course down 14th, something captured his attention: a bare patch of clay cramped between two brick buildings. He jerked a thumb toward the window. "See that park over there, Harlan?"

Metcalfe looked past him to the uneven dirt lot, no semblance of grass, that was passing on the right.

"That's where I played my first football. Talk about road rash. An' man, you wanna be careful where you fall. Needles, used rubbers, everywhere." He shook his head for the tenth time this trip. "Quite an education for a little kid."

The limousine glided on as discarded papers fluttered in its wake and settled amid the garbage that lay decomposing in the gutter.

"Y'oughta come by after dark some time. Dope. Sex. Gangbangin'. Y'know, it's been cleaned up by the white do-gooders a lotta times since I played here. These places all have. But they always end up just exactly like this. What you see is what you keep on gettin'. An' that's never gonna change until we do it ourselves. 'Til we have a stake in the action." His face darkened again. "And no way we're gonna let cocky little hoods like this kid of Barnes's fuck things up."

The car swept past the kiosk, where the guard in an AMPPS uniform snapped to and motioned them through. They pulled up in front of a well-maintained, sixties-vintage, three-story office building. The two men got out, entered the structure, and took the elevator to the third floor.

A receptionist sat behind an immaculate desk in front of a paneled wall. "Go right in, Mr. Mustafa," she smiled. "Commissioner Barnes is expecting you."

Tasteful cherry-wood furniture sank luxuriantly into thick-piled, azure-blue carpet. The office was sumptuous, though its size did not compare with Mustafa's. Floor-to-ceiling windows looked out over the port where several ships were unloading. The soaring 520-foot tower of the new, self-anchored, suspension section of the Bay Bridge dominated the view, dwarfing the ships and structures in the foreground.

Barnes was standing behind his desk. He greeted Mustafa deferentially and offered refreshments. Mustafa declined, as did Metcalfe. Barnes led them to the window for a brief visual tour, explaining what operations were ongoing, how the port had grown to the point that it far surpassed San Francisco in annual cubic tonnage.

Mustafa surveyed the scene appreciatively. "Very nice, Henry. This is very nice. I'll have to come down here more often." He collapsed into one of the two wingback leather chairs in front of the desk. Metcalfe took the other.

"So what's this security crisis all about?" Mustafa asked, beginning the conversation with civility.

Barnes tried to soft pedal it. "One of my young sergeants, kid named Delmar Foster out of L.A. Good kid, basically. He's new. Lotta balls. Sharp, know what I mean? Couple of routine offload assignments, but he jumped the gun, without contacting the command post for the usual coordinating instructions. And this last time he actually made contact with the ship's crew during the offload." Barnes looked away. "Like before, the guy on watch called OPD." He looked back. "We got it straightened out, but, like you said, it's the second time in a month. *Santiago Playa* was the first. I thought we should talk about how to shut it down over at OPD. I'm a little concerned that they might be starting to talk about these situations with AMPPS. I didn't want to get into it without running it by you, be sure we're not working at cross purposes."

Mustafa waited a few beats to be sure he was finished, then said, "I was with you right up to the part where we should be talkin' about it. I would have thought you'd have taken some decisive action on your own. See, this kinda shit simply isn't acceptable, Henry, particularly right now. What the fuck is this Foster's problem?"

"Like I say. He's okay, just a little too fond of the Jumbotron, I guess. But you know, he's young. We all had a little of that goin' at his age." He stopped, and the room went quiet.

"Terminate him," Mustafa said abruptly.

"You mean fire him?" Barnes asked.

"I mean terminate him."

Both men were shocked.

"You don't mean…?" Barnes stammered, searching Mustafa's face to be sure he had it right.

"You heard me."

Metcalfe and Barnes both stared downward, shifting uncomfortably. Barnes was fighting a grimace and losing. This was not possible. Mustafa had always been totally committed to the strict interdiction of deadly force. Occasionally things got a little physical when some kind of impediment had to be confronted, or a point had to be made, but there were immutable edicts about taking a life. It was a business, an organization of college graduates and family men. That was the plan from the beginning. Were they seen as part of the mob, or an arm of gang violence, it would ruin everything. Mustafa's mantra had always been respectability at all costs. No exceptions. It was a religion. This was sacrilege.

"Don't you think that might be overreacting?" Barnes said. "I mean, I know his family in L.A. They sent him up here for me to work with him. I was thinking maybe we could transfer him inside, where we can keep an eye on him 'til we're sure he understands the problem." He glanced at Metcalfe for support, but didn't get any. Metcalfe didn't look up.

"You see, we gave him a second chance," Mustafa said. "We're not going to give him another."

"Then how about we cut him loose? Let him go back to L.A."

"Negative. It's gotta be made clear that we have zero tolerance for this kind of bullshit."

Barnes's head was shaking. This couldn't be happening. "My God, Freeman," he said. "We haven't approached things in that way. I think we all came aboard believing that we would never…" he hesitated when Mustafa leaned forward.

"Well, I guess it's lucky you got an MBA and a pretty good working knowledge of the port, Henry. You've clearly earned your bonuses, but it's obvious you're not qualified to make the important security decisions. From now on, you'll take all those matters up directly with me."

Barnes exhaled through tightened lips.

"Justice has got to be swift," Mustafa rumbled. "You will make it happen, tonight." As he stood and went to the door, Barnes once again registered disbelief.

"Me? But I don't have the—"

Mustafa cut him off without looking back. "Tonight!"

Gripped by emotion, Barnes turned and stared out the enormous windows, but saw nothing.

CHAPTER THIRTY-ONE

"No big thing. Routine petty theft, starts Monday."

It was getting on toward 6:30 at the Oarhouse, and the six o'clock news was still blaring as Sandy babbled about his debut jury trial assignment, trying to conceal his hovering dread. Despite his efforts to make it sound like just another day at the office, he was definitely feeling it, but there was no way he could play any sympathy card; his 484 shoplift came up a little short of Noah's 187.

They were already two-thirds through their first pitcher. After taking a swallow, Noah began the cross-examination. "So what's your defense?"

"Guy had a pint of Jack in his coat pocket in the checkout line at CVS. Says it was just absentminded. Forgot he'd picked it up."

"You buy that?"

"I'm not really sure. He's a pretty decent guy. He's got a semi-regular job, and he did have some other stuff with him that he was trying to pay for."

"Any priors?"

"Three petty thefts and an assault. All pretty remote in time."

"Three petty thefts?" Noah laughed. "He may be a 'pretty decent guy,' but he's a pretty shitty thief. Are they gonna get those in?"

"I don't know. If they do, I'm screwed."

"Any of them involve trying to sneak stuff through a checkout line?"

"Well, yeah. One of 'em was—"

"Lie down, man. You're totally toasted."

"Shit." Sandy's fingers drummed the bar nervously. "DA wouldn't offer me anything. Said he has to go as charged, and the guy's a denial."

"Not surprised. So you'll put it on, and when the jury comes back, you wave goodbye to the guy and move on to the next one. What can you do?" He took another mouthful of the brew and clunked the mug down, gazing at the little bubbles breaking loose and drifting to the surface. "Anyway, it's good experience. That's what everybody keeps telling me."

"I hate this."

"You want some help with the direct and cross?" Noah said. "I could probably patch a couple of hours together this weekend. Pull the old study group out of retirement?"

Feeling miserable, Sandy considered his answer. He could see the jury coming back after ten minutes, hardly time to elect the foreman, who would pass the little paper to the bailiff, who'd give it to the clerk, who'd give it to the judge, who'd give it back to the clerk, who'd read the verdict, and he'd notch up his first loss against no wins. One more disappointment to Howard, who would tell him in the daily briefing from Modesto not to sweat it, but there would be a long silence during which Sandy would know... know that he was wondering.

"Maybe," Sandy finally answered. "Yeah, that'd be good. I'm just not ready for this kind of stuff. I..." He glanced over, but Noah, fixed on the TV, had stopped listening. The Owens interview in front of Giovanni was rolling.

"Just what is the progress of the Ruiz prosecution, Mr. Owens?" Arlen Gates was asking him.

"We're set for trial in a little over six weeks, and it will proceed as scheduled. We have an excellent trial deputy trying the case. Marco Salem has been with me for fifteen years, my Chief Deputy for the last three."

"Do you anticipate anything unusual from the defense?"

"You know, there have been a number of attempts at obfuscation, but that won't change anything. In fact, the most recent subterfuge was a claim by the defendant that he was out of the country in Mexico when the Van Zandt murder occurred. This is, of course, patently false—"

"What?" Noah nearly fell off his stool.

"—there being simply no evidence to support such a contention. We're confident that the People will be vindicated at trial."

Noah pounded the bar in disbelief. "How the fuck did they find out about that?" he railed. "No one outside the office knows anything about the alibi, and here's the fricking DA blasting it all over the six o'clock news."

"How could they have found out?" Sandy asked.

Noah was on his feet and bolting for the front door.

"Wait. Where are you going?"

"Gotta call Buzz."

Sandy's attention returned to the TV as the news segment progressed through other local stories. Noah was back within minutes.

"So?" Sandy queried.

"Left a voicemail. He's working another case. Must be out of cell range."

"What are you going to do?"

Noah slid back onto his barstool and took a long pull of the draft. "Wait for him to call, I guess."

"What are your options? Seems like you been playing catch-up all the way."

"Tell me about it. I mean, these jerks might already have more investigation on the alibi issue than we do. I applied for an expense voucher over a week ago so we could send Buzz to Baja to nail down some witnesses. I haven't heard a word"—he nodded toward the TV—"but Owens obviously has. My guess is their people are down there thrashing around right now, while we're hung up with permits and authorizations."

He paused as he worked through it. "Only explanation is some kind of pipeline to the DA, but how could that possibly be?"

"What can you do?"

"Trial's only six weeks away," Noah said. "What if something we turn up down there suggests some further investigation, or we find something that means we need another expert? We're getting short of time here."

Noah took another beat, another swig, and picked it up again. "I've called Stark three times to press him about the investigation," he said, turning to Sandy, "and about those scumbag cops who thrashed me, by the way. Nothin'. No response. If I leave a message, he doesn't return the calls. If I catch him in the office, he blows me off." He mocked Stark's deep voice: "'No word on the investigation yet.' 'Nothing from IAD on Fitzgerald.' 'They're looking into it.'"

"So, what if you don't get the investigation? Where does that leave you?"

"In deep shit."

"Can't you put Ruiz on and get what a good guy he is? No record? He just says he didn't do it?"

"Jesus, Sandy, with no investigation? I can't put him on without corroborating witnesses. Salem'll destroy him."

"How so?" Sandy asked. "Why can't he tell his story?"

Noah shook his head. "What 'story'? A bunch of admissions on cross that he was in the Van Zandt condo, burglarized him, somehow divined that Van Zandt wasn't going to be there that night. Now he says he was in Mexico, at a weekend party at some Mexican rancho he says, but of course he never said anything about that before. Where are the witnesses who saw him down there? The alleged 'friends' he was with? Can he name even one? Yadda, yadda, yadda. Without corroboration, the whole alibi defense sounds made up, and begins to smack of the needle."

"I guess." Sandy took his point. "But what else have you got?"

"Yeah, well, that's it, isn't it. Pablo wasn't even the one who told me he was in Mexico. His mother did. When I confronted him, he said yeah, he was at this 'Rancho', but he thought it'd just have complicated things if he'd told me." Another slosh of the beer. "Complicate things. God forbid we should complicate things. Can you believe this guy? Then he says he's not sure exactly where this so-called rancho is. Somewhere near San Felipe, he says, Baja California, on the Sea of Cortez was all he could give me."

Sandy topped up their mugs as Noah continued the invective. "He describes it as a 'big hacienda with a red-tiled roof.' Now that really narrows it down, doesn't it?" He shook his head. "Not easy tryin' to carry the ball for a guy who keeps hiding it on you."

"Totally." The concept of hiding cast Sandy's mind back to the times in law school when the pressure was on, and he was glad it was Noah who took the hot seat. He always felt a little guilty about it, maybe more than a little, but not enough to eclipse the relief he found in hiding.

"All I have going for me is Buzz, but I gotta get him looking for this rancho place, like now. I just need for them to approve the frickin' money."

"Speaking of money, have you heard there's gonna be a PD strike?"

Noah finally looked over at him. "No way," he said. "When?"

"I don't know. Sometime in the next couple weeks. Demands are with the county right now. They gotta come back with more money, more muscle in policy-making, or a strike's a sure thing. Michelin says it's unlikely they'll cave, and he's got the votes if they don't."

"How the hell do PDs go on strike? I mean, what happens to the clients? Where does the representation come from?"

"I guess that's kind of the point, isn't it?" Sandy answered. "The county needs to see how critical we are to the system. How would you do it? Write 'em a nice letter and explain it?"

"I don't know, Sandy," Noah demurred, "but I'm not down with any kind of walkout on clients. I've told you that. There's more involved than just teaching the county a lesson. Defenses are bound to suffer. People will end up in the joint. I mean, what if you're in the middle of trial? No way I'd walk out on Ruiz."

"Maybe it'd just be for the day. You know, some kind of symbolic demonstration," Sandy offered. "I can't imagine clients would get hurt. I mean, aren't there ethical issues? State Bar Canons or something?"

"Yeah, really," Noah said. "Something about fiduciary duty? Putting your clients' interests first?"

Their attention returned to the TV. Minutes passed, and finally Sandy said, "You're in, aren't you? It'd go bad for you if you weren't."

"I gotta see what it is. And I got a few other things on my mind right now."

"Like whether we're gonna have another pitcher?"

"More like getting with Buzz about this fucking leak in the office. Like what I'm gonna do about getting him down to Mexico. There's not gonna be any plea, so I somehow gotta find somebody to say Pablo was in Mexico, other than just him and his mother." He glanced at his watch, then at the half-full pitcher. "I gotta go, man. You gonna hang around?"

"I don't know. Yeah, I guess. It's early, and leavin' beer in a pitcher violates a primary tenet of my theology. Think I'll work on it, then pick up some chow mein on the way home. You up for that?"

Noah drained his mug, then said, "I don't think so. I'm beat."

"C'mon. It's Friday night."

"Pass. Gotta save my brain for Ruiz this weekend." Noah threw some crinkled bills on the bar and grabbed his briefcase. "So, we find some time to go over your trial testimony tomorrow?"

Sandy thought about it, but only for a couple of seconds. "Nah," he said. "It's Saturday." Sandy wasn't going to let a little thing like his first trial starting Monday stand between him and his weekend agenda. Party now, worry later.

"Saturday, Monday, Thursday… all the same to me," Noah mumbled. "This trial shit takes a little extra time when you don't know what you're doin'." He stood to leave.

"Right… see ya Monday, I guess." Sandy turned his attention back to the TV.

Noah cut between the tables, flung the heavy brass and dark-wood front door open, stepped briskly into the night air, turned to his right down Eddy, and straight into a woman who was, equally briskly, turning into the Oarhouse. She careened backwards, her bag knocked from her shoulder, and the contents of her purse clattered to the sidewalk.

"Hunnh… hey…?" she grunted, accusingly.

"God, I'm really sorry," Noah mumbled, bending over to pick up the cell phone, lipstick, coins. He looked up sheepishly. "I didn't see you. I guess I… Kate!"

"Noah?"

"Jeezus, did I hurt you?"

They eyed each other awkwardly as the irony of the question hung in the air. They hadn't spoken since Bodega, other than the very occasional frosty hello passing in the office, or at the courthouse. Avoiding her eyes, he bent down to retrieve the rest of the spilled items.

"I-I guess not," she said, straightening her dark wool coat.

He hesitated, then said, "I've been thinking about you, Kate." He bent over again, looking for more purse contents. He'd been determined to let her work it all through, one way or the other. Let her make the first move. But now here it was, her stuff all over the sidewalk, and he was just talking. "I thought about calling a million times. This silence bullshit is making me crazy." He'd imagined this conversation every one of those million times, and it definitely wasn't going according to plan. "I'd hoped we could... uh... straighten things out. I want to tell you, um... how sorry I am about Bodega—"

"No need," she interrupted. "Everything's fine."

Silence, as he considered his options. "Listen, why don't you come in and let me buy you a beer? I mean, I'd really like to—"

"Another time, maybe." Abrupt, brusque. "I was just stopping in to cash a check. I gotta get across the bridge."

There had been periods of distance between them in the past, but never a chasm this long and this wide. Whether she missed their time together or not, there was no way she would expose herself to the insanity again.

"I'm meeting someone for dinner," she said, checking her watch.

He was still staring. He couldn't believe that the woman in front of him was the person he'd been so close to for so long. The face was the same, but behind it, the Kate he had known so well was gone.

He reached out to put a hand on her shoulder, saying, "Kate, please. Can't we just—"

"Sorry," she said, pulling away. Then, as she swept past him, "I've really gotta run." She pushed open the polished brass door without looking back. "Maybe I'll see you at work."

"Yeah..." he muttered, as he watched her melt into the glare of the tavern and make her way to the bar. She chatted briefly with Sandy, smiling, then took out her checkbook and commenced writing.

Turning, he started down Eddy, walking slowly, shivering with the fog that was beginning to settle over the early evening as the kaleidoscope of Tenderloin neon mirrored the jumble of his thoughts.

• • •

A white delivery van pulled up in front of the receiving warehouse in the Ebony Properties yard. Mark Harrison got out, jeans, a white tee, and a blue windbreaker substituting for his usual AMPPS police uniform. Knocking on the entry door next to the truck bay entrance, he glanced back toward the front gate.

How would it go down, he wondered. Unbelievable that it had come to this. The door opened, and Leech Jaqua faced him, a cigarette dangling from his lips.

"I fuckin' hate this," Harrison said, not waiting for a greeting from Jaqua. He stepped into the enormous darkened expanse of the warehouse.

"Gotta be done," Jaqua mumbled. "C'mon in the office."

"I don't know," Harrison said as he followed Jaqua through the dark, vacant industrial space toward the light of a glass-enclosed shipping office. "We work with the guy. I met his brother, for chrissakes."

"Yeah, well… I don't know how you run an organization if you don't have discipline."

"Really? Discipline? This is a little more than discipline."

"All the same to me."

Once inside the office, Jaqua closed the door behind them. Opening the top drawer of a steel filing cabinet, he removed a Beretta 92FS nine-millimeter semi-automatic, extracted the magazine from the grip, checked its contents, and slapped it back in place. Drawing the slide clear, he ensured there was a round in the chamber, then pulled a sound-suppressor from the open file drawer, screwed it onto to the barrel, and handed the rig to Harrison.

"Use this," he said. "Untraceable."

"Fuckin' hate it," Harrison repeated, as he slipped the weapon under the waistband of his jeans at the small of his back and repositioned his windbreaker over it.

"Like I said—"

"I know what you said," Harrison snapped. "But why do I need to be in it?"

"It's a two-man job. I need to meet and greet, or he gets suspicious. You know that."

"Wasn't part of the job description."

"Right. Did you get that that Ruiz kid says he was in Mexico when Van Zandt got done?" Jaqua said, steering it in a different direction.

"No. What's that about?"

"Yeah. Claims he was in Baja."

"So?"

"Just that we know he wasn't." Jaqua cast a sideways glance at the off-duty cop. "He was in the guy's condo. So we got instructions to shut things down before this gets out of hand."

"Meaning?"

"Meaning they want a little encouragement of this fuckin' PD. See if we can't convince him to bring this sideshow to an end."

"What, bring the case to an end? How would he do that?"

"Well, I guess by pleading the kid guilty. What other way would there be?"

"You got something in mind?"

"I got some ideas. Can you get some help from Fitzgerald on it?"

"I don't know. He's usually okay, but he's been talkin' about being a short-timer with the department. He wants to keep a low profile."

"It'd be good to have OPD in on it. Spreads the risk, know what I mean? Maybe you talk to him."

"Well, you have to spell out what you're thinking."

"Never mind. If you can't make it happen, I'll cover it with Mumford."

"I didn't say that, I just—"

There was a knock at the warehouse door.

"Let's go," Jaqua said.

"Where does it happen?"

"In here, but you come with me to get him. Make it look casual." More knocking, louder.

Jaqua opened the door to Delmar Foster, who was standing in front of the exterior light.

"Hey, Jake," the handsome young black man drawled, grinning. "'Sup? Got a call to report down here. We gonna do some sampling of the product, or what?"

"Something like that," Jaqua said. "Got some orders to deal with. Come on in."

As Foster stepped by him into the building, Jaqua picked up the alcohol breath. Definitely a cheap vodka.

"D..." Harrison nodded, acknowledging him as he entered.

"Uh-oh. Must be serious. Got the po-lice here too," Foster observed, still smiling. "So where we gonna have this, uh... tastin'?"

"Let's go into the office," Jaqua said.

"Whatever," Foster muttered, following him into the gloom.

Harrison fell in behind them. Removing the Beretta from his waistband, he shook his head again, his face contorting.

CHAPTER THIRTY-TWO

"Hey Blue, you up?"

Buzz's telephone voice was gravelly Saturday morning. Noah's, however, was not.

"Up? Christ. I'm at Peet's with the sports page, workin' my second latte."

"So, you called last night?"

"Yeah. We need to talk. You been watching the news?"

"Not really. Been out to Pleasanton on that *Drago* case. Why?"

"The DA has the Mexico alibi is all. They plastered it all over the six o'clock news last night."

"Whaat?"

"Yeah. What would that mean to you?"

"Wait. You're not suggesting that I—"

"C'mon, Buzz. It's too early for your paranoia. I need to know how they're gettin' this stuff. They're deeper into our defense than we are. This cannot be happening."

"What Peet's are you at? I'll be right over."

"Turk and Van Ness."

"Have another latte. I'm there in twenty minutes."

Twenty-two minutes later, Buzz bought a large coffee and a currant scone, navigated among the laptop robots and cell phone junkies, and pulled up a chair at the table where Noah had spread his copy of the *Chronicle*.

"The alibi's still front page," Buzz said. "Heard a piece on the way over. I'm mystified."

"You ever have the DA in your pants like this before?"

"Well, I don't know," Buzz told him. "DAs and PDs bunk together every day. A lot of 'em get pretty close over the years. There's always crosstalk, but it's usually just good-natured competition. They don't share the top-secret stuff. You add this alibi leak to those cops going through your car? Say what you want, Blue. This smells bad, and that's not just paranoia. The Buzzard has a nose for this kind of thing."

"Not to mention fixing up a rookie with this catastrophe in the first place."

"Right. And by the way, seems like some stuff might have gone missing from my car, as well."

"What do you mean?"

"I can't be sure, but I'm thinkin' I had a few things in my trunk that I can't find now."

"Like what?"

"I don't know. Some of the lab reports. Maybe a page of my notes. If they've been into your trunk, they mighta been in mine, too." As he took a sip and a bite, Buzz cast a sidelong glance for Noah's response. The governor on his suspicion motor took hold, and he manually reined his conclusions into the credibility range. "I don't know," he said, a little more diffidently. "Can't be sure, but I think there's some pages missing. Might have misplaced them, but I don't think so."

"Jesus."

"Yeah."

"So what do we do?" Noah asked. "You gonna talk to Stark about it?"

Buzz measured him through the Coke-bottle lenses. "Uh, Blue? I know it's early, but this is the Buzzard you're talkin' to, remember? Me talk to Stark? I got a better chance of bustin' into Gitmo to chat with Mohammad."

"Okay, okay. I'll go in on Tuesday. I need to hear what's happening on the IA investigation of Fitzgerald, anyway. Cops beat up PDs, and we're apparently okay with that. Make sense to you?"

"None. And what about the funds to get me down to Baja?"

"Yeah. Put that in the mix, and it's pretty much a full-on stonewall. Are they totally incompetent, or is it something about this case?"

"Well, I think there're some serious problems with the office. Always have. But this's different. There's definitely something going on with this case."

"So, I talk to Stark. What else?" Noah asked.

"I gotta get with Farley Whetmore. He's running some retests on the insect studies in his home lab. Those were the pages that went missing. I was getting them ready to talk to Farley."

"Yeah, what about these 'home lab' studies? How are they ever going to be admissible?"

"Well, now, that's a good question. For a blue, you're starting to make some serious progress. I say his 'home lab' cuz that's where it is. Turns out it's a fully equipped, fully licensed, fully accredited, criminalistics laboratory. Farley consults for lots of folks, not just me. It's just he's giving us a break on the price because we got history."

"Nice. So what's he doing?"

"Time of death is a big deal if we can show it doesn't jibe with when Pablo was in the condo. It'll be key to get the numbers as accurate as possible. Maybe cast some doubt on the ME's studies."

"I've never been wild about that thread. It all comes back to Pablo's word about when he was there. We can't prove it. We don't have anything objective."

"Well, just keep in mind what I said about reasonable doubt. We don't have to prove anything. If their airtight cheese starts to show some holes, jurors begin to wonder if they can buy any of what they're selling. Remember the glove? 'If it doesn't fit, you must acquit.' We don't have to prove whose glove it is."

"All right. See what Whetmore says. I'll talk to Stark. I think the next thing has gotta be some witnesses in Mexico, and we go from there. They've just assigned me to a misdemeanor setting calendar while we're counting down on *Ruiz*. Department Nineteen. So that's where you can find me." He exhaled in exasperation. "Pretty tough focusing on everyday calendar bullshit with a 187 hanging, but there it is."

Buzz returned to his coffee and pastry. Noah drained his latte, folded his *Chronicle*, and stood to go. "Meantime, while we wait for the investigation to come through, we say nothing about anything to anyone, in the office or anywhere else. God knows who's leaking what."

"Roger that, Blue."

• • •

The 9:30 sun shone through the bedroom window, radiating light and heat on the rumpled bedclothes. Kate opened one eye, then the other. Her first awareness was that she had virtually none; the next was that she had a monumental headache extending from the back of her neck to her forehead; and finally, that she was totally naked.

Without moving her throbbing head, she cast her eyes around the unfamiliar room, and slowly, a mosaic of the preceding night began to coalesce, though there were definitely a number of tiles missing. Lying perfectly still to allow the fog to burn off, only two words came to her: "Oh," and "God."

In time, she became aware of a muffled voice from somewhere beyond the room. As it droned, she realized it had a mechanical quality, from a radio or TV. Then another voice was superimposed.

"Morning, beautiful. Sleep well?"

Smiling, she pulled the sheet around her, propped herself with difficulty onto her elbows, and looked up at the figure in the doorway.

"Morning, Jim," she said. "I guess it was mostly okay. I think this throbbing head is a pretty recent development."

Stark's apartment was medium-lavish in a minimalistic way. The furniture was Swedish modern, the adornments sparse, the hardwood floors bare. Opposite the bedroom window was a monster Modigliani print, a reclining nude done all in reds and blacks, below which stood a lonely, black chest. The room was otherwise wall-to-wall bed. Halfway up the hill in Piedmont, the location afforded a commanding view of the Bay and the Golden Gate Bridge beyond.

"Got just the thing for such a malady," he said.

"That's reassuring," she rasped. He wore a white terrycloth robe with a Ritz-Carlton medallion over the pocket. Her first thought was that he seemed remarkably put together under the circumstances. "I was about to call the paramedics," she added.

"This is a better solution. Trust me."

"What is it?"

"Well, see. That's a secret. Starts with tomato juice, but the rest of the ingredients are patent-protected. The full recipe is locked in a vault in the sub-basement."

"Okay," she said. "I'm in. But point me toward a shower, will you? I've got some serious groundwork to do."

He smiled and nodded to a door to the left of the bureau. "There's a robe on the back of the door. Kitchen's down the hall to your right when you're ready. Meet you there?"

"Right," she said. "Give me at least a couple of hours."

Twenty-five minutes later, Kate padded sheepishly into the kitchen, now robed, and drying her hair with a towel. The TV was still tuned to the news, and Stark was at the sink, his back to her.

"Shower felt good," she said, "but I haven't quite decided whether I'll live yet. Any way we could get a couple of Advil into that magic potion of yours?"

He turned and smiled. "Love your outfit," he said.

"Thanks."

"So, I've got the original Dr. Stark's Day-After Remedy all teed up." He opened the fridge and withdrew a tall glass filled with a thick red mixture and a stalk of celery, looking for all the world like a Bloody Mary. "Why don't you hold off on the Advil until you see how this does. If you still need some, we can make it happen."

Kate eyed the glass suspiciously. "There isn't any kind of alcohol in that, is there? One more molecule and I'll have to check into rehab."

"No alcohol," he said as he handed her the concoction. "C'mon. All the way in one play."

As she drank, the word *Ruiz* from the small TV next to the sink caught her attention, and she walked over to listen. The story was a rehash of the Owens interview, a talking head describing the alibi and the District Attorney's contempt for it. Stark looked over.

"Yeah," he said. "That's our case. Getting a lot of media play recently."

"For sure," Kate agreed. "Doesn't it seem like the DA gets a whole lot of the defense material?"

He hesitated, then said, "Not really. There's typically a lot of cross-pollination. Nothing unusual."

She set the empty glass on the counter and continued to follow the broadcast.

"So, you see much of Noah lately?" he asked.

She looked over. "I don't, really."

"Something happen? Seems like you two were pretty tight."

"Both just busy. Not much time for hanging out these days." There was no way she was getting into any Bodega details, so she tried to take it back to his morning-after medicine. "Where did you get that tomato tonic, anyway? I think I feel a little better already. You might be onto something."

"Necessity is the mother of invention, I guess. Lotta trial and error."

"If you bottle it, you might be able to dump this law biz."

They were quiet for a while, listening to the TV until the news went to commercial. Then he said, "Kate…?"

"Ummm?"

"Does Noah ever discuss *Ruiz* with you anymore?"

"Like I say, I haven't really seen him."

"It's just that, after we talked about it, you were really helpful at first, and I could help him more now if I knew more."

"I'm not sure there's much more I can do."

"Maybe you could stoke it up a little again, no? Try to draw him out. See where he's going with it?"

"I don't know, Jim."

"Well, think about it. We're getting to a crucial point. It'd help everyone, especially that Mexican kid he's defending, if I could talk some sense to him."

"Sense?"

"You know that the guy refused an offer that was a total gift. No way he could have possibly understood what he was leaving on the table, and I'm afraid Noah's not making that clear to him. It'd be a terrible injustice if a young kid like that had to spend the best part of his life in the joint."

Noticing her frown, he added: "So maybe you help me help them both?"

She wanted to appear accommodating, but the truth of it was that she just could not bring herself to rekindle any kind of meaningful dialogue with Noah. Too awkward. Too painful. "I'll think about it," she said.

"Do that," he responded as he returned to the fridge. "Now, how about a second dose of Dr. Stark's miracle?"

CHAPTER THIRTY-THREE

"So officer, let's go over this again."

Harvey Cohen began his cross-examination listlessly. "I think you said that the sole basis for your suspicion that my client was the perpetrator had to do with this matter of the knit watch cap?"

Sandy was still sitting second chair to Cohen on prelims, having lost the hopeless petty theft a month earlier. The jury had returned the predicted result: guilty. The victory was that they deliberated for a full forty minutes. Sandy had settled back into prelims while nursing the wound, and today he was scribbling notes as Cohen did his thing. The case, People v. Marquis Ward, was a grand theft person, aka purse-snatch, in which the elderly victim's credit cards and other purse contents were found on the eighteen-year-old Ward some four blocks from, and half an hour after, the mugging.

The last month had seen Noah and Buzz still beating the bushes for prospective witnesses locally, their application for funds to send Buzz to Baja still hanging in administrative limbo. They'd widened the contact net from Van Zandt neighbors to family members, friends, and business associates, but had turned up nothing usable. Baja was Pablo's last hope.

Noah's angst compounded with each passing day as the clock ticked ever closer to trial with no solid exculpatory evidence. At first, he had hounded Stark, who'd responded with evasive excuses superimposed on the well-worn screed about how Pablo should take the deal. Noah had protested that Salem said the offer was off the table, but Stark told him they always tried to dynamite the defense with those kinds of threats. He said they would likely still stand by the original proposed plea bargain, with the caveat that the closer it got to trial, the more enamored they might become with their case. There would be some tipping point at which trial would be inevitable.

After the Mexico-alibi leak, Noah had resolved not to discuss the case with Stark, and he redirected his nagging about the investigation to Bobbi. Her responses had been no less encouraging. "Under consideration." "Going through channels." "Sending an investigator to a foreign country is an unusual request." "Has to be addressed at the highest levels."

The days became indistinguishable from one another. On this one, Noah had finished the calendar in Department 19, and had stopped in at Department 16, hoping to collect Sandy and explore possibilities for the evening's activities. The *Ward* prelim had stretched into the early evening, with Noah occupying a seat in the back while Cohen took a run at dismantling the prosecutor's probable cause. The critical issue was that the incriminating contraband that linked Ward to the crime had been discovered incident to the arrest. So Cohen's cross-examination was aimed at showing the stop was illegal, a Fourth Amendment violation, because all the evidence would then be inadmissible as "fruit of that poisonous tree," and there would be no basis for a conviction.

Judge McCormick sat, not so patiently, listening. The hour was late, and he was long since ready to rule, end a long week, and go home, not so much to a waiting wife as a Bombay martini.

"That's correct, Mr. Cohen. The watch cap was what initially made me think he was involved." In his late twenties, the cop was already an experienced witness, having testified more times than he could remember. It was a major part of the patrol assignment.

"And you said that the victim told you that the man who stole her purse had been wearing a navy blue knit watch cap. Is that what you said?"

"That's right."

"So you would agree that had you not suspected Mr. Ward of wearing a watch cap, you would not have had probable cause to stop him, am I right?"

"That's true."

"And had you not stopped him, there would have been no arrest. Isn't that the fact?"

"I think you could say that."

"But you told us that when you and your partner were patrolling the neighborhood that afternoon, you stopped these three youths, none of whom was wearing a watch cap?"

"Correct."

As he watched the proceedings, Noah's mind went to Kate and her proficiency just days into her assignment to the 270 calendar. Kate was on his mind frequently, but when their paths crossed, encounters had continued in the range of cool to subzero. She was polite and, if she stopped to chat, she was only interested in talking about *Ruiz*, what he was planning, his strategies and tactics. Whenever Noah suggested something beyond that—dinner, lunch, coffee, a beer—there was always an excuse.

"So just remind us, officer," Cohen continued, "how it was that you came to focus on my client if none of the young men was wearing a watch cap?"

"Well, like I said, I noticed your client had a rather prominent afro, and there was a ring of matted hair around his head. From this, I concluded he had been wearing a watch cap recently, but had taken it off, perhaps when he saw our patrol vehicle approaching."

"So, you said there was a 'ring' around my client's head, Officer Gray, is that correct?"

"Yes."

"A 'ring' being a circular configuration?"

"Yes.

"And by that you meant the hair was matted in the back?"

"Yes, it was."

"Did you look?"

"In fact, I did."

"When did you do that?"

"I asked all three to turn around as soon as we had detained them."

"Did either of the other two young men have a ring of matted hair?"

"No. In fact, one had a shaved head, and the other had very short hair."

"And was the hair matted down on the right side of Mr. Ward's head?"

"It was."

Noah turned his head and frowned. *Where could this possibly be going?* McCormick fidgeted and let out an audible sigh, but Cohen soldiered on. He stood and walked over to the jury box to build some suspense. "And I take it you noted that the hair was also matted on the left side?"

"Yes, I did."

Cohen purposefully directed his gaze downward to the floor, as though carefully pondering a complex implication of the testimony, and then cleared his throat.

"Well then, officer, let me ask you this…" *Here it comes. Wait for it. Drum roll. And the point being…* "Did you see any hair matted on the front of my client's head?"

The cop paused, grasping for the meaning. "Well, no," he answered. "The cap had apparently been over his forehead. There was no hair on his forehead."

"Then I submit to you that you didn't see a 'ring' around my client's head at all," Cohen demanded, glaring, his tone accusatory. "Isn't that the truth of the matter, Officer Gray?"

Noah's eyebrows went up and he looked down at his feet.

For the next few seconds, the witness was speechless; all onlookers who had been following the colloquy seemed to be considering its meaning. Finally, McCormick boomed, "Oh, excoriating cross-examination, Cohen! I am overjoyed that the sun didn't set on that revelation. Though given the hour, I'm afraid it may have. So is that it? Or did you have some other fascinating insights into hair-matting with which you might endeavor to impeach this officer's testimony?"

Bowing his head, Cohen's stifled smirk was mostly hidden from the judge's line of sight.

"Are we through here?" the judge demanded, volume increased, face reddening.

"I suppose we are, Your Honor," Cohen muttered.

"Thank God." McCormick exhaled and launched into his ruling, holding Ward to answer for the felony of grand theft before Cohen got back to the counsel table. Sandy turned and regarded Noah with his own surreptitious smirk.

Noah shook his head. *Life in the big leagues. A laugh a minute.*

Ward was remanded into custody, and Sandy gathered Cohen's files as Noah sauntered down the center aisle to the well. "Now *that* was some piece of lawyering," he observed.

Cohen looked at Noah as he took his file from Sandy with a shrug, a tilt of the head, and a thrust of his lower lip. "Gotta pass the time somehow. Still eight years, four months, twenty-six days to retirement."

"Right. So what do we call you now? 'Lord of the Rings'?"

"That'll work," Cohen said, walking up the aisle, "or just Lord'll do."

"So what's up?" Noah asked Sandy. "You wanna grab a quick beer? I'm beat, and I need to get an early start on the *Ruiz* trial prep in the morning, but I got time for one, maybe two."

"I'm in," Sandy said. "Lemme dump these files at the office, and I'll meet you at the Oarhouse in forty-five."

"Done."

Sandy went on ahead. As Noah approached the rear door to the courtroom, Buzz burst through.

"Here you are," he said, somewhat breathlessly.

"Yep. Here I am. What's up?"

"You been back to Oakland Division?"

"No, I been in court all afternoon," Noah said, continuing into the hallway. "Why? What happened?"

"The response on the Mexican investigation finally came through."

Noah jerked around. "What did they say?"

"Denied." Buzz pulled the requisition response from his folder.

"The fuck? Lemme see that." Noah snatched the paper and scanned it, mumbling, "'Insufficient likelihood of success'... 'Misuse of public funds'... 'International investigation'..." He looked up at Buzz, glaring in disbelief. "What are they *talking* about?"

Buzz shrugged and shook his head.

"I may not know shit," Noah seethed, "but I know this. This isn't incompetence. These assholes are totally shutting us down. I have no idea what the play is, but I intend to find out."

"How you gonna do that?" Buzz asked.

"I don't know." Fuming, Noah looked up toward the end of the nearly empty hallway; then he turned back. "But at the moment, we gotta worry about this trial that starts in less than three weeks, and we got bupkis. What I do know is that Pablo Ruiz was in fucking Mexico when the murder went down. Amparo Ruiz is clear about that. And by God, we gotta get someone who can testify to it."

After more silence, he snatched his wallet in a sudden surge of frustration, took out his Visa card, and handed it to Buzz. "Dammit, I'll do it myself. We're outta time, man, and shit outta options. Make the reservation and get down there."

"Tonight?"

"Right fucking now!"

● ● ●

By 9:00, Noah and Sandy had plowed through a full pitcher and a burger as Noah seethed about the denied investigation request. By 9:30, he had set a take-home box of parmesan french fries under the first step of the Larkin for Margaret, and was dragging his hundred and ninety pounds of exhaustion up the front stairs, still steaming, though he'd powered down a notch. The beers had helped, and he was able to begin to get a glimmer of perspective that at least things had come off dead center.

Descending toward him dressed in jeans, a bulky green turtleneck, and white Nikes, Lisa Sanders had her blond hair pulled back in a loose ponytail with wispy tendrils falling onto both shoulders, stark contrast with the black miniskirt-lace camisole-patent pumps she would have been wearing by this time Friday night two months ago. Gone, too, was the flashy neon maquillage, complete with sparkling eyeliner, replaced by soft-colored accents here and there. This was the face of the freshly scrubbed kid from Minnesota she had actually been eight years before when she'd arrived in San Francisco.

"Hi, Lees," Noah managed wearily as she passed. "You look awesome. Where y'off to?"

"Picking Maggie up," she chirped, all perkiness and smiles.

He couldn't muster a response.

"At the foster home. I've got her for the weekend." When she saw that he was dragging, she said, "You're home late. What's up with that?"

"Same old, same old. So what's the current word on your getting her back?"

"I don't want to even let myself think about that for the moment. I'm not going to bring her home until I'm sure everything's right."

"Looks pretty right to me," he said. "You've come a long way, lady. How goes the job search?"

"I ended up taking that gig as a trainee at Kragen. Never thought I'd wind up in auto parts, but it was my dad's racket, so I guess I come by it honestly."

"Hey, it's a job."

"Money's okay, and they seem to like me, and best of all, it's just around the corner on Van Ness."

"That's handy."

She shrugged. "But I'm only sober seven weeks. It's gonna take more than twenty-eight days of rehab and a bunch of AA meetings to convince CPS."

"I'm convinced."

"You're prejudiced. You just miss Maggie."

"You got that right. Give her a hug for me, willya?"

"Sure," she said, leaning in and wrapping her arms around his neck. He returned the hug one-armed. As he looked over her shoulder, his attention was attracted by a white delivery van passing slowly in front of the building thirty feet away, its stocky black driver staring at them through mirrored sunglasses. Noah's gaze followed the van down the block until it turned right onto Leavenworth, at which point he dismissed it.

"I'm proud of you, Lees," he said. "Everything's coming together, just like we said."

"Yeah, well, I was making one hell of a mess of things."

"All good now."

"Thanks to you."

"Nah, you. You're gonna be a great mom. You guys around this weekend?"

"Some. We're going out to the zoo tomorrow. Wanna come with us?"

"You know? I'd love that, but I got this nightmare case heating up, and I'm afraid I wouldn't be much company. Lemme look at things in the morning and see what my day is. What time you leaving?"

"Probably around ten. Try, Noah. Maggie'd be over the moon."

"I'll let you know." He flashed on this image of Maggie on his shoulders and Lisa at his side. The little family making faces into the monkey cage as they wandered by. *What was he getting himself into here?*

"Okay, *Ciao*," she sang, bouncing off down the stairs.

Noah turned his depleted body back to the rigors of the ascent. Once inside his "suite," he closed the door behind him, dropped his briefcase and blazer, and stood, eyes closed, breathing deeply, in the dark. *Maybe a little* Sports Center, *then oblivion.* He flipped on the overhead lights, went to the phone, and dialed voicemail. One message.

At first he thought it must be Buzz. When it clearly wasn't, he assumed it was some kind of solicitation. The deep male voice droned over the speaker, "You one of these guys that doesn't seem to get it without help?"

He shed his jacket and loosened his tie as the message continued. "See, you're gonna find it much healthier if you go with the system. We know you been told to plead this Ruiz guy, and we figure that's what you oughta do."

Noah's head snapped around. *Ruiz? The fuck? Who was this?*

"The guy's been offered a better deal than he'll ever get if you insist on swimmin' upstream. Keep this up and you're gonna find that it gets very painful, very soon. You need to do as you're told." The line clicked and went dead.

Cops? But that wasn't Fitzgerald. There was sort of an Eastern twang, and the voice was lower. Maybe his monster sidekick, Zach? He replayed the message twice. *Some kind of a joke? Not that funny. Definitely the Fitzgerald flavor about fitting in with the system and the 'do as you're told' part, but what could the cops possibly care about Pablo pleading?*

Despite the disturbing message, his thoughts were thick and viscous from the fatigue. He popped a Lagunitas, slumped into the overstuffed chair, and played the message one more time. Then, leaning back, he powered up the TV, and a flow of gibberish washed over him, his mind occupied by a morass of unanswered questions. *Maybe try to find Stark again on Monday? Maybe talk to him about the cockamamie decision on the Baja investigation? Maybe get at the Fitzgerald thing… Maybe pin him down on IAD at OPD… Maybe…*

It seemed like less than thirty seconds had passed when a muffled pounding invaded his deep REM sleep. He blinked through the torpor: the lights were still on; the TV was playing, with the remote in his lap. He was still in his chair, shirt out, tie hanging loosely from his collar. He stood unsteadily, snapped off the TV, and stumbled toward the sound. As he grasped the front doorknob with one hand and the deadbolt with the other, the phone message seeped back through his confusion, and he hesitated.

Again, the banging.

"Yeah?"

"Noah? Are you in there…?" The female voice was shaky.

"Lisa?"

"Oh, God. Help me…" She was weeping when he opened the door and, as she rushed into his arms, he caught a glimpse of crimson.

"J-Jeezus, Lees! What happened?" He held her at arm's length for a better look. The blood under her nose was already starting to clot, her right cheek aflame. On the front of her sweater, a large, dark red streak was drying.

"I-I was on my way to the… to the bus stop… going to get Maggie…" She sobbed convulsively.

"Okay, okay, Lees. It's gonna be okay. Let's sit down." He took her arm and eased her into the chair.

"I stopped at the liquor store to pick up some stuff, candy for Maggie…" She snuffed as the words came in gasps. "When I came out… this van was at the curb, and these two guys jumped me…"

"What did they do to you?"

"One grabbed me, and the other one hit me." She started to sob again.

"Okay, Lees." He squeezed her hands. "Just tell me. What did they want?"

"They told me to tell you…" She was struggling to get it out.

"Tell *me*?"

"Yeah… They said to tell you to 'do as you're told.'"

"What?"

"They said you'd know what that meant."

"Christ… What could they…? Why did they go after *you?*"

"They thought I was…" She took a couple of deep breaths. "They said 'Tell your boyfriend to do as he's told.' They must have thought that you and I were…"

"Wait. Was this a white van? Black guy in shades, blue knit cap?"

"Yes, but there were two of them. Do you know them?"

"No, but I saw a van like that cruise by when we were on the steps before. The driver was staring at us."

"Who are they? What do they want?"

"I don't know. I think it's got something to do with this case I'm handling, but I don't know what." Gathering his thoughts, he glanced at his watch and handed Lisa the phone. "Here, you need to call Maggie. Let her know you're late."

"I guess." She took the phone, but didn't dial.

"God. I'm so sorry about this," he said. "What else did they say?"

"Nothing, really. Just that if you didn't want me to get hurt, you should 'do as you're told.' That was it. They said it a couple of times."

"Shit," Noah said, the gravity beginning to sink in, his face a mask of concern. "You shouldn't be seen with me. Somehow I gotta make it clear to whoever this is that you've got nothing to do with me. You didn't get a license number or anything that would identify them, did you?"

"No license. Just that one was black, kind of round, maybe five ten. The other was taller, white, thin. Pockmarked face."

Noah frowned and shook his head.

"What're we gonna do?" she asked.

"We're gonna report this to San Francisco PD for starters, so they can keep an eye on you and Maggie. Then I'm gonna see if I can find out who these guys are and put a stop to this. In the meantime, you need to stay out of sight, in safe places. We can't be seen together." He looked at the sink. "You want some hot tea or something?"

"You think they're going to hurt us?"

"They already have. We gotta get you outta the Larkin while I'm sorting this out. Is there someplace you can stay?"

She bit at a nail. "Nowhere I can think of…"

"How about Maggie's foster parents?"

"The Goldmans?" She considered it. "Maybe just for a short time. They've got a big place, but I don't know if I'm supposed to be there. I'll ask them."

"Come on. I'll drive you over. If not them, we'll think of something."

"Does this mean no zoo tomorrow?"

He studied her for a moment. *God! He was ruining every life he was touching. What a fucking nightmare!* "Yeah," he said. "No zoo. I can't be seen with you, and you guys gotta stay out of public places. I'll talk to my boss on Monday, and see what we can find out."

She shuddered. "I'm frightened, Noah."

"So am I. But maybe they'll leave you alone if they think I'm doing what they want me to."

"What is it? What do they want you to do?"

"I don't want you to have any more information than you have to right now. I couldn't tell you much, anyway."

They stared at each other for a long moment, and Lisa's eyes began to flood again. "You won't let them hurt Maggie, will you?"

He took her hand in both of his. "They won't hurt Maggie," he told her. "That I promise you. Now let's get you cleaned up."

CHAPTER THIRTY-FOUR

Noah's response to his buzzing cell was medium to moderate irritation. "Yeah?"

The conference-room table at Oakland Division was stacked with books, summaries of investigative contacts, notes on interrogation of witnesses, research memoranda on evidentiary points and search issues, treatises, case reports, and medical texts bookmarked on pathological evidence. It was the Friday before trial, and this was the so-called "war room," where materials could be spread out for maximum visibility for final trial preparation.

At the far end of the table, Noah had the binder in front of him that would be his "trial book," the time-honored tome that Buzz had shown him how to construct. It contained tabbed sections for his witness examination, direct and cross, opening statement and closing argument, exhibit list, relevant legal authorities, the works. Buzz's lectures had been on organization, putting as much critical material at his fingertips as possible. Once underway, he explained, trial is a three-ring circus with everything going on at once, and the less time spent fumbling, the less likely that a jury, which already is doing its best to doze off, will succeed.

The books and materials were in front of him, but the crux of the case was still in Mexico, some semblance of testimony that could place Pablo there at the time of the murder. Buzz had called every day his first two weeks down there, reporting that he was talking up the murder in the local bars and eateries, trying to scout out any possible information source. He'd even gone to the City Hall for maps and aerial photographs. So far, zilch. He hadn't even located the hacienda Pablo had mentioned. Then, the last couple of days, radio silence. Noah's hourly calls had gone straight to voicemail with no response, bringing him dangerously close to freaking.

"Blue?"

Noah bolted upright. "Yeah."

"Buzz, here."

"I know who it is. Where the hell have you been?"

"In San Felipe, where else? It really is a gorgeous little fishing village,

Blue. Lotsa great restaurants. They got the most delicious shrimp. Absolute monsters, and they fix them with—"

"Buzz! Get to it, willya? I don't give a shit about the shrimp... and I hope you're not loading up on them with my plastic."

"What am I supposed to do, Blue? I gotta eat."

"Okay, okay. What've you got? Did you locate the hacienda?"

"Not exactly. I..."

"Christ, Buzz! Two weeks down there and you've found nothing but shrimp. What've you been doing?"

"Bustin' my hump is what. We didn't exactly have a road map, y'know. I get that it's two weeks, but I think I'm finally onto something."

Those two weeks had been torture for Noah. After the disaster with Lisa, he'd finally gotten an audience with Stark, who had agreed that the right thing was to report the attack to SFPD. He was sure OPD cops had nothing to do with it, especially with an IA investigation pending. Item two was the denial of the investigation request. He told Noah it was a committee decision, and there was no point in pursuing it further; their actions were final. Given the leak history, Noah said nothing about sending Buzz to Mexico. Stark went on to assure him that OPD was taking care of the Fitzgerald investigation, in its own time.

Noah had called SFPD and spoken to a uniform in the assault division who had little interest in the attack on Lisa. When he said she was "known to the department," Noah figured he probably had her rap sheet on a screen in front of him, and was unimpressed by just another hooker being slapped around in the Tenderloin. Only when Noah cranked up words like "apathy" and "discrimination" did the guy claim to "guarantee" they would "keep an eye on things." *Right.*

At least the Goldmans had agreed that Lisa could stay with them for a while. Maggie and Lisa were delirious, but they had to keep it under the radar with CPS. It could blow Maggie's placement, and the Goldmans' foster parent status. Noah had checked in on them frequently, in between his regular calendar duties and an all-out sprint with trial prep.

Buzz's cell was bouncing in and out with static, as they both fought to stay with the conversation. Noah was tempted to hang up and call back, but dared not lose him. "I found out that guys at the local... deliver produce to a big place... Rancho Figueroa... isolated stretch of beach... twenty miles... I rented... Zodiac... cruised..."

"You rented a what?"

"Zodiac. You know... boat..."

"A Zodiac? On my card? Why didn't you get a cabin cruiser?"

"Things are pretty... down here."

"They're what?"

"Cheap..."

"So what's this Figueroa place?"

"I don't know if it's... but it's the only... miles... took some... photos... have the hotel fax... you can show him."

"Good."

For reasons unknown, the wireless gods smiled, and the transmission temporarily cleared.

"The hacienda is owned by a guy named Eduardo Figueroa," Buzz was saying. "Apparently a very gay, jet-setting heir of a wealthy Mexico City family. There's some speculation that he might be in over this coming weekend, so maybe I get to him and ask some questions."

"Shit, Buzz. Trial starts Monday. We're slicing it pretty thin here, aren't we?"

"What're my choices? The guy doesn't live here. The compound is like his summer home where he hosts these very private weekend retreats for wealthy, celebrity gay couples who are still firmly in the closet. I'm lucky he's coming in as soon as he is, if he is, that is."

"Gay?" Noah mused. "What was Pablo doing there? You think he's gay?"

"Beats me. Guess you'll have to ask him that, too."

"Where're you gettin' all this?"

"Merchants, mostly, who supply the place. They say there's been a lotta orders for deliveries this week. So they figure there's a thing happening on the weekend."

"Have you called out there? Talked to any of Figueroa's people?"

"Negative. All unlisted, Mexican style. Seems like nobody phones in. They call here when they need something. Totally off the map, like I said. Only thing I can think of is to take a run out there, but it's twenty miles or so by water, and I hear the roads aren't the greatest."

"How sure are you this is the place?"

Just as abruptly, the reception went south again.

"...gotta be it. All... remote beach. ...Figueroa connection fits... parties."

"Okay, fax the pictures. I'll show 'em to Pablo and call you. If he IDs the place, you go out there. But don't be renting any Maseratis."

"Got it."

"What's the name of your hotel?"

"It's... Vaquero Borracho."

"What's that mean?"

"…Drunken Cowboy… my Spanish is…"

"Perfect. Gimme a number."

"…don't have it… on fax."

"Right. Stay in touch from here on in, will ya, Buzz? Email if you have to."

"Email pretty sketchy…"

"Okay, but we're runnin' out of time."

"Roger… Blue."

* • • •

"These pictures aren't very good. They're faxes, and they're pretty fuzzy, but can you tell if this is the place?"

Noah had spread three 8x10 faxed images on the interview-room table. Although the enlargement made them grainy and blurred, one could clearly see a stately, white hacienda with a dark red tile roof, surrounded by palm trees, beyond the beach. To the north were a large patio area and pool.

Pablo examined them carefully. "This is the place. This pool area is where the parties were. Barbecues and mariachi bands. Very beautiful."

"Good. So Pablo, what we're getting, talking to people down there, is that this place is owned by a very rich gay man, name of Figueroa, who gives parties for big-name gays from around the world. You know anything about that?"

Pablo's attention snapped up from the photographs. "Gay? I know nothing about gay parties. Who said that?"

Noah couldn't discern whether the expression was surprise, indignation, or both. *He had to admit, the guy was good. Too bad he couldn't put him on the stand. He'd have made a sensational witness. No more time for wheedling. Trot out the nuclear option.*

Noah abruptly began pulling the photos together.

"That's it. You can get yourself another lawyer. I've had it with your bullshit." He paused, his look severe, and this time, unyielding. Pablo seemed shocked at first, then hung his head like a chastised puppy once again. He'd dodged this bullet before. The remorse card should take care of it, one more time.

"I'm here tryin' my damnedest to wedge myself into your corner, and you stonewall me. You lie. You're evasive. You promise me that stuff is all over, then it starts again, like it never stopped. I've had to prepare this case in a goddamn vacuum. Everything I've gotten has been in spite of you." Another beat.

"We could've been where we are now a month ago if you'd been honest with me. I'm finally getting something here that could help you, something that might prove you were in Mexico when this murder went down, and you're gonna lie to me again. There's absolutely no doubt about this rancho, about what it was used for, that these were gay gatherings. There simply is no way you wouldn't know that." He slapped the file shut and stuck it in his portfolio. "Well, I'm finished, amigo."

Pablo's eyes came up slowly, measuring the threat level. His face still reflected practiced contrition, but there were now hints of apprehension. Could this be the time it was serious?

"I'll have them send down another sucker. Maybe you can get a continuance of your trial to give the new guy a chance to warm to your chronic deception."

Noah marched to the door and started to knock. He knew that in reality, there was no way the court would let him out of the case on the morning of trial, short of his falling off a roof and breaking his neck—which didn't sound like such a bad idea just now.

Pablo's eyes were darting, seeking the emotional escape route. What should he do? Maybe this time there would be no way out. Then no one could help him; no one could fix it; not even this young lawyer. He was the only hope.

"Wait, Noah. Please," he heard himself say, having no idea where he would go from here. It had come down to this. Maybe he always knew it would.

Noah turned and looked at him. "Well?"

"Please."

"What?"

Eyes filled with dread, his voice was barely audible. "Please sit down."

"Why would I?"

"Please…"

Noah returned to his chair, sat, folded his arms and stared expectantly.

Pablo's expression was pleading. He tried several times to begin, but faltered. Finally, he exhaled his resignation, and said, "Do you think they will still let me plead guilty?"

Noah's eyes narrowed, his head turned slightly to one side. "What are you saying?"

"I have been thinking that all of the possible results are bad. I cannot deal with a trial. I cannot deal any more with not knowing. I just want it over."

Another scam? "I'm asking you what you're saying, Pablo. Are you telling me you're guilty?"

Another long hesitation; then Pablo said, "I am telling you I am ready to say that I am guilty in order to finish this."

"But are you guilty?" They were trained never to ask that question. And what did it mean, anyway? How would this guy know guilty from not guilty? That was a legal concept. He might know what he did or didn't do, but not how that shook out under the charges, the law. Still, things had gone too far; he had to keep the pressure on.

"What difference does it make? They do not care if I am guilty. They want me to say that I am, to end this. You told me that. Well, I will say it."

Noah studied him. *Did he do it? Did he really do it? God knew, it would be great to have this mishegoss finally over. But sneak out the back door like this? After everything?* "I don't know, Pablo. If you plead guilty, they swear you in, and I have to ask you under oath whether you did this, whether you killed Van Zandt. Will you say it then?"

"I will say it."

This definitely wasn't in the manual. "What will your mother say about your pleading guilty?"

Pablo closed his eyes. "I could not help her. No matter what I tried to do, I could not help her. I thought I could, but I have failed. Now I just want it over. It does not matter what she says."

"You understand they're likely to give you the maximum sentence if you plead guilty to manslaughter? You get that, don't you? It'd be fifteen years."

"But you said I could get out earlier if I did well in prison."

"Maybe. Maybe parole after ten years. Maybe not. Is that what you want?"

"I can do well."

"Prison is a brutal place, Pablo. There're bad people in there. They do awful things."

"If we have a trial and they find me guilty, they will kill me. And you said that is likely."

"Wait, wait, Pablo. I never said it was likely. I said it could happen, based on the evidence. We don't know what a jury would do." At that, Noah stopped talking so Pablo could have time to think.

In that moment, Pablo fell silent. He was too drained to move, to think anymore. Gradually, the image of a tomb materialized in his mind's eye. Many times since being in jail, he had envisioned what it would be like to be dead. No one would speak, no sound. Only stillness. Forever. What would that be like? Would it be peaceful? Would it be a relief? Would anyone miss him? He had so few friends. What about his friends in L.A.? Would they even know he was gone? What about Mario and Jaime? He had known them since seventh grade. Would they care? Neither had visited him. Only his mother had come. How would she feel if she knew everything? What did it matter? Soon she would be dead, too.

He looked up and studied Noah. And what did this young gringo care? What difference did it make to him? Pablo closed his eyes again. In the resulting darkness, he felt himself drifting down. Only emptiness was below, but so what? The descent was slow, into… nothing. Then, suddenly, his fall began to pick up speed, and he felt himself plummeting, faster and faster. Panic engulfed him and he bolted upright. "No!" he exclaimed.

Noah was watching curiously. "No what?"

Pablo blinked several times, trying to reassemble reality. Finally, he said, "I must have this over."

Noah continued to stare; he had been sorting through the implications. *What about all the denials? How could he have pulled this thing off? His mother said he was in Mexico. That pretty much said it, didn't it? How could he let him be sworn and say he did it? But what else was there to say? It was his decision, wasn't it? It was his life, wasn't it? Everyone says it's the best thing for him to do… But Christ, what if he isn't guilty? There were no options. He simply had to tell Pablo what he thought, express his reservations, and let it come down where it would.*

"I don't know if you've really thought this through, Pablo."

"I have thought of nothing else."

"I understand, and I know that it all seems hopeless right now, that you want it over, to stop having to think about it. But I want you to think about it, at least a little longer. It's probably the most important decision of your life." He leaned in. "Let's get your mother in here, and we'll talk to her about it."

"No!" Pablo snapped, eyes searing.

They stared at each other for seconds; then Pablo said, "I do not want to talk to her about it."

"Don't you want to know what she thinks? The two of you have been so close."

"I know what she thinks."

"What?"

"She is a saint. It is easy for her to say I should not admit to what I did not do. It is not so easy for me. I do not need her to tell me what to do."

"Then let me talk to her."

"No." Less volume, but still resolute.

"She wanted to know what you thought about a plea when I spoke to her last time. That was her first question: 'What does Pablo think about it?'" Noah paused, searching for a more convincing way in. "I'll just let her know what you're thinking, then I'll tell you what she says. You don't have to talk to her. You at least want to know what she thinks, don't you?"

"I do not want her involved in this."

"But she's always been involved in it, Pablo. She was the whole reason for it in the first place."

No response.

"Let me talk to her this afternoon. And get back to you this evening."

Another thirty seconds of silence, and then Pablo said, barely above a whisper, "She works today. She won't get home until this evening."

CHAPTER THIRTY-FIVE

"What changed his mind, Mr. Shane?"

Once again, Noah was seated in the Ruiz parlor. This time there was no coffee, no preparations for his visit. A deeply apprehensive Amparo Ruiz, who again had left work early for their meeting, sat on the chesterfield, with Noah opposite her on the living room chair.

"I don't know, señora," Noah told her. "He's exhausted. That much is for sure. But what's in his mind? Frankly, I haven't had much of an idea about that since the beginning."

Her face was serious and pallid. She was exhausted, too, as she once more wrestled with the impossibility of the circumstances confronting her son, superimposed on her own failing vitality. "I have not changed my thinking."

"He thought you would say that."

"Why? What did he say?"

"He said you're a saint, that it's easy for you to say he shouldn't admit to something he didn't do."

Her expression melted into a half smile. "A saint. Is that what he said?"

"Yes."

"I am no saint, Mr. Shane." The smile faded as she shook her head.

"No?"

"No. No saint. That is not why I do not want him to say he killed someone, when he did not."

"Why then?"

She continued to shake her head. She had never imagined that all this could happen, again, after all the years. "Let me make some coffee. Will you take some?"

"No, thank you, señora."

"I think I will. I'll not be a minute."

Ten minutes later, she returned with a steaming cup and saucer. She put them down on the coffee table and resumed her position. He could see that her eyes were red, wet. She dabbed at them with a tissue, which she then slid into the pocket of her dark cotton apron.

"It is a long story," she said. "But I think you must hear it."

"Of course. Anything you can tell me will be helpful."

She leaned back, straightening a crocheted antimacassar on the arm of the sofa as she organized her thoughts. "You recall that I told you I had made some mistakes?"

"I do."

"I have made many." She pressed her lips together. "You remember that I told you of a terrible time we had in Mexico when there was no money?"

"Yes."

"Well, things were not always so difficult. We were a close family. After my little brother was born, my mother would sometimes clean rooms at the large tourist hotels at the beach when there was work, and I took care of Oscar. He was a wonderful child. So happy," she mused, remembering. "I was only five when he was born, but I learned from him how much I wanted to be a mother.

"Then, when we were teenagers, the hard times came, and eventually we had nothing. As I told you, my father would go away for months to build houses. I tried to find work. My brother quit school. He was nearly fifteen, but he was able to work sometimes on a fishing boat. I was almost twenty, and I worked part-time in the restaurant at a hotel. There were many people and few jobs." She looked up at Noah. "My father wanted Oscar to stay in school, but soon he knew that our family could not survive if we did not all help.

"In time, my brother was making more money than all of us together. My father became suspicious, and asked him how that could be. Oscar said nothing, but my father brought it up many times, and they began to quarrel. Finally, my brother told him the fishing boat he worked on was taking cash crops to San Jose del Cabo for sale, to be shipped to the United States, and that they were paid a lot of money for these trips." She raised her eyebrows.

"Cash crops?" Noah didn't understand.

"Yes, he called them 'cash crops,' but my father knew he was talking about drugs. You can imagine that he was enraged." She shrugged. What a proper man her father had been. In fact, the worse things got, the more rigid he had become. She always wondered whether it was all his religious principles, or whether it was also his inability to support his family. If only he had not been so harsh.

"He demanded that Oscar quit immediately. Oscar refused. He called my father a frightened old man. Oscar said that we would starve if not for his job on the boat." She stretched out her fingers, examined her hands, and sighed. "I will never forget that day. It was terrible. I thought there would be violence." She hesitated, then continued. "My father said that he would not allow this in his house, in his life. He told my brother that he disowned him." She heard herself saying the words she had worked all these years to bury. "My brother said there was nothing to disown, and my father made him leave, saying he never wanted to see him again, that he was no longer his son." The emotions seemed so vivid to her, emerging from the darkness after so many years. "My baby brother," she whispered. "My Oscar." The tears welled up and spilled. Noah wanted to reach out to her, but there was nothing to do but listen.

With effort, she collected herself. "My brother left, and for a long time we did not see him. My mother and I sometimes had nothing to eat. The tourists stopped coming, so there was no more work at the hotel. The church would bring food, but often we would go without a meal for several days. We were desperate," she said quietly, attempting to justify what was about to come.

"I knew how the men had looked at me in the restaurant. Some had asked me to go with them. I always refused." She studied him for a reaction, weighing whether he would judge her. He was impassive. Why was she telling this *abogado* so much? She always thought these memories would die with her. Did he really have to know? Maybe he did. Pablo wanted to plead guilty. This man might be able to convince him what was right. And there was little time left. What was the point of hiding it now? She dropped her shoulders, and continued.

"One night I was at the plaza when a young man began to talk to my friend and to me." A smile. "I remember I wore a light blue dress with small red flowers." A scoff. "It was my only dress." A dress her mother had made that she must have had for ten years. "It was warm. There was music, and he bought us *cerveza*. There were many of us there. We were dancing and laughing. He was very handsome."

Noah noticed a fleeting coy look that seemed a bit out of place. He flashed on the image of the woman before him as a young girl, the brightly decorated square, the mariachis, kids finding momentary joy in the midst of despair, and he wondered where this was going, what it had to do with Pablo.

"Then, late in the evening, he asked me to go with him. I said no. He offered me some pesos, and I… I somehow went." She spoke haltingly as she struggled with it. "I wanted to help my family." No. If she were to be honest, that was not all there was to it. "And I suppose I was flattered that such a young man wanted me. It was a time when no one wanted us.

"After that first time, it was easier. I was able to make some money. I told my mother the money was from a job at the hotel, but there were no jobs."

Leaning forward, she took a sip of coffee, replaced the cup on the table, and leaned back. "I told you that I had made mistakes," she said.

"One day, everything fell apart. My family was destroyed," she said. "My brother was arrested. I had no idea what had happened. I was very frightened, and I went to the jail, but they would not let me see him. They took me to the commandant. This man mocked me and said that he knew what I had been doing in our village. He started to try to take advantage. When I refused him, he had me arrested.

"My mother came to see me. She told me that Oscar was in very serious trouble. He was accused of murder, she said, murder of a policeman who had been killed in a raid on their fishing boat. She said that Oscar told her he was not there, that it was a night that he had been with us." She paused and shook her head with a sardonic smile. "I recalled the night very well, Mr. Shane. My father was away, and it was I who had gone to tell Oscar to come home. My mother missed him so. We had spent the evening together. We both knew he did not kill the policeman.

"Several days later, my father returned to find us both in jail." A grimace flickered. "He was shamed. He tried to bargain for my release, but the commandant refused. He said that he would let me go only if my brother would say he killed the policeman. He said that they knew he was guilty. I told them he did not do it, that he was not there. My mother told them. They would not listen. The choice was that my brother would say he killed the policeman, or I go to prison.

"They would not let me see Oscar, so I begged my father to tell him not to do it." The tears were brimming again. "I do not know if he ever told him." She looked up in misery. Rising abruptly, she picked up her cup and returned to the kitchen without a word.

Noah sat, waiting, not knowing what else to do. After several minutes, she returned with a fresh cup of coffee, resumed her position on the sofa, outwardly composed, and continued.

"They told me that Oscar had said he was guilty, and that I was to be released. My father had made arrangements for us to come to Oakland. He knew a man from Mazatlán who agreed to find him work in the construction here. I tried to see Oscar before we left, but they would not let me in." She closed her eyes. "We just… walked away from him."

Noah now began to understand, where her reticence came from, her abiding mistrust of the system. Then it got worse.

"I never saw my brother again. We learned two years later that he had died in prison. Some kind of sickness. We never found out what it was."

Noah waited to see if there was more, honoring her grief. After a minute or two, he returned the focus to Pablo. "You've endured a great deal, señora." She looked up at him. "I can imagine how these experiences would make you never want your son to agree to anything that was proposed by the DA, but…" He paused. "But isn't the decision his in the end? To take the risk of the death penalty or not?"

"Is it, Mr. Shane?" she said. "I really do not think it is in our hands. At first, I was bitter about Oscar. I blamed the commandant, my father, Oscar, the unfairness. I was angry. But then I realized that what Oscar did, he did for me. He did it because he wanted to do it. His sacrifice was his own choice. He must have thought it gave him meaning, in a time that he could find little meaning. That's when I wondered whether it wasn't his right to make that choice."

"That's what I think," Noah said, immediately realizing how unnecessary his agreement was.

"But when Pablo was offered the same choice, I prayed about it. I realized his was a sacrifice, too, in a situation he does not understand. But after much thought, I decided that, in impossible situations like these, we are powerless. We must turn to God to deliver us. We cannot make such decisions for ourselves. What seems right to us is what we want to be right."

"But how does it help to pray about it? Don't we have to make the choice, ultimately, anyway?"

"Do you not see? It takes it out of our hands. It gives us the courage of our faith, that whatever the outcome, it is what the creation had planned for us."

"But what does that say about Pablo pleading guilty?"

"Pablo must tell the truth. It is only when we tell the truth that God can find us. No matter what the truth, God will decide the best way forward if we have faith." She cast a curious look at him to see if he was following. "Do you understand? I should have stayed in Mexico. I should have persisted in the truth. And Oscar should have, too. I do not know whether we both would have gone to prison, whether we both would have died, but the choice would have been God's. Instead, we made it ours, to my regret… forever." She closed her eyes, shook her head slowly, and then opened them again. "I will not let Pablo make that same mistake."

So there it was. There was only one way forward in her mind, to hold to exactly what happened. No guilt, no plea.

"But how do you know he isn't guilty? He's prepared to say under oath that he killed a man."

She smiled tolerantly. "I know, Mr. Shane. I know that Pablo killed no one. And I think you know that, as well."

"I'm not sure."

"I think your heart is sure."

They sat without speaking. This time, it was Amparo who broke the silence.

"When did he first say he wanted to plead guilty?"

"This afternoon. We were talking about some evidence that my investigator is developing in Baja California. He suddenly said he didn't want to go to trial, that he wanted to plead guilty."

Her eyebrows tightened. "What kind of evidence?"

"It was about the place where the party was, the place where the murder took place. Pablo said he was there."

"I see. And what was this place?"

"I told Pablo that we have learned it was a large resort where very prominent gay men come to vacation."

"Gay men?"

Noah tried to follow what she was thinking, and it suddenly dawned on him. "Wait. Are you saying that's why he wants to plead guilty now?"

She said nothing. The frown remained.

"You think he is unwilling to let you find out?"

"Ours is a very proud culture. There is an ancient tradition for the men. *Machismo.* Pablo was raised in that tradition. His father was a soldier. Perhaps he thinks that it would discredit our family, that I would not love him if I knew."

"My God." He was fixed on her eyes. "My God," he repeated, his mind churning.

Again, she shook her head slowly.

"What?" he asked.

"It is actually quite amusing," she said seriously, her expression entirely inconsistent with the reference. "No, not 'amusing.' Mmmm. What is the word?"

"For what?"

"I have known for several years that Pablo is a homosexual, and I suspected it for many years before that."

"And he hasn't known of your suspicions?"

"Obviously."

He considered it. "I think the word you are looking for is 'ironic.'"

"*Si*. It is the same. *Ironico*. Ironic."

"He's willing to go to prison rather than let you find out he's gay. He was even willing to die before this evidence about the rancho came to light…"

She was nodding.

"…and all the time, you knew."

"I wanted to let him tell me when he was ready. I did not want to invade his private life."

"And knowing about it, you loved him anyway. Despite the *machismo*."

"Of course. He is my son."

"Of course."

"*Ironico*."

"We have to get him to come out," Noah said. "That's the only way he can make a good decision about what to do. If he knows he doesn't have to keep it from you." He reflected on it. "But if you just ask him, he'll probably continue to deny it, even if you say it doesn't matter to you, don't you think? And how would you bring it up in the first place?"

"These are not simple questions," she said. "Yes. It is likely he would deny it now."

Another long silence, then Noah asked, "Does Pablo know about your history, señora?"

"I have never told him about these things I have shared with you. I felt that I could not."

"Why?" Noah realized he was on sensitive ground.

She didn't answer.

"Because you were afraid he wouldn't love you if he knew?" He offered it with considerable trepidation.

The enormity of it slowly coming into focus, she shook her head. "*Ironico*," she murmured.

"Will you tell him now? If he understands what has shaped your beliefs, it might make all the difference. If you tell him why you never told him your own secrets, maybe it gives him the strength to tell you his."

She sat with it for a long moment. "Maybe so," she said, and then, "Yes. I think you are right. I must have this conversation with him. I should have had it long ago."

"Perfect."

"I will see him at visiting hours tomorrow morning." She nodded with the pronouncement, and her attention returned at last to her coffee. She leaned over and picked it up from the table, straightened, and took a sip from the cup. Returning it to the saucer in her lap, she said, "A saint. Indeed."

CHAPTER THIRTY-SIX

"Yes. I was there."

Pablo looked away, flushing deeply.

"The truth is that I have turned some tricks when the money was sufficient to make a difference for my mother."

Noah reflected fleetingly on the symmetry between his experience and the odyssey described by his mother the previous afternoon. "How did you come to be there?" he asked.

"I was at the hacienda that weekend for a gathering of wealthy people. I made an agreement with one of Señor Figueroa's staff at a bar in L.A. I cannot recall his name."

Noah eyed him. Another potential witness remaining nameless.

"No, Noah. It is true. I cannot remember. I was staying with friends in Boyle Heights, trying to find a way to make money."

"You were in San Felipe only once?"

"I was at the hacienda on several weekends. After the first time, it was actually Señor Figueroa himself who would call to invite me. His staff would arrange the transportation and pick me up at the airport in San Felipe. I really do not recall any names. They do not use names very much. Most had nicknames."

"So the only name you can give me is Figueroa?"

"Only that one."

"It'd be helpful if we had a few more names to choose from. We're going to have to bring someone here to corroborate your story, and it would be good if we had a little selection."

"Señor Figueroa is the only real name that I know. I can remember a few *apodos*, a few nicknames. They called the pool boy Calaca. I think there was beach attendant who was Torpe, and the trainer in the gym was Guey. If you go there and ask around, it may be that some of them will remember me."

"Okay," Noah said, scribbling on his pad. "That's a start. Did you have a nickname?"

"They would call me Grahcho."

"Groucho?"

Pablo smiled. "No, Grah-cho."

"What does that mean?"

"It is kind of a *combinacion* for G.H."

"Those aren't your initials."

"No. It was for *'gringo hermano.'* American brother."

"Okay. Grahcho." He looked up from his notes. "Were you going to tell me that if I hadn't asked?"

"Sorry. I did not know it was important."

Noah rolled his eyes. Resigned as he was to this clown act, he couldn't get used to being fed with a spoon. *Butter? Break-in? Mexico? Now Rancho Figueroa? When would it end? What more was there?*

"Listen," he said. "We've both talked to your mother. You've told me you're not going to accept the plea offer, but I need to know that's really how you want to play this. That it's not just your mother talking here. These are high stakes and I have to believe you're okay with it."

"My mother and I have agreed that I will not say I did something I did not do."

"I understand that you agreed, but the decision is yours, right?" In his hesitation, Noah read the doubt, but now he needed to press him. To be certain. "Is this what you want, Pablo?"

"Yes."

"It means you go to trial with a lawyer that's never tried a case before. You get that?"

"Yes. I understand."

"And you might be found guilty by a jury? We just don't know."

"I have said that I understand. What do you want me to say?"

"That could mean the death penalty. You're willing to accept that risk?"

Something snapped. A lifetime of passive appeasement suddenly evaporated, and Pablo thrust his chair back and stood. "*Caray! Que puedo hacer al respecto!*" he shouted, and began pacing, the handsome features contorted. "What can I do? For God's sake. I have no choice!"

"Of course you do, Pablo," Noah said, maintaining his composed tone. "You can plead guilty and avoid the risk."

He whirled and glared. "Then I would go to prison!"

Noah held his crackling stare and waited. He could not rescue him now. This was the bottom line, the go/no-go decision. He alone could make it.

Time passed. Finally, Pablo dropped his gaze. "I cannot say I did it if I did not," he murmured, resigned, shaking his head slowly. "I hate this."

"I know."

They were both quiet, Noah seated, looking down at his file, Pablo standing. At length, Pablo said softly, "I will go to trial."

After taking a beat to see if there would be more, Noah repeated, "That's what you want?"

"Yes."

Noah let it hover a while longer; then he sealed it. "Okay," he said. "Our investigator asks at the hacienda about whether anyone remembers Grahcho. Whether they recall you there the weekend of the twenty-sixth. Meantime, no more games? You tell me everything?"

"I have told you everything, Noah."

• • •

Noah returned to the War Room with a little more bounce in his step, and once again immersed himself in preparation. By 10:00, he felt like he had read about a thousand cases, a thousand medical articles, and rewritten his opening statement about a thousand times. He was beginning to see double and was convinced he couldn't read another word. He decided to grab something to eat and call it a night.

It was after 10:30 by the time he settled onto a stool at the end of the bar at the Oarhouse, ordered a burger and a beer, and tried to focus on the sports page despite the Saturday night bedlam.

"Hi, stranger." It was a woman's voice. Noah looked up into the mirror behind the bar, and saw Kate standing there. He turned.

"Hi your own self," he said.

"So how goes the war? You start pretty soon, don't you?"

"Monday morning, bright and early. You hungry? Sit down." He asked two people next to him to move over a stool.

"Maybe just a beer." Kate looked around the crowded room. "Why don't we get a table? I think I see one."

"Sure," he said. At the moment, he couldn't think of anything more therapeutic.

"Hey, Stork," he shouted, "pint for Kate when you get a chance?" He turned to her and nodded to his burger. "You want one of these? Some calamari?"

"No thanks," she said. "I've had dinner."

He wondered with whom. "We'll be at that table…" He motioned to Stork.

"You got it," Stork yelled over the din.

"So, how does it look?" Kate asked as they sat down.

"Not good. I've always had my doubts about Pablo's guilt, but things are pretty grim on the evidence front. He oughta walk, but it's sketchy. I'm perfectly capable of getting an innocent man a date with the needle."

"So he's really not going to plead?"

"Nah. There was a momentary possibility, but that's gone now. It's going to trial."

"What about the alibi? He was in Mexico, I heard."

"Yeah. I wish I could prove it. Only he and his mother can say he was, and she only knows what he told her. I'm trying to find a corroborating witness. According to his mother, he was down there with 'friends,' but he says there was no one from here with him." He took a hit from the mug. "Buzz's in Baja as we speak, trying to find someone who'll say he was there that weekend."

"Buzz is down there? I thought you said you couldn't get the funding to send him."

"I did say that. Totally pissed me off, so I sent him down on my nickel."

She eyed him. "Wow. So, has he come up with any more leads?"

"Just that it looks like Pablo was at the rancho of a wealthy guy named Eduardo Figueroa, near San Felipe. But we haven't been able to get to him yet, let alone get someone to testify."

"You gonna use the alibi if you don't have a witness?"

"I have to. I mean, it's all I've got. I'm thinking about taking a monster chance and teeing it up in opening statement, even if I don't have anything solid from Buzz yet. I gotta put it in the jury's mind from the beginning, or all they have is Salem's damning version through the prosecution's whole case. Fingerprints in the condo, Van Zandt's jewelry. I'll never get 'em back."

"But it's a gamble, isn't it? What if Buzz doesn't find anything, and you've laid out the alibi as your only defense? Then what? They'll expect you to prove it."

"Yeah, that's it. I don't know. I might have to put Pablo on and get the alibi out of him."

"Won't Salem chew him up?"

"I'm sure, but what choice have I got?" He took a bite of burger and another slug of beer. "Let's just think good thoughts. Buzz'll come back from Mexico with a squadron of priests who played poker with Pablo the whole weekend. Is it a squadron? No... a gaggle. Who knows."

She smiled, remembering just this kind of humor. "Alibi's your only defense, isn't it? You didn't get any expert testimony?"

"I've disclosed a couple of experts, a pathologist and a ballistics guy, just to keep Salem guessing, but we pretty much agree with their people on all the technical stuff."

Stork arrived with her beer. "Hey. It's Kate the lady lawyer. Long time no see. Where you been hangin' out lately?"

He wiped the table with a damp rag and set the beer in front of her. "Thanks, Stork," she said. "Guess I been spending more time in the East Bay. Work and everything."

"Yeah, well, welcome home, kid. Good to see ya." He held out a fist, and they exchanged a knuckle bump; then he returned to the bar as Noah stared into his brew, ruminating on where she'd been all those nights in the East Bay.

"Cases are tough when you can't get squat from your client, you're stonewalled by your boss, the court's jammin' you to trial, DA's breakin' your *cajones* to plead, everyone threatening your—"

"How do you mean your boss is 'stonewalling' you?"

"I'm talking about trying to get Buzz to Mexico to beef up the alibi for a month and a half. I'm on a no-time-waiver, and your friend Stark pitches the request into limbo for weeks, and then the brass finally deny it. Waste of county money, they said." He went back to the brew, then said, "There's something ominous behind all that. I'm totally convinced." He tried to read her reaction, but there was none.

"Anyway, so I send Buzz down there on my plastic, but no worries, I'm independently wealthy, I can afford to bankroll all my clients' investigations... if I ever get any more clients."

"I think you're being kind of harsh with Jim, Noah."

"No, I'm not," he snapped. "I don't know what's goin' on, but whatever it is, that guy's in the middle of it. There's no way a rookie should be defending this case. And after he straps me on the log that's headed for the buzz saw, he gives me no help, no advice, no support, no investigation, no nothing. You think I'm being too harsh?"

"You haven't been very forthcoming with him. How can he help you if you're not?"

He frowned in disbelief. "Not forthcoming? I hounded the guy daily, until he even stopped returning my calls and turned me over to his secretary."

"I'm sure he has his reasons. He's not a bad guy. He's generous, thoughtful, and he's a hell of a lawyer."

"Now how would you know all that?" He was afraid of the answer, but he asked anyway.

She paused and stared at him, questioning. "I've been dating him since September. I thought you knew."

Seconds passed as he processed it. Then, with a mock smile, he shook his head. "Astounding, Kate. Not only did I not know, but don't I remember a night, in this very establishment, when someone who had just interviewed with the guy we're talking about here was describing him as 'a pompous, overblown idiot'? Lemme see. Who was it said that? It'll come to me."

"I know I said that. But I really didn't know him then."

"And, baby, I guess you do now."

"I think I do, Noah," she said, her tone now strident. "You think that's some kind of crime?"

"You know what I think it is? I think it's a damn shame. Because I thought you were better than that. And since you ask me, what I think is that you shouldn't give that guy even a nanosecond of your time, let alone whatever else. I think he's a two-faced, incompetent, sly sonofabitch who makes up for his shortcomings with deceit. I don't believe a word he says. And by hanging out with him, it tells me you've turned into a bit of the same. That's what I think."

Kate's jaw was set. She'd had enough of his neurotic bullshit. Who did he think he was? Unbelievable. All this, and after Bodega. "I think who I spend time with is my business." The words were clipped, defiant, steaming.

"Sure it is," he said. "But you asked me. I told you." It was flowing now, and he couldn't let it go. "And you wanna know what else I think? I think you're gonna go far in this office, what with how adept you are on the casting couch and all—"

Her open palm caught him heavy on his left cheek; she'd hit him hard. Bright lights danced. His left ear rang.

Conversations at the neighboring tables stopped as patrons gawked. Kate stood and looked down at him, teeth clenched, nostrils flaring, the silence between them crackling. She leaned forward and picked up her beer and, for an instant, they both thought she was going to dump it on him. Instead, she stomped off to the bar with it. He sat for a full minute, breathing deeply and gathering himself; then he returned to his unfinished burger. After one bite, he threw it down, smacked a twenty on the table, got up, and stalked out.

Kate watched him go in the mirror behind the bar. He turned right out the front door, and disappeared. She left her seat, made her way through the crowd to a relatively quiet place in the rear restroom alcove, extracted her cell phone from her purse, and dialed.

"Hello?"

"Jim, it's Kate."

"Hey. Long time no see, since dinner anyway. I was just thinking about you."

"I've been speaking with Noah. I think we should talk. How about I stop by?"

"Wow, it's late. What's up?"

"Well, you said you wanted me to tell you—"

"You're right, I did. Come on over."

CHAPTER THIRTY-SEVEN

SUNDAY, NOVEMBER 11ᵀᴴ, 2:30 PM:

"Yeah, I know it's a long way down. And no, we are not going back for some shrimp. We gotta see this thing through. Trial starts tomorrow."

Buzz guided the orange '92 Ford Escort wagon as far from the sheer cliff as he could. The rubber bird swung languidly with the bouncing of the ancient vehicle, its painted eyes scanning the surroundings as it twisted one direction, then the other. The road, to use the term loosely, snaked dangerously close to the edge of a four-hundred-foot drop-off, below which the violent surf crashed onto black volcanic rock. What must have been substandard blacktop twenty years ago had now eroded into nothing but potholes and rubble.

"I know you'd rather have the Jeep, but there was no way." He took one hand from the wheel, balancing it precariously with the other, and batted the yellow duck into submission. "We had to satisfy the Blue, didn't we? And his fixation on his precious plastic."

The car was gutted except for his seat, though the engine and radio functioned, at least so far. He had opened all the windows to keep from being asphyxiated by exhaust wafting up through the floorboards. The rental place, "Honesto Ernesto," swore that the engine had been rebuilt, but English had failed on the question of when.

Fortunately, the afternoon sun was still warm, deep into autumn. Buzz worked a finger into his ear as the Escort bounced along at fifteen miles an hour to the blaring strains of mariachi harmonies competing with background static. At the moment, static was winning.

The road, winding down toward the beach, was barely wide enough for one car. Of course, there had never been such a thing as a railing. God only knew what would happen if another vehicle came up from the opposite direction. How the hell did they get the trucks out here with party provisions? Must come in by boat.

The roadway straightened as it leveled out onto the sand, and

Buzz breathed a sigh of relief. Nearly a mile ahead, the blacktop led directly to a ten-foot chain-link fence with a gate defended by a small, well-kept wooden guardhouse. To the right, the fence ran straight to the cliff, then followed along its base. To the left, it extended out onto a breakwater that protected the beach. Clearly no easy way in. Two large

Alsatians lay side by side near the kiosk, chained on long leashes inside the fence.

"Yeah, I see 'em," Buzz muttered. "Can't sweat it." He flicked the swinging bathtub fowl with his index finger. "They're chained up." Downshifting, he navigated the old orange wreck out onto the beachfront roadway and stopped in front of the guardhouse. One of the two Mexican guards, whose eyes had followed the vehicle's approach from far up the road, emerged, binoculars hanging from his neck. No hacienda in sight. No building of any kind, other than the checkpoint.

"*Buenos tardes, señor.*" The guard was about 5'10" and slim, dressed in khaki pants, a short-sleeved khaki shirt, and a khaki military hat with brown leather brim. No insignias. No signs on the fence or guardhouse. No stinkin' badges. He looked into the dilapidated Escort, then at Buzz's brightly colored ALOHA shirt over brown Bermuda shorts, and then at the duck hanging from the mirror. His features tightened into a frown.

"Afternoon," Buzz said. "I'm looking for Señor Eduardo Figueroa. Am I in the right place?"

"And who is asking?" The English was excellent, the bearing well-mannered.

"Name's Hoogasian. I'm an investigator for Alameda County. That's Oakland, California… U.S.A. I'd like to talk to Señor Figueroa about a case we're handling."

Eyeing him suspiciously through mirrored aviator sunglasses, the guard said, "You will wait here one moment, *por favor.*" He turned, went back to the kiosk, and picked up a phone.

"Sure…" Buzz muttered, but the guard was already gone.

He returned in less than a minute. "I am sorry, señor. There is no one here who can help you."

"Well, I wonder, is this Mr. Figueroa's rancho? Can you at least tell me that?" Buzz opened the Escort's door and stuck out a skinny white leg, at the end of which his bony foot was clad in a huarache sandal. No sock. The guard stepped forward and put a firm hand on the door, obstructing any further plan to disembark.

"I said there is no one who can help you, señor." The tone was still polite, but firmer. "You will have to leave the premises immediately."

The second guard, six inches taller and fifty pounds heavier, stepped out of the blockhouse and moved into position next to his companion, his hand resting on the holster on his right hip.

"See, I wonder if I could just get some information before I go," Buzz said. "I've been trying to get in touch with Mr. Figueroa, and I've come all the way from—"

"Perhaps you did not hear me, Señor Hoogasian." The smaller guard was definitely more forceful now. "I told you there was no one here to help you. You will please to turn your vehicle around and go back from the direction you have come." He increased the pressure on the door, squeezing Buzz's leg. Buzz thrust the door outward, jerked his leg into the car, and the door slammed shut. There was a low growl from the other side of the fence, then a bark.

"Yeah, well, thanks anyway," Buzz said. "Appreciate the hospitality."

He backed the Escort, cranked it around, and pulled back onto the road, kicking up a cloud of sandy dust as the car rattled away from the gate. In his rear-view mirror, he could see the two guards standing side by side, watching him. The big one still had his hand on his weapon.

"You believe that?" Buzz griped to the swinging bird. "Didn't even let me tell 'em what I'm about. So, whaddya gotta make, a fuckin' appointment? Good luck with that."

As the diminutive station wagon bounced over the crumbling asphalt toward the cliff, Buzz could see that the chain-link fence surrounding the rancho angled away from the roadway and disappeared behind an approaching bluff. There was simply no time to waste another day going back to town and renting the Zodiac to approach from the sea. This had to happen now.

"See, now?" he told his rubber companion. "If I get in there, I get a witness. Simple as that." The painted blue eyes regarded him vacuously.

At the gate, the fence extended to the breakwater on the beach side, in full view of the guards. No way to get in there. But behind the bluff on the mountainside, the fence was out of sight.

Once around the bluff, Buzz pulled the Escort off the road, nestled it close to the cliff, and stopped. He got out and squinted up the rock face, into the glare. About fifteen feet above, a narrow ledge led to a natural break in the cliff, opening into a dry wash that extended upward to the crest beyond. Ridges and cracks here and there might accommodate a handhold, a foothold, some kind of purchase.

"Awright, Daf," he said. "You stay here and watch the car. I'm gonna find this guy, Figueroa." He threw off his slippery leather sandals and started up.

When he got to the ridge, he saw that he was surrounded by sand, rock, and chaparral, thick and tall enough to hide him as he made his way into the compound. To the south, he could now see the large hacienda in the distance, standing between the cliff and the beach, beyond view of the road. He could barely make out a number of people milling about, some in the pool area, some out on the clear white sand, and some in the water.

Scrambling down the steep embankment to a chain-link fence below, he checked in both directions for a place to climb. Nothing. He would have to get over it in his bare feet. The ascent was painful, but quick, both feet bleeding by the time he reached the top. Throwing one leg over, then the other, he let go and dropped about ten feet into the warm sand. He then got low, sprinted to a nearby stand of chaparral, and worked his way along the rocks at the foot of the cliff.

Now inside the fence, he would still have to get past the guardhouse to reach the casa. As he came within fifty feet of the kiosk, it became obvious there was no way to bypass it unseen in daylight. The dogs could be a problem, but the breeze was on shore, so with any luck they wouldn't pick up his scent. He hunkered down behind the cover of the chaparral to wait for nightfall.

About 9:00 a warm wind began fluttering the vegetation in which Buzz had been dozing. Rousing, he blinked and shook his head. The sky now completely dark, countless stars glittered overhead. A couple of hundred yards down the beach were the glimmering lights of the casa; a number of figures cavorted in the water under large floodlights illuminating the surf.

Moving cautiously, keeping the base of the cliff close beside him, he set a bead for a point beyond the casa so he could pass around and come up from the sea side, hopefully undetected. He glanced toward the gatehouse. A spotlight above it cast a beam beyond the fence and down the approaching roadway, silhouetting the guards inside. Both dogs were lying next to the fence, the sea breeze ruffling their bushy, tan-gray manes, as they occasionally shook their massive heads.

Working his way down toward the compound, Buzz crab-walked until he reached the sanctuary of a tall oleander hedge between the casa and the cliff. He jogged along in the lee of the ten-foot bushes that were laden with sweet-smelling white flowers. Passing quickly around the building, he made his way toward the beach, where he could see a handful of revelers still splashing in the warm, shallow foam that washed up onto the sand and receded. Most held large bamboo cups containing various potions, probably what was fueling the shouts and guffaws that resounded above the surf. As Buzz watched, a dozen or so merrymakers started for shore.

Wading from the shallow water, the partiers moved toward the hacienda and began to disperse. Buzz glanced toward the casa, over the wide-open expanse of lawn between his position and the patio, and concluded there was no way he could cross to the main house undetected on his own. His mind went to Noah, whom he knew was hard at it, preparing for trial, and he told himself his move had to be now. Taking a deep breath and exhaling, he fell in with the group of g-stringed carousers.

A young Mexican steward nodded as Buzz made his way across the patio, then through an adobe portico adorned with flowers and a flowing waterfall, nearing a glass conservatory filled with towering, broadleaf tropical plants that reached toward a glass ceiling twenty feet above. Spotlights peeked through the fronds, casting a verdant glow throughout the glass enclosure.

Just as he was about to enter, Buzz spotted one of the guards from the afternoon confrontation approaching from the other side of the conservatory. He averted his eyes and walked quickly by the entrance, ducked off the tiled walkway behind a cabaña, and hid in a clump of large ferns, hoping he hadn't been seen. The sounds of conversation in German, then laughter, emanated from several stragglers who sauntered through the glass house and into the thick-walled casa beyond. Buzz waited in the darkness as they passed, then started tentatively back toward the tile walkway.

His last awareness was the sound of a sickening crack that seemed to come from behind him, then brilliant red, yellow, and orange quavering lights, a display that surpassed any Baja sky, and then everything went black.

CHAPTER THIRTY-EIGHT

"Peeble versh Pablo Rueeeszh!"

The immense ornate courtroom was packed with press and curiosity seekers.

Noah stepped forward as Judge Erhardt perused the file. Salem was already seated in the well with his usual staff.

"Ummm, yesss," the judge droned, peering through the bottom of his blended lenses. "*People v. Ruiz* is on for jury trial this morning. Are the parties ready to proceed?"

"Ready for the People, Your Honor," Salem said.

"Ready for the defense, Your Honor," Noah echoed.

"Very well. Time estimates, gentlemen?"

"Perhaps three weeks, Your Honor," Salem told the court without consulting Noah or looking in his direction. Never the recognition that Noah was even present, let alone a foeman worthy of his steel.

"Mr. Shane?" Erhardt had the courtesy.

"I would agree, Your Honor," Noah said, having no idea how long it would take to try the case. Three weeks seemed like an impossibly long time to fill with what he knew about anything.

Having discussed the judge draw with Roger Moreland and a few others in the office, Noah realized this was critical. He had hoped to get Buzz's guidance coming down to the wire, but once again, his numerous voicemails, texts, and emails had gone unreturned since their conversation Friday.

Three judges were purportedly available. The first, Remington Scully, a former civil attorney, was a Pete Wilson appointee from the Dark Ages and a member of the Christian Right. Sally Broughton was an African-American former DA who had only tried a handful of misdemeanors before her appointment. Definite prosecutorial leanings. The Moreland advice, if either of these was drawn, was to exercise an immediate peremptory challenge.

The third possibility was Donovan Pulansky, the former Public Defender of Alameda County, described by Buzz as brilliant, irascible, tyrannical in his courtroom, and eminently fair. He knew firsthand what it was to be walking way out on that plank defending a guy who would go into endless free fall with an adverse verdict. Noah would have sold his soul to get Pulansky.

"All right," Erhardt mused, scanning his calendar and the list of courtroom assignments. Noah was riveted, breath caught in his throat. Salem looked disinterested. "Let's seeee now… mmmm," the judge hummed, as Pablo's life hung in the balance. One in three. *Les joux sont fait.* "There's a note that Judge Scully's robbery didn't finish as scheduled," Erhardt said. The little ball circled, circled, bounced and caromed, then rattled into a slot. "And I understand Judge Broughton has a sick child in the hospital. So, this matter will be assigned to Department Twenty-six, Judge Donovan Pulansky. Thank you, gentlemen."

Yesss! Noah exhaled audibly, mentally pumping his fist. *Over the first hurdle and running comfortably.* For the first time since the beginning of this nightmare, it was his turn. He didn't favor Salem with even a glance, but he knew for sure he wasn't happy.

There was a scurrying as the media people and reporters scrambled to their feet to troop across the street to the Administration Building that housed Department 26. Noah picked up his bulging, antiquated, government-issue, leather trial bag—on which the long-ago embossed label, "Alameda County Public Defender," was nearly rubbed off—and turned to leave. As he walked up the aisle, he glanced into the gallery to his right, where Chris Connelly raised his chin, smiled, and gave a thumbs-up. Noah felt a surge of adrenalin. *No point in being tentative. Best to go for it. Brazen it out. Think confident, act confident, be confident… maybe.*

As he crossed the street, a cluster of press surrounded him.

"Noah! What do you think of the judge assignment?"

"Does Ruiz have a chance?"

"Did they offer you a plea?"

Careful. Nothing definite at this stage. Can only step in it. "We have a strong defense. Mr. Ruiz would have been satisfied with any judge. We just want a chance to tell our story." *Right. What the hell was the defense? Was there an alibi witness or not?*

As he arrived at Department 26, pushed the front door open forcefully, and marched in, images came flooding back. *Cleats clomping down a tunnel, cannon firing, bursting out into Saturday afternoon sunlight gleaming off a dazzlingly green field, butterflies gyrating in savage anticipation. Bumping chests… butting helmets… tee it up, motherfuckers… let's get it on.*

"Judge'd like to see counsel in chambers," the bailiff announced as Noah slid his bag under the defense side of the counsel table. Salem, who had held his usual press conference at the elevator bank before entering the courtroom, strolled up the aisle, followed by his assistant, and took a position on the prosecution side nearest the jury box. Noah grabbed a legal pad and stepped forward, every nerve in his body humming. *I got the best judge in the fricking courthouse, by God. Let's go do this thing.*

• • •

"Mr. Hoogasian? I am Eduardo Figueroa. Welcome to my home."

As Buzz groped through shadowy unconsciousness, his eyes twitched but had yet to open. Then a brilliant shaft of morning sunlight blazed through the upstairs window, casting a golden glow on the deep brown oak of the heavily carved bedstead. It was already 9:30 AM, and this was Buzz's first sign of life.

The squat, dark Mexican attendant had been the first to notice Buzz's initial movements and had called down the hall in an eruption of rapid Spanish. Minutes later, a tall, aristocratic, light-skinned man with angular European features and semi-darkened glasses had entered the room and quietly closed the door behind him.

"My guard at the gate tells me that you are an investigator?"

Buzz grimaced as he put a hand to the back of his throbbing head and, bringing it forth, examined the crusted and smeared blood. He stared at Figueroa. "Where am I?" he managed, weakly.

"You seemed to be interested in my little gathering last night, but somehow you injured your head, so I thought we should keep you until morning, to give you a chance to recover. Fortunately, we have three rather pre-eminent physicians here this weekend. One evaluated you and, though he thought you were not seriously injured, it was his recommendation that you get some sleep, so he gave you a mild sedative."

It gradually came back. The guard must have seen him. Christ, then what had happened? He reached under the covers to find that he was unclothed. Instinctively, his hand went to his crotch, as if he expected to find something missing.

"What have you done to me?" He rose with effort onto an elbow. A wave of aching pain from the back of his head seized him, and he grimaced and collapsed back onto the blood-smeared pillow.

Figueroa laughed, the lines around his eyes making it clear that this was not an uncommon activity.

"Have no fear, Mr. Hoogasian. You have not been violated. Of course, we invited you to participate in our gaiety last evening. I assumed you would not be here if you did not want to join in the merriment." The twinkle in his eye left no doubt that he was enjoying the banter. "Unfortunately, no one found you attractive. Can you believe it?" He smiled broadly and chuckled. Figueroa was strikingly handsome, his thick black hair brushed back in graying waves. His dress was affluent casual: a gleaming white guayabera over gray slacks, with black Italian loafers.

Buzz was not amused. "You... you better not have fucked with me."

"So, Mr. Hoogasian. My guard tells me you are with the county of Alameda? In California? Suppose you explain to me what prompts you to honor us with your visit."

Buzz tried again to get up, but the room again began to revolve as he moved, and again he fell back with a long sigh. It dawned on him that Noah must be in court right now, getting assigned out to trial. He had to make this happen quickly if they were to have a chance.

"I came to see you," he said. "Your guards wouldn't let me in."

"I see. And what business did you have with me?"

"I'm an investigator with the Public Defender in Oakland. We represent a guy named Pablo Ruiz, who we understand came down here to your functions."

"Pablo? Yes, Grahcho. I know him. Fine young man."

"Groucho?"

"Grahcho. A pet name we have for him. Is he in some kind of trouble?"

"He's charged with the murder of a local big shot up in Oakland, name of Warren Van Zandt. Pablo says he was down at your place here when the murder happened. I flew down to hopefully find a witness that could confirm that."

Figueroa looked surprised. "Pablo was charged with the murder?"

"Yeah," Buzz responded, squirming to find a comfortable position. "Did you know about it?"

"I had some information. Warren Van Zandt was known to me, as well."

"To you?" Buzz was lost. This was a bit much to grasp, especially given the current sluggishness of his brain. "How did you know Van Zandt?"

"Warren also came to my home, to some of my gatherings, from time to time."

"Your gatherings?"

"Let me explain." Figueroa drew a chair from the writing desk that stood against the wall, placed it on the brightly colored area rug near the bed, and sat down.

"For many years, I have been sympathetic with men in high places, in the public eye, who find themselves in love with a person of their own sex. You may know that many members of our community have, over the past decades, been increasingly able to practice their chosen lifestyle with openness. Often that is not true, however, for men of responsibility who must live highly visible lives as politicians, actors, business leaders. You cannot imagine what torture it is to love someone and have to hide that love, hide who you are, in order to serve your community or your country, particularly if you do your job well."

"What does that have to do with Van Zandt?"

"In time, the frustration begins to affect one's ability to function, especially where the work in which one finds oneself is highly demanding, as it is in the kinds of positions of which I speak. And yet, due to the narrow-mindedness in many countries of the world—for example, our machismo culture here in Mexico—it is simply not yet an alternative to such men to make their choice of lifestyle public. You see the dilemma? The frustration affects their ability to function, and because these are men upon whom we all rely, we all suffer, do we not?"

"So?" Buzz still didn't have it.

"So, some years ago I resolved to provide such individuals a place where they could come and be themselves, in comfortable surroundings, enjoy recreation, world-class cuisine, and wines. I wanted to give them an open, supportive environment where they could show their feelings for the men they loved. Rancho Figueroa is such a place."

Figueroa stopped and shook his head. "But forgive my lack of hospitality, Mr. Hoogasian. You have not eaten. Would you like some breakfast?"

The thought was slightly nauseating. "Uh, no... but thanks."

"Some orange juice, perhaps? A sweet roll and coffee?"

"Well... maybe a little orange juice."

Figueroa rose, went to the door, and opened it. "*Carlos, un vaso de jugo de naranja, por favor.*" The small man disappeared quickly down the hall.

"As I was saying, Mr. Hoogasian, I created the Rancho with the thought in mind that prominent men from around the world could join me on occasion, to live without fear of the ridicule which would disrupt their important work. Fortunately, I come from an old family in Mexico

City that affords me the means to accomplish such an ambitious goal. It was, let's see, some fourteen years ago now, that I found this beautiful old hacienda, which happens to be very convenient to the United States and its international airports."

He stood, walked to the window, and surveyed the courtyard below. After a few moments, he turned back to Buzz and continued.

"I converted the property into the compound that you see. Since then, friends have come from around the globe to enjoy the facilities, to celebrate their lives, in absolute privacy. Of course, complete discretion is the primary issue, so we have a very robust security. We do everything necessary to insulate our guests from prying eyes. You will understand that extortion of such men could change the course of history."

He smiled proudly. "We have wonderfully erudite and powerful people who join us. The conversation is always fascinating. The ideas that are exchanged here are most uplifting. Many important agreements and decisions are made.

"Of course, attitudes are changing. The Rancho may be experiencing its last days. We hope that is so. There will certainly come a day when Rancho Figueroa will become just a conventional resort. But in the meanwhile, we are committed to serve, so long as that may be necessary."

"And, so? What about Van Zandt?"

Figueroa went on to describe the comings and goings of Pablo and confirm that he had, in fact, been at the Rancho on the weekend in question. But that wasn't all that Figueroa had confirmed. When Buzz had heard the whole story, his only thought was to get hold of Noah, quick.

CHAPTER THIRTY-NINE

Seated at his desk in chambers, Pulansky smiled at the DA. "Good morning, Mr. Salem," he said.

"Good morning, Your Honor."

"And, let's see, you must be Mr. Shane," the judge added, glancing down at his court file as Noah stepped in and closed the door.

"Noah Shane, Your Honor. Public Defender. I represent Pablo Ruiz."

"Yes." Pulansky continued to peruse the file in front of him. "Well, have a seat, both of you," he said, not looking up.

He was compact and square. Some years earlier, his hair had been jet black and wavy. Now it was salt-and-pepper, flying unattended. A high-strung and nervous man, Pulansky had a blazing metabolism, his fingernails chewed to the nubbin. His body movements were almost as quick as his mind, both in perpetual motion.

Awkward in social situations, he found small talk a monumental chore. In his early twenties, Pulansky realized that his special gifts rendered him unsuited to the world of ordinary mortals, and he had taken refuge in the law. His unswerving devotion to this "jealous mistress" had cost him two marriages, both devoid of offspring, after which he had abandoned the institution. Later, his sanctuary became his courtroom, where there was no requirement that he suffer fools. A tireless worker, he knew his evidence code intimately, and demanded the same from the lawyers who appeared before him.

Pulansky, now sixty-three, had a face permanently flushed from the years of abusing fine scotch, his medication of choice to salve the neuroses and to mercifully slow the rapid mental firing rate at sundown. The aged single-malt tincture, stocked in his desk drawer, was often shared, neat, in fine crystal old-fashioned glasses, with counsel during evening chambers sessions. Of late, an occasional dose after lunch was added to ease the tensions of particularly long afternoons.

"You're a PD, Mr. Shane? Haven't seen you before. You been around awhile?"

"I have, Your Honor," Noah said, smiling. "I think it's a couple months now."

The judge raised his eyebrows, tilted his head, and jutted his lower lip. "I'm impressed. They must like your style."

"I wouldn't know, Judge."

"I was a PD three years before I got a 187, and I thought I was pretty hot stuff," Pulansky reminisced. "Course we had a pretty light compliment of lawyers in those days, and the case was only a battle for a sandwich between two old homeless drunks at the shelter out on Fifty-fourth. Never could figure why they charged it as a 187. My guy ended up going down on a second."

Both lawyers nodded dutifully.

"Turned out it was a famous victory, though I didn't know it at the time. My client was sentenced to three squares, room, daily showers, clean clothes, and all the books he could read for the rest of his life, all courtesy of the State of California." Pulansky shook his head and smiled. "Checked in on him a year later. He was happier than a butcher's dog. Figured he'd won the lottery."

Twenty-six years as a public defender had cured Pulansky of taking himself too seriously. An artist with words, he had a style that extended to the pun, the occasional off-color double-entendre, and the wielding of sarcasm like a sword. His sense of humor was apt to be quirky, and thanks, but he would handle the jokes in his courtroom. As a lawyer, he had been deadly in battle. As a judge, he was not to be crossed. Still, the deeply ingrained love of humanity, so difficultly expressed in his interpersonal relations, emerged frequently in his decisions and rulings. Example: taking a chance on Buzz Hoogasian when everyone else had written him off.

"So, I hear there's a bit of a labor dispute brewing over at the office." Pulansky took a gulp from a brightly colored, hand-painted coffee mug that bore the inscription *Drug of Choice*. "Rumor mill says some kind of 'collective action' might be in the offing. Association stirring it up again?" He was scrutinizing Noah somewhat severely over his horn-rimmed glasses.

Unfortunately, Noah missed it. "I don't know much about it, Your Honor," he said dismissively.

"No?"

"I've really had other things to attend to."

"I see." Pulansky reflected for a beat, then, clearing his throat, changed the subject. Another swing and a miss, again unnoticed by Noah.

"I assume you gentlemen have exhausted all efforts to resolve this matter by now?"

"We offered an involuntary before things got too far, Your Honor," Salem responded. "It's hard to imagine our having gone that low, knowing the case as I do now. But there was never any formal response from the defendant. Of course, the offer is no longer on the table. We're ready for trial."

The judge was again focusing on the file in front of him. "That true, Mr. Shane?"

"That they offered an involuntary? Yes, Your Honor. That's correct."

"And your client wasn't interested? From the little I see of the facts here, it seems a pretty generous proposal."

"I suppose it might be considered quite generous by some, Judge," Noah said. "The problem with it was that Pablo didn't kill anyone."

"Got the wrong guy, did they?" the judge said, now considerably more brusque with Noah than when he had walked in. "Well, we've seen that defense a time or two, haven't we, Mr. Salem?"

Salem smiled, and scoffed.

"In this instance it happens to be true, Your Honor." Noah was slightly indignant at the judge's tone. *Could they have been wrong about this guy?*

"We'll see." Pulansky was noncommittal. "Like I say, he's not the first to claim he was somewhere else when the beef went down. I've probably pitched that defense in over a hundred trials myself." He looked at each of them in turn. "So, is there any point in further discussion of a negotiated disposition, gentlemen?"

Noah was the first to answer. "I don't believe so, Your Honor. Pablo simply isn't guilty."

"Mr. Salem? Are you through talking?"

"I guess some cases just have to be tried, Your Honor."

"So I have your binders with exhibits and proposed jury instructions. I didn't see any paper on any motions. I take it there are no motions to be heard now?" He was referring to Motions In Limine to exclude evidence before the trial began so that sensitive matters wouldn't come up and prejudice the jury before an objection could be made.

"No motions at this time, Your Honor," Salem said. "The People are content to deal with the evidence as it comes."

Pulansky turned to Noah. "Mr. Shane?"

"Agreed, Your Honor." Again, without Buzz, Noah was hamstrung on some of the niceties. He'd consulted Roger Moreland on putting the exhibits and jury instructions together, but Roger had little knowledge of the case, and less time to get into it. Noah had decided to let the pretrial motions go and concentrate on the testimony.

The judge straightened. "All right." He punched the intercom and shouted to the bailiff. "Sid! Summon the panel. We got us a horse race." He turned back to the lawyers.

"Mr. Salem knows that I run a tight ship. No games. No ups, no extras. I allow the lawyers to conduct their own voir dire, particularly in cases of this magnitude, but if it wanders too far afield, I will take over. There will be no speaking objections. I don't like you coaching the witness, so save your speeches for your closing. When I have ruled, I expect you to move on. No whining. Sidebars will be held to a minimum. If you ask for one, make sure you have good reason. We will be traveling light and moving swiftly. Mr. Salem knows all this, am I right?"

"Indeed I do, Your Honor," Salem responded.

Perhaps it was lack of sleep, but Noah somehow interpreted the warning to be brief as not wanting to hear Pablo's excuses, and the comment got away from him before he could corral it. "Why am I not surprised?" he muttered.

Pulansky's retort was instantaneous. "Now see? That's exactly what I'm talking about. I said I like a crisp, businesslike approach to a case. What I don't like is wisecracks. When I was a defense counsel, there were judges who let the lawyers run the courtroom. This is simply not conducive to solid public opinion of the judicial system. I take it you have heard of the Chicago Seven trial? Well, I am no Julius Hoffman, and the William Kunstlers of the world do not find life easy or enjoyable in my court. There will be no liberties taken with respect. And if I hear any impertinence in the presence of the jury, I will not hesitate to award jail time for contempt… the first time out, Mr. Shane. I trust you have your toothbrush with you, just in case?"

"I'm sorry, Your Honor," Noah said, looking down to avert Pulansky's dagger-eyes.

"I'm glad we understand each other. Now, if you gentlemen will excuse me, I believe the panel will be arriving shortly."

Salem and Noah returned to the courtroom.

"You want your client brought in now, counselor?" the bailiff asked Noah.

"Please."

He drew the bronze key from his holster, unlocked the secure door to the holding cell, then ducked in and emerged with Pablo and a guard from the jail. Pablo was dressed in a dark blue suit, a white shirt, and a conservative blue tie, all bought by Noah. He was clean-shaven, his hair combed perfectly, immaculate. After leading him to the counsel table, the jail guard unlocked the shackles. Pablo sat down next to Noah, and the deputy took a seat at the rail several feet behind.

Noah whistled under his breath. "You look killer, amigo. Oh, sorry. Mmm... how y'doin?"

"I am very nervous, Noah." Pablo managed a brief smile. "How about you?"

"Medium, getting better. We got the best judge we could've hoped for. He's gonna be awesome," Noah whispered behind a hand, despite feeling unsure of this prediction. He opened his trial bag and was laying out his materials when the door opened at the rear of the courtroom.

They turned to see an assistant jury commissioner leading seventy-five prospective jurors into the room. Salem stood, faced them, and smiled. Noah and Pablo followed suit. The panelists were escorted to seats, nearly filling the gallery. When the shuffling had settled, the clerk pressed a buzzer that sounded in chambers, and the bailiff announced the arrival of the judge.

"Remain seated and come to order. Department Twenty-six of the Superior Court is now in session. The Honorable Donovan Pulansky presiding."

Pulansky entered with a flourish, almost walking out of his robe, and took the bench.

"Good morning, ladies and gentlemen. I am Judge Donovan Pulansky," he said as he settled in. "Let me begin by conveying, on behalf of the County of Alameda, my gratitude to each of you for taking the time from the important activities in your private lives to participate in our system of justice. Trial by jury is perhaps the finest social structure yet devised on this planet, but it cannot function — no, it cannot survive — without the dedication of citizens like you.

"Now, I want to tell you a little bit about *People v. Pablo Ruiz*." The judge opened the file in front of him. "This is a case in which Pablo Ruiz, whom you see at the counsel table next to his attorney, Public Defender Noah Shane, is accused of a violation of Section 187 of the Penal Code, pre-meditated murder. Will you stand, Mr. Ruiz, and you as well, Mr. Shane?" Noah and Pablo stood and turned, facing the panel like Butch and Sundance at the edge of the breath-taking precipice, smiling hopefully, before leaping into the rushing river far below.

"The prosecution will be handled by Marco Salem from the District Attorney's office. Will you stand, Mr. Salem?" Salem rose and nodded. "If anyone knows Mr. Ruiz or either of the lawyers, please raise your hand. I'm not asking whether you have seen them on television or in the papers, only whether you know them personally." He paused. No hands.

"Good. It is alleged by the prosecution that Mr. Ruiz took the life of a Mr. Warren Van Zandt. Anyone who knows Mr. Van Zandt please identify yourself." Nothing.

"All right. You have all been given questionnaires that you have filled out concerning your backgrounds, and your general views. We will now begin the voir dire process, in which the attorneys will have the opportunity to ask each of you some additional questions. Please understand that they do not intend to slight anyone by dismissing a juror. The effort to ascertain that you would be impartial does not imply that you are not fair-minded. I'm sure you are. But we all have biases that we bring into the courtroom with us. We're simply trying to find out whether your particular biases might resonate with the case in front of us in a way that would make it hard for you to keep an open mind. For example, as a recovering cigarette smoker, I might have trouble with a case for a smoking injury against a tobacco company. I have actually disqualified myself in one such case, and have let the lawyers know about my bias in others.

I will now ask the clerk to swear the panel and call the first twelve jurors into the box. Madam Clerk?"

Pablo, at the counsel table, his back to the gallery, closed his eyes and prayed silently. Noah crossed his fingers in his lap.

CHAPTER FORTY

True to his word, Pulansky had ridden hard. Jury selection was swift. By 4:00 on Tuesday, they had a jury, seven women and five men. Three women and three men were African-American. There were two housewives, two clerks, a schoolteacher, two owners of small businesses, three government workers, a banker, and an engineer. No Hispanics on the jury panel, but two alternates were selected, both women, one Caucasian, the other Hispanic. Four Hispanics had been seated and questioned, but Salem managed to challenge them all, except the alternate. He was down to his last peremptory challenge—one that he did not have to show any reason for—at that point, and most seasoned trial lawyers didn't want to waste the last one on a questionable call, in case someone god-awful to their cause was the replacement, and they would be stuck.

Salem asked each prospective juror to promise in voir dire that he or she would have no trouble convicting if the evidence pointed to guilt, notwithstanding that the People were seeking the death penalty. Noah objected, but Pulansky allowed it, since the law was clear. The California Crime Victim Justice Reform Act made such questioning of candidates kosher in the presence of the full panel, in the discretion of the court. Noah figured if the DA was allowed to raise that kind of fanfare, the defense should be permitted to ask each prospective juror if he or she would like to wield the hypodermic. He was a little fearful that a couple would have said they would.

Still no word from Buzz, and Noah had been unable to reach him on his cell throughout the day. Trying to buy as much time as he could before having to go one way or the other on the alibi in opening statement, he stretched out the voir dire, but his options rapidly dwindled down to none. Notwithstanding the lateness of the hour, when the jury was finally impaneled and sworn, Pulansky took a ten-minute recess, telling counsel they would proceed to opening statements when court reconvened.

Salem went first, strutting back and forth in front of the jury box as he laid out his assortment of incriminating facts. He spurned the podium for the opportunity to get as close to the panel as possible, the jurors occasionally casting suspicious glances in Pablo's direction.

"And the People will show that the defendant entered the condominium of the victim, Mr. Warren Van Zandt, at the East Gate Plaza, an inhabited building, at about one-thirty AM on August twenty-sixth for the sole purpose of burglary.

"Unfortunately, Mr. Van Zandt returned home unexpectedly, surprising the defendant. Then, to avoid being exposed, the defendant violently strangled this peaceful and kind man, to death"—pause—"…shot him to obscure the trail, probably with Mr. Van Zandt's own gun, trying to make this appear to be some kind of execution"—pause—"…proceeded to steal his jewelry and his gun"—pause—"…and disposed of Mr. Van Zandt's body in the Emeryville Sewage Treatment Plant." He looked from face to face, all intent on his every word, several grimacing.

"Now, how do I know all this?" Salem went on, walking slowly to an easel on which a four-foot by six-foot cardboard diagram of the floor plan of the Van Zandt condo was resting. "Because the defendant's fingerprints were found in Mr. Van Zandt's condominium." He picked up the pointer and indicated. "Here, in the study on the desk top, and on the middle drawer… here, in the bedroom on Mr. Van Zandt's bureau and on a jewelry box in the top drawer… and here, on the inside knob of the front door and the outside of the door and the jamb." He laid the pointer on the tray and returned to his position in front of the jury box.

"It was at this point that your police department got very lucky in its investigation. The defendant had just been arrested and incarcerated on a burglary charge, and his fingerprints had been placed in the computer system." Noah cringed ever so slightly, realizing he had given him the opening to tee up the burglary by asking one too many questions at the prelim. No matter. They would have gotten there anyway.

"Officers Tony Lockhardt and Mike Roberson immediately obtained a search warrant from Judge Howard Simmons of the Alameda County Superior Court." Again personalizing, trying to cast the image of all the players being friends and neighbors—the entire county, its police, courts, DAs, and its jurors—united against Pablo Ruiz, public enemy number one. "And they searched the defendant's home.

"Tragically, Warren Van Zandt cannot stand before you this afternoon and tell you what happened that night, but Tony Lockhardt and Mike Roberson will come into this courtroom, raise their right hands, and explain how they found Warren Van Zandt's jewelry under"—he pointed at Pablo—"…this defendant's bed."

Salem went on articulating a prosecution case that sounded increasingly airtight. Finally, he had placed it all before them. "When we have finished presenting this case to you, ladies and gentlemen," he concluded, "we are convinced that you will be satisfied, beyond any reasonable doubt, that this man, Pablo Ruiz," he turned, again pointing at Pablo, this time glaring fiercely and for the first time using his name, "took the life of Warren Van Zandt coldly, calculatingly, and with malice aforethought." He stood motionless for several seconds, stretched to his full height, his solemn countenance moving from one juror to the next. Then he turned, strode back to the counsel table, and continued.

"Now, notwithstanding all this was undoubtedly the case, His Honor will instruct you that, in order for you to convict of first-degree murder, the prosecution need not show that the defendant intended to kill Warren Van Zandt, only that he intended to commit a burglary, to invade the sanctity of Mr. Van Zandt's home, and that the homicide took place in the course of that felony. This is what we call the felony-murder rule." Salem knew that felony murder without the intent to kill would not support a death sentence unless it could be shown that the defendant acted with reckless indifference to human life, but that would be a discussion for the penalty phase. For now, he would simply pitch all the concepts at once, as equally reprehensible.

"We believe that, after hearing the evidence, you will conclude that this crime was committed by the defendant. At that time, we will ask you to return a verdict of murder in the first degree." He nodded definitively, then abruptly sat down.

"Thank you, Mr. Salem," Pulansky said. "Mr. Shane, does the defense wish to make an opening statement at this time?"

Noah stood and buttoned his coat, "Yes, Your Honor. Thank you." He looked down at the table, breathing deeply to calm the butterflies as he had done so many times before, breaking the huddle and walking up to the line on the first play from scrimmage.

He looked up solemnly. "Ladies and gentlemen…" he said. "At this moment, I find myself in circumstances I have never been in before. I stand before you—an impartial jury of citizens of this community—with the awesome responsibility of addressing you in a murder trial. I speak to you on behalf of Pablo Ruiz, who is also having an experience for the first time. Not only has he never been the defendant in a murder case, he has never been the defendant in any case before today." He paused. "It is a humbling experience, I assure you."

He also rejected the podium, but unlike Salem, elected to stand next to Pablo at the counsel table, underscoring their connection. He looked down at his trial book. Most of the elements of his opening, and even the phraseology, had been put together in consultation with Buzz. Finding his place in his notes, he raised his eyes to the box and continued.

"Not only have I never tried a murder case, I have never tried any case. Yet because of this great system Judge Pulansky was talking about, I have the honor of representing Pablo Ruiz here today, in this court. But I ask your indulgence with any errors I might make. They would be due to my inexperience, and I ask that you not hold them against Pablo, whose very life is at stake in this proceeding." He and Buzz had decided that he might as well get it out in the open early. In fact, two of the moms, one black, one white, were smiling, but Salem wasn't. As Noah was silently congratulating himself, Salem climbed to his feet. Ordinarily, he wouldn't object during an opening. It just called attention to the defense position. But here it might be well to trump the 'lovable ignorant kid' card, and get in the first body blow.

"Your Honor," Salem purred. "I'm not sure we're all quite as enamored with Mr. Shane's lack of skill and experience as he is, but I believe that it is Mr. Ruiz we're concerned about here. I would ask that Mr. Shane be admonished to adhere to the facts of the case."

"Yes, Mr. Shane," Pulansky chided. "The statement about your level of experience will be stricken. Please confine your introductory remarks to what you believe the evidence will show." He turned to the jury and smiled. "Ladies and gentlemen," he said, "from time to time I will sustain an objection by counsel, and material will be stricken from the record. You are not to consider that material for any purpose. In this instance, Mr. Shane's qualifications or lack thereof, however endearing, are not evidence, and are not to be considered by you as mitigation in this case, or for any other purpose. Continue, Mr. Shane." A prosecution sympathizer in the back row identified himself by shaking his head and snorting.

"Thank you, Your Honor," Noah said, convinced that it was worth drawing the objection to make the point. "The evidence will show," he went on, "that Pablo is a fine young man, with no criminal record, who comes from a hard-working, respectable family." He turned and smiled at Amparo in the first row of the gallery, just in case any of the jurors hadn't yet guessed who she was. She acknowledged with a slight nod.

"While the death of Mr. Van Zandt is a tragedy, not only is Pablo Ruiz not the kind of person who could ever commit such a crime, but the evidence will show that he could not have done so in this instance. We will show that he was out of the country when the murder was committed, spending the weekend in Mexico with friends."

There it was. Rolled the dice. If Buzz couldn't get a witness, no choice but to put Pablo on to say where he was. That would lay him bare to the flashing teeth of the hyena for the prosecution on cross-examination. Maybe Pablo could never stand up to that, but what were the choices?

"This is simply a case of coincidence that solely on the basis of circumstantial evidence has been turned into a monstrous web of unsupported guesswork. Pablo admits to you that he entered the condominium of the decedent. We will show you that, due to a terrible disease his mother has contracted, and her need for expensive treatment, this man with no criminal record committed a burglary in an effort to raise money for a lifesaving surgery for his mother. That is a fact."

Major risk number two. The prosecution didn't have this information, and Salem would love to pump Pablo's terror of his mother dying into monumental motive for anything, including murder. But Noah needed the sympathy factor to offset the community sentiment for Van Zandt. The problem was that, as with the alibi, he couldn't prove Pablo's commitment to saving his mother without putting him on the stand, exposing him to cross-examination. He would try to get it in through Amparo, whom he considered his key witness, but what could she really say about Pablo's state of mind or his motivations? That would all be speculation, conclusions on her part. All inadmissible. He never really told his mother about his thoughts, and it would be hearsay even if he had. Noah couldn't say how it would play out. Maybe she could sell it. What was clear to him, even as a neophyte, was that he couldn't imagine a better witness. Wouldn't anyone be understanding of Pablo's trying to move heaven and earth to help his mother in such a situation?

Hearing the mention of Amparo's cancer, Salem fleetingly eyed Noah, then let it go. The prosecution always wanted the defendant to take the stand, and Salem was relishing the prospect of cross-examining him.

Noah addressed a handful of additional facts; then, checking his notes again, he went on to his conclusion: "We will explore all of this together in detail. We concede that this burglary, however understandable, was misguided. But burglary was all that took place." *He and Buzz had thought there was no harm in admitting that now. The burglary wasn't charged. Could they charge it later? One thing at a time.* "The death was not caused by Pablo Ruiz, so it is not felony-murder." Noah put a hand on Pablo's shoulder, looked down at him, and then from juror to juror. "Pablo Ruiz did not kill Warren Van Zandt," he declared, letting it sink in. "He was not present the night the killing took place. He was not even in the country.

"So we submit that the District Attorney's case is not what he would have you believe. We ask that you keep an open mind while Mr. Salem puts on his evidence, remembering that it is his responsibility to prove the charge—to prove what he promised you he will prove—beyond any reasonable doubt. We hope you will listen carefully to both sides, and when you have heard all the evidence, we think you will be satisfied that Pablo has not been, and can never be, proven a murderer."

He sat down and exhaled again, this time in relief. *It all sounded good, but how the hell would he pull it off if Buzz didn't come through? That was maybe the only question right now.*

CHAPTER FORTY-ONE

"Bastards. Can't put shit back where they found it."

Noah dropped his hefty trial bag on the floor and collapsed into a chair. The war room was pretty much as he had left it, except that his mountain of books and articles, notes, and materials, had been pushed up to one end of the conference table to accommodate some kind of office meeting. Most of it had gotten shuffled. Noah fumed as he sorted it out. After a long day of thrashing about in the murkiness of criminal trial practice, he was drained.

By the time Pulansky's marathon had finally subsided after opening statements, it was well on the way to 7:00. Noah had packed his bag and left the courtroom. In the hall outside, he passed a still-scintillating Salem, holding his obligatory séance with the press. Several reporters had broken away and shown signs of trying to corner Noah, but he dodged into the stairwell, sprinted down a flight, and out on the third floor before they could follow. He hustled down the hall to the elevators at the far end and absconded, still wary of saying something that might come back to haunt him.

The drive back to Oakland Division, over on Washington in the Broussard Center, had been mechanical; the Captain knew the way by now. With the adrenalin flowing all day, Noah felt no mounting fatigue, but riding up in the elevator, the exhaustion suddenly hit him.

Football had been different. Anxieties always pumped before a game, evaporated with the first hit, then returned in the tight spots, but the pressure was firmly attached to the clear challenge at hand. In trial, there was a continuous low-grade apprehension with occasional moments of stark terror when it seemed that things were getting away. And always the façade. God forbid anyone should perceive anything outwardly other than absolute confidence. Of course, the fuel expended in keeping up that little charade could fill a medium-sized tanker. When the end of the day rolled around, the reservoirs were totally depleted, only it wasn't until the adrenalin titer fell that the message seeped through to his higher brain centers that he was running on empty.

Just as he pulled out the Evidence Code and tried to remember what it was he wanted to research, the door opened, and Sandy barged through.

"Saw you come in," Sandy said. "Pulansky must have gone pretty late."

"Tell me."

"So how goes the war?"

"Okay, I guess. I haven't been shot by the bailiff yet. Everything else has been somewhat questionable."

"Why? What's happening?"

"Well, yesterday I managed to piss off the judge. Today Salem embarrassed me in front of a jury that's fully prepared to give Pablo the needle by their own sworn statements on voir dire."

"Wow. So you're well into it."

"Two days to get a jury and open. Is that 'well into it'?"

"I'd say. I thought you'd be a week getting a jury, at least."

"Yeah, me too. Pulansky served notice that he's gonna keep everybody running at a dead sprint."

"You heard from Buzz yet? Has he found a witness down there?"

"Nothin'. And if I don't get something from him pretty quick, I'm screwed. I told the jury in opening that I'd prove that Pablo was in Mexico when the killing went down. I better be able to deliver."

"Shit, Noah."

"Well, what the fuck else've I got?" The fine-tuning on his mood-modulation regulator was definitely fried. "These decisions are based on my many years of solid experience as a trial lawyer. Y'learn to wing it after a while."

"Right." Sandy had something on his mind and wanted to maintain things on an even keel until he got to it. "So, uh, why don't we duck over to the Oarhouse. Lemme buy you a beer. You can get to bed early and pick it up again in the morning."

Noah stared in disbelief. "You crazy? All I'm gonna do is put on a pot of that PD mud out there, dive back into the case, and get ready for tomorrow. Gotta spruce up my cross of the pathologist, try to get hold of Buzz, and do some research on an evidence issue, if I could remember what it was. Some of us actually have a full day planned." He went back to the stack of materials and began sorting through for the evidence folder.

"Okay, so…" Sandy rose tentatively and turned toward the door. Maybe just let it go? Nope. Now or never. He looked back. "Oh, uh… Noah?" The 'afterthought' that was the real reason for the visit.

"Yeah?"

"I-I just wanted to let you know that negotiations have broken down with the county, and the Association is declaring a sick-out for next week. It's not public knowledge yet, but Michelin told me today, and asked me to give you a heads-up so you could plan your trial around it."

Noah's cerebral synapses weren't firing anywhere near baseline, let alone in the optimal range. He stared at Sandy as the neurotransmitter molecules groped for the tiny receptors, trying unsuccessfully to lock on. "The fuck is he talkin' about, 'plan my trial around it'?"

Sandy knew full well this wasn't a good time, but he'd lit it up now, and he had to see it through. "You are going out with us, aren't you? As far as I know, the whole office is behind it. It's only for a week, no matter what the county does."

Noah continued to stare, still wondering if he had it right. *A week? What did that mean? They didn't expect him to walk out of his trial for a week. No. Wait, did they? Sounded like they did.*

"A week?"

"That was the decision."

"You gotta be nuts, man. Ruiz's life is on the line. I may not know shit about what I'm doing, but I sure as hell am going to give it my best shot. You think I'm going out on some strike and give this hanging jury a whole week to imprint on everything Salem told them before I get a chance to put my case on? Not a chance. If I'm goin' down, I'm goin' down swingin'."

"Jesus, Noah."

"No way."

Sandy had been to the meetings. He knew how big a deal this was for the Association, for the office. First time in their history they'd actually taken a stand on something, let alone collective action. "You'll be screwing everybody. Don't you see that? You've got the highest visibility case in the office right now. Michelin talked about your case specifically at the meeting. The media'll pick up this labor dispute and run with it if you're in. You could be the guy that holds the press conference and makes the whole thing happen. But if you're not, it makes you the hero, and the rest of us look like greedy jerks."

Noah's eyes narrowed. *Not only was this freaking union trying to disrupt and upstage the trial, but they expected him to take the point?* He lacked the capacity to censor it, and the venom flowed.

"What are you thinking? Do you get what's at stake here? Do you get that I'm trying this death case my first time out, for an innocent man that this very same county's fitted up with a murder, jammed out to trial, cut my fricking nuts off on the investigation, and tried to get my client to cop to an involuntary on a killing he didn't do? Do you see that?"

He stood, continuing the diatribe.

"Meantime, these mysterious dudes—cops or someone—beat up a friend of mine and are threatening to kill me, and her, if I don't make a plea go down." He began pacing, reached the far end of the conference room, stopped, and turned. "And I don't have a clue why it's all happening. I don't know enough to figure out whether I'm crazy or the whole friggin' system is bent, but when I try to find out, this goddamn office turns its back on me. What does my boss say? 'Keep your head down, Noah. Show a little backbone...' and he doesn't give me shit. Why? Because he's too busy balling Kate to sweat the small stuff, like killing an innocent client.

"Now you come in here and say this same goddamn office wants me to tank the fucking trial so it can get a quarter-an-hour raise?" He picked up *Dressler on Criminal Law* and slammed it down on the table. "Are you kidding me? Are you *kidding* me? Are you in on this whole fucking fraud? Or are they just using you?"

He took two steps back toward Sandy, stopped, looked him straight in the eye. "What's happened to you, man? Where the fuck did your commitment go? All those times you pulled my head out of my ass and made me hang in there. What happened to all that?"

"That's pretty funny, Noah," Sandy snapped. "You talkin' about commitment. Kate said you'd probably be the only hold-out."

"Kate said that? Kate said?" Months of frustration and self-doubt was hemorrhaging. "Kate sold her fucking body to get a leg up in this office. Anything she'd say doesn't mean shit to me anymore. But you... The fuck's happened to you?"

Sandy wasn't retreating. The issue was bigger than one trial, no matter whose, or how high the visibility. He was needed by this movement, valued, maybe for the first time, and he wasn't going to let anyone rob him of that, even Noah. "Easy for you to criticize. You always were the hotshot. Here you are with your name all over the papers. Trying a 187 in your first three months in the office. Some of us aren't like that."

Noah waved an arm dismissively. "You don't know what you're talking about."

"Listen to me, will you?" Sandy was struggling for control. "I'm talking about plodding along in the pack, agonizing whether I can pull off a petty theft defense. I'll never be able to do what you do. I know that. I've always known that. But I tell you what. I can make it as a team player.

If I put what I want second to what's best for the office, I'll get there. It may take me longer, but I'll get there." Pausing, he looked away, then back, eyes intense. He buried his shaking hands in his pockets and tried to keep his cool. "We're the fucking linemen, Noah, layin' the blocks up front so guys like you can grandstand."

"Grandstand! I'm trying to save a guy's life, for chrissakes! What would you do? Even linemen gotta pick up a fuckin' fumble and run with it sometimes!"

"That's not how I see it. In my book, you're turning your back on the people who need you, on the people you need too, if you think about it. You say it's about Ruiz, but you could make that work if you wanted to. You're turning your back on the people who help make this office happen. But you don't get that, do you? It's all about you, and not looking bad."

Noah couldn't take any more. "Get the fuck out of here," he snarled. "You don't have a clue. Never did."

Sandy stared, trying to think of what to say next, but coming up dry. So many times he'd made it right, smoothed it over. He just couldn't bring himself to do it this time. So was this it? Were they really oil and water now? Had it taken some time out in the world to realize it? He had no idea where things would go from here. He turned and left, closing the door behind him.

Noah watched him go, then picked up *Dressler* and winged it at the closed door. His mind was blank. He turned his back, running a hand through his hair, and started to pace. After about five minutes, his heart rate began to slow. He sat, cracked open the Evidence Code, and tried to get back what the issue was, but the pages started to blur. He leaned forward and rested his head on his crossed arms as consciousness faded.

An hour later, the vague sound of a phone relentlessly jangling seeped into his unconsciousness. Opening his eyes, he found himself still slumped on the conference table. His head had been resting on both arms, and they tingled violently the instant he moved. In a mush-minded haze, Noah turned and squinted at the black telephone on the bookshelf behind him. The back line was blinking, and he struggled to pick it up with a numb hand.

"Hel-lo?" he mouthed, gravelly.

"Thank God I finally got someone. Who is this?"

Noah sat up.

"Buzz?"

"Yeah, who's this?"

"Noah."

"Jesus, Blue. Didn't sound like you. Couldn't get through on your cell. I been callin' everywhere tryin' to find you."

"God. I forgot to turn it on when I got out of court. What's happening? You got a witness?"

"Not exactly. See what you think… I finally got with Figueroa. Spent the last couple days at the Rancho. Lost my cell when I got roughed up, but that's another story. They only have one phone down here, and they won't let anyone from the outside use it. Big storm rolled in so I had to stay an extra day, and they wouldn't give my phone back to me until I left. Weather's still pretty grim, lotta wind, but I left as soon as I could so I could call you. The—"

"Great, Buzz. Did you find a witness?"

"—good news is that Pablo *was* here the weekend of the murder."

"Outstanding!" Noah slammed an open hand on the table and recoiled from the bolt of electricity up his arm. He shook it violently and grunted, "Will… Figueroa testify?"

"No way. I asked him. He's got a gig goin' down here that he thinks a lotta people in the States would like to put an end to, and he thinks they might stick it to him, arrest him or something, if he comes up there. I'll tell you—" The line had been passable but it suddenly went south, static rasping over Buzz's voice.

"Buzz? Hello? Buzz?" Noah barked. "Buzz? You're breaking up."

"I'm here— Hel—?" The connection was becoming impossible, the cells being few and far between in Baja. The crackling continued for several more seconds; then, "Blue? Can you hear me?"

"Yeah, that's better. Listen, if I lose you again, call me on a land line, okay?"

"Well, I'm on my way back to San Felipe and there's nothin' out here, but I'll call or email when I get back to the hotel."

"Okay, so tell me. Figueroa won't testify. Will anyone else?"

"Figueroa says he won't expose any of his people, but I'm checkin' further. I'll see what I can do. That's not the worst of it, though. You might not want him to testify when you hear the rest."

"Christ, what now?"

"Turns out Van Zandt was actually killed down here, not in Oakland. They took his body out the morning after—"

"Whaaat?"

"Yeah, and that's not all. Pablo was the last person Figueroa saw with him…" More static. "…body was found…"

"Are you shittin' me?"

"This is the word from… it was… he…"

"Buzz? Buzz? You're cutting out again. Buzz? Dammit!" This time, it was hopeless. Noah dialed him back four times, but the connection was gone.

He stared at the table in front of him, struggling to get his mind around the enormity of it. *Pablo killed him. So that was it. Could there be any doubt about it now? But even with everything, it just didn't seem possible. It wasn't just his being gay that he had wanted to keep secret. Had the whole thing been an act for Amparo's benefit? He hadn't been able to confess any of it to his mother? Maybe things just got away from him somehow; he killed the guy and just can't even admit it to himself.* Noah looked at his watch. Almost 8:00. He jumped up, grabbed a tablet, and headed for the North County Jail.

● ● ●

"So… Now you know. I guess I knew all along that you would find out, finally."

Noah sat limply at the table in the holding cell, eyes half-closed in a combination of exhaustion and incredulity. He knew he should never ask the questions he was about to ask, but he was incapable of preventing himself. For his part, Pablo was every bit as depleted. The impossible strain of it all: the responsibility of saving his mother, the terrible events in Mexico, the crimes he was accused of, the death penalty, the trial, and now this. He was helpless to defend against it any longer. Both were enmeshed in a web of tragedy from which there was no escape, powerless to do anything other than play it out.

"You killed him."

"Yes."

"Tell me."

Seconds passed.

"Tell me."

Pablo took a breath, trying to find the strength. "It was the first time I had been in Mexico when Warren was there." Pause.

"Yes?"

"He liked me. I knew that."

"The murder, Pablo."

"Yes." Pause.

"Pablo?"

"I am trying." Pause.

"Tell me about it."

"I met him on the beach. We talked, had a few drinks. He offered me twenty-five hundred dollars to come to his room." Pause.

"What happened?"

"We drank more rum, did some coke, and we had sex. And… and when he gave me the money in hundred dollar bills, it made me think how rich he was. So I told him about my mother. That it would take fifty thousand dollars to save her. I asked him to help me."

Pause.

"Pablo?"

Nothing.

"What did he say?"

He grimaced. "He… he laughed."

"Okay."

He straightened angrily. "He laughed. He said my kind were all the same, that I would say anything to get money. I swore that it was the truth."

"Okay."

"It was like he was laughing at my mother."

"I can see that."

"I was filled with rage. I told him… I told him that I would tell people in Oakland about our having sex if he did not give me the fifty thousand dollars."

Noah's eyes slowly descended. *Jesus. Extortion now.* He looked back at Pablo. "So, what did he say?"

"He just kept laughing. He said I could say anything I wanted. He was tired of being in the closet. He was planning to come out anyway, to change his life." Pause. "I guess I lost control. I shouted at him. I hit him with both fists. He just kept laughing."

"And you choked him."

"No."

"What happened?"

"I ran. I had to be alone. I could not think. My mind was mixed up, full of drugs. I kept thinking the same thought."

"What were you thinking?"

Pablo averted his eyes and rasped, "That I wanted to kill him."

Silence.

"I was crazy. I *did* want to kill him. I had failed at everything. My mother would die. This man could save her, but he refused. And he laughed." The tears welled up and spilled. He pulled a folded handkerchief from his pocket and wiped his eyes.

Noah waited, then said, "What did you do?"

"I sat on the beach. The sun was going down. I was wild. I walked back and forth. I thought to get him away from the casa and kill him." He looked away. "The coke…" He shook his head. "I have never been so angry."

"So what did you do?"

Pause. "It is all very hazy. I do not remember much after that. I must have blacked out, because I next remember being in a small place in the rocks." He wiped his eyes again, as if keeping them dry would control the emotion. "The rocks by the beach. I do not know what time it was. It was dark. I stood up to go back to the casa, and then I saw Warren, lying a few feet away." His voice diminished to a whisper. "I thought he was sleeping."

He hung his head to hide his face and sobbed silently, gasping. He tried several times to speak. Noah put a hand on his shoulder as the weeping continued, his upper body racking spasmodically. Then the gasping slowed, and he tried to make his breathing regular as he spoke. He would tell it now.

"I tried to squeeze by him… without waking him… to return to the hacienda. I brushed him… his body was cold… he wasn't breathing…" Noah started to speak, but Pablo held up a hand, insisting upon finishing.

"I… I was terrified. Paralyzed. I had no memory… but there was no one else there."

They sat in silence, both imagining it. Seconds ticked by as stillness hung in the tiny room. Finally, Pablo said, "I ran. I ran as far as I could. Then I went back to the hacienda and gathered my things. They took me home." He searched Noah's face for reassurance.

"Who else knows about this, Pablo?"

"I have told no one," he said and shuddered. "I have destroyed everything. I killed him. Now they will kill me. What will happen to my mother?"

Noah's instinct was rescue. "No," he said. "We don't know that. You have no memory of what actually happened. The prosecution has to prove all this. It's not over." But that's not what he was thinking. "When you thought of killing him, what was the picture in your mind?"

Pablo thought, focusing on the image. "I was strangling him."

Noah's shoulders fell and his chest tightened, his thoughts racing.

My God… He did do it. Now what? And what about Amparo? He had to think of something, or they would both die. What about the trial? A plea? But there was no more offer. He couldn't put Pablo on the stand and let him lie, say he was in Mexico, try to sell that the murder was in Oakland when they knew it wasn't.

Wrenching his mind back into the holding cell, he said, "I have to think this through. No one can testify about what happened to Van Zandt. Not even you. The truth is, you don't know." He stood.

Pablo was slumped over, eyes closed.

"You have to stop assuming that you did it," Noah said. "No way I'm giving up, and neither are you. I just need a little time."

He stepped to the door, banged for the guard, looked out through the little window, and saw no one. Closing his eyes, he rested his forehead against the cool glass until the lock clicked and the door opened.

"I'll come by before court in the morning," he said, as he left the room without looking back. He didn't want Pablo to see his trepidation.

● ● ●

Noah left the jail in a trance and walked straight to the parking structure. Before firing up the Captain, he tried Buzz on the cell. Zilch. Then he headed back across the bridge, agonizing.

Never had he felt more alone. Hanging in the spotlight of media heat, he was dangling from a rope that had just frayed to a single strand. He was sweating, hands clammy, his mind careening out of control. No one between Pablo and destruction but him. *Gotta get some input. Who to call? Buzz was in Mexico, God knew where. In less than twelve hours, the world would demand answers. Stark? Useless. Sandy? No clue. Kate? Forget it.* He wondered what his mother would say. *"A murder case? Nice, dear. Gotta run." And where was his father at that moment? The sonofabitch who had never been in his life?*

Nobody but Pablo to testify that he'd been in Mexico. Shit, there wasn't even an alibi anymore. The murder had happened down there. But did he have to tell Salem that? The bastard was trying to kill Pablo, wasn't he?

It was all his fault. Should've let Pablo take the deal when he wanted to, no matter what his mother said. Now it was gone, and he would have to put him on to testify. But why put him on now? He couldn't let him deny the murder if he actually did it.

He had to get out of this thing. Show up tomorrow morning and withdraw. There was still time. Trial had just started. He would tell

Pulansky he had a conflict of interest but couldn't disclose it without prejudicing his client. The judge would have to continue the trial, and they would get Pablo another lawyer… wouldn't they? Someone who knew what the fuck they were doing? Someone who saw Pablo as just another killer? Let him slide downhill into the death penalty. "Sorry, did the best we could." Wasn't that what they always said?

As the Captain glided back across the bridge toward the lights of San Francisco, it suddenly it hit him. *Wait! The body was found in the sewage plant. Emeryville! How the hell could Pablo pull that off? It was one thing to schlep it over from Oakland, but someone had to get it back from Mexico, didn't they? How could they find out who that was? They were in trial. Too late.*

No! Put Pablo on and let him deny it. He would say he was in Mexico. Forget about where Van Zandt was. Was that suborning perjury? Did you lose your ticket if it came out you put a witness on to testify to half-truths? But who knew that Van Zandt was killed down there? Pablo? Buzz? That guy Figueroa down in Mexico knew, and God knew who else at the hacienda. And wouldn't Salem ask him point blank on cross whether he killed Van Zandt? Then what? Would he have to say he doesn't know? Not much of an answer in the face of this mountain of damning evidence.

Once over the bridge, he took the 9th Street off-ramp into the Tenderloin, then drove around for fifteen minutes trying to find a parking place. Finally spotting one on Eddy, he backed in and locked up the Captain for the night. As he turned the key, it occurred to him that he never used to lock his car—that is, until the cops entered uninvited.

It was nearly 10:00. As he walked briskly up Eddy, he glanced up at the stars and shivered. Sounds of laughter down the block attracted his attention, and he glanced up toward the corner, saw the warm lights of the Oarhouse, and changed direction.

"Christ, you look like shit." Stork's Saint Bernard nature blossomed as Noah climbed mechanically onto a stool. He drew a frosted mug of the usual and set it down on the bar.

"Lemme have a shotta scotch," Noah said.

"Wow. You are in the wars." He poured a dose of the anesthesia and set it next to the beer. "Wanna talk about it?"

"Nah." Noah pounded the scotch, drained the mug, laid down a few bills, and slid off the stool. Stork watched him curiously as he plodded from the tavern, turned right on Eddy, and made his way toward his sanctuary.

Totally zoned, Noah stripped, threw his clothes onto the chair, and slipped into bed. Mercifully, the alcohol did its job and sleep came quickly, but once again, the demons appeared in short order to do their usual dance.

"Get in the car, Noah, we're late."

"Can't I stay here, Mom? We're almost done with our game. It's thirteen to ten, bottom of the eighth."

Noah stood on his expansive front lawn beside a makeshift home plate with his bat in hand, his blue Dodger cap shading his eyes. Four other seven-year-olds were scattered around the yard. A taller eight-year-old, standing on a piece of cardboard that served as a pitcher's rubber, impatiently tossed the ball up and caught it. Until a few moments ago, it had been heaven on a Saturday afternoon.

"No. I told you we're going to Rachel's today. Your aunt hasn't seen you in several months. Now, we talked about this."

"But it's still early."

"Well, I've got a date tonight, and I made an appointment at the beauty parlor before we go to Rachel's. I've got nowhere to leave you, so you'll just have to come with me. Get in the car."

"But, Mom…"

"Get in the car, Noah! I've got a lot on my mind, and I don't have time for this! Don't make me come after you!"

He stomped across the lawn to the driveway and the white Mustang convertible where she stood. The other boys looked on in exasperation. The pitcher started to smirk.

"Randy's mom is next door. She can watch us while you're gone. You could come back and pick me up. What am I gonna do at the beauty shop?"

"You'll read a magazine or something. Now let's go."

"Lemme stay… please?"

Glaring furiously, she was grinding her teeth. "I said no… dammit! Now get in that car!"

"All the other kids get to stay. You're not a very good-"

Before he could finish it, she lashed out and slapped him with her open hand. His eyes flew wide as he looked up, startled and humiliated, his cheek on fire. Her face was contorted, ugly, eyes squint-flashing. Overcome with rage, he tried not to cry, but he couldn't help it. He turned and ran as fast as he could. Behind him, he could hear her yelling as the boys stood and watched.

"Noah! You come back here! Noah, do you hear me? Get in this car!"

He ran, on and on, far from the diminishing sound of the voice behind him, from the inability to cope, from the smallness that entrapped him, from all of it. His strides grew rhythmic, and there was a growing sense of lightness, of freedom. His feet hardly touched the ground, and he felt a gush of elation.

Almost imperceptibly, he became aware that he was splashing through water. Soon it was ankle deep; then it was up to his knees. The water was still, dark, murky. He kept sloshing through it as fast as he could, frightened to think what might be lurking below the surface. Everything was cold, turbid liquid, getting deeper, holding him back as he tried to run, dragging him down.

Ahead he could see a wooden bridge. He struggled toward it through the flood that was now up to his waist. From a distance, he could discern someone sitting on edge of the span, legs dangling, leaning toward him, a hand extended. Getting closer, now submerged to his shoulders, he could see that it was an older woman, calling to him softly, her expression gentle, reassuring, something white around her head. The water was up to his neck, beginning to swirl. He reached for her as he started to go under, trying desperately to take her hand. Just as his fingers closed around hers, the current took him, breaking his grasp and sweeping him away.

He was awakened by the sound of spasmodic gasping. He realized that it was his own sobbing. He lay there a long time, unable to stop. Shattered, consumed with sadness over the isolation, the abandonment, he wept for a seven-year-old who was utterly powerless to help himself.

CHAPTER FORTY-TWO

It was almost midnight. Noah had finally gotten back to sleep when he slowly became aware of buzzing. He located the annoying vibration, picked up his cell, squinted at the yellow screen that read "Unknown Caller," and tapped the answer button.

"Here's the thing, Shane, we been friendly about this fucking Ruiz thing up to now, but we're apparently not getting our point across. We thought it'd be good to have a little meeting to discuss it in plainer terms."

"Discuss what?" He peered over at the blur of glowing numbers on the nightstand clock. Even through his haze, it was clear this was the same voice he'd heard the night Lisa had been roughed up.

"We need to talk about a plea," the deep male voice rumbled.

Noah sat up and switched on the bedside lamp. "Who are you?" he said.

No response.

"There is no more plea. Why is this so important to you?"

"See, that's the point. You had your chance on the involuntary, and you blew it. Now Ruiz's gonna have to take what he can get, plead as charged if that's all they'll give him. But he's gonna have to plead."

String this out? Think of something. "Why would he do that? He'll spend the rest of his life in jail. No parole."

"Because he's guilty. And it's the healthy thing to do."

"Why are you calling me?" *Hang up and call SFPD? Could they somehow get a trace on this guy?*

"We think it'd be a good idea to get together and talk this over. We think you need to know how serious we are."

"Sorry, don't think I'd be interested in—"

"You will be," the caller growled. "There's a warehouse at 1201 Crescent, an alley off Fifth, between Bryant and Brannan. Be there in half an hour. Got it?"

"Why would I do that? I don't know you."

"Because there'll be someone there you do know, a little friend of yours who'd like to see you. Say hello, Maggie."

Noah bolted to his feet. *Jeezus! It couldn't be. Please God.*

"Noah? Is that you?" The voice was small and sounded frightened. It was unmistakably Maggie.

"Maggie? It's me, Noah. Listen, it's gonna be okay."

He could hear her talking, but he couldn't make it out. Then the male voice again.

"Be there in a half hour."

"You bastards better not hurt that kid. I swear I'll—"

"No threats, Shane. And no cops, no social workers, no foster parents. Just you. Unarmed. We have eyes on you, and it's important to Maggie. One half hour." A click, and the line went dead.

Noah fought the panic as he climbed into his jeans. *My god! How could this happen? How did they get her?* It came to him that Lisa was in L.A. for a week-long Kragen training seminar. *They must have taken Maggie from the foster home, or maybe from school. That couldn't be right. If she didn't come home on the bus, the Goldmans would have called. They had his number when Lisa was away. She didn't sound hurt, only terrified. No way to get hold of Lisa. Had to call SFPD. Call the Goldmans. They couldn't know she was gone yet.*

He pulled on a T-shirt, sat on the bed, grabbed his cell, and then leaned forward, elbows on knees. *What was he thinking? They'd kill her. Couldn't call anyone. Gotta just go get her.* He kept shaking his head. *All his fault. His fault. Gotta go get her.*

• • •

The Captain cruised slowly down Crescent, a dingy back-alley in an industrial section south of Market lined with brick warehouses, all with corrugated sheet-metal roofs. Dumpsters, garbage cans, empty crates, and boxes were propped against the grimy buildings, making passage, even by a single car, tight. Most of the places didn't have posted addresses.

Creeping by, Noah caught a number on a building to his right, 1164. A few doors up, a number was slashed in faded white paint above a steel bay door on a dilapidated building, but what was left appeared to be 1201. He pulled to the right and stopped.

Walking back, he surveyed his surroundings. The alley was dark, totally deserted, devoid of illumination except for a single light on a façade down the block. No sound but his footsteps, which he did his best to dampen.

He was suddenly aware of the vulnerability of being unarmed. He didn't own a weapon. Never needed one, even living in the Tenderloin. He'd gotten into a few scuffles with drunks and crackheads, a punch thrown here and there, but never anything life-threatening. He wasn't wild about the idea of walking straight into this pit alone, defenseless, but there was no other option.

Access had to be through the bay door or the metal one beside it. To their right, a single window was boarded up. Noah would have to make contact with whoever had called him sooner or later, but for the moment, his instinct was to maintain radio silence. Taking hold of the knob on the smaller door, he twisted, half-hoping it was locked. No such luck. The door creaked open a foot, and he peered into darkness. Cautiously, he pressed forward, listening for any sound from inside. Once he was through it, the door began to swing shut behind him, smothering the little light from the alley. Gasping, he grabbed for it, but it slammed with a loud thud. *No need to say hello now.* He pulled out his cell and illuminated the flashlight feature. The light was pinpoint and directional, but he could see he was in an empty room with another door on the far wall. Moving toward it, he stumbled over some boxes, then steadied himself. At last he swallowed hard and opened the door.

"Maggie?" he rasped, his voice thunderous in the silence. No response. Holding his phone light like a beacon, he crept, short steps, into the second room.

"Maggie?"

As he shone the light around the room he saw an open door in the far wall with darkness beyond, and he started for it. Suddenly he was seized from behind, a vice-like arm around his neck. A hand knocked his phone away and covered his mouth. Lashing out with both arms, he grabbed backwards ineffectually for his attacker. A blinding torchlight seared into his eyes.

"You need to get just how accessible you are, asshole," a voice snarled into his ear. "You, Lisa, Maggie." The arm ratcheted tighter around his neck. "You fuckin' wanna bear that in mind."

Noah tore at the arm, grappling desperately with both hands in an effort to relieve the pressure constricting his airway. He turned his head, exposing his mouth slightly, and grunted, "What… do you want?"

"Shut the fuck up!"

The hand again covered his mouth, and the pressure on his larynx increased.

"Here's the message: You make this plea go down, Shane. This trial ends today. That's it. Otherwise, some things are gonna happen that can't be taken back."

Knowing it was only seconds until he would black out, Noah gave one last wrench of his whole upper body, simultaneously biting down hard on the hand that covered his mouth.

There was a scream, and for an instant the grip on his neck loosened, then it tightened unbearably. A fist drove into his kidney. "God... damn... you fucking asshole!"

Noah tasted blood as he flailed. Another fist shot out of the darkness into his gut, just under his sternum. The breath exploded out of him and he went limp, collapsing to the floor. Though he tried to cover up, he was unable to protect himself against a flurry of sharp kicks to his ribs and the back of his head. The blows seemed to come from everywhere. Something caught him on the right temple, and he saw stars.

Clinging to a thread of consciousness, he thought he heard jumbled footsteps, obscenities, a door slamming, an engine racing, tires squealing. Unable to move, he struggled for shallow breaths. He lay alone in the blackness, not knowing how much time had passed. Gradually, his awareness returned, and he was consumed by excruciating pain and intense nausea. *Maggie! Gotta find Maggie.*

Staggering to his feet, he lurched erratically in the dark, groping with both hands. His shin hammered something hard, and he went down again, his shoulder striking a large, solid mass as he fell. He supported himself on the wall to his right, stood, and frantically felt his way along, yelling, "Maggie! Maggie!" His hands came upon a doorjamb, and he stumbled through, entering another darkened room.

"Maggie! Are you okay?" *Christ, where was she?* Fighting images of what he might find, he ran his palms along the ancient walls on one side of the door, then the other. A light switch! He snapped it on, and the room was dimly lit by a naked bulb hanging from a ceiling wire. It cast enough illumination for him to see that the room he just left was an office, probably not occupied for years; the one he now found himself in was some kind of storage space. Dust and cobwebs were everywhere. He spotted his cell phone near the door, and stepped back to retrieve it as he continued to yell for Maggie.

Retracing his steps, Noah rushed back through the office and into a larger room filled with dilapidated metal shelving. The place looked like an auto mechanic's shop. This had to be the parts area, with rows of old oil barrels and an adjacent five-foot-deep pit for working under vehicles.

He stumbled on, thrashing through the entire place yelling Maggie's name, searching every room, throwing open closet doors, groping in cupboards, backtracking, and searching again. After several repetitions, it was clear that no one was there.

• • •

Driving up 5th toward Market, Noah fumbled with his cell. What now? Cops? He'd heard that the longer kids were missing, the more the hopes for recovery dimmed. But first, the Goldmans. There was no reason not to call now. He found the number in his contacts and tapped it in. After several rings, a somnolent female voice answered.

"Hel-lo?"

"April? It's Noah Shane. Do you know where Maggie is?"

"Noah? What? What time is it?"

"It's after two. What's happened to Maggie?"

"She's here. Asleep. What's going on?"

"Are you sure?"

"Where else would she be at two o'clock?"

"Would you check? I need to know."

"What do you mean? We went to bed early. Of course she's here."

"April, some men called earlier who said they had her. I've got to know. I've been searching. Will you check for me?"

"Okay… all right. Hang on a minute." She put the phone down.

He pulled the Captain to the curb and waited for her answer, muttering continuously, "Please God, please God, please God."

"Yeah, she's here. Noah, what's going on? Tell me."

"Oh, thank God." He slumped his head against the steering wheel.

"Noah?"

"I've gotta come see her. I'll be there in ten minutes."

"Can't you come by tomorrow? It's really late."

"I know. But I gotta come now. This is all my fault."

"What is?"

"I'll explain in ten minutes."

It was almost 2:30 when he arrived at the gray-shingled, four-story Victorian in the lower Fillmore. All the way over, his mind had been a knot of relief, conflated with confusion and dread. *How in the name of God did they do that? I heard her voice. Some kind of tape? Jeezus! They can get to her any time they want. Gotta frigging put a stop to this. But how?*

It seemed as though all the first-floor lights were on. April Goldman, short, round, clad in flannel pajamas, responded to the bell. Maggie was with her. Noah knelt and hugged the child, almost crushing the breath out of her.

When he stood, April took one look and said, "Noah. What happened?"

"What?"

"Your face."

Maggie looked up. "Yeah, Noah. Your face," she said, worry in her voice.

He put a hand to his cheekbone, already swollen twice its size. A sharp pain rippled as he touched it, and he winced. "Um, nothing. Just bumped into a doorjamb in the dark."

"Wow. It's all purple," Maggie said.

April was about to follow up, but she looked down at Maggie and thought better of it.

Balding and bearded, Marv Goldman padded sleepily downstairs in his bathrobe. Noah laid out the events of the last several hours, then checked his contacts for Lisa's cell and dialed her in L.A. He wanted to be sure these thugs hadn't gotten to her, as well.

Lisa was asleep when he called.

"Noah? What's going on?"

He gave her the summary, then said, "It was the same guys who beat you up. They're trying to strong-arm me about this case I'm trying. For some reason, they want the trial to stop. I've been doing everything I know to stay away from you and Maggie, but they're trying to show me how they can take both of you any time they want... and I'm convinced."

Silence. "My God. Who are they?"

"I don't know. I really don't. But I'm going back to SFPD with it."

"Yeah. Lot of good that seems to have done."

"I know, but I'll get them to listen. Meantime, you need to watch your back, stay out of places where you're not with other people. Don't answer the door without knowing who it is."

"How're you gonna be sure Maggie's okay?"

"I talked to April about that. She'll keep her home from school, stay with her until this trial's over. Maybe as much as three weeks. They'll get her lessons from the teacher. April says Maggie can help with the little kids during the day. And Maggie's up for it."

"I'm really frightened."

"I know. I'm so sorry. I'd make them stop if I could. I've gotta believe everything'll be fine once this trial is over. Until then, we'll hunker down and do whatever it takes to keep you and Maggie safe."

"I don't know if I can deal with this, Noah."

"I hear you, Lees." He knew what she was saying. "Stay close to your sponsor. You can't let this destroy everything you've worked so hard for. Maggie's depending on you. I'll check in with you every day."

"Yeah…"

While Noah phoned SFPD, April made some hot chocolate for Maggie. It was after 3:00 by the time he reached them. This time, he bypassed the assault division and went to Juvenile, where he talked to a middle-aged inspector who knew nothing of Lisa. After giving his statement, he related how he'd reported Lisa's assault by these same guys, yet no one had even interviewed her. There had been no surveillance. And now her daughter had been threatened. The cop took copious notes as Noah made it clear that if either Lisa or Maggie was the subject of further criminal activity, there'd be a report to the police commissioner and a civil suit for dereliction of duty. He had no idea if there was such a thing, but it got the attention of the rather serious Juvenile officer who had promised a full investigation, and beefed-up protection. They would take Maggie's statement tomorrow and work out a protocol for round-the-clock surveillance.

Noah left the Goldman house after 3:30. He made April promise not to let Maggie out of her sight, then asked her if Maggie had talked to anyone she didn't know on the phone. Yes, April said; there had been a call.

"He said it was you, Noah," Maggie said. "But I didn't think it was, and he hung up. It kind of scared me."

"It wasn't me, sweetheart. But I want you to tell me if there are any more calls, okay? April, best you don't give her any calls except Lisa or me." April nodded.

"Who was it, Noah?" Maggie asked.

"I don't know, squirt. It's some guys who are after me, not you. I don't want you to worry, but I do want you to be careful. Don't talk to any strangers, and tell April and me if anyone calls."

"Okay."

"Now listen. I was talkin' to your mom, and when this trial I'm in is over, we're all goin' to the zoo, then out to dinner, okay?"

"What's a trial?"

"You know. In court, like on TV. *Law and Order?*"

"You're in trials?"

"Yes, ma'am."

"What's it about?"

"It's a muuuurder case." He made a face and held up both hands, wiggling his fingers like Frankenstein.

"Wow. Will you tell me about it?" Her eyes were saucers.

"I sure will," he promised, taking her hand as they walked to the front door. As he opened the door, he waved to April. "Thanks for humoring me. I'll call you tomorrow."

"Get some sleep," she said.

He looked down at Maggie, squeezing her hand and trying to manufacture the confidence she needed to see, even though the fatigue was rapidly returning. "'Night, squirt. This is all going to be okay. We'll all talk tomorrow."

A serious expression crept over the sleepy little features. "Noah?" she said.

"Yeah?"

"I love you."

He nodded slowly, biting his cheek. Then he squatted in front of her, holding her by both shoulders.

"You're one special kid, Maggie," he said, and gently kissed her forehead. "I love you, too."

CHAPTER FORTY-THREE

"Heard about the PD walk-out. Kinda thought you might turn up missing this morning."

Pulansky was back on the loyalty to the old "firm" theme. "And yet, here you are. And looking like you got the worst of it in a bar fight, at that. Rough night?"

Noah sat, subdued, in his usual place during the morning ritual in chambers. *Rough night? For sure.*

The judge puffed on his first cigar of the day, his shirtsleeves and suspenders a contrast to the formal suits of the two lawyers.

After finally getting to bed at nearly 4:00, it had taken Noah a while to slow the adrenalin enough for sleep. It seemed like only minutes later when the alarm rang at eight. He had set it for as late as he dared. It wasn't until he attempted to rise that he had pulsating updates on every kick he had sustained the night before. He slid a leg out of bed and cranked himself into a semi-standing position. He'd taken a lot of hits at Stanford thanks to a weak offensive line, but this was definitely something special. He hobbled, bent over, to the bathroom, downed four ibuprofen, and dragged himself under a steaming shower. After half an hour, he emerged somewhat more erect, but not much.

He checked the phone and laptop for email from Buzz. Nothing. *Okay. Bad weather and no cells on the way back from the Rancho, but where the hell was he now? And when was he getting back?*

During the ride to Oakland, his thoughts returned to last night's revelations from Pablo. He gradually became aware that the constellation of events, panic about Maggie's safety, the flat-out ass-kicking, and then the indescribable relief on finding her unharmed, had been somehow therapeutic, focusing him on the people who needed him. Still, the impossible questions remained, and any answers were definitely obscured by an aching body and sleep deprivation. His mind first went back to whether he could get out of this trial, this case. *What about ginning up some kind of claim of conflict of interest, and then withdrawing? Nobody would know. But they would have to hire some hack outside the PD's office, who would be willing take the minimal fee they paid in conflict situations. Would Pulansky even grant a continuance for a conflict? No one would know he had made it up. No one but him, that is. Suppose the new hack tried the case and got Pablo the needle? How could he ever forgive himself? No. There were no choices. Put one foot in front of the other and see what developed. Maybe Buzz gets back tomorrow.*

At the jail, he found Pablo clinically depressed, withdrawn, unable to sleep. Noah said nothing about his own night's events, reiterating the doorjamb-in-the-dark story before the question of his battle scars came up, though in his current state, there was some question whether Pablo would even have noticed.

They walked through the "remaining alternatives," among which was the possibility of a plea to first-degree murder. Should the DA accept it, such a plea would preclude a death sentence, though it would likely mean life without parole. Pablo sat mute, nodding feebly after Noah repeatedly asked him if he understood. *No way to know if he did.*

Noah went on to cover the ethical dilemma of putting Pablo on the stand and letting him spin his being in Mexico as an alibi now that it was clear that the murder had actually taken place down there. Of course, if the DA asked the right questions, such a strategy would be life-threatening. Again, the question of whether he understood. Again, the feeble nod.

So, Noah told him, they would simply play it by ear for now, see what the prosecution's case was, then revisit how to proceed. Kicking the can down the road was certainly no solution, but given Pablo's state of mind, he didn't want to try to explain the apparent lack of any remaining defense.

Amparo arrived, and Noah went out to the lobby to greet her. She was shocked to see his face, and he once again repeated the explanation. They then proceeded to the glass-windowed, telephone-communication visiting room, where all but the attorneys visited the inmates. For Amparo's benefit, Noah repeated the dwindling options; Pablo did not speak.

"Pablo seems to have little awareness of what is going on," Amparo remarked, as she and Noah left the visiting area.

"Yeah, I noticed that."

"Do you think he is all right? He did not speak this morning. He was not like that yesterday when I saw him."

"He's pretty depressed."

"Can they arrange for him to be seen by a doctor?"

"I think he's probably not sleeping, not eating."

"But he must. He must keep his strength up. He will become ill."

"I can only imagine the stress of being jailed, facing murder charges, and now being in trial."

"Is there anything that can be done?"

"I'm afraid what we are seeing may be part of the consequences of facing that truth you were talking about, señora. But if he doesn't improve, I'll take it up with the judge. Maybe they can have him looked at."

Having already finished several calendar matters, by 9:45 when Noah and Salem had arrived, the judge was settled in his chambers, sucking down his third mug of coffee, surrounded by the plaques and framed awards that memorialized his lawyering and judging achievements. The room was devoid of the usual photos of wives, kids, grandkids, or fishing trips. Had Noah learned to take cues about his judge from the trappings of his natural habitat, he would have taken note of the large bronze-plated tablet prominently displayed behind his desk. It was an engraved Certificate of Appreciation for outstanding service as the Alameda County Public Defender for the twelve years before Pulansky's appointment to the bench. Obviously an accolade he valued highly.

Hoping for a pass on the judge's question about his bar-fight appearance, Noah focused on the inquiry about the strike. "Yeah. I heard about that, Your Honor. I think it's actually all next week."

"Next week?" The surprise on Pulansky's face was followed by a faint smirk. "They're going out for a whole week? So what did you have in mind about this trial?"

Noah hesitated, one eyebrow up, one down. "About the trial?" he said, wondering if the judge actually thought he would suggest they disrupt a murder trial for this labor strike. Finally, realizing an answer was expected, he shook his head and shrugged. "Nothing."

A few more years in the saddle would have sensitized him to the notion that this man across the desk, the one about to don the black robe, had his life—and even more so—his client's life, in the palm of his hand. But, lacking such a perspective, he strode carelessly through the haze of uber-fatigue and full-body ache into the maw of the beast, from where he delivered yet another sadly miscalculated line: "I've got no time for that kind of nonsense, Your Honor."

Pulansky's eyes narrowed. "Really," he said. "If the lawyers had had the bollocks to exercise some muscle when I was the PD, I think they would have had unanimous support. Might've gotten a few things changed around here by now. You think many of your brothers and sisters will be working next week?"

Unlike Noah, Salem understood it perfectly. He sensed a widening of the chasm that had already opened between Noah and the judge, and had long since learned to keep his mouth shut and let things develop when they were going his way.

"Well, I don't know, Your Honor." Noah couldn't fathom how this piddling labor issue could be of any real significance to Pulansky in the middle of a capital murder trial. But then, he hadn't been around in the old days, when PDs had camped in the County Law Library because there were no offices, or when they worked a sixteen-hour day for a few bucks a case, if they were paid at all. All costs and expenses had to be approved by the county and were often mired for months in bureaucratic red tape because no one cared about "that kind of nonsense." Pulansky, on the other hand, had most definitely been there.

"My guess is," the judge said, his tone now caustic, "if you show up here, you'll probably be the only PD in court." The judge let it linger, fully appreciating the high visibility of the case they were trying and the impact Noah's actions would have on the Association's collective efforts. He waited, and when Noah didn't respond, he moved on in a barely concealed smolder.

"So, anything else we have to deal with before we get started this morning, gentlemen?"

Noah was finally picking up on the judge's animosity, but still didn't comprehend it. "No, Your Honor."

"Your Honor, I know it's irregular," Salem interjected, now that the time was ripe. "But based upon recent information that has come to light, I would request leave to briefly supplement my opening statement. I would stipulate to the defense supplementing as well, if Mr. Shane wishes."

"Any objection, Mr. Shane?"

So long as Noah sat perfectly still, he experienced almost no pain. That, coupled with not wanting to make things any worse than they seemingly were by appearing the obstructionist, prompted him to respond: "I guess not, Your Honor." He turned to look at Salem, and winced from the stab of pain from his ribs. "This information doesn't add any new issues to the case, does it?" he grunted.

"Of course not. Just some new evidence. The issues are all the same."

"All right then," Pulansky said. "We'll start with your supplemental opening. If you have anything by way of response, Mr. Shane, we'll hear that next. Then you can expect to call your first witness, Mr. Salem." He rose, stepped to the clothes tree in the corner, snatched his black robe, and barked, "Let's go to work, gentlemen."

Both lawyers returned to the courtroom. The jury was already in place;

Pablo sat gazing down at the counsel table as before. Noah greeted him, forced a smile, and again put a hand on his shoulder, lingering for the jury to see the contact. Pablo didn't look up. The bailiff snapped to attention.

"Remain seated and come to order," he droned, as Pulansky took the bench, recited appearances for the record, and the day began.

"Ladies and gentlemen, the District Attorney has asked for an opportunity to address you further on what he plans to prove. Without objection from the defense, I have granted his request. Please give him your attention." He turned to the prosecutor. "Mr. Salem?"

"Thank you, Your Honor." Salem stood and again moved out from behind the counsel table, buttoning his pinstriped jacket, again adopting his position in front of the jury box.

"Ladies and gentlemen," he began. "Since our session yesterday, I have received word that two young men were found in Mexico— Baja California—who have very important information concerning the circumstances surrounding the death of Mr. Van Zandt. They are Rodrigo Sanchez, a sixteen-year-old boy, and Miguel Gallegos, his friend, who is fifteen. Miguel and Rodrigo live near San Felipe, a small fishing village on the Sea of Cortez, a hundred miles south of the Mexican border. The People will bring them to Oakland and will call them to testify, through an interpreter, that on the morning of August twenty-sixth, they were on their way out to go shrimping when they discovered a body among the rocks near the beach. We will prove that this was, in fact, the body of Warren Van Zandt, who had been murdered in that place the night before."

Even in his haze, Noah was struck dumb, riveted on Salem in total disbelief.

"The People will demonstrate that although the boys reported the whereabouts of the body to authorities, they took a small necklace from around the neck, a necklace with a pendant on which Mr. Van Zandt's name was engraved. They thought no one would miss it. The evidence will show that this necklace was actually a gift that was given to the victim at his birthday celebration that very night by a friend, one 'Pepito,' whose name also appears engraved on it. There can, therefore, be no doubt that this was, in fact, the body of Mr. Van Zandt."

Noah groped for an explanation. He tried to take some notes on what Salem was saying, but his pen barely moved.

"We will further demonstrate that what counsel told you is correct; Mr. Ruiz was in Mexico that weekend. We will produce an additional witness, who will say that Warren Van Zandt was last seen alive in the company of the defendant, and that same witness will say he saw the defendant walking down the beach, toward the precise area where the body was found the following morning by these two boys."

Somehow, Noah's mind seemed stuck. He wanted to act, but he couldn't get a handle on a response. *This cannot be happening again! How the fuck are they doing this?*

"We will satisfy you that the reason the defendant knew no one would be home in the Van Zandt condominium when he burglarized it was because he knew the victim was dead, having committed the murder himself. The defendant returned the body to the United States, or had it returned, shot it several times to make it appear to be some kind of an execution, and dumped it into the sewage plant. It was later that he broke into the condominium, and that is why there was no sign of a struggle, no shots heard, at the Van Zandt premises. It is expected that the evidence will be convincing that the defendant likely committed these acts himself, but was most certainly complicit in…"

The magma finally reached the surface and erupted. Noah's adrenalin gushed, his awareness of physical pain now numbed by endorphins. He bolted to his feet.

"Objection, Your Honor!"

All eyes turned.

"The defense vigorously objects to the District Attorney changing its theory at this late date. These three witnesses were not on the prosecution witness list. This is obviously an end run—"

"The objection will be overruled, Mr. Shane," Pulansky interrupted, trying to quell the insurrection before it gained momentum. "I will permit Mr. Salem to supplement his witness list in light of this recent information. It's the truth we're after here. I don't perceive any prejudice to the defense."

"In that case, Your Honor," Noah persisted, "the defense requests a continuance of this trial to conduct investigation of its own into this new evidence, and to research whether trial of this matter in this jurisdiction is appropriate when it is claimed that this death occurred in a foreign country."

Pulansky turned to the prosecutor. "Response, Mr. Salem?"

"Jurisdiction is appropriate, Your Honor. Mr. Van Zandt was a resident of Alameda County. His body was discovered here. The defendant is also a resident of this county. The interests of Alameda County are served by the prosecution occurring in this forum. As to the investigation, the public defender has had the same opportunity to look into these matters as our office. We are now in trial. Mr. Shane cannot stop the proceedings every time a new piece of evidence arises of which he was previously unaware. We'll be trying this case until next November."

Pulansky considered it at the speed of light, the mental AutoCAD turning it in every direction in seconds. It was a major new wrinkle that the killing had been in Mexico. Jurisdiction was sound, but Ruiz had been painted as a barrio kid, acting alone. How could he get the body back, solo? This was a huge opening for the defense, if they could capitalize. But a continuance? What would that accomplish? It was all investigation that should have been completed by trial time.

"Denied, Mr. Shane. You'll have your opportunity to cross-examine these witnesses. The defense has had the same time to investigate as the prosecution, and moreover, I fail to see how any further investigation might be revealing. Now, as to jurisdiction, both the accused and the alleged victim are residents of this county. The body was discovered here. I think that jurisdiction is intact. Unless you have some supplemental opening, I will ask the People to call their first witness."

"Your Honor!" Noah was shouting, now clinging to the end of his rope. *This judge had either been bought like the rest of these crooks, or he was playing games because of comments that a murder trial was more important than some bullshit PD strike.*

He was shaking imperceptibly, desperately reaching back for control. "Pablo Ruiz is on trial for his life," he began again. "And this court will not allow him the opportunity to review and investigate the evidence against him. This case was jammed to trial. For this court's information, my client was, in fact, not afforded the usual rights of investigation. Application was made by the defense for out-of-state investigation, which was denied. Now we see that the DA has obviously been given far superior access to potential out-of-state evidence and witnesses. Not only that, but the statements of the District Attorney and other public officials in the press have been highly prejudicial. Pablo Ruiz has been railroaded in every way, at every turn, since his arrest." The words were coming furiously. He was helpless to stop them, his natural inhibitions lagging far behind his rage. "Your ruling now appears to be more of the same, either part of an obvious conspiracy to rush Mr. Ruiz to a conviction, or based on some personal animosity towards me. I will take this matter—"

Pulansky had heard all he was going to hear. "That's enough, Mr. Shane! I've changed my mind. I am going to allow you that continuance you requested after all. You will spend it in the County Jail. Bailiff, take counsel into custody."

The deputy moved toward Noah, who stood motionless.

"I warned you about this." Pulansky's jaw was set. "You are in contempt of this court. You will be incarcerated until further notice. Between now and tomorrow morning, you will carefully evaluate your conduct, and you will consider your remarks. At the morning session, the court will entertain the matter of your release if a full—and sincere—apology is offered. We will be in recess until tomorrow morning at nine o'clock, when the sheriff will bring defense counsel to court for further proceedings on the contempt citation."

Pulansky turned to the jury. "Ladies and gentlemen, you will return at nine-fifteen tomorrow morning and remain in the jury room until you are called. In the meantime, I remind you of the admonition that you not discuss this case among yourselves, or with anyone else, especially the press."

He stood and stormed off the bench to a chorus of shouts as representatives of the media sprinted from the room to file their stories. In shock, the jurors slowly rose, looking vacuously around them, and began to file out, unsure of what had just happened.

"Okay, counselor, hands behind you," the bailiff instructed. Noah complied, mindlessly, as the two jail deputies moved Pablo into the holding cell. After they had cleared Pablo from the area, the bailiff took a dumbstruck Noah through, into the elevator, and down to the basement. Their footsteps, echoed off the concrete walls as they marched without speaking through the brightly lit, concrete tunnel leading from the administration building, under Fallon Street, and into the basement of the Main Courthouse. With a firm hand on his biceps, the bailiff led Noah into the secure elevator that would lead only to one other stop: the old courthouse jail, now used to hold prisoners whose cases were in court, at the building's top floor.

It wasn't until the five-by-five lift began to slowly ascend that the horror began to sink in. *Jail? How the fuck was he going to do this?* Noah's mind struggled to comprehend; the panic began in the pit of his stomach and spread through his body. He tried to resist, to fight it, but it rose higher and faster. *God Almighty. How did this happen?*

Once upstairs, he was placed in a holding cell where he sat, alone, while the guard phoned to summon a separate van to North County Jail. They would not transport a public defender in with the regular prisoner population. Each slow, shallow breath elicited stabbing rib pain.

Forcing himself to hang on, Noah became progressively light-headed. In an effort to clear his perception, he stood and paced unsteadily.

After about fifteen minutes, he was taken to a subterranean carport, where he was loaded, still cuffed, into the secure van and driven the five minutes to North County. He was booked in; his clothes were checked; he was issued an orange jumpsuit, sneakers, and a blanket, and then taken up to a cellblock on four.

As the guard led him, shuffling down the windowless hall in his underwear and sneakers, a blanket and jumpsuit in his arms, he tried to keep his head down, but first one inmate, then another, recognized him. In short order, shrieking catcalls and whistles resounded off the concrete walls. As the noise increased, he was guided into an empty solo cell. Furnished with only a cot and a mattress, a stainless-steel sink, and a commode, the cubicle had no window, only a barred sliding door that thudded shut behind him, clicking loudly as the automatic lock engaged.

Standing in the gloom, his back to the bars, breathing hard and trembling, he could feel his heart beating wildly as the raucous din rose to consuming proportions. He grimaced and held both hands to his ears, trying to block it out. Sweat was cold on his forehead. He walked the two steps to the cot and sat, naked except for his shorts and laceless shoes, the blanket and jumpsuit on his lap. In the hall, the shouting reached a continuous roar, laughter and catcalls throbbing, louder and louder. He tried to will his mind to a place of calm, but the perfect storm of physical and mental pain, superimposed on exhaustion, rendered it hopeless.

Staggering to his feet, he started to pace. Two steps in one direction, two steps back. *He had to get out! Get out!* Breath coming in gasps, eyes darting, he lunged to the bars, hung on, and peered down the hall. His face, dripping and contorted, pressed against the cold steel as the chorus of shouts reverberated through the cellblock. Everything was distorted. Leering, grinning faces. Rhythmic banging. Metal on metal.

He jerked back into the tiny room and dropped, face down, onto the mattress, covering his head with his hands, squeezing his eyes shut. An intense, high-pitched sound, merging with a searing white light, consumed him. He couldn't think, couldn't breathe. *He would not scream... God-damn-fucking-sonofabitch, he... would... NOT... SCREAM!*

PART THREE

SURVIVAL

He conquers who endures. —Persius

CHAPTER FORTY-FOUR

"Yes, Celia?"

"Mr. Owens on line two, sir."

"I'll take it."

Mustafa punched an outside line. "Ben. What's the news from the courthouse?"

"Disaster."

He sat up abruptly. "Why? What's happened?"

"Chaos. Pulansky threw Shane in jail this morning."

"He *what?*"

"The way I get it from Salem, after it came out that the murder went down in Mexico, Shane moved for a continuance to do more investigation. When Pulansky denied it, Shane had a meltdown, accused the judge of being part of a conspiracy to obstruct justice. That didn't sit too well with Pulansky, who runs his courtroom about like Patton ran the Italian campaign. So I guess Pulansky cited him in contempt and had the bailiff cuff him right there in front of the jury, the media, everybody."

"Shit!"

"Right. When the media reports that this kid-PD is accusing the system of railroading his client, they'll turn this into a total circus. We're talkin' national exposure."

"Cha-rist. This's all we needed. Another endless, fuckin' O.J. passion play."

"And maybe he takes a writ on being denied a continuance when he was turned down for investigation that we were able to get. So it looks like we either go back to the involuntary, or put our heads down and just plow through it when Pulansky lets him out."

Mustafa considered it. "Negative. Can't give him a parkin' ticket now, not after it's all in the media. The whole system'd look weak, or worse. And if the fuckin' trial continues, this Shane kid's gonna cause trouble all the way. It's his style. We take a chance on some sensitive matters coming out, along with the trashing of Warren Van Zandt." He thought for another moment, then added, "And God knows who else."

"Maybe, but I'm not seeing many options."

There was a long silence; then Mustafa said, "I don' know. Lemme think on it. I'll get back to you."

"Right."

Mustafa punched off and hit the intercom.

"Metcalfe."

"Gimme a minute, Harlan."

"Be right there."

Metcalfe entered without knocking and closed the door behind him. Mustafa waved him to a chair.

"What's up?" Metcalfe asked.

"This Ruiz case has taken a nasty turn. It's gonna require some kind of immediate action."

"Why? What's happened?"

"Well, let's just say we always knew that if the case went to trial, the chances that sensitive information would become public would increase dramatically. Unfortunately, it's come to that. We've tried everythin' to avoid a trial, all the damage, but we're at a point where our chances of success in sneaking out of this are looking pretty grim." He paused.

"Okay." Metcalfe never had grasped exactly what Ruiz had to do with Mustafa or Ebony Properties, but he didn't probe. There was clearly a connection, and he'd be told what he needed to know.

"This fuckin' judge is unpredictable. He's a former public defender who's too bright for his own good. He's all over the place. Jailed the PD."

"Jailed the lawyer? Why?"

"Apparently he accused the judge of bein' part of a conspiracy. Course, that's wide of the mark, but the problem is that it's high visibility, and it implicates the whole fuckin' county organization." Mustafa turned his gaze out the window, to the lake, then back to Metcalfe.

"Fuckin' kid," he growled. "We pitched him a deal no rational lawyer could refuse. He refused. We cranked up the pressure. He's still not on board."

Metcalfe had seen this before, Mustafa bouncing ideas around the room like volleyballs, formulating his thoughts as he spoke. He hadn't made a decision yet, or else he'd be barking orders.

"It's come out that the murder was in Mexico. There's some volatile shit down there that'll become troublesome if this goddamn trial continues. And Ruiz is liable to walk now that we gotta explain how he got the body back up here. We can't let that happen. This thing'll hit the media in the evenin' news. Can't help that, but it's gotta be stabilized."

"What'd you have in mind?"

More silence... then Mustafa slowly leaned forward. "We gotta put an end to the trial."

Metcalfe said nothing.

Mustafa nodded. "There's gonna be risk, but we gotta put an end to the trial."

"How?"

"We put an end to Ruiz."

Metcalfe was stunned, but he would never outwardly express doubt. He didn't drop a beat. "How do we get to him in the lock-up?"

Mustafa's words came slowly as he thought it through. "By sundown today, Leech Jaqua will be arrested for petty theft. He'll be arraigned and incarcerated in that same lock-up. At some point during the night, we can expect that Ruiz might try to make homosexual advances on Leech..." He was formulating it as he spoke. Metcalfe was impassive.

"When Leech resists, it becomes physical, and in a struggle to defend himself, Leech will seriously injure young Señor Ruiz. Those injuries will unfortunately prove fatal. In light of these developments, the trial will not be completed, and the press and the public will clearly accept the District Attorney's theories about the charges."

"What happens to Jaqua?" Metcalfe asked. "Doesn't this get back to us?"

"There'll be a complete investigation, of course, and it'll be found that Leech was exercisin' his right of self-defense in the face of a deadly attack by a murder suspect under conditions of abominable overcrowdin' in the County Jail. I predict that the District Attorney will accept a plea from Mr. Jaqua to the petty theft, and he will be given community service hours, pickin' up papers in the park. This never comes back to us. Trust me."

Metcalfe stared, his face still devoid of emotion, as Mustafa regarded him, waiting for some sign of validation. After a beat, Mustafa returned dismissively to the papers on his desk.

"See to it," he said.

• • •

The bedlam in Cellblock 4b of North County Jail continued unabated as two day-shift guards stood at the end of the hall, bemused by the tumultuous reaction. Though they would ordinarily take control and extinguish such an outburst, it was a rare event having a PD as a guest in their charge, and they weren't about to disrupt the entertainment. The caterwauling and beating of cups and plates on the bars was deafening.

In the confined one-man cell at the end of the hall, Noah lay sprawled on his belly on the cot's bare mattress, his near-naked body racked with pain as it shook with seizure-like convulsions. Eyes clamped shut, nose exuding fluid, intense nausea generating waves of retching, he was helpless, virtually unable to organize any voluntary movement, his consciousness devoid of thought, dominated by the pounding reverberations.

Approaching the limits of his endurance, drenched in sweat, on instinct alone he raised his head and stared into the swimming distortion. The remnants of his focus were drawn to a darkened corner of the cell where, just beyond the throbbing frenzy, he could dimly make out the gossamer form of an older woman, her head wrapped in something white, a serene smile on her unlined face, extending a hand to him.

CHAPTER FORTY-FIVE

"Okay, asshole. Now, I'm just gonna have you stand over here and hold that number up. No, a little lower. Like you thought it made you look pretty."

The beefy guard pulled Leech Jaqua firmly by the arm of his orange jumpsuit and positioned him over the two white lines taped on the floor. "Don't s'pose this is the first time you been a guest at this hotel. Put your feet on those two marks there, and watch the birdie. No smiling."

Several recent arrests had led to a line of new arrivals outside the booking office, and Jaqua's turn had come. He put one of his jail-issue high-tops on each line, and the camera flashed. As he held up the number, the guard noticed the blood-soaked bandage over the middle and index fingers of his left hand.

"What happened to you?" the deputy asked, nodding at Jaqua's hand.

"Cut m'self slicing pickles."

"Oughta leave that pickle alone."

The deputy reset the camera, stapled Jaqua's papers together, and tossed them into a wire-mesh basket.

"Okay, that's it for you. Through the sliding door over there, down the hall to the first room on the right, and find yourself a bunk. Pool opens at three. Cocktails at five on the veranda." He turned to the line behind him. "Next asshole," he barked. "Yeah, I'm talkin' to you, dickhead. Step over to the concierge desk here. Don't got all night."

Jaqua padded sullenly to the sliding panel of heavy bars and waited for it to open. A guard approached from the other side with another orange-jumpsuited inmate. Passing through the ingress corridor that was separated from egress by a single wall of bars, Jaqua watched the prisoner, who was on his way to the Reception Center to be processed out.

The exiting inmate continued down the hall, then turned right to the checkout desk, where the guard pushed a pen and a printed form across the counter. "Sign here, counselor."

"What's this?" Noah asked.

"Says you got everything they brought you over here with."

"Everything but my sanity." Still a little shaky, he slashed a signature across the card. In the midst of the chaos that had engulfed the cell block that morning, his state of mind had ultimately risen from rubber-room into the critical-but-stable range, and he had found himself overcome with exhaustion. He had drifted into a deathlike, dreamless sleep that only ended about half an hour before the guards came for him. In the noiseless jail, he lay on his back, emotionless, drained, alone with his thoughts and the pain in his ribs when he inhaled. The walk back through the cellblock toward the Reception Center had rekindled the pandemonium, somewhat more subdued than before, but Noah had found himself impervious to it this time. Now, standing in front of the Reception Room deputy, he was surprised to find his mental processes falling into near-normal alignment.

"So Pulansky decided not to hold me?" he asked the sheriff, sliding the form back across the desk.

"I don't know what the story is. Way above my pay grade. By the way, there's somebody waiting for you in Receiving."

"Who's that?" Noah asked.

"Beats me. Like I say, they don't consult me on the high-level stuff. Your suit's hanging over there with your shoes. After you change, just push the green button, and the deputy'll buzz you out." He jerked a thumb toward a gray-metal egress door with a small wire-reinforced glass window.

The guard outside the secure area directed Noah to the Receiving Room, where a familiar figure stood, back toward him.

"Buzz!"

"Christ, Blue," he said, turning. "Can't leave you alone to do anything. Your assignment was easy: try this case without winding up in jail. And yet, here you are." The grin diffused when he looked closely at Noah's face. "Whoa, what happened to you?"

"Long story. We'll get to it, but what happened to the contempt citation? Pulansky said I was going to rot in here until court tomorrow morning."

"Yeah, I heard about that. But hey, why don't we grab some grits?" He gestured toward the exit. "I got a lot to tell you, but I'm starved."

"So what happened? Did you bail me?"

"Yeah. Or no, no bail. I'll break it all down."

As they stepped out onto the sidewalk, Noah endured some painfully deep breaths of evening air. Then his thoughts returned to the case.

"Pablo's screwed, Buzz. They've got the kids who found the body. The prosecution knows all about it, that he, and the murder, were down in Baja."

"I know. I gotta fill in all the blanks for you. That's what we need to talk about. Woulda emailed you, only that storm knocked out the power in San Felipe... but what happened to your face?"

They walked the three blocks down Broadway toward the produce district. Noah began relating the story of Maggie's apparent kidnapping, his evening groping in the back alleys south of Market and, as they ducked into a dingy hamburger joint, he felt his anger rising again.

"I know what you think about Pulansky," he said, "but the guy's either up to his hairline in this whole conspiracy, or he went off on me because I'm not going along with the PD strike. You hear about that?" Noah didn't wait for an answer. "The one thing that's totally obvious is that whoever's behind all this is scared shitless about what's gonna come out in the trial. Scared enough to put the full court press on me." They settled into a booth.

"Who do ya think it is?" Buzz asked.

"It has to be somebody who thinks Pablo knows something, and he definitely might. I'll never know if I've gotten the whole thing from him."

"That's for sure."

"Maybe they're afraid it comes out that Van Zandt was gay? But that couldn't be a big enough deal to get into kidnapping, assault, obstructing justice."

"Yeah, well—"

"Whatever, it's gotta be pretty heavy duty to try to stop a high-profile capital murder trial by muscling the defense lawyer." A pause. "And what makes them think I can do anything about it, anyway? If they know all about the case, why don't they get that I can't make Pablo do anything? He's not goin' for any plea."

"Pulansky's not in on it, Blue. You don't know him like I do."

Noah regarded him a beat. "We'll see. That's kind of the whole problem, isn't it. I don't know anything about any of them. What I do know is I should never have been sitting in that chair in the first place. And also in that column of known facts is that somebody set this whole thing up, tied my hands on prep, beat up my friend, faked the kidnapping of her daughter, and kicked the shit out of me when I tried to find her. And if I continue to connect the dots, I see that the next morning, this hero judge of yours throws me in jail in the middle of the trial. So what does that say about who's in and who's out?" His jaw was taut, eyes narrowed.

Buzz studied him. There was something different, though he couldn't put his finger on it. "Okay, I get it, and I agree it's been a setup from the get-go. And I don't blame you for being uber-pissed."

Noah turned away. "You know? I'm not sure I can even identify with pissed anymore." He struggled for the right word. "I guess it's more like I'm just done."

Buzz hesitated. "Meaning?"

"Meaning I've had it with this whole charade."

Buzz's eyebrows gathered. "Wait, Blue. You're not gonna pitch it in? What happens to —"

"Nah, there's no way to pitch it in. God knows I've thought about it, but they wouldn't let me out anyway, and I just can't fake some exit strategy that's likely to do Pablo in." He paused as Buzz stared, somewhat amazed. "Nah. I'm locked in. So I guess I'm really saying the opposite. I'm talking about finding a way to get to the bottom of the freakin' thing once and for all, and deal with whoever's behind it."

"What did you have in mind?"

"Yeah, well, that's the part I'm not sure about yet, but I'm working on it."

An overweight, oily-skinned teenager arrived and set down two glasses of water. Buzz ordered them a couple of dogs with sauerkraut, but Noah interrupted and said he'd have a burger instead. When the kid left, Noah said, "Tell me what happened with Pulansky. How did you get me out?"

"I think I told you that Donovan was pretty heavy into the hooch when he hired me. Not as bad as me, but still, we definitely shared more than a few snorts together before we both swore off... mostly swore off. He went back to it, but I guess he can manage it better than I can. Anyway, we were pretty tight in those days, in more ways than one."

"So?"

"So when I got off the plane this afternoon, my first stop was Oakland Division to look for you, and they told me about your little calamity. I knew it was gonna require some drastic measures, and it occurred to me I might still have some juice with Pulansky, so I called him." He took a sip of the water, musing. "I've never asked him for anything in all these years."

"Wait. You called the judge? Perfect. So now I gotta deal with some kind of ex parte communication along with everything else?"

"No ex parte communication. I don't say anything about the case. I just tell him I been doing the investigation, and that I gotta get you out to prep the thing. I promised to lay out the rules of the road for you, and I asked him if he could see his way clear to spring you a little early. That's it." Then he added, "And he had some nice things to say about you."

Noah's frown deepened. "He what?"

"Yeah. He said you were one smart kid, maybe a natural at trial work."

"He did not."

"He did. But I gotta tell you he also said you might be some kind of self-absorbed egotist who couldn't give a shit about what the PDs had been through during the very tough old times."

"So then it was the strike that set him off."

"From what he said, I don't think that was it."

"What then?"

"He wasn't happy about your attitude about the strike, but it really sounded like it was your mouthing off in front of the jury, accusing him in open court of being part of some kind of conspiracy. That's what got to him."

The dog and burger arrived. Buzz slathered his with mustard and ketchup, then started to devour it. Noah only sat, not eating. Finally he said, "We gotta do something… and it's gotta be something radical."

Buzz looked up, cheeks bulging. "Not that I disagree with you, Blue, but what kind of radical are you thinking?"

"He's not guilty," Noah chafed in a low voice.

"Yeah, I know."

"No. He's really not guilty. The amazing thing is he thinks he is, but he's not. I wasn't sure, but now I am."

Buzz swallowed and stared. "He thinks he is?"

"I had this kind of vision."

"Vision?"

"In the jail."

"Jesus, Blue. Visions of not guilty? You're starting to sound like me. So what happened?"

"I don't know, exactly. I was pretty fucked up when they locked me in there, and this sort of image came to me."

"Image?"

Noah hesitated. His experience had been so personal; Buzz wouldn't get it, anyway. He let the vision part go. "Everything started to slow down, and after a while I found myself thinking about Pablo, that he was right there in the same jail, maybe only a few feet away. The only difference was that he might never get out."

Buzz gawked through the Coke-bottle lenses, mouth half open, kraut plainly visible. "Uh… yeah, so, uh, lemme tell you what happened in Mexico."

"No. I'm not finished."

"Uh, right…" Buzz went back to the dog. "Not finished."

"I remembered Pablo saying that after he left Van Zandt, he was on the beach and watched the sun go down." He studied him for some sign of comprehension. "He said he 'watched the sun go down,' and was by himself at that time. The last memory Pablo has is the sunset, but the autopsy report places the time of death at two AM."

"So?"

"Well, I couldn't figure that out. What time is sunset? Seven-thirty? Eight? Van Zandt is alive until two. Could Pablo have been conscious, walking around, but lost that entire time? Six or seven hours? From what? Some kind of intense emotion? Could he have stayed so enraged that he remembers nothing? Somehow got up, went back, and killed Van Zandt in some kind of fugue state? Or he gets angry again for some other reason he doesn't remember, and kills him in some new and different rage?" He shook his head. "I don't think so. It just doesn't compute. I think he passed out in the rocks down by the beach, wasted on coke and booze, exhausted from anger, and was unconscious the whole time. I think he was totally zonked when this guy was murdered. Gotta be that someone else did it."

Buzz tried to add it up. "Wow," was his only response.

They sat quietly for several beats; then Noah picked up his burger and said, "So, uh… Mexico?"

Buzz related the whole Baja odyssey. "Turns out that Figueroa's a solid guy. Very erudite, rich Mexico City family that made its money in silver mining. He discovered fairly young that he might have a slightly different gender orientation, a way of life that wasn't all that popular then, especially in Mexico. I guess he decided to make some chicken salad out of it, so he bought the Rancho Figueroa and turned it into this four-star resort. Beautiful grounds. Great service. Gourmet kitchen with world-class chefs. Now he maintains the place as a kind of retreat where gay couples from around the world can come and have a totally private, like marital, relationship among friends, if only for a weekend.

"Course, it ain't cheap, so he only caters to the rich and famous. Has these very sophisticated gatherings for some of the great and near-great artists, musicians, business people, and politicians of the pink persuasion."

"So?"

"So, yeah. All extremely discreet and confidential, of course. He's got the place guarded like a bunker. Makes the case that he's saving the world. Way it looks to me? He may be."

"Aren't there a lot of gay resorts, like in the Caribbean, the Mediterranean, and such?"

"Sure, but the deal is that none of 'em take the pains to ensure this kind of anonymity, total security, along with the high-end amenities. That's what brings in the top-level clientele. And the word gets out. Lotta repeat trade. Eduardo's the premier guy, and just a stone's throw from California. International airports and such."

"Funny we never heard of the place."

"I guess that's kind of the point, isn't it."

"And what about the murder?"

"Well, they were having one of their dos that weekend with a bunch of international notables, and included on the guest list was one Rowland Murphy."

Noah cocked his head, trying to get whether he'd heard it right. "The mayor?"

"None other."

"He's gay?"

"Very, so Figueroa says. But it gets better. Murphy was down there with his long-time partner. Guess who?"

Noah thought for a minute, then looked up slowly. "No," he whispered. "Not Van Zandt?"

"Bingo."

"Dammit! God-dammit! All that rhetoric from Murphy, kicking Pablo's ass on the murder? And all the time, he was there too?" His mind was racing; and he struggled to grab the thoughts as they sped by. "He's totally hiding something. Can we get anyone from down there to testify?"

"Negative. Figueroa's rock solid on that. He won't let any of his people take the stand. The DA apparently found a server who Figueroa had fired a few weeks ago, American guy who agreed to testify about Pablo. Thing is, Figueroa feels safe down there, even with this murder, as long as he stays put beyond the court's subpoena power. But he did say he'd help if he could. He liked Van Zandt, and he liked Pablo. Murphy? Not so much. Says he's a *serpiente*."

"*Serpiente?*"

"Yeah. Same thing I said. A snake."

Noah sat with it a few seconds, then said, "Jeezus, Buzz. We're getting close here. But how are we gonna prove all this? There's gotta be a way."

"I'm not sure. Figueroa said he didn't know who killed Van Zandt, and he didn't want to know. But here's something else. Apparently Murphy and Van Zandt had been attending functions at the hacienda for years, and every time they'd come down, one or two of Freeman Mustafa's goons would come with them. Figueroa says 'to keep order'."

"Freeman Mustafa?"

Buzz frowned, and then it came to him. "That's right. You are a definite blue, aren't you? So, Mustafa is Ebony Properties. Huge developer, one of the wealthiest entrepreneurs in the Bay Area. Big philanthropist. Heavily connected politically. A major power player in this part of the world."

"So what does Mustafa have to do with Figueroa?"

"Nothing, according to Figueroa. Seems Mustafa's guys were down there hovering over Murphy."

Noah pondered it, then shook his head. "What the hell is the connection between all this and the murder? And how do we get at it? We're in the middle of trial. We aren't exactly gonna stop everything and convince the grand jury to launch an investigation."

"No way Pulansky would grant a continuance of the trial without bulletproof evidence that something is pretty clearly going on that casts some heavy doubt on the process."

"Well, we sure aren't gonna get to the mayor. He's surrounded by security. No way he'd talk to us, anyway." Noah was running the mental checklist. "Subpoena someone in Mexico? Can't. No jurisdiction. Wait. Pablo said he was with friends in L.A. when he ran into Figueroa's people the first time. Maybe they know something?" He shook his head. "Nah. Never find 'em in time." He pounded a fist on the table. "Mustafa. That's the only way. We gotta get to Mustafa, like now. We got no witness. No evidence. No nothing. No other way." He took a beat. "So what're the options?"

"Beats me, Blue."

They sat, brooding over it. Eventually, Buzz began a slow oral rumination. "I don't know. Maybe if we could get some documentation that Murphy and Mustafa's people were down there together with Van Zandt the night the murder went down, we might have enough to raise some question in Pulansky's mind. Like you say, Murphy's been pretty bloodthirsty in the press. Could piss Pulansky off that the mayor's been firing all those rockets at Pablo but neglected to mention anything about being down there himself." He paused to clear the surplus sauerkraut from between cheek and gum with an index finger. "Pulansky's been a defense guy for a lot of years, y'know. I think if we turned up something semi-solid, he'd be sympathetic about the stonewall we've gotten. Might at least give us the continuance to follow up on some of this. I mean, what else have we got?"

"Keep going. I like it. What kind of documentation do you think we could find?"

"Who knows? Maybe there's some travel receipts? Something that proves Mustafa's people were down there with the mayor at the time of the murder... and no one came forward?"

"Yeah. That'd at least raise an implication that Pablo was being set up, wouldn't it? That the murder had nothing to do with any break-in at the condo? That there was this big corporate interest involved?"

"Something like that."

"But how do we get those kind of documents? Call Mustafa up and ask him?"

"Sort of," Buzz said, a faint smirk materializing. "Mustafa's office is in the Lake Merritt Plaza over at Twentieth and Harrison. I say we go up there after hours tonight and do a little discovery. I know the night security. He's an old PD client."

Noah stared in disbelief, searching Buzz's face for some sign that the suggestion was one of his far-out cons. Reading nothing, he looked away, then looked back and scoffed. "Of course you're joking."

Buzz's smirk had disappeared. "Dead serious."

Noah shook his head. "Wait, Buzz. I said we had to come up with something radical, but I've only had this ticket for a few months, and I was hoping to keep it for a few more. B and E and burglary are felonies in this state, not to mention subverting the justice system and a few other offenses you've got wrapped up in this."

"We're just looking for a peek at the discovery they wouldn't give us from the beginning. And besides, who's gonna know?"

Noah turned it over in his mind. Then turned it over again. *Really? Yeah, these assholes are all in this together for sure. And yeah, it's time to pull out the stops for sure. But really?* "No freaking way," was all he could say.

"Well, we're kinda outta choices here, aren't we? How about just a quick check of the accounting department. Find some credit card slips, maybe airline reservations? Even a copy of a ticket with Van Zandt's name on it. Prove Mustafa's office made the reservations for him?" He was peering at Noah out of the corner of his eye. "Hell, maybe there's tickets for all of them, Blue. What if we get lucky and score the whole package. Then we'd really have something, no?" He stopped to let it settle in.

After nearly a minute of hands in lap, rocking back and forth in his chair like a davening rabbi, Noah slowly straightened, eyes narrowed, teeth grinding, and delivered it in a low but steady voice. "How did you say we get into the building?"

CHAPTER FORTY-SIX

"C'mon man, ya gotta eat somethin'. Fuckin' wastin' away."

The enormous man seated next to Pablo was a behemoth by any reckoning. Big Hermie wasn't the sharpest tool in the shed, but he was most definitely one of the largest. He had to go at least 350.

The dining room at the Glenn E. Dyer Detention Facility was a high-ceilinged, yawning, windowless expanse, reminiscent of the Great Hall in Hogwarts Castle. With 400 orange-jumpsuited inmates gathered for dinner, the din was just about as deafening. All sat at metal tables anchored in concrete, each equipped with four built-in stools in the round, eating from metal trays with large soup spoons. No knives, no forks. Even spoons became knives if cut and sharpened properly, prompting the sheriffs to count them at every meal.

This was an assortment of some of the baddest in the country, fresh off the streets of Oakland. Some awaited trial on third strikes and had nothing left to lose. Others were already in transit to the penitentiary for the duration. If these guys could gain an advantage in any violent way, deadly or otherwise, there would be no hesitation. Little wonder they counted spoons. No shoelaces, no pencils, no pens.

Somewhere near the middle of the room, Pablo sat in silence in front of his metal tray, oblivious to the cacophony and altogether disinterested in the two gray, leathery slabs drenched in a watery brown liquid which, according to the chalkboard menu behind the cafeteria line, was liver and onions. The menu may have identified the mysterious entree, but it couldn't make it appetizing.

For the last two weeks, as trial approached, Big Hermie's interest in Pablo increased in inverse proportion to Pablo's appetite. Over a lifetime of institutionalization, Big Hermie had learned to be alert for the depressed inmates whose appetites were dwindling. He'd always had an eye on Pablo, but after the recent erosion of his future prospects, Pablo had become his full-on protégé.

The comfort that the feedbag brought to Big Hermie in these unhappy circumstances no doubt derived from a doting mama in his distant past. Some folks said "I love you" by demanding galoshes or a sweater as an offspring left the house. Others, by showering delicacies on their growing boys at mealtime.

Completing the symbiotic loop, Big Hermie warded off the various vultures who would feed off Pablo's weakness in any way they could. He asked for no financial or sexual favors in return, but he was always there at chow time. Occasionally he'd show up after Pablo's table-in-the-round was already fully occupied, at which times a jerk of the head or a menacing look was usually sufficient to clear a seat to Pablo's left or right. Now and then, he would have to clench a shirt and whisper some encouragement to confirm his accommodations.

"How you gonna keep yo' strength up for this fuckin' trial, you don' eat?" The monster's soup spoon was poised, his voracious eyes surveying Pablo's plate. "Say, you gonna eat those mash potatas?"

Pablo didn't respond. Smiling, Big Hermie heaped the mushy spuds onto his own metal tray, shoveled an immense spoonful into his mouth, and mumbled on, cheeks distended.

"Mah mama always said, whatever come 'round, y'still gotta eat."

The shorter man next to Big Hermie picked up the line without looking up. "Seems like yo mama musta tol ya t'eat whatever comes 'round. Why don'cha leave the fuckin' brother's dinner alone, man?"

"You talkin' 'bout, niggah?" was the high-pitched retort. "I'm the onliest thing keep this man alive these past weeks. Ain' that right, Pablo?" He eyed the tray again. "Lissen heah, man. Have somma 'dis soup…" Big Hermie pushed the soup toward Pablo and tried to hand him the spoon. When Pablo didn't move, Big Hermie cast a quick glance up at him, then put the spoon down. "Y'all ain' gonna eat 'dis cupcake, is ya?"

Several tables away, Leech Jaqua pawed listlessly at the substance on his plate with his unbandaged right hand, staring down in silence. Occasionally, his predatory eyes would stray ominously in Pablo's direction, though his head didn't move.

After the meal, Jaqua strolled to the lounge, where he sat smoking with forty other inmates in front of a TV blaring *Jeopardy*. Blue-gray smoke hung in layers under the lights like a Newark pool hall as Alex Trebek fired questions about seventeenth-century composers, the history of the Indo-European wars, and the prayer rituals of the Dalai Lama, all of which flashed over the heads and past the vacant stares of a roomful of fourth, fifth, and sixth-grade grads. Some dozed; others played cards or paged through magazines until, at 9:50 sharp, the buzzer sounded its warning that ten minutes remained before lights out. Jaqua roused and ambled with the other prisoners to the large, windowless, green-walled dormitory next door. His was one of twenty-four double-decked bunks, six rows of four, all spoken for.

Pablo had gone straight to the dormitory after dinner, and had lain in his upper since. After lights out, he stared at the ceiling in the dim illumination of a nightlight. On a bottom bunk three rows over, Jaqua closed his eyes and waited. An hour later, sounds of snoring and deep breathing filled the room. Jaqua gave it another half hour to be sure, then silently slid from his bunk and moved toward Pablo, crossing the three rows in seconds, and creeping up Pablo's row undetected.

• • •

"So what do we do now, knock?"

As Noah stood in front of the massive, black-wooden, double doors on which EBONY PROPERTIES, INC. was emblazoned in gold letters, his current second thoughts about the whole enterprise were a product of his novice status at B and E. No stranger to the process, Buzz had the two-way radio to his ear, and he waved Noah to be quiet. "Yo… J.B." he said in a stage whisper, as if someone might overhear.

"Go, Buzz," John Beacham responded from the lobby.

Ten years earlier, Buzz had investigated Beacham's freeway-salute assault case, and Beacham had been acquitted on a self-defense theory, largely on the testimony of two witnesses Buzz had lined up after the rest of the defense team had given up. Like the many other beneficiaries of Buzz's relentless determination, J.B. was grateful, and the appreciation of former clients eased Buzz's job immeasurably. Tonight, J.B.'s contribution was access to Lake Merritt Plaza through the service entrance in the basement; he would be arming Buzz with the two-way radio system in case of "emergency." Buzz knew that the risk of this accommodation to J.B.'s job was high, so he told him they were on "PD business," that they'd have a subpoena for him to "cover his ass" tomorrow. Buzz explained that the Ebony Properties folks might not appreciate the visit, so J.B. should sound a warning if there was any chance of their being disturbed.

"We're at the front door of the suite. You say you don't know the IES setup?"

"IES?" Noah said.

"Internal electronic security system," Buzz mouthed, a hand over the two-way. Buzz figured Ebony Properties probably kept little in valuables in the office other than the decorative artwork, but it was certain there would be a fairly elaborate system to protect trade secrets and to keep would-be "competitors" at bay.

"Right," J.B. told him. "They all have different rigs. What I can say is that the alarm control panels are set up in the utility closet. On the penthouse floor, left out of the elevator and right at the end of the hall."

"Roger that. We're on it."

Lights burned all night throughout the building, so no trouble with visibility. Returning to the elevators for orientation, they followed Beacham's instructions to the utility closet. Buzz reached into his pocket and extracted a square leather case containing a high-quality twelve-in-one tool and a set of lock picks. He examined the doorjamb and pocketed the case. "Don't need these," he said. "Lemme have your credit card."

"Haven't you done enough damage to that thing already?"

"Lucky I don't have expensive tastes."

Buzz slid the card into the jamb and had the door open in less than ten seconds. Not too complicated, but inside was another story. After switching on the closet light, he gave a low whistle when he saw the array of telephone and other utility wiring.

Noah looked on, bewildered. "Jeezus, looks like spaghetti."

Sorting through the various panels, Buzz located the two security systems that were fortunately labeled with suite numbers. Not high-tech so far. He pointed to a small flashing red light. "ATD," he murmured.

"ATD?"

"Anti-tamper device. Guards the box cover. Usually it's wired separately, so if the bulb burns out it doesn't risk shorting out the whole..." He was reaching in behind the box with the flat blade of his twelve in one. "There..." The red light went out, and he opened the box. "Ummm. Not too bad," he said, sorting through the jumble.

"Where'd you learn this shit?"

"All those years in the service got me a little more than a Prozac habit and an eye twitch... but"—he squeezed his fingers in between the terminals as delicately as possible—"I'll admit... not much... more..." He strained to extract two separate sets of wires. "Damn."

"What?"

"See these twisted pairs?" Buzz held up several sets of wires under his index finger.

"Twisted pairs?"

"I think they control the perimeter and the interior vibratory sensor— that's a beam that senses any movement inside the suite and sets off the alarm once it's armed."

"So?"

"So, it's like there's two separate systems here. Short story is, I think

I've disarmed the perimeter and the vibratory beam, but I don't know what the rest of this is. Goes to the inner offices, no doubt, but it's hard to tell. We don't have time to map it."

"Why don't you just disable the whole system?"

Buzz glanced at him. "It's a thought. But most of these rigs ring the alarm when the whole system goes down if you don't punch in the code first, which you gotta do inside."

"Yeah, well, just a suggestion. What do I know?"

"It means we'll have to be careful when we get in there."

They returned to the front door, where Buzz made short work of the lock with his picks. Entering, they quickly found Mustafa's office.

"Whoa," Noah said with a whistle. They stood in an immense room with dark paneling and burgundy carpet. He began to wander around, inspecting the various photographs and other mementos on the walls. "You weren't kiddin' about this guy being a power broker. Looks like he's into about everything."

"Uh… while I think we're okay so far, I'm thinkin' we really don't have time to work up a resume for him, tonight anyway."

"All right, all right. I'll check out the desk in here. See if you can find the accounting office."

"Roger that." Buzz strode off down the hall.

Noah scanned the office, then walked to the wall near the door and perused the memorabilia, his gaze moving among the Little League teams, school classes, hospitals, elder care facilities and the kids… everywhere, kids. *Guy looks like the real deal.* He could feel his apprehension rising as he flashed on a hearing room at the State Bar, the proceeding in which his ticket was on the line. His thoughts went to his old civil procedure prof, Graham Kennedy. He could just hear the old fart's testimony: "I knew all along this guy was a thief."

He slid into the black-leather-and-chrome desk chair, unsure exactly what he was looking for, let alone where he might find it. Swiveling the chair around to the credenza, he started in on the drawers. He began to imagine he'd find a gun, or God knows what else, and the adrenalin started to pump. But the contents turned out to be pretty routine, files of the various current projects, nothing. His attention fell on the black steel three-drawer file cabinet beneath. Its fireproof construction was clearly heavier than the other cabinets, and the combination lock also made it stand out. He tried the drawers. All locked. He was up and into the outer office.

"Buzz!" It was a little louder than a stage whisper as he came up behind him in Harlan Metcalfe's office.

"I need your safe-cracking skills down the hall."

"Hold on, Blue." Buzz was absorbed in a sheaf of papers.

"Whaddya got?"

"This is the Visa file. There's a September statement that reflects a general aviation airplane rental, NorCal Aviation, on a round trip to San Felipe the weekend of August twenty-sixth. No names, but it's a start, no?" He had his cell phone out and was snapping photos of the documents.

"Great. But photos aren't going to help much. It really has to be the originals if we want to get them into evidence. And there's a file in Mustafa's office you gotta help me with."

● ● ●

Jaqua crept silently up the row of bunks. As he neared Pablo's, he stopped abruptly. There was a faint, but unmistakable, sound of voices in the hall. As he listened, the voices grew louder; then there were more of them, and the sound of a scuffle. He retreated to his bunk, sliding under his blanket just as the alarm suddenly blasted, all lights blazed, and three guards burst into the room. Two more stood at the door to the dormitory, one with a truncheon, the other with a Taser at the ready.

"Awright, assholes. Everybody up. Feet on the fuckin' floor. NOW!"

The deputies marched briskly through the room, rapping nightsticks on the tubular-steel bedsteads as the groggy inmates dragged themselves from sleep.

"Everybody out in the hall. Form it up, ladies. You know how to make a line, don't you?"

The guards herded the sleepwalking roomful of gangsters, junkies, thugs, and pimps, all in various stages of undress as they shuffled into some semblance of a double line. The mood was ugly, and deteriorating.

Down the hall, three burly guards wrestled a short, wiry, wild-eyed prisoner to the floor. He bucked, twisted, and shouted, his shaved brown head glistening with sweat in the brightly lit hall.

"Get offa me, mothafuckah! Get cho… fuckin' hands… off!"

"Easy, Marvin," an older guard soothed, a hefty arm around the squirming man's neck, straining to subdue him. "It's all over now. Just chill and you won't… get… hurt," he grunted, as he draped himself over the smaller convict, forcefully pinning both shoulders.

Ten feet away, on the polished green-tiled floor, another inmate lay writhing on his back as guards tried to hold him. He moaned weakly as blood pumped from a pulsating artery in his neck, drenching his head and chest, and collecting in a large dark-crimson pool underneath him. Four more guards stood in a perimeter, trained not to touch him without the necessary safeguards. Finally, another officer wearing rubber gloves, safety goggles, and a surgeon's mask, ran up, squatted over the hemorrhaging prisoner, and applied digital pressure to his spurting neck.

The throng of near-dormant inmates from the dormitory up the hall slowly became aware of the situation and stood in silence, watching it play out. Ultimately, the guards cuffed the struggling aggressor and dragged him into the secure wing beyond an electric steel-barred panel that clanged behind them. Two paramedics arrived, also dressed for a moonwalk, and bent over the injured man.

Somewhere in the middle of the assemblage in the hallway, Pablo was almost oblivious to the drama, eyes vacant as he gazed at the floor. The group stood facing the wall as guards conducted an interminable search of every bunk, and all belongings, for weapons. Standing fifteen feet from Pablo in the line, Jaqua occasionally glanced in his direction.

● ● ●

The razor-thin metal pick danced gently against the tumblers. Prying repeatedly, feeling for alignment, Buzz craned, listening for the telltale sound, his ear brushing the face of the filing cabinet. Within several minutes, the mechanism fell into place, and the drawer slid open.

"Yesss!" Noah exulted.

"Noooo!" Buzz exclaimed simultaneously, as he spotted the barely visible wire, little larger in diameter than a human hair, leading to the contact electrode on the left side of the cabinet.

"What happened?"

Buzz stood abruptly. "We tripped the fuckin' alarm. They're gonna be here in minutes." He turned for the door. "We gotta get outta here."

"Wait," Noah said, stooping down to the space Buzz had just vacated. "Lemme just see what's so important it has to be stashed in this heavy-duty vault." He started thumbing through the files, each with a handwritten name on the tab.

"Martin Silver. Isn't he the Commissioner of Education? And Henry Barnes. That's the Port Authority Commissioner." Noah paged through what appeared to be some kind of report, and a handful of photos that smacked of cheap, soft-core pornography.

Buzz ran down the hall to grab his leather kit. He stuffed the Visa statements into his jacket pocket, carefully replaced the accounting files, then sprinted back to Mustafa's office. "Come on, Blue. We're outta here. I'm tellin' ya, in minutes we're gonna be toast."

"These are some kind of dossiers! I think this is what we're looking for. Let's see. I, J, K, L, M... here's one that says Rowland Murphy." Noah tried to scan the file quickly as Buzz looked over his shoulder, but it was reasonably thick. There were reports, transcribed statements, grainy telephotos, snapshots. He looked up. "Jackpot!" A CD dropped out onto the floor, and he snatched it up. "Lemme just see what I can get—"

"This stuff isn't gonna mean shit if we're both dead. We gotta split. Now!"

Beacham's voice crackled over the two-way. "Condition Red. Repeat, Condition Red."

"Jesus. That didn't take 'em long. Come on!" Buzz shouted.

"But—"

"Condition red!" Beacham shouted over the radio. "Buzz, get out of there! Don't use the elevator. Condition red!"

Bounding across the room to where Noah was stooped over the files, Buzz seized him by the jacket collar and dragged him to the door, yelling, "NOW!"

The Murphy file dropped to the floor, scattering papers and photos.

"Dammit! Lemme get these." Noah grabbed for them with both hands, like a game show contestant told he could keep all the dollars he could gather in thirty seconds. As Buzz pulled him to the door, he stuffed papers in his shirt, photos in his pockets. They sprinted down the hall, past the elevators, and into the stair well as the UP light came on over one of the elevators and the arrival bell dinged.

"Ohhhh shit, ohhhh shit..." Noah wailed, as they took two and three steps at a time. It seemed like they covered the nineteen floors to the basement in less than a minute. Bursting out into the garage, they raced for the service exit, out the door, and down Harrison Street to where Captain America was parked. Noah jumped behind the wheel as Buzz slid in and slammed the passenger door. After several excruciating attempts, the Captain fired up, labored away from the curb, and lurched down Harrison.

As the old Dodge skidded, metal grinding, through a wide left onto 20th, past the front of the Lake Merritt Plaza, four men in night camouflage, dark clothing, and watch caps, spilled out the front door and onto the sidewalk, running toward a white panel-delivery parked across the street.

"Jeezus! Jeezus! Jeezus!" Noah chanted, as the Captain fishtailed through the intersection and straightened out onto 20th. Buzz was rigid, both hands on the dash in front of him. Fighting the wheel with one hand, Noah reached under his shirt and into his pockets with the other, extracting his treasures and throwing them on the seat between them, craning for a look at each item as he struggled to keep the Captain on course. *Somewhere in this mess there was bound to be gold. He could feel it.*

CHAPTER FORTY-SEVEN

THURSDAY, NOVEMBER 15ᵀᴴ, 1:00 AM:

The night at North County Jail had been a long one. By midnight, the inmate whose throat had been cut—over who would sleep on the top bunk—was bedded at Highland Hospital, listed as critical. The guards and officers had completed a shakedown and search that had turned up seven shanks, fourteen stashes of crack, and five bags of heroin with two kits. During these two hours, the entire population stood in the hall in skivvies, and tempers became frayed and ragged. A couple of additional scuffles broke out that were quickly quelled. It was almost 1:00 AM when the all-clear sounded. The prisoners trooped back into the dormitory, returned to bed, and the lights went out.

Within half an hour, the sounds of sleep again filled the capacious residence hall, and Jaqua silently left his bunk and crept the three rows to where Pablo was sleeping. In the dimness of the nightlight, he placed a bandaged hand tightly over Pablo's mouth, then shook him. Pablo's eyes opened, and he woke with a jolt to find himself looking into an unfamiliar, pockmarked face, mere inches from his own.

"Shhhh… I got a message from your lawyer."

"Wha…? Shane?" Pablo groped through the fog.

"Yeah, Shane. I got a message from Shane. I just came in this afternoon and he asked me to tell you something."

"What… is it?"

"Not here." Jaqua glanced one way, then the other. "I need to explain it. C'mon into the head."

"Wh… who are you?" Others had come on to Pablo at night in the jail, and he had learned to maintain a healthy distance. But now sleep, superimposed on depression, clouded his judgment.

"Shane represented me when I was busted," Jaqua whispered. "He asked me to deliver a message. Said it was important. C'mon. Let's go." Jaqua pulled his arm.

Half awake, in only a T-shirt and shorts, Pablo obediently slid down from his bunk and followed unsteadily into the large lavatory situated between the two dormitories, servicing both. A single nightlight burned at the far end of the white-tiled expanse, next to the sinks; a medicinal odor of Lysol permeated the room.

The instant they were through the door and could no longer see the closest row of bunks, a fully alert Jaqua snaked an arm around Pablo's neck, clapped a hand over his mouth, and dragged him to the floor. Then both hands were around his throat, fingers closing around his trachea as he gasped and kicked. Jaqua was only slightly larger, but Pablo, in his somnolent state, was no match.

• • •

Transmission whining, Captain America swung left off 20th, and powered west on Broadway through the heart of downtown Oakland. Third gear was worthless, but second could generate some torque, though the Captain was clearly in pain and was letting Noah know about it.

After midnight, the streets were mostly empty, but here and there the whores, pimps, and night people still crowded the sidewalks. For them, the evening was young.

Noah knew that the four operatives he'd seen sprint from the Lake Merritt Plaza and scramble toward the white van couldn't be far behind now. So far, he hadn't seen them in the rear-view mirror, but it was just a matter of time. The Captain might have been doing about fifty-five, but his heart was racing at well over a hundred.

"Okay, Blue," Buzz said, elated with their narrow escape. "Just aim it toward the Police Administration Building. You know, the jail on Broadway." As far as he was concerned, they were safe. They'd pull into the back lot at the Admin Building, now just a few blocks away, and the threat level would descend into the green zone.

Noah continued to finger his trophies from Mustafa's office, and his hand fell on the unmarked CD. "There's a CD player in the back somewhere. Grab it, willya?"

Buzz ignored the non-responsive statement. He looked ahead to Broadway. "A right in two blocks, onto Sixth. OPD lot," he said, pointing his index finger.

Noah reached a hand over the seat and began blindly turning over the piles of papers and clothes. With his other hand, he swung a left onto 7th, a block short of the Police Administration Building. "It might be under some of this shit. Just look around. Black CD player." He flew through a very late yellow at 7th and Webster.

"What the fuck are you talkin' about? Are you nuts? Get this goddamn heap to the station. You turned the wrong way."

Noah cast a fleeting glance over at him, then returned his attention to the nearly vacant street ahead. "Cops? Really? You're the one who's crazy. We just broke, entered, and burglarized the offices of one of the most powerful guys in this city. We lose our jobs. I never practice again. And for sure we get a healthy vacation in the joint with a few former PD clients who might not see us as pals. That's your idea of a game plan?" He looked over again. "Get the frickin' CD player."

Lake Merritt was passing on the left as the Captain continued gnashing down to where 7ᵗʰ joined 8ᵗʰ and the two streets turned into International Boulevard.

Buzz shook his head, mulling the situation, and started to rummage under the clothes, newspapers, and KFC boxes. "Who cares?" he said. "These guys'll blow us away if they catch us, and they will catch us. Where were you thinking we'd go?" He looked back at Noah. "Whaddya want the CD player for?"

For the moment, Noah was more focused on the CD than on their circumstances. "You see this?" He held up the disc. "This fell out of Murphy's file. Considering the other stuff that seemed to be in that file, what's on it might be of some interest. You gotta find that player." He was almost shouting.

"Okay, okay." Buzz propped himself on his knees, leaned into the back seat, and sorted through the clutter. "Jeezus. Whaddya do with all this crap? Fuckin' car's a health hazard." Then, success. "Okay, I got it."

Noah handed him the disc. "Cue it."

Slipping it into the player, Buzz cranked the volume. Even through considerable surface noise, they could hear a voice. It was a truncated conversation, apparently on a cell phone. The recording initiated with the conversation already in progress.

"...*Okay, okay*..." the deep male voice was saying. "*Now calm down. Tell me exactly what happened.*"

"...*you gotta help me,*" came the agitated response. "*I KILLED him. Oh my God!*"

"*All right, I understand.*" The reply was soothing. "*Now, just tell me how it happened.*"

"Killed him...?" Noah glanced over. "Jesus, Buzz, is that the mayor?"

"*We were on the beach. Warren told me that he... I don't know how it happened... I just lost it. What am I gonna do? Everything's over.*"

"*How did you kill him...?*" No answer; just rapid breathing. "*How? How did you do it?*"

"*I choked him, I guess... I don't know exactly.*"

Noah and Buzz were silent, spellbound by the enormity of what they were hearing.

"*When did this happen?*"

"*God, I don't know, you gotta help me.*"

"*When did it happen?*" The second voice was steady, insistent.

"*I don't know…*"

"*What did you do with the body?*"

"*I pulled it up into the rocks.*"

"*Did anyone see you?*"

"*No! There was someone in the rocks. Lying there, passed out, I guess. I don't know who it was. I thought…*"

"*Thought what?*"

The conversation clicked off, and Noah exploded. "Unbelievable!" "That's gotta be the mayor. It's in his file. Murphy killed Van Zandt! It wasn't Pablo!" He hammered the steering wheel with the heels of his hands.

"Whoa, Blue. We don't know whose voices those are, let alone whether this CD'll ever be admissible in any court."

"But don't you see? Whoever that is killed Van Zandt. It wasn't Pablo."

The CD player began to croak again. A second conversation could be heard, this one clearer than the first, and obviously more measured. It began with the basso male voice that sounded like one of the voices from before.

"*…if I'm going to help you, you have to tell me exactly what happened.*"

"*I don't remember, exactly.*" The voice might have been the killer from the first recording, yet it sounded less agitated; this, together with the earlier track's poor quality, made the comparison difficult. Squinting, Noah strained to make the identification, but it was wishful thinking.

"*Sunday night was Warren's birthday. He and I had dinner at the hacienda about nine-thirty. After dinner, we went out to the pool.*"

"*What time was that?*"

"*Umm… it was a long dinner. I guess it was near midnight. Anyway, we were drinking margaritas and doing some lines at the pool.*"

"*How much did you have?*"

"*I don't know. But toward the end, I was pretty ripped. It was warm. Warren was charming.*"

"*How long were you there?*"

"*Well, I gave him a birthday gift. We were dancing. Everything was wonderful.*"

"*What kind of a gift?*"

"*It was a beautiful little gold chain, with a pendant.*"

"So, what happened?"

"Warren seemed to get serious. At first I thought he was just tired. But he asked me to take a walk. It must have been after one…"

"Shit!" Noah saw the van fall in behind them, maybe a block back, as they passed Fruitvale. When he stood on the accelerator, the Captain coughed a couple of times and heaved forward, whining, then choked again.

Buzz clicked off the CD player. "We'll get the rest later… if we're still alive."

"Dammit." Noah pumped the pedal, and the gas finally fed smoothly.

"So what now, Blue? Can we go to the cops? If that's Murphy, it's pretty clear he killed Van Zandt. No one's gonna say anything about how we got the CD."

Noah couldn't believe it. "You don't fuckin' get it. You know we can't prove that's Murphy on the CD. All we know is that it was in a file in Mustafa's office with the mayor's name on it, and we don't get that without putting ourselves in there. But the bigger problem is that this whole thing with Pablo has obviously been a set-up to make him on the Van Zandt murder and clear Murphy."

The pedal was all the way to the floor.

"God knows how deep it goes, but it's clearly into the DA's office. That's why they offered Pablo that unbelievable deal. No doubt it's into the PD's office, too. It's the only way their keeping me on the case makes any sense, refusing us investigation, assigning you to the case because everybody thought you were a whack job who stacked facts." Noah made a sliding left onto Foothill. "The goddamn court might even be involved, jamming this thing out the way it did." The van was closing. "We take this CD to the cops, it'll never see the light of day, and neither will we."

He swerved left onto 35th, then right onto Galindo, trying to keep turning, keep winding through side streets. He had no clue where he was going, but what he did know was that the Captain could never outrun this van on a straightaway.

"Holy shit," Buzz whispered, mouth open, eyes fixed and dilated, the enormity of it finally coming home, that they were out there twisting, with no safe harbor. "I don't know which is worse, these assholes chasing us, or the cops."

"Amen."

Neither spoke, both of their minds racing, as Noah careened right at one block and left at the next.

Gradually, an awareness crept into Noah's eyes. "Yes there is," he said.

Buzz looked over at him. "Where?"

"Pulansky…"

Buzz mentally turned it over. "Pulansky, yeah. Yeah!" He checked his watch. "But we can't get to him at one in the morning. I don't know where he's living now. I don't even have a phone number. I called him through his clerk before."

"Right," Noah told him. "We'll just have to get him in chambers tomorrow, before court."

After a beat, Buzz said, "Perfect, Blue. Why don't we just grab a couple of beers and a movie and we'll check with him in the morning?"

"Yeah." Noah took his point. "We gotta get off the street somehow."

CHAPTER FORTY-EIGHT

THURSDAY, NOVEMBER 15TH, 1:30 AM:

The land line on the nightstand had rung three times before Mustafa, wearing only shorts, stirred, reached over, knocked the receiver off its cradle, then picked it up and answered, his voice six tones deeper than usual, shrouded in gravel. "Yeah?"

"It's Carl Mumford, Mr. Mustafa. Sorry to wake you, but we got a situation here. Thought y'oughta know."

"Yeah…" Mustafa stared blankly at the back-lit digital numbers on the alarm clock, struggling to clear his head.

"While ago, the security system in the Oakland office went off. I responded with the regular crew. When we got there, the place was broken into, and there's like shit all over the floor in your office—"

"My office?" Mustafa sat up.

"They got into your desk, and that black file cabinet behind it. Seems like that's what set the alarm off."

"Wait a minute. You're sure they were into the black filing cabinet behind the desk?" He was suddenly wide awake.

"There was papers all over the floor."

"Who was it? Did you get 'em?"

"Nah, they got away, but we seen 'em, and followed 'em. It's two white men who got in this old car. Young guy and an older one. We're about a block behind 'em right now. Just turned south on Foothill, gettin' near Thirty-fifth."

"Did they get anything?" Mustafa was now on full agitation, mind reeling with the potential of some kind of surgical strike, like they were after something specific.

"Tough to say."

"Tell me exactly what you saw on the floor."

"It was like stuff from a file outta that black cabinet. Mighta had somethin' to do with the mayor. I didn't really look at it," Mumford lied.

"Shit!" Mustafa swung his legs around and sat on the side of the bed. "Now listen carefully. This is very important. Was there a CD in the file?"

"I didn't see one, Mr. Mustafa. I mean, I didn't look through the stuff, but it was me pulled it together. They was some papers and pictures. No CD. Think I'd a seen it if it was."

Mustafa stood. "All right, I'm gonna get the car and stand by. I want you to call me every five minutes and let me know where you are. When they stop, I'll join you. You follow?"

"Yes, sir."

"And Carl… Don't let these guys get away. They have some very confidential materials. Those things must be recovered. Do you understand?"

"Yes, sir."

"I want you personally to take custody of those materials when you catch up to them."

"Yes, sir."

"No one is to question them about any of this but me. Do you understand?"

"Yes, sir."

Mustafa hung up, retrieved his cell phone from the nightstand, and went to contacts. He looked up Henry Barnes's home number and dialed.

"Hul-lo?" a groggy voice answered.

"Henry?"

"What."

"This is Freeman Mustafa, Henry."

Nothing.

"Henry, are you with me?"

"Yes." Vacuous.

"Okay. Now, there's been a serious breach of security tonight that could be very dangerous to all of us. The perpetrators got away. My personal security people are close behind them right now, but they're gonna need backup."

Silence.

"Henry? Are you gettin' this?"

"Yes."

"I don't think this is necessarily a job for Oakland PD at this point, but I'd like you to send a couple of AMPPS units. Can you do that?"

"What kind of security breach?"

"There's been a break-in at the Ebony Properties office. Some sensitive material may be missing. These guys have gotta be stopped before they go public with any of this. Am I clear enough?"

"I'll get right on it. Where are they now, d'you know?"

"Yeah. Foothill and Thirty-fifth a couple of minutes ago. Mumford is behind them, but I'll be catching up with them personally as soon they get them cornered. We'll phone in the coordinates, and you can get your people out there."

"I'll have two units rolling right away. Who do they contact?"

"I'll give you the cell number."

• • •

Noah continued to zigzag deeper into the San Antonio Neighborhood of East Oakland. Each time he made a turn, he hoped he had lost the van, but within moments it would again fall in a block behind them. He couldn't outdistance it, but so long as he kept making turns, it didn't seem to be gaining on them, either. When Noah glanced at the gas gauge, he shook his head. "We can't keep this up forever," he said.

"You got any ideas?" Buzz asked.

"Not really." Then, within moments Noah's attention focused on a passing sign for 44th Street. "Wait. Maybe I do."

He made two quick consecutive right turns and, before the van could make the second turn, bounced the Captain into an alley and backtracked. After another right, he squealed left into the Ruiz driveway, drove back behind the frame bungalow, stopped in front of the garage in the rear, and killed the engine and lights.

Instinctively ducking down, Noah and Buzz waited nearly a minute, then slowly raised their heads in time to see the van fly past in the opposite direction on 46th. Sanctuary, but probably not for long.

Noah pulled out his cell, went to his recent call history, and found Amparo Ruiz's number. He didn't want her to wake up in the middle of the night, find a car in her back yard, and call the police.

"Hola."

"Señora Ruiz?"

"Si?"

"This is Noah Shane."

At first it didn't compute; then, "Mr. Shane… has anything happened to Pablo?"

"No, Pablo's fine, but I have a problem that I need your help with."

"What can I do?"

"My investigator and I are being chased by some men who have something to do with Pablo's case. We have a CD with information on it that may clear Pablo of the charges against him, and they want it back. We were nearby, and I was hoping we might stay at your place until things settle down a little."

"But of course. Where are you?"

"Well, to be exact, we're in your back yard."

Long silence. "I see…"

A light came on at the rear of the house, and Noah could make out Amparo's face in the window as she drew back the curtain.

"No, señora," Noah said quickly. "You must turn out the light. The men who are chasing us are close by."

The light went out. "Please come to the back door. I will let you in."

"No, no. We'll just hide in the car in the back, and leave when things calm down. I don't want to involve you in this. These men are armed and very dangerous."

"I do not think that is sensible. You must come inside. If there is important information as you say, and they find you, all will be lost. If you come in, we can hide it."

"But…"

"Pablo is my son, Mr. Shane. There is no risk I can take that is greater than the one he faces."

Noah looked at Buzz. "Okay," he said. "We'll be right in."

He brought the CD player and the file materials. Once inside, he whispered an introduction in the dark. "Señora Ruiz, this is Buzz Hoogasian, my investigator. He's working on Pablo's case with me."

"I am honored, Mr. Hoogasian."

"Likewise."

"May I offer you gentlemen some coffee?"

"No, no, thanks," Noah whispered. "We better keep the lights out and maintain a low profile."

"I understand. But you mentioned something about a CD?"

"Right. We'd like to listen to it now, if you don't mind."

"I would like very much to hear it. Please come with me." She showed them into the darkened kitchen and pulled a small penlight from a drawer. "This is the farthest room from the street. We will be safest here."

She shined the little light on the Formica kitchen table, and they all sat down. She handed Noah the tiny flashlight, and he began to cue up the CD.

"But what is your thinking?" Amparo asked.

Noah explained that although they didn't yet know exactly whose voices were on the CD, it had come from the office of Freeman

Mustafa, a prominent Oakland businessman, in a file marked with the mayor's name, a file that contained a number of other items pertaining to Murphy.

"The CD may show that these men have conspired to blame Pablo for the Van Zandt murder," Noah said, "which might actually have been committed by Mayor Murphy."

She considered it, confused. "But why would the mayor kill this man?"

"We think it may have been some kind of lovers' quarrel."

Her brows went up, and her eyes widened. "Lovers' quarrel?"

"Yes, it appears that the mayor and Van Zandt had been lovers for some time. But the most important thing is that they apparently have tried to cast suspicion away from the mayor, and Pablo fell into their hands at a time when he was trying to raise money for you."

"So this is what Pablo meant about being at gay parties in Mexico. He was engaged in prostitution?" Her face was expressionless.

"I think it all fits together," Noah said.

She nodded. "Shall we listen?"

He pressed Play and set the volume on low as they leaned in.

"How long were you there?"

"Well, I gave him a gift. We were dancing. Everything was wonderful."

"What kind of a gift?"

"It was… a beautiful little gold chain, with a pendant."

"So, what happened?"

"Warren seemed to get serious. At first I thought he was just tired. But he asked me to take a walk. It must have been after one…"

There was a long silence.

"Okay, you took a walk," the second said, urging the other to continue. *"If you don't tell me, I can't help you."*

"Yeah, Warren said he didn't want us to see each other anymore." More silence.

"What did you say?"

"I couldn't believe it. Four years we'd been together. I just couldn't believe it. He said he couldn't stand sneaking around like this any longer. He said he loved me, but the energy it took to keep from being exposed was killing him. He said he was doing it all for me, for my career. He wanted a different life. He said he was getting too old for all that. Can you imagine? Warren? Too old?" The voice made an awkward scoffing sound.

As the conversation played on, Noah paged through the other file materials with the penlight.

"So, what happened?"

"Of course I told him I didn't believe it. And I didn't. He was interested in someone else, I knew that's what it was. I told him that. He insisted there wasn't anyone else, but he said he thought we should see other people." Pause. "I told him I'd quit my job. I said he didn't have to worry about the high visibility anymore. I told him he was everything to me." Pause. "Warren said that was nonsense, that I couldn't quit. I said of course I could, that we could be together, be happy." Pause. "That's when he said it wouldn't make any difference. He needed some time away from me." Pause. "I knew then what it was. I guess I lost it. My memory isn't too clear. I just went off. I must have gone crazy." Pause. "It was like I was watching myself from a distance, but I was powerless to stop."

"Stop what?"

Noah elbowed Buzz and shined the light on an 8x10 photograph. It was black-and-white and grainy, obviously taken with a telephoto lens. Two men were sitting next to a lavish Mexican-tiled pool. Even from distance, it was clear that one was the mayor. An older man sat on the adjacent chaise longue, a tropical drink in his hand. Infrared equipment had to have been used; the photo was dark except for several tiki torches. The mayor was smiling widely, probably laughing. Clad only in a G-string, he was arrestingly handsome in a youthful, boyish way, a shock of dark, wavy hair spilling down onto his forehead. Noah was struck by the resemblance to Pablo. Though this man was significantly older, it could almost have been Pablo in the blurry photograph, if one only glanced quickly. His companion was smirking, amused. Comfortably round, softly appealing, he had an engaging smile, a glint of torchlight reflecting from the triangular gold pendant dangling from his neck.

"I was choking him. I was out of my mind." The voice became quiet, strangely matter-of-fact. "I choked him until he wasn't breathing. I killed him. I loved him, but I killed him."

"Then what did you do?"

"I don't remember exactly. What I do remember is waking up on top of him. It was so dark. I've never been that scared. I dragged him up the beach. And then I saw someone else. There were two legs sticking out of a breach in the rocks. It had to be someone from the hacienda, passed out in the sand. I thought whoever it was would wake up and see me, but he didn't. I pulled the body in next to him. I guess I hoped maybe it would look like he had something to do with Warren's death. Then I ran. When I got back to the hacienda, I called here."

"And when you got back—"

Suddenly, there was a loud banging at the front door, accompanied by a demanding voice. Noah instantly doused the penlight, and Buzz killed the CD player. Amparo put a single finger to her lips and motioned for them to follow her into the back bedroom, next to the kitchen, along the rear of the house. Without a word, she held out a hand; Buzz gave her the CD player and the remainder of the file. Standing on a chair, she secreted the materials above a loose ceiling tile, then opened a closet door and pointed silently inside as the pounding continued out front.

Through the window, Noah and Buzz could perceive movement in the back yard. They ducked into the closet as Amparo pulled her robe tightly around her and hurried to the living room.

In the darkness of the closet, Noah yanked out his cell phone, then hesitated. *Jeezus. Who to call? Who can help now? Cops? No way. Sandy? What could he do besides call the cops? Pulansky? No number. Dammit! No one.*

Amparo unbolted the door and opened it. Two of Mustafa's people burst into the living room, weapons drawn, with two more behind them.

"Don't move!" Mumford ordered, pointing his semi-automatic at Amparo's head. She stood motionless, regarding him without visible emotion. Mumford took her roughly by the arm and seated her on the couch.

"A'ight. I'll see to her," Mumford told the others. "Search the place." The three men started toward the rear of the house, and Mumford turned back to Amparo.

"The two guys who came in here… we know they're still here, lady. We seen their car in the back."

"I have no idea what you are talking about, señor."

Mumford raised the gun and put his face down next to hers. "Sure you do…" he hissed. Her expression did not falter.

There was a knock at the front door, and it opened slightly. A young white officer, dressed in the white shirt and black pants of the AMPPS, leaned his head inside.

"Port Police," he said. ""We got two units out front. Everything secure in here?"

"Everything's under control, officer," Mumford responded. "Maybe you just stand by."

"Will do."

Within minutes, one of the operatives searching the rear of the house opened the bedroom closet, and thrust a Smith & Wesson nine-millimeter inside. There was movement from among the hanging clothes and boxes. He opened the door wide, revealing a blinking Buzz.

"Whadda we got here?" he said.

"Would you believe a slumber party?" Buzz mumbled.

"Out," he ordered, yanking Buzz from the closet by his jacket.

"Didn't think so."

The barrel of the semi-automatic sorted among the clothes and exposed a squatting Noah. "Okay, let's go," the mobster growled, throwing Buzz toward the living room and motioning Noah out.

"Easy, big fellah," Buzz said. "Anyone ever tell you it's not nice to push?"

Noah stood and walked slowly out of the closet into the hallway. As they passed the swinging kitchen door, he suddenly bolted through it and sprinted for the back yard.

"Need some help back here!" the thug shouted. "One's running!" In seconds, another hood appeared from the living room and grabbed Buzz, jerking him toward the front of the house, as the other took off through the kitchen after Noah.

By now, Noah was over the back fence, into the alley, running hard. *Gotta get to Pulansky! Only way to cool this situation off. But how?*

The hoodlum scrambled over the fence after him. Just as he neared the end of the block, one of the AMPPS units bounced into the alley, bar lights swimming, roaring toward him. Noah stopped short, grabbed the top of a six-foot wooden fence to his right with both hands, and vaulted over, sprinting the instant he hit the ground, through a back yard, down the driveway toward the street. *Shit! Shoulda gone over the other side. This way's gonna be crawling with 'em.*

Nearing the end of the driveway, he saw another AMPPS car slowly cruising down 46th, and he was suddenly illuminated in its spotlight. Reversing direction, he scrambled back toward the alley as the squad car screeched to a stop, the sound of running footsteps coming from the driveway behind him. When he reached the back fence, he again launched himself and swung a leg over just as the gate opened and two AMPPS patrolmen banged through. On the alley side, Mustafa's man stood, semi-automatic in both hands, pointed squarely into his face. "That's it!" he shouted, and four handguns clicked simultaneously.

Breathing hard, Noah slid slowly into the back yard; he was immediately grabbed by the hair and thrown forward, his arm yanked up behind him. A shoulder in his back shoved him forcefully through the gate, and he stumbled back down the alley toward the Ruiz house.

"Okay, I got him," Noah's captor yelled as they entered the back door. When they reached the living room, the man thrust Noah, still panting, onto the couch next to Amparo and Buzz.

Out front, a black limousine glided ominously to the curb.

CHAPTER FORTY-NINE

"Good evenin', Señora Ruiz. My name is Freeman Mustafa."

The heavy, cream-colored cashmere overcoat added to his substantial dimensions. Stylized, the image was nonetheless him; there was no sense of veneer. After he took an instant to orient himself and unbutton his coat, his face softened by degrees, adopting a more genial aura. Having recognized Pablo's mother from newspaper photographs, he now locked in eye contact, inclined his head, and smiled slightly in an effort at equanimity.

"These criminals have broken into my office this evenin' and stolen some things that belong to me," he drawled, gesturing toward Noah and Buzz. "I deeply regret your becomin' involved. I know you must be under a great deal of strain of your own right now, but these men were followed to your home."

Amparo studied him, her face devoid of expression. Mustafa turned to Noah.

"You're the public defender representin' Señora Ruiz's son. Shane, is it?"

Noah didn't answer. He had no idea where this was going, but he certainly had no intention of hastening its getting there.

"I'm deeply shocked by your conduct. Engagin' in burglary and this kind of criminal activity. This is hardly what I'd have expected from our public defender. I've had a lot of respect for your office in the past." He moved closer to Noah, his face darkening.

"Now, as I said, I believe you have some of my belongin's."

"I don't know what that would be," Noah said.

"You know exactly what I'm talkin' about," Mustafa snapped. "You stole a CD and some other materials from my private office. You might be able to avoid a whole lot of personal discomfort by givin' them to me right now."

There being no response, he nodded to Mumford, who walked behind the couch, grabbed Noah by the hair, jerked his head back, and placed his weapon to his temple.

"I'll tell you where it is," Noah grunted. "But only if you agree not to harm her."

Buzz sucked in a breath. Amparo dropped her head and closed her eyes.

Mustafa chuckled. "I think that's a bit much to ask. We'll clearly find the disc anyway. It can't be far from where you're sittin' right now, can it? We'll tear this house apart until we find it, and, if somehow we don't, we'll burn the place down.

"See, I'm gonna have to assume that by now you all know what's on it. That doesn't strengthen your bargainin' position much, does it." He glared menacingly at Noah, then, with effort, softened again. "No, I don't think you can change the outcome in any real way, but there could be a whole lotta physical pain for all of you, dependin' on your choices."

"She knows nothing about any of this."

Mustafa set his jaw, staring at Noah, not looking at Amparo. "Even if you're plannin' on bein' a hero, I wonder how she does with pain."

In the heavy silence that followed, Noah could hear a clock, ticking. His gaze fell on the altar behind the front door, the lone candle long since extinguished, and he felt a sudden gush of remorse.

Finally, Mustafa jerked his chin toward the back of the house. Letting go of Noah's hair, Mumford walked out from behind the couch and yanked Amparo up roughly.

"Wait!" Noah pleaded.

"Why are you doing this?" Amparo asked.

Mustafa regarded her. "This is my community. It might surprise you to know that its safety is of great importance to me." He paused, looked down, then back at her. "Your son murdered a dear friend of mine. By makin' an example of people like him, we ensure this city is a place where we can be proud to raise our children."

Amparo held his eyes. "We both know that Pablo did not do what you have said."

He remained locked on her for a long moment, then turned abruptly to Mumford, all business, the charm gone. "Have two of your people get 'em to the compound," he ordered. "I'm right behind you. I let the Port Authority people go, so you stay here until the others find that CD, then catch up with us. Call me in an hour if you don't find it."

Mumford nodded and seized Amparo, and then he motioned Noah and Buzz forward at gunpoint, moving them toward the front door, as another of the operatives joined them. Mustafa opened the door, and they stepped out onto the porch into the blackness, then froze, all realizing simultaneously that a number of people were milling about in the near darkness in front of the house. Many vehicles had stopped near the curb. A single light, perched on a tripod standard, switched on somewhere near the front walkway, illuminating the lawn area.

"Mr. Mustafa?" a voice intoned from a silhouette near the light. They all squinted into the glare to see a man holding a microphone in his hand. "Mr. Mustafa?" he called again.

"Who is that?" Mustafa growled.

"It's Arlen Gates of KXTV News, Mr. Mustafa. Do you have a statement for us?"

Mustafa was completely bewildered.

"We understand that you have an important announcement concerning the *Ruiz* case? We were told it was critical we be here immediately?"

There were consecutive loud thuds as klieg lights switched on, bathing the entire front of the bungalow in blazing light and heat. "We're on camera one," a female voice called.

"Shut that camera off!" Mustafa snarled. "No cameras!"

For several moments no one moved, no one spoke; the small red light on the handheld camera burned steadily.

"All right," Mustafa said. "We were just on our way out, but I'll give you a short statement." The charm resurfaced as Mustafa's two agents receded into the deep shadows, obscuring their weapons.

"As you know, Mr. Gates," he began. "I am a staunch proponent of equal justice in our community. Many of my skirmishes on that issue have been reported by your station, even by you, yourself, if I recall." He smiled broadly, then slowly became serious, staring into the camera as he had so many times.

"I've watched the developments relatin' to the murder of my good friend, Warren Van Zandt, with interest, and I am now in a position to release evidence that I have been under extreme pressure not to make public, evidence that a grave injustice may be threatened against one of our own."

Noah's features gathered into a quizzical frown as he struggled to follow what he was hearing.

Mustafa paused again as he surveyed the surrealistic scene in front of the bungalow. Lights had come on in the surrounding houses. Neighbors were emerging on porches and spilling out into the street in bathrobes and all manner of sleeping attire. They wandered among the cables, cameras, and TV engineers, craning for a better look. Somewhere, a baby was crying.

"I am now satisfied that there may be evidence that Pablo Ruiz was not involved in the killin' of Mr. Van Zandt," Mustafa went on. "I had intended to present this evidence to the proper authorities tomorrow morning for their further consideration. I suspect that is what you may be referrin' to, Mr. Gates, but I don't know who told you I would be makin' a statement tonight."

Gates interrupted. "What evidence would that be?"

"I cannot say more about it at this time, but I certainly wish the community to know that I am doing everything in my power to prevent any injustice."

"Thank you," Gates shouted. "But can you tell us anything more about this 'evidence' you mentioned, Mr. Mustafa? I'm sure our viewers would like to know what was so important that we were called to Ms. Ruiz's home in the middle of the night."

"Ah… yes," Mustafa answered. "I certainly understand your curiosity. But it was not I who summoned you here. I regret that I cannot detail the nature of the evidence just now, but I am certain that all will become clear. Now, if y'all will excuse us, my friends and I must be on our way." Mustafa started down the front steps, and his two men followed.

Recognizing Noah, Gates turned to him. "Mr. Shane, do you have a statement for us?"

"I most certainly do," Noah responded, watching Mustafa walk across the grass toward his car. "Do you have an envelope with you?"

Gates was puzzled. "An envelope? What kind of envelope?"

"A large manila envelope."

"We may," Gates answered, nodding to a nearby crewmember. "Why?"

"If you'll excuse me for a moment while you're checking that. I'll be right back." Noah turned and entered the front door.

Within a minute he returned to the porch and held up the disc, along with the handful of papers and photos. "I have here a CD and certain other materials which were just discovered this evening. They contain evidence—statements and photographs of a high-ranking government official—that will clear Pablo Ruiz of all charges against him. I intend to present this evidence to the court tomorrow morning."

The crewmember brought a large manila envelope forward and handed it to Noah, who raised it to the camera, placed the CD and the other materials inside in full view, then sealed the envelope, and wrote *People v. Ruiz* on it with his pen. Mustafa stood by the open back door of his limousine, watching and listening, as the camera zoomed in for a tight shot of Noah.

"If you will give me your word that you will accept custody of this evidence, safeguard it tonight at the KXTV Studios, and deliver the envelope with the seal unbroken to the chambers of Judge Donovan Pulansky, Alameda County Superior Court Department Twenty-Six, tomorrow morning at eight forty-five AM, I promise to give you an exclusive interview at the morning recess in that department in which I will explain precisely what is on this disc, and detail this entire matter for your viewers."

"Can you tell us a little more about it at this time?" Gates asked. "Is this the evidence Mr. Mustafa mentioned?"

Noah knew he had set the hook, but he had to play it just a bit more to be sure the bait was swallowed.

"I can say only that it contains evidence of a conspiracy that reaches to the highest levels of local government. That conspiracy goes to the core of the *Ruiz* case."

"What kind of conspiracy? And where was this evidence discovered?"

"I cannot say more at this time, without risking prejudice to the case. However, as I have promised, KXTV will be guaranteed to be first to report these developments if you will take custody of the envelope and ensure its safekeeping overnight. I will also say that you are at liberty to report the facts as you know them now, but you must assure me that you will not break the seal on this envelope, in order to preserve its admissibility. Agreed?" Noah held up the envelope. He knew the answer.

"Agreed." In full view of the camera, which had pulled out for a longer shot, Gates stepped forward and took the envelope, intensifying the drama.

"I caution you," Noah said as he handed it over. "There may be serious risk in keeping this evidence safe. There are very powerful people in this community whose careers, whose lives, are at stake by virtue of its content. And remember, you are not to open the envelope unless something happens to me, to my investigator, or to the accused's mother. This is critical evidence in a murder trial."

"Understood," Gates responded solemnly, now apparently satisfied that he had gotten what he came for.

"Tomorrow morning then," Noah said, turning and walking into the house with Amparo and Buzz, as the camera continued to roll.

Mustafa stood at his limo door, glaring. He turned to get into the vehicle, then glanced back, one eyebrow dropping slightly. Then he snorted and slid into the sumptuous rear seat. Within moments, the limousine floated past the news vehicles, down the block, and out of sight.

"Whooooeee," Buzz whooped once they were safely inside the house. "You are *smokin'*, Blue!" He grabbed Noah's hand and pumped it as Amparo stood by nodding, a smile finally appearing. "But Gates…" he said. "When did you get the message to him?"

"I didn't have anything to do with that. Wouldn't know how to reach him without some research we didn't have time for."

"Then where in hell did he come from?"

"I have absolutely no clue. But talk about timing."

"Seriously. How could he possibly have known we were here? This is some kind of major magic. You definitely have got the gods flying in formation."

"Could they just have been monitoring police calls, and followed the cops out here?"

"Negative. I didn't see any Oakland cops out there."

"But there were cops. They jumped me out back."

"Port Authority, Blue. Those guys work for the AMPPS."

"So then I don't get it… I just don't get it."

"Would you take that coffee now?" Amparo asked.

"That'd be great," Noah told her, and she disappeared into the kitchen.

"Well, whatever, it definitely went well out there," Noah said, laughing.

"You think you can trust Gates?"

"What choice did I have? Besides, this is such a mammoth story, I don't think he'll blow it. Even if he did crack the seal early, I doubt he'd leak what's in it. He knows he can play what he's already got on the morning news, pump the suspense, and be the first with the full story. Probably wants to open the envelope on camera at the courthouse." Noah considered it a beat. "Bottom line, he knows it's all front-page headlines by noon tomorrow anyway. He might as well be the one to get the byline."

"What about chain of evidence if he's carrying that stuff around until tomorrow?"

"Yeah, that's the main reason I didn't want him to open it until the morning session. I put a light pen mark on the flap of the envelope to check if it was opened, and one on the disc so hopefully we can see if it's been played, or at least convince Pulansky we can."

Buzz was shaking his head, grinning. "You are definitely gettin' some litigation chops, Blue."

"Yeah, well, here's the bigger problem. We're not home free yet. We're convinced that's the mayor on the CD, but I don't know if we can prove it. What do you know about voiceprints? Can we get it in that way?"

"Not likely."

It occurred to Noah that this was the first note of pessimism about any kind of evidence he'd heard from Buzz. *Maybe they were both 'gettin' some chops.'*

"The burden is pretty stiff to establish that a print's good enough to be admissible," Buzz said. "There's still a lot of controversy about it. We'll run one for sure, but the likelihood of getting it into evidence in a high profile case like this? Not that great."

"So what we can prove is that whoever's speaking on the disc is the killer. Might also be able to prove that's Mustafa's voice. His is a lot more distinctive."

"Yeah. But we still gotta rely on some kind of technical identification."

"We also know that the speaker gave the victim a gold pendant that's already lodged with the trial exhibits."

Buzz cocked his head and frowned. "With the trial exhibits?"

"Yeah. Salem was waving it around when he told the jury that those two kids found the body. They stole the pendant off the corpse, which is how Salem intends to identify the body down there as Van Zandt's. He said he can show that Pablo was with him that night."

"So..." Buzz nodded, beginning to comprehend. "But that still doesn't get us that Murphy is the one on the recording, admitting to the murder."

"That's the problem. In fact, the pendant apparently has the name 'Pepito' engraved on it. So that's who gave it to Van Zandt, according to Salem. A little less Irish than 'Murphy,' but maybe not than 'Ruiz,' wouldn't you say?"

"Still, it's gotta be Murphy. Murphy's 'Pepito,' no doubt. Why else would Mustafa have had this stuff in his vault?"

"We know that, but proving it is something else." Noah was still reticent. "I can't just put you on to testify to the details of our extracurricular discovery."

They both sat with it, then Noah said, "Wait. I think there's a case, *Fonville*, maybe? You don't have to have the parties to a recorded conversation testify in order to get it in if it contains information that was unlikely to be known by anyone other than the speaker. Remember that photo of Murphy and Van Zandt I showed you?"

"So?"

"So it had the date, August twenty-sixth, the night of the murder, on it. Murphy's in it, and clearly Van Zandt was wearing the pendant. Murphy says on the disc that that was when he gave it to him. Not only does that prove that the mayor was in Mexico with Van Zandt the night of the murder, but maybe I can convince Pulansky that that talk about the pendant on the disc by Murphy is something only the speaker on the disc would have known. Murphy knew about the pendant because it's in the photo."

"That'll work!"

"Maybe." Noah was more cautious. "Pulansky might say there are a lot of people who could've seen Van Zandt with that pendant. Especially with this Pepito stuff. Salem is going to say that whoever Pepito is gave it to him. That's the killer, and it doesn't have to be Murphy."

Amparo returned to the room with the same silver tray and service that Noah had admired previously. "I still do not understand how the television people were aware of what was happening here," she said, as she began to pour.

"Yeah. I don't either," Noah said. "I'll check it with Gates tomorrow, but thank God for whoever it was. We'd all probably be swimming in sewage by now."

Amparo sat down with her coffee. "I do not know how to thank you, Mr. Shane."

"It's Noah. And I feel awful about involving you in this nightmare."

"I would not have had it any other way. I wanted so much to help. It was I who caused all Pablo's difficulty in the first place."

"You didn't cause anything."

"No. I should have known how he would react to my illness."

"He made his own choices, didn't he?"

She looked up and gazed at Noah for a beat. "You know, when I found out that the Public Defender had put someone on Pablo's case who had no experience, I was filled with fear, and then anger. I thought to go to the office to complain, to try to make them change it."

"Why didn't you?" Noah asked.

"Because then I met you, and I saw that you cared deeply about the case."

He continued to regard her as he considered that. "I have to confess to you that I really wanted more than anything to get out of it."

"I could see that, but it was because you cared so much. I was certain you were not like some of the older ones who have worked for the government for many years. Such people would have abandoned Pablo."

Come on... Really? "Well, I'm getting to be one of those older ones pretty fast." He grabbed a piece of his kinky locks. "I think I can start to see some gray hairs."

Amparo laughed. It was the first time Noah had seen her laugh. They rehashed the evening's events while finishing their coffee; then, as Noah and Buzz got up to leave, Noah told her, "Be in court early tomorrow morning, señora. Good things are going to happen." As he hugged her, she asked whether they could get word of the evening's developments to Pablo.

"We can't contact him tonight, but we'll tell him in court tomorrow morning." He wished he were as sure about things as he was trying to sound.

Day was close to breaking as he and Buzz emerged through the back door. "We gotta pin this thing down, Buzz," he said. "It's still too uncertain. I need you to make a call to Mexico, to the Rancho. Maybe there's something you can pull out of Figueroa that'll hook things up now that we've got something to go on. You said he wanted to help."

"What kinda thing you got in mind?"

Noah didn't answer. He was gaping through the predawn gloom in the back yard to where the Captain was parked in the driveway. Ransacked, violated, the seats were pulled up, upholstery ripped, glove compartment trashed, trunk open with the spare pulled out and slashed, and all his back-seat treasures unceremoniously strewn over the adjacent lawn and flowerbeds.

"Those SOBs mangled the Captain," Noah moaned, stooping to pick up a blanket and a KFC box.

"Might not of noticed," Buzz responded, trodding on extremely sensitive ground.

"I knew I shoulda gotten the insurance."

"Waste a money, Blue. Whole damn heap isn't worth the deductible."

CHAPTER FIFTY

"Refill, Arlen?" Karen Bessemer, the cute blond assistant producer, stood in front of Gates, steaming thermos of coffee poised.

The report of the events at the Ruiz home on the morning KXTV newscast had guaranteed that the hall outside Department 26 was dense with humanity. Three television crews were set up and ready to roll, two network affiliates in addition to local KXTV, Oakland.

Arlen Gates sat on a bench in front of the courtroom, absorbed in a thick black binder of notes, clippings, and photographs, his "bible" on the *Ruiz* case, preparing himself for any interview that might present itself before the court day. He wore the usual immaculate pinstriped suit coat, light-blue dress shirt, and green paisley tie, as well as Levis and Nikes, his face crusted with a bilious pink pancake makeup. Next to him, his cameraman, Sam Billings, sipped from a Styrofoam cup, handheld resting on the floor, propped against his knee, ready for action.

Gates glanced up from his notebook. "Um? Oh, yeah. Thanks, Karen." It was full anchorman timbre as he held up his cup for her to pour.

"Sam?" Karen asked.

The camera jockey robotically extended his cup, staring blankly ahead, brain drained by the hour and the events of early that morning.

Down the hall, the crowd parted to allow Noah, also bleary-eyed, to pass; then it closed behind him. When Noah reached the front door to Department 26, Gates stood.

"Morning, counselor. You look like you mighta been up late."

Noah grinned. "Funny thing. Seems like I saw you at that same party. Maybe I'd look better if I tried a little of that pink Crisco you use on your face."

Gates snickered. "Oh, you don't want to do that. You take it off and you look eighty, kind of like Dorian Gray. Only us evil guys are allowed to wear it."

"So, you got my evidence?"

Gates turned to his towering security guard and held out a hand. "Leroy? The envelope, please."

The guard unlocked a canvas bag, produced the manila envelope, and handed it to Gates.

"Sam," Gates alerted the cameraman, "let's get him taking it on camera."

"Nah," Noah demurred. *Just as he had suspected.* "I promised you the full treatment at the recess. I just want to get in and get going right now."

"Okay, counselor. Your show."

He handed the envelope to Noah, who glanced quickly at the tiny pen line that was still visible and intact across the flap.

"So, Arlen," Noah said, trying to make it sound like an afterthought. "How did you guys know anything was happening out at the Ruiz place last night?"

"Got a call saying Mustafa wanted to make a statement about the *Ruiz* case. That we ought to get out there Code Three, lights and sirens."

Noah canted his head slightly. "Really. Who was the caller?"

"Now that, Counselor, is protected. You should know that."

"Well, maybe. But in this case, the guy might be a material witness in a murder trial."

"Can't be helped. Sources are sacrosanct."

Noah studied him a beat, then figured he'd best get inside. He shrugged, turned, and began to work his way through the crowd.

"I'll be right here at the recess," Gates called after him, and Noah waved.

Inside, the courtroom day was beginning. The clerk was engrossed in the judge's calendar. Sid, the bailiff, had the *Ruiz* exhibits spread out on his desk, putting them in order, as Noah entered through the door from the rear hallway.

Sid looked up. "Well, counselor, didn't think you'd be in this early, and without that jewelry you were wearing last time I saw you. They let you out? Or did you manage some kind of jailbreak?" The events of the day before had been a definite highlight-reel item for Sid.

Noah tilted his head, pasting a grin, as he walked over to the bailiff's desk. "Speaking of jewelry, do you have that pendant that the DA was talking about yesterday? I think it was Exhibit P-16."

Sid shuffled through the materials and produced a gaudy gold chain and pendant, wrapped in a plastic sleeve. Noah turned it over and examined the inscription on the back of the small golden triangle. *Warren – Love, your little Pepito.* He returned it to the bailiff.

Though teetering on the edge of exhaustion from six total hours of sleep over the last two nights, and still aching all over and bearing the facial scars from going a couple of rounds with the would-be kidnappers, nothing could possibly derail Noah's mood this particular morning. He took a seat at the defense side of the counsel table, opened his trial bag, pulled out his trial book, and set it on the table in front of him. Then he extracted the CD player and laid it next to the manila envelope. Turning to the bailiff, he said, "Deputy Cooper, I wonder if counsel might meet with Judge Pulansky in chambers before court is convened?"

"Maybe. I don't know if you're going to be so welcome after your little rock-and-roll contempt disco yesterday."

"Be an angel and check with him for me, will you, officer?"

Sid gave him a polite curtsy, then walked over and knocked on the door to chambers. An unintelligible response came from within, and the bailiff disappeared, the door closing behind him.

A moment later, Salem made his entrance through the rear door, followed by his bespectacled sorceress, laptop in hand.

Noah smiled. "Morning, Marco." He turned to the backup staff. "Ma'am?"

Salem sneered at him, slightly taken aback by the first-name familiarity. "Man, your guy's gonna wish he'd taken the deal."

"You must be a late riser," Noah said. "Guess you didn't see the morning news."

Salem's slightly puzzled frown confirmed he hadn't, but there wasn't time to respond as the bailiff emerged from chambers and said, "Judge'll see you now."

"Morning, Your Honor." Noah clutched the manila envelope as he stuck his head inside the door. "May we chat for a moment? I have something I want to inform the court about before the morning session."

"Mmmmm..." Yesterday's contempt was obviously fresh in Pulansky's mind as he projected a contorted scowl.

Taking that as a yes, Noah turned and nodded at Salem, who followed him into chambers.

When everyone was seated, Noah began. Despite lingering doubts, he figured it best to open with a flourish, make it at least appear that he was confident he had the silver bullet.

"Your Honor," he said. "Last night I came into possession of a CD, and certain other materials, which conclusively prove that my client, Pablo Ruiz, has been the victim—"

"Just a minute, counsel," Pulansky interrupted, and Noah stopped. "Aren't you forgetting something?"

"Am I, Your Honor?"

Pulansky studied him through slit-like eyes. "Yesterday I held you in contempt of this court and told you that before anything else happened in this case, I would have a full and complete apology from you. Do you recall that?"

"I do, Your Honor, but—"

"But nothing." It was clear that Pulansky was harboring no lost love. "Before you make any presentation to me about anything, there will be a full apology."

"All right, Your Honor. I apologize." It seemed to hang in the air.

"You apologize for what?"

"I apologize if I offended you. Now, if it's okay, I wanted to play this—"

"Dammit, Shane! Don't you get any of this? Here you are, waltzing around out on your own. You got this big murder trial. And, by God, you're gonna milk it, solo, and in a way that undermines the authority of this court at that. No loyalty. No regard for the needs of your colleagues. Now, if you aren't prepared to own up to your transgressions in my courtroom and satisfy me that you understand you were wrong, and that this kind of behavior isn't going to be repeated, I'm throwing you back in the cooler. Do I make myself clear?"

"Yes, Your Honor." Now a bit more subdued, Noah had finally begun to read the graffiti, despite his impatience to get on with it.

"So?"

"So, I never should have implied that Your Honor was part of a conspiracy—"

"Damn straight you shouldn't. What about your tone?"

"I had no business raising my voice to you, Your Honor. I understand that now."

"Why is that important, Mr. Shane?"

"Because, if the jury and the public are expected to abide by the law, they must accept the rule of law, and in order for that to happen, they must respect the judge, who is interpreting the law and making the rulings. Disrespect from lawyers, who are officers of the court, challenges the court's authority and threatens the very foundation of justice."

Salem's eyebrows had risen to his blow-dried hairline.

"Not bad," Pulansky observed, nodding. "May I assume that we have this kind of conduct behind us?"

"Most definitely, Your Honor. You may rely on that."

"Very well. Now, you had something you wanted to bring to the Court's attention?" He obviously hadn't seen the morning news, either.

"Yes, Your Honor. I would like to inform the Court that this envelope contains material evidence, evidence that has been held in the custody of KXTV television news overnight."

"Oh?" He now had Pulansky's attention.

"May we have the court reporter present for this meeting, Your Honor?" Buzz had instructed him that that would be critical.

"You think that's necessary?"

"I do, Your Honor. I am about to reveal evidence that will change the course of this case."

"Very well," Pulansky said, only a hint of doubt drawing down an eyebrow. He picked up the phone and dialed the bailiff. "Sid, would you tell Nora to come in? Thanks."

Within moments the middle-aged reporter came in, pulled up an armless chair, situated herself, and nodded to the judge.

"You may continue, Mr. Shane," he said.

"Before I break the seal," he began, "I would like the court to note this small ink line that shows that the envelope has been unopened since I placed it there on camera during a television taping in the early morning hours. Should it be necessary to establish the chain of evidence, we can view that video clip at the court's convenience."

Pulansky scrutinized the envelope. "I see it."

Noah broke the seal and extracted the disc. "Last night I came into possession of this CD." He held it up for the judge. "It, along with some other materials that came with it, demonstrate beyond doubt that the case against Pablo Ruiz for the murder of Warren Van Zandt is the result of a massive conspiracy to suborn perjury and obstruct justice in order to protect the Mayor of the City of Oakland, Rowland Murphy, who is, in fact, the murderer."

Pulansky's eyes were bulging, but he said nothing. Salem sat transfixed. Noah cued up the CD player.

"This disc was obtained from Mr. Freeman Mustafa, who, I believe, is known to Your Honor?" He paused.

Still bulging, Pulansky remained mute.

"Mr. Mustafa has indicated in the television interview I mentioned that he will cooperate fully and support the effort to bring the guilty parties to justice. That statement aired on the morning news on KXTV."

Noah didn't know precisely how Mustafa fit into all this, but just then, he didn't care. He was satisfied that the full implication of the association between Murphy and Mustafa would sort itself out in the days or weeks to come, and Pablo was his only concern. For now, if he could get this CD into evidence, it was Pablo's ticket out.

"Well?" Pulansky managed. "Is there any objection, Mr. Salem?"

No matter what he thought, there was no way Salem was going to be able to prevent the judge from listening, and he knew it. He was savvy enough not to try to swim upstream. "No, Your Honor," he responded. "The People are certainly keenly interested in any evidence that will further the cause of justice."

"Let's hear it, Mr. Shane," Pulansky said.

Noah hit Play and the voices spewed forth.

Before the recording concluded, Salem was all over it. "Your Honor, this is preposterous! Counsel is implying that is the voice of the Mayor of Oakland, and that he was therefore somehow involved in this murder! How can we possibly know the identity of the voices on this—"

"Yes, Mr. Shane," the judge interrupted. "Just how do you intend to authenticate this smoking gun of yours?"

"I thought Your Honor might ask. I have here a photograph taken on the night of the murder. It shows the mayor with the victim. As Your Honor can see, the laser imprint of the date clearly shows August twenty-sixth." He handed the photo to Salem, who examined it and passed it on to the judge.

Pulansky took the photograph and scrutinized it. "Mr. Salem?" he said, after several moments.

"I don't see where this photograph gets us, Your Honor. We still have a recorded statement that's obviously highly prejudicial, and inadmissible without an iota of authentication. We don't know the identity of either of the speakers. We don't know who recorded it, when, or where. Mr. Shane would have us believe that it's the mayor confessing to the murder of Mr. Van Zandt, but there's no evidence that that's the mayor's voice. It could be anyone's, even Ruiz's. In fact, even assuming any of this is to be given credibility, the speaker says that he gave the victim the necklace and pendant as a birthday gift, and the inscription on the pendant is that of someone named 'Pepito'. Just because counsel has a photograph of the mayor with the victim, even if that photograph can be authenticated, which is doubtful, and even if it was taken the night of the murder, doesn't add anything to what's on the CD."

"I would tend to agree," Pulansky said, hovering, ready to rule. "Any response, Mr. Shane?"

Noah started slowly, trying to reflect that he knew what he was talking about. Maybe a slight stretch at the moment, but after digging up all the authorities, by God, he was going to use them.

"Your Honor, I would concede that the usual method of laying a foundation for the playing of a recording is to call a participant on the recording to testify as to the identity of the speakers, and to the accuracy of the recorded material, but the law is clear that this approach is not exclusive. Evidence Code Section 1421 provides that a writing, which a digital recording is considered to be, may be authenticated by matters it contains which are unlikely to be known by anyone but the author. Here, Your Honor, the speaker on the disc talks about having given the victim the necklace, and we have a photograph obviously taken that night, just shortly before the murder, showing the mayor with the victim, and the victim is wearing the pendant. These are therefore unique facts, known to the speaker on the recording, that others wouldn't know."

"Nonsense," Salem boomed. "All the photograph shows is that apparently the mayor and the victim were together that night, and that the victim had a necklace that somebody gave him. Any number of people could have known about that necklace, could have seen it. Besides, it's clearly someone named 'Pepito' who gave it to him. That, no doubt, is who is speaking on the recording, *if* the recording is authentic. If it is, the voice could just as easily be that of the defendant. What is important is that it has not been authenticated, and should not be admitted. This is precisely why we have rules of evidence. It's outrageous—and if said outside this courtroom, perhaps defamatory— that counsel seeks to sully the name and reputation of the Mayor of Oakland with this kind of drivel in some last-ditch hail-Mary attempt to extricate his obviously guilty client from the charges against him. This kind of misconduct should be reported to the Bar Association and—"

"All right, Mr. Salem," Pulansky intervened. "Let's not get carried away. Anything further, Mr. Shane?"

"No, Your Honor."

"I have to agree with the prosecution. The CD is highly prejudicial, and it has not been authenticated. It's out."

Noah's head dropped, eyes closed. *All this. This close, and they were all just going back to the charade? It couldn't be. They knew that Pablo wasn't guilty.* He could feel his face flushing, his pulse quickening, as the probe careened wildly through his memory banks searching for something, anything.

"Then I would point out, Your Honor," he said, volume increasing, "that even if the court does not admit the recording, the photo indicates that the mayor and the victim were together on the night of the murder, apparently in Mexico. The mayor has made damning attacks on my client in the media. He has implied that Pablo Ruiz is the murderer.

Never once did he indicate that he was also with the victim that night, that he was quite clearly in Mexico at the same time. He is obviously a material witness. I would renew my request for a continuance to undertake further investigation into his involvement, and its impact on the case against Pablo Ruiz."

"Denied," Pulansky said, without dropping a beat. His volume was also dialed up, Noah clearly not being one of his favorite people just now. "You're missing the point. We don't have authentication for any of this. While the mayor's often-inflammatory statements, many of which I have seen in the media myself, are of interest, they do not have sufficient bearing on the facts of this case to justify the risk of maligning a public figure, disrupting this trial, and inconveniencing jurors, witnesses, and the court. You're free to call him as a witness and go into these matters, but you'd better have a convincing offer of proof. I'll rule on any objection to his testimony if it comes up."

At that, Pulansky rose. "Are we ready to go to work, gentlemen?"

"Your Honor." Noah was almost shouting as he blathered on in desperation: "May I at least have time to brief—"

Pulansky's head jerked around, his jaw set. "Goddamnit, Shane! Are we going to start this again?"

The door suddenly swung open, and the bailiff stuck his head in. "Your Honor?" he said. "Mr. Hoogasian is asking to be admitted to chambers. He says that it's urgent."

Pulansky, poised to ring Noah up again, turned and walked to the clothes tree in the corner and grabbed his robe. "All right," he growled without looking around. "Let him in."

Buzz burst into the room. "May I speak with Mr. Shane privately for a moment, Your Honor?"

"Couldn't this have waited until I took the bench?" Pulansky demanded. "We're on the record, here."

"I'm sorry, Your Honor. But it really couldn't. It'll just take a second. If Your Honor could just remain in chambers for a minute, I think we have something of importance."

"Oh, very well. But make it brief. Let's go off the record."

Buzz drew Noah aside and opened a file folder, showing him the contents, while whispering animatedly. "You were right! Figueroa did have a picture."

As Noah studied the faxed photograph, a broad smile slowly crept over his features. Then a chuckle escaped, despite his effort to stifle it.

"Something funny, Mr. Shane?" the judge spat, dagger-eyes again fixed on Noah.

"Actually, it is, Your Honor. A little."

"Back on the record," Pulansky said.

Noah opened the folder. "This is a photograph faxed to Mr. Hoogasian this morning by one Eduardo Figueroa, a prominent Mexican citizen, and owner of Rancho Figueroa, the resort where Mr. Van Zandt's murder took place. The original photograph will arrive tomorrow, and we can connect all these dots with sworn testimony. As the Court can see, it is a photograph of Mayor Murphy seated at his desk at City Hall, a photograph that the mayor has signed with the nickname by which he was known at Mr. Figueroa's establishment. If I may read the inscription: 'To my dear amigo, Eduardo Figueroa, with gratitude, Rowland 'Pepito' Murphy.'" I'm sure that handwriting studies will demonstrate the authenticity of the signature." He handed the photograph to the judge, who examined it briefly, then moved abruptly toward the door, radiating anger and determination.

"If counsel will return to the courtroom, we will begin the morning session."

Noah stared in disbelief, thinking the judge was dismissing even this clearly damning evidence. He was about to relight the rant and dial it up even higher, but Salem had the judge's reaction to the photo right, and thankfully beat him to it.

"But, Your Honor," the prosecutor protested, trying to slow things down. "The defense is slandering the name of a public official. We still haven't authenticated—"

"Your indignation is laudable, Mr. Salem," Pulansky broke in, "but at this point, I would encourage you to save it for another forum. I am exceedingly familiar with the mayor's handwriting, and his signature, and also his voice by the way, having known him for a number of years. In fact, I believe I could be called as an expert witness on any of those subjects.

"Until we had this photograph, I did not believe there was sufficient corroboration of the far-reaching implications of the unauthenticated recorded statement and photograph. Those implications, of course, being a potential 187 charge against the mayor of this city. Under the circumstances, I had no choice but to proceed by the numbers. Whether some other body might have proceeded to investigate all this was not my concern, but I could not justify permitting the introduction of this evidence into a criminal trial on the authentication such as it was.

"That has now changed," he continued, and then paused to give force to his decision. "For present purposes, I have no questions, and no need of further corroboration. However, that should be a lesson to you, Mr.

Shane, in the formal, and practical, evidentiary requirements of the court."

"Noted, Your Honor."

Pulansky stared for a beat, then gave him a brief nod, and finished buttoning his robe.

Back out front, the courtroom was packed, jurors all in place. As he took his usual position at the counsel table, Noah smiled at Amparo in the first row, then noticed that Pablo had not yet arrived. Puzzled, he walked over to the bailiff's desk to find Cooper on the phone. Noah shrugged and frowned, holding his palms up in a silent inquiry.

"I don't know," the deputy answered, cupping a hand over the receiver. "There was apparently some trouble at the jail last night. I'm trying to find out what happened."

"What kind of trouble?" Noah was immediately alarmed. "Is he okay?"

"I don't know. That's what I'm trying to find out. They say he was attacked by another inmate."

"Attacked?"

The deputy returned his attention to the phone, shaking his head and waving an ashen Noah to be quiet. An instant later, the bailiff bolted to his feet, the phone still to his ear, as the door to chambers opened and Pulansky took the bench.

"All rise. Department Twenty-Six of the Superior Court of the State of California, County of Alameda, is now in session. The Honorable Donovan J. Pulansky presiding. Be seated."

The courtroom sat as one. Noah was still glued to the bailiff. "What are they saying? Is he okay?"

Cooper, whose attention was into the phone, frowned and again waved him off, trying to listen.

Suddenly the holding cell door swung open, and Pablo, wearing a soft neck collar and his suit without a tie, was led in by a deputy. As before, he appeared only vaguely aware of his surroundings and the capacity crowd. As he and Noah went to the counsel table, Pablo managed a half-smile at his mother and took a seat between Noah and Buzz. Noah was focused on the collar.

Pulansky greeted the assemblage brusquely. "Good morning, ladies and gentlemen." He paused and looked down at the court reporter. "Madam Reporter?" he said.

"Ready, Your Honor."

"Very well. The record will reflect that this is day four of the trial in the case of *People v. Ruiz*, Action Number OS659331. The defendant is present, as are counsel for the People and the defendant, and all jurors are present.

"Ladies and gentlemen," he began. "Certain reliable evidence has come to the Court's attention this morning that casts grave doubt on the guilt of the defendant, Mr. Ruiz, for the crime of which he stands accused."

Hearing his name, Pablo's brow tightened as he stared at the judge, groping to follow, as usual. Seeking reassurance, he glanced at Noah, who smiled and nodded.

"I now have deep concern not only about the defendant's guilt," the Judge continued, "or the absence thereof, but also about the manner in which this case has been prosecuted. In light of these troubling developments, I am making the following orders:

"First, the trial of this matter is hereby suspended, and the jury dismissed. I thank you, ladies and gentlemen, for your time and effort, and for your commitment to your civic duty. I am sorry that you were unable to see this case through to verdict, but I believe justice will be served by the action I am now taking. You will remain in place until the conclusion of the morning session."

The jurors blinked at one another in confusion. Agitated murmurs began to rise and build from all areas of the courtroom. The judge rapped once to obtain silence.

"Second, in light of the unique, and extremely worrisome, circumstances before us, I am referring this entire matter to the office of the United States Attorney for a full investigation by the Federal Prosecutor as to just how deep this conspiracy may go, with an eye toward bringing the matter before a Federal Grand Jury for consideration of charges against the individuals involved.

"Third, I assume that the Oakland Police Department has already taken the mayor, Mr. Rowland Murphy, into custody for questioning, but if that has not been accomplished, I instruct that it be done immediately, and that Mr. Murphy be held without bail until further investigation sheds light on his flight risk."

The room exploded into bedlam as the crowd tried to make sense of this. Pulansky again pounded for quiet.

"Fourth." Pulansky's tone became more severe. As he glared at Salem, it was as though he found some kind of vindication in it all. "The court will continue this trial for ninety days, and will take under submission a motion to dismiss the charges against Mr. Ruiz in the interests of justice pursuant to Section 1385 of the Penal Code, Mr. Salem. I will rule on that motion at the completion of the investigation that has been ordered here, and the further verification of the evidence that has now come to the Court's attention." He stopped and waited.

Nada.

"Mr. Salem?"

"Oh… uh, yes, Your Honor," a shell-shocked Salem muttered. "The People so move."

"Thank you."

Looking down at Pablo, Pulansky continued, "Mr. Ruiz, it appears that your community may have done you an outrageous injustice. If that turns out to be the case, please know that this Court will do everything in its power to see that that wrong is righted. In the meantime, you will be released on your own recognizance. This court will be in recess until one-thirty this afternoon." With a final thump of his gavel, he bolted from the bench.

Still confused, the gallery burst into a chaotic din, members of the press stampeding to the exit. The uproar continued as the jurors stood and began to file out of the box. Most of the onlookers lingered, as if they thought somehow all of this would be explained if they remained long enough.

Pablo hadn't grasped it yet. He looked around vacuously, at Noah, at the gallery. To his immediate left, Buzz was pumping Noah's hand as a handful of remaining reporters shouted questions. Looking over Noah's shoulder, Pablo saw his mother, still standing at her seat in the first row, regarding him with a soft smile. Slowly, the realization that something cataclysmic had happened began to settle over him, a comprehension that for some unfathomable reason, it might be over. He went to Amparo and gently put his arms around her.

Noah turned and started through the crowd toward them as reporters continued to mob him, demanding explanation, clarification of Pulansky's statement.

"Mr. Shane! Is the mayor accused of murder?"

"Can you make a statement as to where things are going now that Ruiz has been released?"

"Can we hear the CD?"

Noah tried to push through. It was hopeless. He stopped and held up his hands. "Look, folks. This will all become clear shortly. For now, I've promised an exclusive to Arlen Gates at KXTV, and I intend to honor that promise. I'll be happy to talk to you all after that. Now, if you'll excuse me, I've got to speak to my client." He started through the crowd again. "Excuse me. Please."

When he reached Pablo and Amparo, Pablo turned and hugged him, hanging on for a full thirty seconds. Noah could feel him shuddering, sobbing silently, unable to contain the emotion any longer. Finally, holding him out at arm's length, Noah looked into his face and said, "I guess you understand what this means?"

Tears streaming down his cheeks, Pablo answered without a moment's hesitation. "It means I did not kill him, does it not?"

Noah reflected on this before responding. Not the answer he had expected. "Yes, Pablo," he said. "That's what it means. You didn't kill him. But it also means you're free. Free to go home."

"I do not know how you did it. I am sure you will tell me."

"I'll tell you."

"I will never forget this moment."

Smiling, both hands on Pablo's shoulders, Noah shook him gently.

Amparo, who had been standing next to them, put an arm around Pablo and looked up at Noah. "Thank you, Noah. Thank you for everything. You have given to Pablo and to me a gift we can never repay."

Noah took her hand. "No, señora. The gift is from you. You gave me the strength I needed."

"That is not true," she said. "You had everything you needed."

He started to protest, but let it go.

EPILOGUE

"Large latte for Noah!"

Picking up the steaming cup of wonderfulness, Noah stopped at the condiments bar to sprinkle chocolate powder and apply an insulating sleeve, then found his way to a table and spread out the *Chronicle* in front of him.

For the first five days after the trial ended, the paper had been full of stories about the case, the corrupt Oakland government, speculation about a federal investigation, and Noah's heroics. Then it had dwindled down to an op-ed or human-interest column here and there, with Noah being interviewed a number of times. This morning, thumbing through the front section and the local news, he found no reference, and concluded that the celebrity ride was finally petering out. Scanning the Bay Area section, however, his attention was attracted to a two-column-inch news piece:

PORT AUTHORITY COMMISSIONER RESIGNS

Henry Barnes, Commissioner of the Port of Oakland, resigned yesterday after eighteen years in the post, and thirty-two years of public service, citing disillusionment with the corruption in local government. Mr. Barnes made reference to the criminal activity that was uncovered by the alleged obstruction of justice in a recent murder case as the motive for his decision. "Things have gotten out of hand," Barnes said, "when powerful people can manipulate the courts and county agencies to their own advantage. We have only seen the tip of the iceberg, an attempt to subvert the court system in this case, but I am convinced the problems extend far deeper into massive criminal conduct." Mr. Barnes promised to cooperate with the pending Federal investigation, and any State investigation that might be forthcoming. In his retirement he looks forward to spending more time with his family, including six grandchildren, four boys and two girls.

"Hey, Blue," came the familiar voice from behind.

"Hey, Buzz. Pull up a chair," Noah said, kicking it out for him. "Did you see this article about Barnes in the Bay Area section?"

Buzz set down his large coffee and leaned back. "Negative. Barnes?"

"That Port Authority Commissioner, Barnes?"

"No."

"You remember. One of the dossiers we found in the Mustafa files?"

"Oh, yeah."

"He resigned, citing corruption in the wake of the Ruiz thing. Offered to cooperate with the investigation, which says to me that he must know more than he's said yet."

"And that's a big deal?"

"The timing of it is what struck me. Right now? After the trial? With all this looking behind the curtain at the mayor, and Mustafa? Now he goes public?"

"Meaning?"

"Well, I told you that Arlen Gates wouldn't tell me who called in the report to KXTV about Mustafa being at the Ruiz place that night. Protecting his source, he said. I guess this article got me wondering whether it might have been Barnes. Especially since, like you pointed out, the only cops that were out there that night were Port Authority. No OPD. Barnes must have known about the call to AMPPS cops, don't you think?"

Buzz shook his head. "Your mind just never stops grinding, does it. Does it hurt? All that electro-cranial bluesification?" He took a cautious sip from his steaming cup. "But you might be onto something. You gonna check into it?"

"Nah. Doesn't matter. Might come out in the ashes if there's an investigation."

"Right," Buzz scoffed. "The ashes."

Noah was still scanning the paper. "What I'm wondering now, is why you called this meeting."

"So, we need to talk."

"About?"

"About how I resigned from the office."

Noah's head jerked up from his paper. "Whaaat?" He leaned forward, stunned.

"Affirmative. Resigned."

"Why would you do that?"

"Because they gave me the option before firing me."

"Firing you? You just brought in an outstanding result. How could they even think about firing you?"

"Yeah, well, like I thought, you weren't the only one who got his car busted into. Someone lifted those preliminary police reports with the DA's fax header out of my vehicle."

"But you had nothing to do with coming up with those."

"Whoever it was stole the reports from me gave 'em to the PD brass. Said they thought I'd broken into the DA's office and faxed the stuff to myself. Accused me of havin' some kind of nefarious second story skills. Can you imagine?"

"No way, Buzz. That was me who got those reports, from…" He hesitated as the full catastrophe suddenly washed over him. *Oh my God! Becca! What was gonna happen to Becca?* "It was me. I'll explain to them it was me."

"Hold on, Blue. No need to get excited. I was definitely due for a change of scene, anyway."

"But it wasn't your deal, Buzz. I can't let you take the fall for something—"

"I'm telling you that I was gonna move on anyway. No big thing."

Noah stared at him. *This couldn't be happening.* "Who? Who reported it?"

"No clue. But it was around the time I was going to Mexico. I think whoever it was had in mind running me out so I wouldn't be snooping around down there. They might have succeeded, too, but I wasn't checking in with the office, so I missed the memo telling me to come in and face the charges."

Noah considered it. *There was a major conspiracy from the beginning. That much was dead-ass clear. God knew how deep it went, but no chance Buzz was gonna be the last casualty in this war.* "I'm not letting you do it, Buzz. We'll fix it. I'm gonna tell them the DA must have sent the fax to me by mistake."

"No, you're not. They'd never buy that. There's codes you gotta key into the DA's fax to prevent that kind of thing. Besides, I've already turned in my notice. I called Eduardo Figueroa, and he offered me a job at the Rancho, consulting on their high-powered security down there. Gave me an offer I couldn't refuse. I've rented a place in San Felipe, and I'm gonna commute. It's all done, Blue. I leave tomorrow."

"Tomorrow?" Noah shook his head slowly, still shocked.

"Yeah. I told you what a great time it was in that little town. I'm really lookin' forward to some serious livin' on sponge cake, and on my own plastic this time."

Noah continued to stare. *Couldn't let him do this. He would step up and admit to it. Take the hit himself. No way they'd fire him right now. But wait… what if Buzz wants it this way? Maybe it was his parting gift, protecting them both, him and Becca. No way he could rob him of that.*

"Jesus, Buzz, what am I gonna do with you?" A beat, then, "Hell, what am I gonna do without you?"

"You'll manage."

Noah took a deep breath and exhaled, fighting the emotion. "You taught me everything, man."

"We had some great times for sure."

They were quiet. Finally Noah said, "You didn't have to do this, you know."

"Yeah, I did. It's the right thing. And if anything comes up, you know where to find me."

Picking up his latte, Noah raised it to his lips to hide the dampness that was invading his eyes. Then, setting it down, he sniffed unabashedly. "And you know where to find me, Buzz."

Raising his cup to him, Buzz said, "Roger that, Blue."

• • •

"All right, the Court finds that the defendant understands the plea as explained to him by the Public Defender, and his plea of guilty will therefore be entered. The defendant will be released from custody and referred to probation for a complete report and arrangement of a payment schedule. This matter will be placed on the calendar in forty-five days for review of the probation report and sentencing. A date, Madam Clerk?"

"January eighth, Your Honor?"

"That'll be the order." Noting that that was the last case of a short calendar, Judge Krousse added, "This court will stand in recess until tomorrow morning at nine AM." She stood, then paused to look at the large institutional clock on the wall as she left the bench. "Five o'clock sharp," she said. "Not bad for a Monday. Let's go home, people."

After gathering her files and packing her briefcase, Kate turned and walked up the aisle behind the members of the gallery, who were shuffling out. As she arrived at the rear door of the courtroom and started to push it open, a voice from the back row of the gallery addressed her in a low, theatric register.

"Hey, you a PD?"

She looked back. "Yes, I am."

"I don't want no PD," Noah continued in the deep basso. "I want a real lawyer."

"Well, I knew you didn't want this PD," she responded when she saw who it was. "Maybe someday you'll find your real lawyer."

"Ouch. Waaay too serious, lady."

"Unless memory fails, seems like last time I saw you, you were the serious one."

He caught up to her and pushed the door open.

"Now, Kate. Don't be like that. How about a little won ton soup as a peace offering?" They walked out together.

"One-ton soup? Is this another poundage pool joke?"

"Whooa…" He nodded appreciatively. "Nice. And so quick. That little place over on Franklin okay? Chow Ming Ling? I told Sandy to meet us."

Kate glanced at her watch. "Okay," she said.

He hadn't seen her since *Ruiz* had broken open and, though he'd planned this encounter for a while, he was still definitely surprised with her response, the first social invitation she had accepted from him in months, and pretty readily at that. "Think you can fit me into your tight social schedule?"

"Maybe."

On the two-block walk, there was no talk of the case. Noah asked her about the "270 biz," how things were going with Judge Krousse. They arrived at ten after five, and the darkened restaurant, done in red and black, was nearly empty. A young, impeccably dressed maître d' seated them in a back booth, and Noah ordered a carafe of the house vin ordinaire blanc, with three glasses. The waiter brought the wine and poured them each a healthy slug in tumblers that were once jam jars.

"So," Kate observed. "White wine. Is this about your big victory?"

"No, it's to toast your success defending the deadbeat dads of the world. You're getting quite a name for yourself."

"It really was a spectacular win."

He was reveling in how well this was going, given the history. "Well, considering those bastards seemed to have everything we had, almost before we had it, we were pretty lucky."

"Noah?" She eyed him sheepishly, having dreaded this moment for weeks, knowing it would come.

Uh oh. "Yeah?"

"I… I'm afraid I might have had something to do with that."

"Oh?"

"Yeah." She avoided his gaze.

"Tell me."

"Well, I was totally livid after that fiasco at Bodega," she began, glancing at him hesitantly. "I guess you can imagine."

"I suppose I can. Not my best night."

"Anyway, I told you I had been dating Jim Stark."

"Yeah, you did say that."

"It was just after Bodega that he asked me out."

JUSTICE BY THE POUND [409]

"Okay."

"I probably shouldn't have let it happen, but I was really down, and alone."

"You don't have to tell me this."

She shook her head. "Yes, I do. You have a right to know."

"I... have a right to know? Why?"

"Because it's about you... and Ruiz."

"How so?" *He had no idea where this was going, but her eyes were brimming with contrition. Something had happened, and there was no way he wasn't going to hear it out.*

"Stark told me he wasn't sure you could handle the case on your own. He asked me to keep an eye on you, to let him know what you were doing, what you were thinking."

Noah was dumbstruck. "Why didn't you tell me?"

"He told me not to, that it might undermine your confidence. Anyway, I mentioned the things you told me. He kept pressing for more."

Oh... my... God... So that's how they did it. Oh... my... God... There was a wave of total disappointment, grief, down into his gut. He looked at his hands and closed his eyes. *How the hell could she? He'd known her so well.* Then, right on the heels of self-pity came remorse. *Hold it... wasn't all that totally predictable? After the mess he had made of everything?*

"I passed along what you were telling me, but after a while, I didn't think it was just the normal interest of a supervisor, so I refused to talk about it anymore. He got pretty insistent. The jerk actually threatened my job."

"Jesus."

"It took me a while to work up the courage, but I finally told him I wasn't going to see him anymore. I figured I'd be on the Santa Rita run, or worse, out the door maybe." Her voice trailed off.

"Hypocritical scum. Somebody has to take him down."

"That's what I thought, only I was obviously never going to do anything publicly. He gave me the silent treatment, but the funny thing is that he didn't retaliate. I finally got the nerve to go to County Human Resources, and they wanted to pursue it. I told them I'd have to have total confidentiality, and they agreed. Turns out I'm not the first assistant PD to be the object of his affections. They're investigating him for sexual harassment."

Noah smiled approvingly. "Nice work. That sonofabitch definitely needed thrashing. I hope he loses his job."

"Well, we'll see. I just hope they don't have to call me to testify."

They were quiet for a beat, during which she bowed her head and bit her lip. "I hate that I was so stupid," she whispered.

He covered her hand with his, and said, "I'm the one who screwed things up, Kate. I'm so sorry."

Looking up at him tentatively, she turned her palm up and interlaced her fingers in his. He met her eyes.

"So, it's the conquering hero and his lady fair. Am I too late to get in on this?" They both looked up to see the maître d' arriving with Sandy in tow. He glanced from one to the other. "Uh... am I interrupting something?" Once again demonstrating his vast store of sensitivity.

"Just disturbing the peacemaking," Noah said. "Siddown."

Sandy slid into the booth next to Kate, and Noah squeezed her hand, placing the bookmark, then poured Sandy a tumbler of the dernier cru. Raising the glass to Noah, he toasted. "To the protector of the downtrodden."

Noah extended his glass in return. "And to the champion of the working class. I got a newsletter that said the county bumped us eight percent and agreed to a twenty percent increase in the 401k contribution. Had your fingerprints all over it. All without a strike, no less. Very cool."

"Yeah," Sandy said, pouting. "Came out okay... no thanks to you."

Noah looked down into his jar and smiled. "You're better at that stuff than I am, anyway."

"So what've you been up to?" Sandy asked. "I haven't seen you around since your big triumph."

"I've been around, but they did give me a week off. I was more wiped out than I thought."

"Yeah?" Kate said. "What'd you do with your time off?"

"Not much. Went out to the zoo with some friends, among other things."

"The zoo?" Sandy snickered. "What, to visit your relatives?"

"Hey, easy now. I'd rather be raised by simians than the nut-cases I got stuck with."

"Explains a lot," Sandy said.

"Come to think of it, maybe I was raised by simians."

"I'll buy that," Kate said. "All that hair, the long arms." She pulled his hand up above the table. "Let's see if there're some scabs on those knuckles."

Noah clutched his chest and mimed a deeply wounded façade.

"So, what'd Pablo think about the victory?" Kate asked. "It must have been an enormous relief."

"I guess. You know, he was damn-near killed in the lockup?"

"I didn't know." She looked concerned. "What happened?"

"A guy tried to strangle him for reasons unknown. That jail's a pit. Take it from someone who knows."

"Yeah, I heard about that. You want to mind how you go off on judges," she told him. "So what happened with Pablo?"

"I don't really know. Story I got from Sid Cooper"—he looked over— "...you know, the bailiff in Department Twenty-six? Was that some thug dragged him into the head in the middle of the night, and was choking the life out of him. This behemoth they call 'Big Hermie' followed them, stormed in, grabbed the guy, and pulled him off Pablo. I guess he picked the dude up by the hair and bashed his face on the floor."

"My God," Kate gasped. "Did it kill him?"

"Knocked all his teeth out. But Cooper said he's gonna live to be prosecuted."

The waiter checked in, and Noah ordered three bowls of the Wah Won Ton, specialty of the house. They continued to guzzle the wine while Noah fielded questions about the case.

"So what's gonna happen to the mayor?" Sandy asked.

"Hard to say. You following the news? OPD's been on his trail since this whole thing broke, but so far they still haven't found him. And with the international flavor, the Feds'd like to ask him a few questions too."

"What about Mustafa?" Sandy said. "He definitely sounds pretty evil, the way he went after you guys?"

"Yeah. Pretty powerful guy. I'm sure he'll be at the top of the grand jury's list of possible RICO defendants."

The soup arrived.

Noah spread the white napkin in his lap. "Speaking of questioning, I'm gonna be a witness myself."

"What's that about?" Sandy asked.

"Internal Affairs finally decided to bring charges against those two cops who worked me over."

"You think there're a lot like them around?" Kate wondered.

"Two's too many in my book, but probably."

Gazing down into her steaming bowl, Kate picked up the ceramic spoon. "Well, you got what you wanted, didn't you? You proved Pablo was innocent."

He hesitated. "Did I?"

"What do you mean?"

"I mean, was he really innocent? He broke and entered, stole, turned some tricks, tried to extort Van Zandt, sold dope, and lied to me about all of it. All for good reason, maybe. But I don't know, is that the test? Seems like what matters is what he's charged with, and it's not my job to judge him. In theory, we paint our pictures, the DAs paints theirs, and the jury decides." He slurped another spoonful. "There're no bright lines in the courtroom… pretty much. No truths. Only ashes."

Sandy frowned. "Ashes?"

"Just something Buzz said."

"So, is there a lesson there somewhere?"

"Well, I guess the take-home is that you just stay in it."

"What's the point?" Kate asked. "Is it even worth doing if it's always so unclear?"

"The point is, you hang in, keep swinging, even when it's unclear. Over time it works out," Noah said, helping himself to another touch of the brutal white.

"The prophet Woody Allen," Sandy said. "'Eighty percent of life is just showin' up.'"

"That's it." Noah leaned back with his jam jar, closed his eyes and rested the back of his head on the cool leather of the booth. As he drifted with it, a smile played at the corners of his mouth.

Kate looked over. "What?"

"That really *is* it, isn't it." He slowly opened his eyes and returned his attention to her, still with the slight smile. "Staying in the crucible. Screwing it up, and coming back. Day by day… Inch by inch…" He scoffed. "Pound by pound."

• • •

The maître d' coaxed the stack of immaculately folded white linen napkins into a cubby in the dark mahogany buffet, sorted the various silver into their appropriate partitions, then slid into a booth around the corner from Noah, Kate, and Sandy at the rear of the nearly empty restaurant, a vantage point from where he could see any customer who might enter. There were only a handful of patrons out front, and the usual Wednesday afternoon social group in the back banquet room. One waiter to cover them all was plenty. He wrapped a hand around the blue-and-white porcelain cup to ensure that the tea was still hot. It was early yet. The rush wouldn't begin for another half hour.

The evening *Tribune* was spread out on the table in front of him.

He took a sip from his cup and paged through until he reached the East Bay Breaking News section. As he scanned the columns, a piece below the fold on page three that contained the name of a frequent customer caught his attention. He read with interest, but was only halfway through when a party of four stepped in the front door, laughing and chatting. The maître d' rose to seat the new arrivals, leaving the paper open. He would finish later. His venerable father would have most assuredly rebuked him for this bit of untidiness, but the table was sufficiently obscured from view. It would not be noticed.

FORMER PORT AUTHORITY COMMISSIONER FOUND DEAD

The bullet-riddled body of Henry Barnes, former Commissioner of the Port of Oakland who retired from his position just last week after eighteen years of service, was found by refuse workers in a dumpster behind Giovanni Restaurant on Broadway in Oakland during early morning routine collections. Restaurant management had no insight into the matter. A joint police investigation is ongoing today involving Oakland and Port Authority law enforcement agencies. Morris Garfield, vice mayor and current acting Mayor of Oakland, was quoted as promising the full support of his office in the investigation, saying he knew Mr. Barnes well, and that the former commissioner would be deeply missed by his family, his colleagues, and the citizens of Alameda County. Commissioners of Education and Public Works, Martin Silver and Philip Lewis, lauded Mr. Barnes's abilities and his contributions to the county administrative structure, assuring the Tribune that the Port of Oakland was in a strong position due to the former commissioner's efforts. These sentiments were echoed by prominent Oakland businessmen including Mark Siden, the CEO of local tech giant, Symmetrics, and recently appointed CEO of Ebony Properties, Harlan Metcalfe. Mr. Metcalfe indicated that he had dined with the decedent at Giovanni last night, and said that he had been in good spirits during dinner. Barnes had been scheduled to give testimony before a Federal Grand Jury regarding local government corruption next week.

ACKNOWLEDGMENTS

So many thanks to my lifelong friend, Steve Cannell, an internationally-acclaimed writer, best-selling novelist, and producer of television, who moved me to write fiction in the first place, then mentored me. Thanks to Sheldon Seigel, a master of best-selling legal thrillers, who provided so much encouragement. Thanks also to my friend Annie Lamott, best-selling author and all-around smart and hysterical human, for helping me with some direction at the times that I was in danger of pitching the whole thing, a blessing that she's given to so many.

I'm grateful to my agent, Mitchell Waters, and his assistant Steven Salpeter. Their expertise is so appreciated. Thanks to Wayne Williams who did the initial edit and contributed some great ideas, to Scott Heim who did the final edit and most definitely made it a better book, and again to my son Bo for the freshness and youth added by his many suggestions. Thanks to Greg Mortimer for his excellent cover ideas and for bringing the whole thing together. And thanks to my son Aaron who was the master photographer.

Special thanks to my right arm, Pete Epstein, who has had my back and covered me brilliantly over all the years, bringing so much within reach.

I lost my sweetheart Marilyn just now, just before *Justice by the Pound* became a reality. It has been the most painful experience of my life. She was my inspiration. She gave me her council, her encouragement, and her love, which most definitely made me the world's luckiest man. Her spirit is all over this story... and all over me. I miss her terribly, but she will never be far away.

Made in the USA
Middletown, DE
21 July 2020